ABBOTT
IN
DARKNESS

BAEN BOOKS by D.J. BUTLER

Abbott in Darkness

The Cunning Man with Aaron Michael Ritchey
The Jupiter Knife with Aaron Michael Ritchey

The Witchy War Series
Witchy Eye
Witchy Winter
Witchy Kingdom
Serpent Daughter

In the Palace of Shadow and Joy

ABBOTT IN DARKNESS

D.J. BUTLER

BAEN

A Baen Books Original

Baen Publishing Enterprises
P.O. Box 1403
Riverdale, NY 10471
www.baen.com

ISBN: 978-1-9821-2609-4

Cover art by Dom Harman

First printing, May 2022

Distributed by Simon & Schuster
1230 Avenue of the Americas
New York, NY 10020

Library of Congress Cataloging-in-Publication Data

Names: Butler, D. J. (David John), 1973- author.
Title: Abbott in darkness / D.J. Butler.
Description: Riverdale, NY : Baen Books, [2022]
Identifiers: LCCN 2022001551 (print) | LCCN 2022001552 (ebook) | ISBN
    9781982126094 (trade paperback) | ISBN 9781625798633 (ebook)
Subjects: LCGFT: Novels.
Classification: LCC PS3602.U8667 A63 2022 (print) | LCC PS3602.U8667
    (ebook) | DDC 813/.6--dc23/eng/20220114
LC record available at https://lccn.loc.gov/2022001551
LC ebook record available at https://lccn.loc.gov/2022001552

Printed in the United States of America

10 9 8 7 6 5 4 3 2 1

For Abid

CHAPTER ONE

"This is just as nice as the margrave train in New York." Ellie smushed her face against the window, made a kissing shape with her lips, and blew an enormous raspberry. When she pulled her face away again, a sheet of condensation on the glass surrounded an archipelago of negative space remembering the presence of her nose, cheekbones, and chin.

John stopped his pacing to admire his daughter.

Beyond the glass, deep blue sky and bright green foliage stretched in all directions. The train was fast; only three hours earlier, the family had come down the ramp from the shuttle bay onto the concourse at Central Transit Station.

Ruth handed each girl an animal cracker. She offered John one, and he waved it away. She did all this without releasing her grip on one of her bags—it was the bag into which she'd packed her mother's jewelry, once the steward of the starship *Oberon* had retrieved it from the ship's safe.

"Maglev," Sunitha said, correcting her sister. "It means magnetic levitation."

"Fine," Ellie shot back, "but *margrave* means you float."

Animoosh barked. Her ears were rotated into their forward position, which meant that she was alert, curious, and a little on edge. She pressed against John's knee.

Ellie was five years old and Sunitha eight. They shared a cinnamon complexion midway between the peaches and cream colors of their mother's face and the dark walnut of their father's. Ellie also had her mother's features, with a long nose, narrow, full-lipped mouth, and strong jaw, framed by a shock of unruly dark red hair. Sunitha's face looked like her father's, angular, with fine features and high-arching eyebrows. Except, of course, that she didn't have his protruding eyes or the ears that poked out perpendicular to the sides of his skull. Her hair was a deep golden color, and tightly curled.

"We call this kind of train a maglev train," John said to Ellie. "You're right, it does float. It levitates on giant magnets, which keeps the drag down and lets the train go really, really fast. This train is much newer than the ones in New York, so it's cleaner and shinier." Also, the Sarovar Company employees seemed less prone to writing vulgarities on the train walls than New Yorkers were, but he wasn't going to point that out to his young daughters. "It doesn't go to as many places, though."

"Because Sarovar Alpha is unexplored!" Sunitha said.

Ruth smiled. She still had that part-fretful, part-hectoring expression on her face that she had put on when John had told her they'd be traveling to Henry Hudson Post by train. She fretted and hectored from a good place, from the best of all possible places: she didn't want John to die of heart failure, if the train accelerated too fast.

He knew why she worried, but it was still too much. He wasn't *that* fragile.

"Sit down, John," she said. "Stop bending your wrists and fingers back."

"Yeah, Dad," Ellie said. "You're going to break off your hands!"

John clasped his hands together to stop himself from bending his wrists and fingers backward. It was a lifelong habit, like cracking one's knuckles.

Ruth fretted in part because they had sold everything and borrowed all the money they could to get here. They had a suitcase each full of clothing and small domestic items plus John's computer, but no other possessions.

John had a life insurance policy, but it wasn't very big, because they couldn't afford much in the way of monthly premiums right now. The Company salary had started getting deposited in their Sarovar Depository account when they boarded the *Oberon* in orbit above New York and had therefore become visible immediately upon their emergence from the Saravor end of the wormhole, but life insurance premiums were high for John. If he died, Ruth would be economically stranded, with two children.

"Is that what Doctor Doctor tells you?" John asked. Doctor Doctor was the AI tutor he had installed on both girls' multitools in New York. "Sarovar Alpha is unexplored?"

"The planet has been surgeried!" Ellie cried, before pressing her face against the window again.

"Surveyed. Yes, but not *explored*," Sunitha said, slipping into her faux aristocratic-English accent. "*Surveyed* just means that they flew around it a few times and took measurements from space. All of the planets of Sarovar System have been surveyed but not fully explored. There are satellites orbiting Sarovar Alpha right now, but they're mostly for communication. That's how our multis work here. There are just a few large posts on the planet, and although there are many minor posts, they are really small. The train lines mostly connect the major posts with Central Transit Station—that's the spaceport we just left. Cataloguing of indigenous species is only at an estimated forty percent completion. Of course, any planet has an awful lot of species, given all the bugs and microbes and stuff."

Ellie detached from the window. "Some planets are just rocks."

"Yes, but I mean habitable planets," Sunitha said.

"There are still many unknown species," Ruth said. "What are the most famous ones we do know about?"

"Weavers!" Ellie shouted.

"Shhh," Ruth urged her.

John bent his left hand back until his knuckles nearly touched his forearm and shrugged. "We're the only ones in the car."

It was true. The car in front of them was empty and the car behind them held several men who had embarked with them at Central Transit Station. They wore heavy boots and jumpsuits, and accompanied several large crates marked *TOOLS* and *PROPERTY OF THE SAROVAR COMPANY* on a long, narrow sledge.

"Good," Ruth said. "They can practice acceptable manners while there's no one around to hear them fail."

John laughed.

"Weavers," Ellie whispered. "But what about the other ones? Zoofoos and ills?"

"You mean Zaphons," John said, "and Illig. There's only one known wormhole connecting to Sarovar System, and its other end is near Jupiter. That means that to get here, you have to go through Earth. It's like we're on a dead-end street, in terms of space travel. You might see nonhuman sentients here, but I think they would have to come as Company employees, so there can't be very many of them."

He'd had a Zaphon lecturer at NYU, Professor Tzaark. Not for an accounting class; the sedate extraterrestrial, who looked half wolf and half lizard, had lectured on the experience of encountering alien life-forms—while at the same time providing in his own person an object lesson. Zaphons were nocturnal, so the class had been held in the evening, and Tzaark had always arrived yawning and blinking, newly roused from sleep.

"But Sarovar Alpha has lots of its own species," Ruth said. "Doesn't it, girls?"

"The Sarovari Weavers," Sunitha explained, "have a three-sided geometry rather than being bilaterally symmetric, as so many of Earth's life-forms are. They produce the Sarovari Weave, which is one of the exports of the Sarovar Company from the Sarovar System."

"Those are some awfully big words to come from such a delightfully small girl," John said.

Sunitha smiled.

"Did you just memorize the words, or do you know what they mean?" John asked. Sunitha was capable of parroting back enormous amounts of data, but he worried she didn't always process what she learned by rote. "What is 'bilaterally symmetric'?"

"Bilateral symmetry means that a creature's left and right sides mirror each other," Sunitha said. "Like you, mostly, when you don't slouch or bend your hands back."

"Thanks." John grinned. "I didn't really have a good posture coach until I got married."

"Daddy slouches." Ellie laughed.

"The Weavers are radially symmetric, and three-sided. On Earth, bilateral symmetry is associated with cephalization, which means having a head." Sunitha frowned. "Doctor Doctor doesn't know whether the Weavers have heads or not."

"They're sentient," Ruth said.

Sunitha grimaced. "That doesn't mean they have heads. Maybe

they have brains, and whatever else they need to be sentient, in some part of their body other than a head."

"Souls," Ruth suggested. "They need souls."

"Doctor Doctor doesn't mention whether the Weavers have souls."

"I'm glad to hear that Doctor Doctor doesn't know everything," John said. "That means there are a few things left for us to explore."

"Like sixty percent of the species," Sunitha said. "Estimated. Maybe we'll see the Weavers close up ourselves."

"I don't want to explore bugs," Ellie said.

"The Weavers have diseases," Ruth said. "Diseases that can be especially lethal for human beings, even though they don't seem to bother the Weavers themselves."

"That's what we've heard, anyway," John murmured. "So we'll be careful."

"I know." Sunitha stamped a foot. "I mean, maybe the post we end up at will have a zoo. Or a stuffed specimen, or something."

"I just want it to have a decent church," Ruth said. "I don't even care much what kind, at this point. I grew so tired of hearing the triple-chewed mush of the *Oberon*'s chaplain."

"Ew, he was boring," Sunitha agreed.

"I'm not sure you can really put sentients in a zoo," John murmured. "Maybe a *museum*. For artifacts."

"Do we know yet what post we'll end up at?" Ruth asked. They had had this conversation many times before. She was really asking whether he had received any messages on landing.

"I have to imagine Henry Hudson," John said. "Surely, the bookkeeping data is all transmitted there from the smaller posts for the financial planning and analysis work. And my boss works there. Stands to reason we'd be there, too, doesn't it? Of course, they could send us anywhere. Maybe we'll be sent to the southern continent and we won't be dealing with Weavers at all. We'll be mining and watching out for Riders."

"Henry Hudson is as big as a city." Ruth's eyes were hopeful. Her family tree was heavy with pioneers, missionaries, and explorers, but she was herself a city girl. She liked plays and art galleries, and had thrived in New York City, even having to drag two little girls along with her everywhere she went. "A small city, anyway."

"I bet Henry Hudson Post will have a zoo. And a museum." John nodded. "And there'll be school, so you can ask your teachers about how to get a good look at a Weaver. And maybe a Rider. Does Doctor Doctor say whether there are Riders on the northern continent at all? At least, there must be better pictures of Weavers here than are available on Earth."

"How do we trade with the Weavers?" Sunitha asked. "Doctor Doctor says they don't speak any human languages."

"I have no idea," John admitted. "Maybe we learned *their* language. Maybe we have some way of trading without language." Professor Tzaark had told stories of the first encounter between Zaphons and humans, out beyond the orbital ring of Pluto, at which he had been a young participant. They had initially communicated by laborious pantomime and pictures sketched in a smear of strawberry jam, which had more than once nearly caused the parties to attack each other.

"Do we give them money?" Ellie asked. "What do they spend money on?" She took another animal cracker from her mother. "Do they like cookies?"

"I have no idea." John shrugged. "I've read...well, in the orientation materials the Company sent me, that there are some funny new words we're going to have to learn while we're here. Like setty."

"Isn't that a sofa?" Ruth laughed out loud.

"You're thinking of set-TEE," John said. "SET-ty is a Sarovari word, and it means something like 'guy' or 'person.' The example sentence that the orientation material gives is, 'My toilet is backed up. Do you know the number for the water-setty?'"

Ellie laughed. "I'm going to call you my Dad-setty and my Mom-setty."

"Just Mom will do fine," Ruth said. "What does the word 'setty' have to do with how we trade with the Weavers?"

"It suggests there's a pidgin," John said. "Probably the traders here didn't make the word 'setty' up, so maybe they borrowed it...for instance, from the Weaver language. But that's just a guess, because how exactly we trade with the Weavers isn't something I've been able to figure out yet. It's a...trade secret, you could say." He grinned.

"Is that a dad-setty joke?" Ellie smiled.

John chuckled. "Guilty. You can ask your teachers all about the Weavers."

"I have a teacher now." Sunitha sounded cross. Had he talked too much about what he knew, and let her talk too little? "Doctor Doctor."

"Father meant a flesh-and-blood teacher," Ruth explained.

John frowned. *Father* made him feel old. He preferred Dad-setty, given a choice.

"I want a real live teacher," Ellie said. "What's a margrave, then?"

Ani pressed against John's leg, so John sat and stroked the dog behind her ears. Her color-changing coat had become somewhat confused during the five months aboard ship, shifting from chocolate brown to autumn red, and then stopping. Ani was an abstemious dog, if there was such a thing—some dogs would gorge themselves whenever there was food available, but Ani only ate when she was hungry. As a result, she still had her boxy, muscular frame, whereas John and his family had all gotten a little soft on the voyage. As he stroked his dog, he could feel her relax. Her ears slid back to their rear position, and she yawned.

"A margrave is a title of nobility," John said. "We've never had those in the United States, but they used to use them in many parts of Earth. They still have them in a few countries. Like a queen or a king, only a margrave is a much lower title."

"Like Uncle Christopher?" Ellie asked.

John raised his eyebrows at Ruth, inviting her to explain.

"Uncle Christopher is a cardinal," she said. "That's sort of like a margrave, but instead of being a title the government gives, it's a title the church gives."

"He's a priest," Sunitha said, in a very margrave-like accent.

"A senior sort of priest," Ruth said. "He leads other priests."

"Can Uncle Christopher float?" Ellie's eyes were pinned to the forest canopy beneath the train's elevated track. John followed her gaze and saw rich green vegetation, growing over gray rock and sliced into sections by green and brown streams.

"Neither margraves nor cardinals can float," John said. "Maglev trains float."

"Oh yes." Ellie's voice was distant, her imagination captured by the forest below.

"Is Sarovar part of the United States?" Sunitha asked.

"I'm sure you've already tried to figure out the answer for yourself," John said. "What do you think?"

Sunitha frowned. "It seems like a Territory. Like Puerto Rico used to be, or Oregon. The Weavers don't vote."

"They're hostile to humans," Ruth said. "And savage and unpredictable. Whether we can communicate with them or not."

Little confirmed information about Sarovar Alpha, or its Rider and Weaver populations, was available in New York. But years of informal meetings with Company recruiters had left a stew of rumors, suggestions, and innuendo in NYU's student population. At parties and in study groups and in private conversations, Ruth and John had both absorbed that stew.

"And I don't think the U.S. government really does much here." Sunitha puckered her lips in thought. The accent had disappeared. "It doesn't even collect taxes."

"It collects taxes upon remission to Earth," John said.

"And the judges are all Company employees," Sunitha continued. "Is there even law here?"

"Some U.S. federal law is applicable in Sarovar System," John said. "Taxes, murder, a handful of big crimes. Most day-to-day kinds of law are covered by the Company's bylaws and code of conduct."

Sunitha nodded. "So I think that makes Sarovar something like a condominium."

It was John's turn to frown. "You mean, like in an apartment complex?"

"Ha ha," Ellie said. "Sunitha got a word wrong."

Sunitha shook her head, her good mood abruptly restored. "A condominium is where two powers jointly control a territory." Her aristocratic tones had returned. "Like Oregon once was."

"Well, Doctor Doctor has already taught you more than I know." John shook his head. "But the Sarovar Company is a federally chartered United States corporation whose principal operations are in Sarovar System. It operates under a charter that gives it the right to basically run the system, so long as it pays taxes to the U.S. and guarantees all indigenous sentient species certain rights."

"I don't think a whole system should be turned over to a private company," Sunitha said.

"Well, *someone* has to run the place," John said. "It's slow and dangerous and expensive to get ships through the wormhole, both directions. And private companies are much better than the government at controlling costs and running efficient operations. If not the Company, then who do you think should be in charge?"

Sunitha shrugged. "Maybe the church."

John nodded. "Mom would like that."

Ruth smiled.

"Uncle Christopher!" Ellie cheered. "Uncle Christopher can run the system!"

"He might be too busy trying to keep the Anglicans and the Mormons from jumping out of the United Congregations," Ruth said. "Being a cardinal is already a lot of work."

"Just before we left New York," John said, "they accidentally printed a missal with the Angel Moroni on the cover. Again. It nearly caused a shooting war in West Africa."

"Nobody shot anybody," Ruth demurred.

"Thanks to Uncle Christopher," John said. "So we should leave him right where he is."

"I know one more thing about Sarovar and the Sarovar Company." Sunitha's voice had a sly tone, as if she were prepared to spring a punchline.

Ani rolled over onto her side and John scratched the dog's belly. "What's that?"

"That the Company is about to get one new trader!" Sunitha beamed.

John's heart melted. "Accountant, at least," he said. "We'll see about trader."

Ruth's brows furrowed.

"Certainly, trader," he said. "If not immediately, then very soon."

"That's how Company employees make their fortune," Sunitha informed them all, as Ruth needled John with her eyes. "They can trade for their own account, buying Sarovari Weave and other exports and selling them back home."

John nodded, his throat dry. "Of course, they have to pay their share of the Wormhole Transit Fee. And unless they want to take the risk of loss on the shipment, they may want to sell to a broker here on Sarovar. Only then they make less money."

"But the risk isn't high," Ruth said, "is it?"

"It's not zero," John said. "But that's what an entrepreneur is—it's someone who puts his own money in and his own hard work and is willing to take the risk."

"We're willing to take risks." Ruth smiled at John, but there was steel in her smile. She didn't look at her daughters, who were forty light-years from home and riding a train into a new life with unknown perils. "And we'll do our best to manage the risks."

John reached across the gap between the train seats and took her hand. "Of course."

"We might end up rich," Sunitha said.

John laughed. "Let's start by trying to end up debt-free."

The maglev began its deceleration, approaching Henry Hudson Post.

CHAPTER
TWO

"John Sanjay Abbott."

Director Ryan English was the kind of thin that made people think a person was tall, but John knew from having shaken his hand at the door that English was of average height—probably one hundred eighty centimeters, compared to John's one hundred ninety. His angular, downswept face, complete with slightly pointed, elfin ears, was spoiled by a jutting nose that was knobby and rounded like a small potato. His teeth, though, were perfect, shining bright white every time he opened his mouth. His hair was perfectly black and full, but receded above each temple to leave a dramatic V over the center of his face.

From what John had read about English, he had to be fifty years old, but he looked thirty. John had been assured breathlessly by other NYU students that Company officers enjoyed access to cutting-edge rejuvenation spas, generally believed to be located on the moons of one of Sarovar System's other planets. Perhaps that explained English's unlined face and thick, glossy hair.

English's signature had been on John's offer letter, and all the communications from the Company had been from 'the Office of Director English.' Those communications had instructed John to report here. Light flooded in though tall, wide windows, overlooking green forest, and spilled all over the director's desk, coffee table, and chairs.

The office was elegant, but its real sense of power came from the fact that John had reached it by an exclusive lift at the back of Company House's lobby. The elevator stopped only at the lobby floor and this office.

"That's me," John said.

"Sanjay is an Indian name, isn't it?" English leaned back in the chair behind his desk, steepling his fingers.

John nodded. "It's very common; you get in an Indian neighborhood, you can't swing a dead cat without hitting five Sanjays. It's like being named Dave."

"When did your family immigrate to the U.S.?"

"All in the last two generations. My mother's people are from southern and central India. My father immigrated from Nigeria."

"Masters in finance and accounting from New York University? Top ten percent of your class."

Why did this feel like a job interview? John nodded. "I put in the work."

"How is Gotham these days?" The director smiled. "I haven't left Sarovar System in nearly a decade."

"Recovering," John said.

English fixed him with a piercing eye. "I read that, after the riots, fundamentalists moved in and took over whole neighborhoods—the Bowery, Hell's Kitchen, the Upper East Side."

John managed, by force of will, not to fidget in his seat. "I don't know that I'd call them fundamentalists. For sure, the United Congregations have gained a lot of ground in New York recently. That's not surprising, people who are willing to change their lives enough to take a new religion are people who are looking for something. That's way more likely to be the case for poor people than rich people. For the same reason, poor people are generally more likely to be interested in religion, and energetic about their faith, if they have one."

"The Unity Church targeted New York."

John shrugged. "They saw an opportunity to reach people who were in need. But yes, some U.C. missionaries did come into New York to serve."

"Is that why *you* went to NYU?" English asked.

"I'm not U.C. I'm not any kind of believer, really. My family has a long tradition of cheerful, live-and-let-live agnosticism."

English frowned down at his multi. "Your wife is the niece of Cardinal Ruocchio. You're not a member of the Unity Church?"

"*She* is," John said. "From the Catholic side. It's hard to call a movement fundamentalist when its whole reason for existing is that it brought lots of Christian groups together into one alliance."

"All the most morally traditional Christian groups," English said. "Some would say, the most severe or the most puritanical."

"I've had Christmas dinner with way too many of these people to think they're Puritans."

"You're bending your fingers so far back, I don't see how they don't just snap off."

John chuckled. "Old habit."

English met John's gaze. "Is it difficult, being married into that family? Are you a permanent outsider? Do you feel judged?"

John shrugged. "No. I don't think *they* feel judged by *me*, either. We're family. We can get along." He was, however, starting to feel more than a little judged by English.

"Touché." English chuckled, then he paused and seemed to think. "And tell me what it means that you have Marfan's Syndrome."

"It's a genetic disorder that affects the connective tissues," John said. "It means I can bend my fingers and wrists really far." He demonstrated his wrist flexibility. "It's also why I'm such a goofy-looking bastard."

English guffawed. "You're more handsome than I am. But Marfan's can kill you, too, can't it?"

"Weak connective tissues mean that the heart isn't as firmly anchored in place as it should be," John said. "So sudden physical shocks might cause my heart to detach, leading to heart failure. It's why I couldn't be a pilot."

"Like your father was. Victor Abbott."

John hesitated. "That wasn't in my application."

English shrugged. "We run a thorough background check on all applicants. But what I really meant to ask was, how does a twenty-second-century American end up with a genetic disorder? How was that not screened out and corrected in utero? I thought maybe your parents might have had religious reasons, but that doesn't seem to be the case. And you grew up in Ohio and Illinois, not out in some technological backwater."

John clasped his hands together and leaned forward, resisting the urge to stand and pace. "You know, there was a lawyer who said very similar things to my parents. They caught my Marfan's when I got my physical to apply to the Space Force Academy. I was summarily rejected, of course. Can't even have an office job in the Space Force, if you have Marfan's. And this lawyer showed up at our house the next week. He told my parents that the hospital where my mom had me was guilty of negligence, and we should sue for millions of dollars. I remember the scene very well, sitting at the dining room table over coffee and dates. My dad said, 'There's nothing wrong with my son.' The lawyer said, 'We don't even have to prove negligence. *Res ipsa loquitur* is the applicable legal theory here. It means your son is defective, and because the Sisters of Mercy entirely controlled the means of detecting and correcting that defect, they're liable. Open and shut. We'll have your money inside a year, and your son will be taken care of for life.'"

"Many parents would have jumped at that," English said.

"Not unreasonably." John nodded. "But my dad said, '*Res ipsa loquitur*, that's Latin. I have a Latin dictionary in the other room. It's a large book, with lots of words inside and very sharp corners.' 'Yes?' said the lawyer. 'And if you don't leave my house this instant,' Dad said, 'I will shove that entire dictionary up your ass.' And that was the end of that."

"Your father wanted you to fend for yourself."

"My father wanted me to be a whole human being, and he didn't think the Marfan's would stop me."

English laughed, softly. "I would like to have met your father."

John didn't waste time saying what English must already know; that his father had died two years ago, while John was in the first year of his masters' program, of heart failure. Which had made John wonder whether his father had also had the disease. Victor Abbot hadn't had his son's ectomorphism and flexible joints, but he and John had shared slightly bulging eyes and prominent ears.

His father's death had sent John to his files, to look again at the test results for both his daughters, results that said they did not have Marfan's. Though John's parents had received very similar results for him, once, and had believed them.

And Marfan's, if not caught in utero, was not correctable. A defective heart or liver could be replaced with a simple bioprinted organ, but medical technology didn't yet allow for the replacement of all the body's connective tissues.

"Of course," English continued, "this whole conversation would make the human resources professionals shudder with discomfort."

John shrugged.

"Good thing we fired them. Right after we fired all the lawyers. In Sarovar System, we only have room for the productive. You sedjem good, mar?" English asked.

John smiled. "I read the word list. But mar is 'boss,' isn't it? That's what *I* should call *you*."

"Very good. You're going to want to do more than understand Sarovari words; you're going to want to pepper them into your speech. Generally, you'll find that the more time someone spends away from Henry Hudson, out at the smaller posts or in the forest, the more he sedjems. So getting that right is an important part of earning trust from people in the field."

John nodded, imagining himself sitting in a neat office, interviewing grizzled traders to confirm accounting data, jawing away in comfortable Sedjem.

"John," English said. "I have good news and bad news."

John kept smiling as his heart sank. He was in debt over a million dollars for his education, and couldn't even afford a journey home. He and Ruth were fully committed, the ship metaphorically burned on the beach. Any bad news that English could give him, he would simply have to live with. "I'm excited to hear them both."

"You like bad news, do you?"

"I like information. Information is the basis of all trade, and all relationships, and that includes information that's sad or frightening."

"Interesting," English said. "As a manager, as a leader of men, I have to say, I like lack of information. I like the darkness."

John frowned. "I don't understand."

"In darkness, you see who a man truly is. When no one can see him, when he has to act without perfect knowledge . . . then you see character."

John cleared his throat. "I can understand that perspective."

"Bad news first, then. The job that was supposed to be vacant at Henry Hudson Post has stayed filled. I expect it will come available again, maybe in a year or so, but for now, there's no job for you here."

John took a deep breath. He had horrible visions of his daughters begging with tin cups and Ruth singing for coins. "I saw what looked like a commercial district near the train station," he said. "Shops and restaurants. Am I right to think those are not all Company-owned, that there might be other sorts of jobs and businesses on the planet?"

"There are, you're correct." English steepled his fingers in front of his face. "But you're getting ahead of yourself. There's no job for you at Henry Hudson Post, but there's still work for you at the Company."

"Oh, excellent." John's heart pounded; he felt his pulse throbbing in his temples. "Will I report to you?"

"Absolutely. I need an auditor to go to Arrowhawk Post and investigate possible malfeasance there."

"Does 'malfeasance' mean theft?" John asked.

English nodded. "I suspect some of the traders are skimming from the Company."

"Isn't this the kind of thing Internal Audit should investigate?"

"I'd really like to have my own person look into it," the director said. "And you need a job. And the post could use another accountant, in any case."

"I can see how theft would be tempting," John said. "If they could sell whatever they skimmed for their own account."

"Exactly. Which brings us to the good news."

John smiled and sat up straight.

"Obviously, having just arrived, you can't be a trader."

John fixed his smile in place. "The offer letter was ambiguous on the point." He had been careful to tell his family that he might not be a trader immediately, but he had certainly hoped he'd be able to quickly buy and sell, and begin to crawl out of the enormous hole of debt he was in.

"I suppose that's deliberate," English said. "So we don't have to adjust the text for the occasional offer we make to someone who will start as a trader. Someone with a lot of experience, for instance. But here's the good news: you're a factor, as of right now, and that means that you can bargain with any Company trader and sell to him."

John nodded slowly. "So I'll need to make trader friends at Arrowhawk Post."

"No, we can do better than that. I'm a trader, obviously, and I'll ship your goods with mine. This is actually to your advantage, because my shipments have priority over the shipments of ordinary traders, without having to bid for it. That's one of the better perks of my office. That means you'll get paid faster."

"And you'll do this . . . for free?" John suggested, smiling.

English frowned. "Sadly, I can't. The code of conduct requires that I charge you at least one percent. But I can probably make that up to you in volume, if you can get Sarovari Weave in quantity."

"Shesroo," John said, using the Sarovari word.

English smiled his acknowledgment. "And I can push for a raise for you, once you've had a performance review."

John nodded; it seemed unlikely he could get any more. "So Arrowhawk traders buy Weave, then? Arrowhawk must be here on the northern continent?"

"They do, principally, and it is. Arrowhawk is a small post, and remote. The train only goes there once a week, ordinarily, and it's about an eight-hour ride."

John frowned, trying to remember Arrowhawk in his orientation materials. "Is it on the beach?"

"In the mountains," English said. "But low, old, eroded mountains, thickly forested. Think Appalachia, not Himalaya."

"What's my job title?"

"Auditor," English said. "You'll be one of two auditors, reporting to the audit chief. In addition, as we discussed, you'll report to me."

"I'm to help the audit chief find out whether any of the traders are skimming revenue?"

"Heavens, no. I suspect the audit chief is a coconspirator. His name is Keckley, by the way. Audit Chief Keckley. Who's in a better position than the audit chief to simply miscount bales of Weave, steal the difference, and sell the bales on the side? You're going to find out who's skimming revenue at Arrowhawk Post, and how much, and the very first person you're going to investigate is the audit chief."

"Shouldn't it be easy to tell if the audit chief is stealing?" John asked. "If his shipments of Weave jump way up, he's getting extra."

"But what if he steals Weave, and then sells it at a discount to other traders, who in turn have it shipped back to Earth?" English suggested.

John considered the possibility. "The banking system here is all contained on this side of the wormhole. If he's receiving payments, it might show in his Depository accounts."

"Unless he was receiving payments in cash," English pointed out. "You noticed the markets on your way in; the Company prints Company Dollars, called Sarovars or Sars for short, to allow those markets to exist. Sars are exchangeable for U.S. dollars at a fixed one-for-one rate, not only here, but at Depository branches on Earth."

"So he could collect a pile of cash, planning to deposit it when he gets home," John said. "Or buy U.S. dollars with it."

"He could also be collecting wealth in some other form—gemstones, promises, land, who knows. He could be consuming the wealth in the form of liquor, food, sexual services."

"At the expense of the Company."

"And at a time—I don't want you to worry about this, it's an issue that a different task force is looking into—when Sarovari Weave is getting harder to come by."

"Is something wrong with the Weavers?" John asked.

"Don't worry," English said, "there's plenty of shesroo still coming through to let you pay off your school loans quickly, as well as save up for a house."

John nodded. "I'll be investigating the audit chief."

"And after him, Post Chief Carlton. She's smart and ambitious. I respect that, but sometimes smart and ambitious people lead themselves astray. Naturally, I will require your complete discretion. I do not know whom to trust."

"Of course."

"*Complete.*" English's stare drilled into John's face. "This is not something to discuss even around the kitchen table."

John nodded solemnly. "And how will I communicate with you? We'll need some means that resists eavesdropping."

English set a knob of metal with two stubby metal leads protruding from one end on his desktop. "Insert this in the comms panel at Arrowhawk Post when you contact me, by ethermail or otherwise. It will encrypt your messages, and only I, as the possessor of the counterpart device, will be able to read them. It will encrypt audiovisual messages as well as text." He handed over a slip of paper with a long number hand-printed on it. "This is my personal encrypted comms address."

"The communications run over satellite?"

"There's also a physical line. It runs parallel to the train. We have redundancy in case of a catastrophe. The post is remote, and bad things can happen. If worst came to worst at Arrowhawk, an emergency signal from the post might lead us to carpet-bomb the area."

John hesitated. "Carpet bomb? What would necessitate that?"

English shrugged. "An uprising of the natives, maybe. A breakout of a virulent and unknown disease. It hasn't happened yet."

John nodded.

English stood and extended his hand. "Your train leaves the day after tomorrow. I've had a bag of the uniforms you'll need delivered to the hotel ahead of you. The steward of the *Oberon* knew your sizes."

CHAPTER THREE

Ruth and the girls waited in the Company House lobby. They were just where he'd left them, sitting on deep leather sofas beneath a ceiling-height mural that showed three humans with surveying tools, standing at the top of a rocky cliff and looking down on a stream-riven, forested valley. In the valley were creatures that looked like giraffes, and sloths, and something that might have been a bear, if it hadn't had six legs. John put on his best smile as he exited the lift to meet them.

"Dad-setty!" Ellie charged across the glowing white plastic floor to hurl herself at John's knees. He scooped her up and hugged her. Ani padded slowly behind Ellie and moved in a slow circle around John, ears cocked forward and tail wagging. "Mom-setty said it was probably taking so long because they wanted to go ahead and make you a director right now!"

"Mom." Ruth stood. Her eyes were tired; she was surrounded by a mound of luggage on wheels, the handles still extended. She continued to grip the bag containing her mother's jewelry. Had she let go of that bag once since they had packed up for landing in the starship's cabin? John didn't think so.

Sunitha had her multitool open, and her eyes were glued to it; the screen was full of the animated gestures of Doctor Doctor, and earbuds were visible in Sunitha's ears.

"Actually," John said, "it took a long time because Director English wanted to fire me and hire my daughters instead, because he heard from the starship crew that they were smarter than I am."

That got a smile from Ruth, and her eyes relaxed. "IQ isn't everything, John. I'm not sure either of the girls can analyze a balance sheet like you can."

"We were singing, Dad-setty!" Ellie told him. "Church songs!"

"Oh, I hope you sang the pirate one," he said.

"That's still a hymn, John," Ruth said.

"I know, and I love it." He grinned. "It makes me want to clash my ale mug with the other pirates' mugs, brandish my cutlass, say arrr, and bury my treasure."

"There might be a limit to how much joking God is willing to take from you." Ruth smiled, but her voice had a slight edge.

"Based on what I know about the universe and how it works," John replied, "I'd say that God has a really good sense of humor."

"Where's our housing?" she asked. "We should go get settled in."

"Well, speaking of God's sense of humor," John said, "our housing is in Arrowhawk."

"Is that a street name?" Ruth's eyes narrowed.

"That's a different post." Sunitha stood up. She pulled out her earbuds.

Ruth's shoulders slumped.

"What can you tell us about Arrowhawk?" John asked. "I'm surprised Doctor Doctor even knows anything about it."

They had asked Doctor Doctor for all the information he had on the Sarovar System during their journey here. It hadn't been very much. John certainly didn't remember hearing about Arrowhawk Post. He hadn't known the name of Henry Hudson Post, other than from his offer of employment and the orientation materials.

"Old Doctor Doctor didn't know about Arrowhawk," Sunitha said. "New Doctor Doctor does. But look, he's changed." She held up her multi for John to see, thumbing an icon to change the audio channel.

The Doctor Doctor avatar was the same rumpled, balding, stocky figure John had carefully selected for his avuncular, nonthreatening appearance. He stood in front of a bookshelf, which was his default welcome screen, with a meerschaum pipe in one hand, and the other hand in his pocket.

But now he wore a jacket with the stylized S of the Sarovar Company on its breast, like an old-style letterman's jacket, except that its body extended down to Doctor Doctor's knees. The body of the jacket was a rich blue and its sleeves were buff, blue and buff being the Company's colors, and beneath it hung a blue kilt.

The image sensors of the multi detected John's presence, and the avatar smiled at him. "Hello," it said, "I'm Factor Doctor. What's your name, and what can I tell you today, about the Sarovar System or about the universe in general?"

"What did you do?" John asked Sunitha.

"When we sat down, I connected with the ethernet," she said. "I thought we might have ethermail from Grandma."

"Ethermail doesn't come through the wormhole by itself," John said, "it comes on starships. So any new ethermail from Grandma could only have come on the ship with us. You'll get ethermail later, as other ships arrive from Earth. It has to come and go in big batches, or else it would take years to arrive."

"I know that," Sunitha said, dropping into Received Pronunciation. "Only, I thought wouldn't it be neat, if Grandma surprised me with an ethernet message? And that would be just like her, to do something sweet to remind us of her. But when I connected, there was an update for Doctor Doctor instead."

"Hello," the multitool said again, "I'm Factor Doctor. What's your name, and what can I tell you today, about the Sarovar System or about the universe in general?"

"My name is John," John said. "I don't want to know anything right now, thank you."

"Come back anytime!" Factor Doctor lit his pipe.

"Arrowhawk Post is the end of the western maglev line on the largest continent in Sarovar Alpha's northern hemisphere," Sunitha said. "The continent is named Wellesley. The largest continent in the southern hemisphere, by the way, is named Bonaparte."

"Arrowhawk is the end of the maglev line," John said, "but it's not on the coast, right?"

Sunitha stood very straight as she declaimed. "The western coast of Wellesley, with its famous Muir Archipelago, is approximately five hundred kilometers west of Arrowhawk. It is reachable by air, by sea, and by land transportation other than maglev train. Factor Doctor says that flyer and all-terrain vehicle are the modes of transportation preferred by traders in western Wellesley, although historically, some traders have used mules and horses."

"Mules and horses? Not hovercars?" This was all news to John, who had trained as an accountant and committed to the Sarovar Company to make his career because of the opportunities for trade, and because professionals back from Sarovar were so broadly in demand, across industries and territories.

"Start in Sarovar," Alan Bannister, his professor of Forensic Accounting had urged him. "Once you have Sarovar on your résumé, you can go anywhere."

Was he going to need forensic accounting in Arrowhawk? It seemed that he might.

Although, revenue... if Director English was right, and what was being falsified was revenue, that might not be a forensic question, so much as a matter of going out into the forest or down into the warehouse and counting bales. John didn't mind the thought of getting his hands dirty—it was kind of an exciting prospect, to get out into the field with the traders—but the farther he got from a calm desk job, the more nervous Ruth would be.

What if, for instance, Audit Chief Keckley *was* stealing? What if he found out that John was investigating him, and didn't take kindly to the investigation? If he had stolen a lot, and risked severe punishment... how far would the audit chief go to protect himself?

And how much of all this should John tell Ruth? Complete discretion, English had said. Not even around the kitchen table.

John sighed.

"Weavers, by the way," Sunitha said, "have only been encountered on Wellesley."

"Okay," Ruth said, "this is not a problem. God has taken care of us so far, and He will continue to do so. Just because we don't yet see how this latest development is a blessing doesn't mean that it isn't one. One day, we'll look back and marvel at what a wonderful thing it was that we got to live at Arrowhawk Post."

She offered John an encouraging smile.

He took a deep breath and smiled back. "Yes. And I'll be trading directly with Director English, which is great for all kinds of reasons. So we just need to get some cash in and start buying Weave, and before you know it, we'll own our own businesses in New York. What businesses should we invest in, girls?"

"A cupcake store!" Ellie cried.

"An engineering firm," Sunitha suggested. "Or medical technology design."

"Maybe a combination of the two?" John raised his eyebrows.

"So when does our train leave, Dad-setty?" Ellie asked.

"A day and a half." John smiled at Ruth. "For two nights, we'll stay at the Sarovar Company Hotel, right across the street from the train station."

They left Company House, John and Ruth pulling wheeled suitcases and Sunitha dragging her sister's bag behind her as well as her own. John had a chit that English had given him, a featureless white plastic oval, telling him it would pay for all their transportation and food and lodging for the rest of the day, as well as their train tickets in the morning. On the street, with cool rain splashing down the front of Company House and pooling in depressions and potholes, a tall man in Company blue and buff flagged down a wheeled cab for them. They climbed into the back where two broad seats faced each other over a shared space for feet, not unlike the seating on the train. Ani hunkered down among the luggage and closed her eyes.

John pressed the chit against a reader and said, "Sarovar Company Hotel."

The cabbie saluted and drove into the rain, whistling a tune John didn't recognize.

The girls were both quickly engaged with their multis; along with Factor Doctor, the local update had a Sedjem Swami app, and they quickly dove into learning the traders' patois.

"Et," the Swami said. "Food. Especially, bread."

"Et," the girls repeated.

"Where et-setty, mar?" the Swami continued. "Repeat after me: where et-setty, mar?"

"John," Ruth murmured. "Tell me how you're really feeling about this."

"I think the opportunity is good," he said. "The opportunity *is* good, and, anyway, it's the opportunity we *have*. English is going to help me sell, so that should work in our favor. Hopefully I can quickly move from factor to trader, so I won't need his help anymore." Especially if he did a good and quick job of uncovering the truth about Audit Chief Keckley.

"You're tense," she whispered.

"Sorry. Tired, maybe. Caught off guard. I thought we'd be in the city, not out in the boonies, doing audit work on the Company's tiniest post."

"You think it's dangerous?" she asked.

"Well, inside the post it's got to be relatively safe. Hard to say about outside the post. Sounds like we'll be pretty remote."

"Our nest egg is gone."

John felt weighted down. "The amount of energy necessary to open the wormhole is variable. The cost is borne by passengers and shippers pro rata—it was an expensive journey. This will happen to us from time to time when we ship goods back, too."

"I know."

She looked out the cab's windows at the rain. They passed brightly lit signs advertising food and flicks and ATV repair. The stores huddled together more densely as they approached the maglev station.

The cabbie unloaded their bags onto the smooth slab of concrete beneath the plastic awning in front of the hotel. He had a haggard face, features beaten into incongruous crags and crannies by years of weather, but he smiled at them.

John dug into his pocket. "Sorry, I've only got a few bucks in cash and it's U.S., we're new to the planet."

The cabbie waved John off. "The Company chit tips at twenty percent automatically." He handed John a plasticated business card. "You're not the first new arrival I've ferried around. You need a ride in Henry Hudson, give me a call."

Once they were checked in, to a beige, pink, and avocado green suite with two bedrooms and a kitchenette, the girls took to jumping on the couch. John inflated two large disposable foam beds from the dispenser, the first dialed to a firmness of three for the girls, and the second dialed to a seven for Ruth. For his own weight, John would have chosen a nine, but he preferred to share a bed with his wife. He examined the booklet of available services and entertainment. "There are flicks on the console," he said. "But there are going to be flicks at Arrowhawk. I think you'll see lots of flicks, so many you'll be sick of them. The hotel also has a pool, and I don't know when the next time will be that you'll see a swimming pool."

"And after swimming," Ruth said, "Dadi Abbott sent a treat for you to have on your first night on Sarovar Alpha."

"A treat?" John was surprised.

"Jalebi," she said. "Vacuum-packed, so it should still be good. She also made me pack a can of condensed milk."

"Yay, Dadi Abbott! Yay, Grandma-setty!" The girls hallooed their way into the bathroom to change into swimsuits.

Ani took the opportunity to claim the couch for her own, curling up where the girls had been jumping moments earlier.

"I want you to take my mother's jewelry," Ruth said.

"What?"

"I'll take the girls swimming. If you want jalebi, we'll save you some. You take the jewels down to the street and sell them for all you can get."

"Ruth . . . that's all you have from your mother."

"Wrong." Ruth smiled. "I have all my memories, and all her love, and half her genes, and her two grandchildren. The jewelry is no big deal."

John sank into a soft chair and buried his head in his hands. "Do you want to buy passage home already?"

"You idiot," she said gently. "I want you to have cash to invest in trading, right away. This is how we're going to buy the future for our daughters, and I don't want to wait until we've scraped together enough from your pay packet, I want to jump in now."

"Maybe I can pawn them," John mused. "If I can borrow enough to get us started, then I can buy the jewels back in six months or a year."

"To get our money quickly," she said, "we'd have to sell to a trader here on-world. Which means a lower return, doesn't it?"

"Yeah," he said. "But maybe . . . maybe I can make it work. I'll have to see the numbers."

"You look at the numbers, John," she told him. "But understand this: I'm happy to sell the jewels, not pawn them, if it means we can get started building the business that will pay off our debt, send the girls to school, and eventually buy ourselves a hundred meters of the Oregon coast."

"And a house," John said.

"You know I hate tents. And, John . . ." Ruth looked at the bathroom to be sure the door was still shut, and lowered her voice.

He raised his eyebrows.

"If you're worried about safety, buy a gun."

"If the post is dangerous," he said, "they'll have guards, or they'll issue me weapons that we need." But would that be true if the threat was a cornered Audit Chief Keckley? Or would Keckley be able to cut off access to security when John and his family needed it?

But maybe Keckley was innocent anyway, and this was all fretting over nothing.

"I would have brought a gun from Earth, if I'd thought we needed it." Ruth opened her suitcase, took out the small zipbag that contained her mother's jewelry, and handed it to John. "All I am saying is, here are the jewels. I don't need the jewels, I need you and the girls and our future. Things are turning out slightly different than we planned, so I want you to take the jewels, and do what you think is best."

John nodded, then slowly reached out and took the zipbag.

He gave Ruth three of the four hotel keycards and a kiss, and then he headed back down to the street.

"Save me some jalebi!" he called, just before the hotel door shut.

CHAPTER FOUR

The rain had let up, but the breeze blowing across Henry Hudson Post was wet with the possibility of more squalls. John considered summoning the cabbie, but decided against it; stores of all kinds crowded right up against the hotel and the train station, so he was confident he'd find a pawnshop or a jeweler.

Running up extra charges on the Company chit seemed like a bad way to start his relationship with Director English.

Two valets stood at the hotel entrance; one was opening the door of a sleek blue groundcar and helping its passengers step out, so John turned to the other and asked directions to a jeweler or a pawnshop.

"There's a jeweler right there." The valet nodded. "There are two pawnshops farther down that street, both on the right side."

John gave the man five dollars, the last of his U.S. cash.

He was a little surprised by how little blue and buff he saw, once he stepped out onto the street. If these people weren't Company employees, who were they? Former employees, who had quit or been fired, and weren't able to afford the trip home?

Some were small merchants; just in crossing the street to the jeweler, John passed a noodle shop, a tattoo kiosk, a multitool repairman working out of a two-wheeled cart pulled by something that looked like a yak, and an oxygen bar.

Drones hummed overhead. Some carried visible packages—what did the others do? Were they messengers? Surveillance drones?

A two-wheeled rickshaw narrowly avoided running John over in the middle of the street. He stared as it continued past; its two yoke-poles rested on either side of a rolling ball, about one meter in diameter. At the corner, the ball abruptly swiveled right, and the rickshaw neatly pivoted in train.

There was no sign on the front of the jeweler's indicating what its business was. The name *Seteng* glowed from one window with a steady blue LED light—or did *seteng* mean jewelry in Sedjem? All three windows were protected behind screens of thick, black iron bars.

The metal door was shut and barred from the inside. John pressed a button beside the door, and moments later a panel opened in the door at face level.

Two eyes and a dark brown nose appeared. "What you meri, mar?"

"Ah . . ." John said.

"What you want?"

"Looking for a jewelry-setty," John said. "Seteng-setty? I want to sell."

The face behind the door laughed. "Seteng is a name, mar. Hold it up, let me see what you have."

"You don't want to go in there." This came from a new voice, behind John.

John took a step sideways and turned, fearing a mugger and wishing he had purchased a gun before doing anything else—though he had no cash, and was stretched too thin to have good credit. Maybe he could have used the Company chit.

But the man standing in the street looked harmless. He'd been walking, because his gray, wide-brimmed hat was awash with water. A transparent rain jacket hung from his shoulders, revealing a shabby blue suit beneath, with thin gray stripes and a short, fat tie. He clearly hadn't shaved in several days, and his heavy jaw and protruding forehead were set in a broad grin.

"Good day," John said.

The door opened, and was filled by a thin man with long facial features and skin the color of caffè Americano with extra milk. "We're buying, mar," he said.

"You don't want to go in there," the heavy-jawed man repeated. "You're clearly from off-world, and you don't know this, but Seteng has a reputation for ripping off sellers. You're new here, right? Trying to pawn something to get a little cash?"

"I'm Seteng," the man in the door said. "Show me the jewelry."

"Do what you want," the man in the rain jacket said. "I get it, I'm a stranger, too, and you don't know who to trust. But I'd strongly recommend that if Seteng makes you an offer, you at least try one of the pawnshops in town to get a second opinion."

He turned and started walking away, humming something... operatic. John wasn't especially musical, but he thought it might be Verdi. *The Chorus of the Hebrew Slaves*, or something like that.

Seteng shook his head. "If I make you an offer, it's take it or leave it, on the spot, mar. You don't get to shop me around town and try to force my prices up."

"Never mind." Without waiting for Seteng's sudden sputtering to resolve into anything else, John broke into a trot, aiming to catch up to the man in the suit. "Excuse me!"

At the corner, as he turned, the man stopped beneath a glowing sign that read ET HANKET NOOB. "Ah, good," he said. "You took my advice. Seteng is a thief. There's a reason he's willing to pay more in rent to be right next to the train station and the hotel. He's trying to catch new arrivals before they know any better, and he gives the hotel valets a cut when they direct customers to him."

"John Abbott." John extended a hand. "As you guessed, I'm new."

They shook hands and the other man looked John up and down.

"I'm Bangerter Cheapside," he said. "Lawyer. New York Bar, not that it really matters here."

"How did you know I was a new arrival?" John asked.

"That shirt and those pants. Not Company issue, bought off the rack from a department store, not worn full of holes. Let me guess, you're some kind of engineer."

"Accountant," John said.

"Ah. I knew it had to be one of the nerdy professions."

"Could have been a lawyer, then."

"Except the Company doesn't fly any lawyers in."

"Did you fly yourself in, then? That's expensive. You must have a prosperous practice."

Cheapside scratched his nose. "I was a Company employee, once. When they fired me, they weren't going to send me back to Earth. I just hung out my shingle here, instead."

"You were one of the lawyers English talked about?"

Cheapside laughed. "Still telling the same damn jokes, is he? No, I was a pharmacist. Worked at the Company clinic here in town. But I was a qualified lawyer, too."

"What does a lawyer do on Sarovar Alpha?"

"Same as a lawyer anywhere, basically. I resolve private disputes. I execute and write wills. I help people negotiate contracts. Sometimes, I represent people in front of the Company's executives, arguing about Company bylaws and code of conduct issues, or the very few actual U.S. federal statutes that apply here. Once in a very great while, I sue the Company, and try to hold it accountable to its own conscience."

"That sounds interesting."

Cheapside laughed. "Does it? Did I mention that I'm single, poor, and possibly alcoholic?"

"I'd invite you to get a bowl of noodles with me," John said. "Or maybe a bowl of Et Hanket Noob, if that's something edible. Et is food, right? Not sure I remember the other two words. Only I have no cash, and it doesn't seem right to invite you to buy me dinner."

"Hanket is any drink," the lawyer said. "Though, properly speaking, it's beer, in the same way that, properly speaking, et is bread. Noob in this context means cash, though it can also mean gold. This is a convenience store. In Brooklyn, the sign would read, 'Groceries, Ice cold beer, ATM.'"

"I guess I'm going to have to knuckle down and learn this patois." John sighed.

Bangerter Cheapside shrugged. "Everyone speaks English. All the humans do, anyway. But you'll sound less new when you can sedjem a bit."

"All industries have their shop talk," John said. "But I admit, I find this one especially strange."

The lawyer nodded and seemed to be considering something. "If you have any extra time here in Henry Hudson, you should check out the Stone Gardens."

"I've seen some nice murals in Company House."

"The Stone Gardens," Cheapside said again. "You can get there by car, or a longish walk, if you have good shoes. I can tell where to find a cobbler who's worth a damn. And you'll look less new when you're wearing a Company jumpsuit, or at least something that's locally made. I can point you to tailors, too, if you want."

John shook his head. "But the pawnshops, or more reputable jewelers, would be very helpful. Thank you."

The lawyer gave John quick directions to two pawnshops farther from the hotel than the ones indicated by the valet. They shook hands again, and parted company.

The rain picked up again as John turned left off the main street. The buildings here were three meters apart, and awnings from both left and right entirely covered the space, turning what was technically an alley into a tunnel, with flat-packed gravel underfoot and a rough gutter to one side. The gravel drained water better than asphalt did, so the tunnel was something approximating dry.

And lined with shops.

John passed two clothing shops, a cobbler, and a bar, but then dawdled a bit at a fruit seller. He'd spent time on five of Earth's continents and seen all kinds of trees, but he still couldn't immediately place half the fruits that stood piled up in wooden trays. "What does this taste like?" he asked the vendor, brushing his fingers across a heap of blue, hard-shelled spheres.

"Very tasty." The vendor looked East Asian. "Like watermelon, but a little sweeter, and not as wet. Chewier. You can eat the seeds, if you don't mind a bit of extra crunch. Two bucks."

"I'll be back." John kept walking.

A hundred meters from the street, he found the first pawnshop. Cheaper wares were stacked near the front of the store: clothing, boots, multitools, battered paperback books. The shop was narrow enough that John, despite being the thinnest man he knew, had to turn sideways to get inside. In the rear of the store, under clear plastic counters, lurked the pricier items, including firearms and jewelry.

A burly man with thick red hair on his forearms leaned on the plastic counter and chewed a toothpick. "Looking for a little extra protection?"

John realized his gaze had been lingering on one of the pistols. It was bulky and square, and lay between a pair of semiautomatics. "I guess I *am* curious about that one," he admitted.

Forearm Hair unlocked the panel behind the counter, reached in, and placed the weapon atop the clear plastic. "It's an energy pistol."

But wasn't that illegal? John blinked and bit his tongue. He could see the slot at the back of the weapon where an energy cell would be inserted.

"You're thinking, 'This is illegal, unless you're in the military.'" Forearm Hair laughed. "But that's because you're new here. U.S. firearms laws are inapplicable in the system. Company policy might restrict where you can carry something like this, but you can wear it around on the street, no problem, or in the forest."

John picked up the weapon and sighted down the barrel. "How many shots do you get out of a cell?"

"With this model, one. With some of the newer models, as many as five. You see the switch on the side—that lets you toggle between a wide beam, which will stun a crowd of attackers or light a forest on fire, and a narrow beam, which will punch a hole through steel."

John set the energy pistol down. "I'm here to sell. Do you buy jewelry?"

"I do." Forearm Hair set a clear plastic tray on the counter. "Let's take a look."

John felt ill setting his wife's jewelry down, but the pawnshop owner seemed thoroughly competent. He looked closely at the necklace, bracelets, and earrings through a magnifying class, holding it all carefully with a soft white cloth and doing everything fully in John's view.

"These are nice pieces," he said. "I can give you ten thousand dollars."

"They're antique," John said.

Forearm Hair nodded. "You'd get more for them in Los Angeles or Hong Kong, but I have to resell, and I don't have the children of billionaire moguls walking through here, looking to drop a hundred thousand bucks on new shinies for prom."

"Can you go twelve thousand?" John suggested.

"Ten-five. That's it."

"What about a loan?"

"I can lend you eight thousand bucks. You'd have six months to buy it all back for eighty-five hundred."

"If you can buy it for ten thousand five hundred, you can lend me ten thousand," John said. "But I need a year to buy it back."

"New trader, eh?" Forearm Hair chuckled.

"Arrowhawk." John laughed along, not disabusing the man.

"You might make your first shipment within a year. Or at least, sell to a buyer at Central Transit."

"It belongs to my wife, and it has sentimental value. I'll do whatever's necessary to buy it back."

"A year's going to cost you," Forearm Hair said. "You can buy it all back within one year, but it's going to be for twelve thousand dollars."

"You have a competitor just down the street," John said.

"And you should absolutely go ask for a bid from him. His name is Leafty, and he won't go as high as I can, because he doesn't sell as much jewelry. My name is Joe Monson, but everyone calls me Red. Tell him the bid you got from Red, and see if he'll top it. He won't, because he can't, but he'll try to wheedle you into taking his offer, anyway. He's from the 'Oh, I am a poor man, why do you want to rob me?' school of negotiation. And then come back here and get your cash. I'll get your ticket filled out in the meantime, that's how confident I am."

Red scooped the jewelry back into John's zipbag, and John carried on down the tunnel of shops. Next to a pink-awninged kiosk selling bright blue and green liquid in fist-sized plastic bubbles with drinking straws punched into them, he found Leafty's.

Even after hearing Red's offer, the best Leafty could do was nine thousand dollars. "Repeat business," he said in a husky voice, "I'm a repeat player. Maybe I can't get you the best price on this jewelry, but you're going to want to come to market again, when you need crates for all the Weave you'll ship, or pretty shoes for your girlfriend, or a new hat. I'm the most connected man in Henry Hudson, and if you want something exotic, you're going to come back, I promise."

"What I want," John said, "is as much money as I can get for the jewels."

Red had the ticket all but complete when John returned to his shop. John filled in a few final details and took a receipt, and Red asked, "How do you want the money?"

"Two hundred in cash," John said, "and the rest in my Depository account."

"I don't have U.S."

"Sarovari is fine."

Red transmitted the money and John got the receipt message on his multi, pocketing the two hundred dollars.

"Take this." Red pushed the energy pistol across the counter, and three energy cells with it.

"I need the money for other things."

"I know," Red said. "This is my gift."

"Do you think I'll need it?"

Red grinned. "I get the most money if you come back, soon, and buy back the jewelry. The gun is just a way to increase the odds that you come back."

CHAPTER FIVE

In the morning, despite having exhausted themselves in the swimming pool, the girls were up before the sun, awake and bouncing on the couch when John returned from a short jog in the hotel's fitness center.

"Still on *Oberon* time," Ruth grumbled over scrambled eggs and fruit at the buffet in the hotel lobby.

"How far away are the Stone Gardens?" Ellie asked.

John tapped his multi. "The app says it's a twenty-minute drive, let's see . . . twenty-two kilometers."

"I'm glad we decided not to walk," Ruth said.

"Well, it might rain."

Sunitha swallowed the last of her cocoa. "And how long until the cab gets here?"

"Should be about thirty seconds." John threw his plate and utensils in the disposal, where they'd be sterilized, ground up, melted down, spun out again as new thread, and reprinted as something else. He picked up the blue-and-buff grip bag and slung it over his shoulder; inside were the energy pistol, several liters of water, and snacks. They all wore their own jackets.

"We could swim again," Sunitha said. "There will probably be hiking at Arrowhawk."

"But there won't be the Stone Gardens," John said.

"What are the Stone Gardens?" Sunitha asked.

"They're magnificent," John said. "And they're a surprise."

"You have no idea what they are," Ruth said.

"I have no idea what they are. But someone told me last night we should go see them, and I think he was a pretty reliable source."

The cabbie who picked them up was the same one who had driven them to the hotel. The minute the family was sitting down, Sunitha whipped her multi out of her pocket.

"Hey," Ruth said. "I told you I would take the pictures, and you could leave your multitool at the hotel."

"Only you take pictures of all the wrong things, Mom," Sunitha said. "I don't need more pictures of Ellie or Dad—I know what they look like. I want pictures of the things we're going to see."

"Okay, but you don't need a picture of the inside of the cab," John said, trying to head off Ruth's ire.

Sunitha put on her aristocrat voice. "Obviously, I'm looking up the Stone Gardens."

Four minutes' drive was enough to get them out of Henry Hudson Post. The streets he had walked the previous evening were pale and tame by morning light, with a few shop owners sweeping up cigarette butts and throwing absorbent powder onto puddles of urine and vomit. Drones still zipped by overhead, but the larger vehicles were few and far between.

John sat facing backward, his arm around Sunitha as she banged away at the screen of her multitool. John himself scanned the list of Sedjem words in the orientation packet on his multi, trying to commit the strange words to memory. There were also notes on syntax, which made no sense to him at all. At their first turn, John chanced to look behind them and saw a white groundcar on their trail, several blocks away.

"First of all, they're not gardens," Sunitha said.

"Right," John said. "They're actually a lake."

"No," Sunitha said.

"A pool of lava," John guessed. "A prison. A hole in the ground."

"Ruins." Sunitha shoved her multitool back into her pocket.

"I feel like I was close," John said.

Ruth kicked him softly.

"What else?" John asked.

"That's it. They're ruins, and we don't know who built them."

"Could be the early surveyors?" John suggested. "Or the Weavers?"

"Do the Weavers build anything?" Ruth said. "I know people say they're intelligent, but I always had the sense that they were only semi-sentient. Like, really smart dogs. And the smartest dogs aren't going to build . . . whatever it was that turned into the ruins."

"Maybe the ruins are all three-sided buildings," Sunitha suggested. "Radiating out from the center. And then we'll know."

"Ooh," Ellie said. "Gross."

"Why would that be gross?" Sunitha asked.

"It just sounds disgusting. Like a cow pat."

"What? Have you ever even seen a cow pat? Besides, it sounds like a sunflower or a daisy to me."

"I haven't heard that they build," John said. "Is there a longer article on the Weavers in Doctor Doctor now? Or rather, Factor Doctor?"

"Yes," Sunitha said, "and it says they live in the forest, and possibly in caves. It doesn't say anything about buildings, one way or the other."

"Humans," the cabbie called from the front of the car.

John turned around to look at the driver. They rolled along a road that was still paved with asphalt, but now cut through a patchwork of green fields and thin forest. "You've seen them, then?"

"Yes, mar. I don't know about the Weavers building, but since they don't have hands, I don't think so. But these were built by someone with hands, had to be. So I say it was the first settlers, the first human settlers, back before the Company took control of everything."

"I didn't think those numbers were very big," John said. "Were there really enough early settlers to leave ruins?"

"Bigger than you'd think, mar," the cabbie said. "There are whole towns out there where the Company doesn't control the trade or the courts. They hack into the Company's satellites, but they usually set up their own power. They farm. They raise animals. They colonize."

"Are they politically organized?" John wondered. "It seems like sooner or later there must be a conflict."

"There's plenty of room. They stay out of the Company's way, and just come into the posts when they need a replacement machine part, or want a bowl of noodles. It's a bit like the Amish back on Earth— they want to be left alone, in their own towns. You might work here twenty years for the Company and never see them. I know they exist because they hire me for rides, sometimes."

"And you think the ruins are theirs?"

"You'll see what I mean."

John turned back around, and saw again a plain white groundcar.

It might not be the same one; it looked very nondistinct, a sedan with soft, rounded edges, one of the nearly identical models that every manufacturer offered. And if it was the same car, that might be coincidence; there just couldn't be that many roads, and so it must often happen that drivers imagined themselves to be followed.

"You're seeing the car," the cabbie said.

"I figure there just aren't that many roads," John said. "So it feels like we're being followed, when really we aren't."

"I'm pretty sure he's following us," the cabbie said. "That's Sarovar Company Security Services."

"You mean . . . police?" Ruth turned to look out the back window.

"You work for the Company, don't you? I'm pretty sure they're just taking care of you while you're in town. It would be a shame if you went to the Stone Gardens on your first day here and something ate you. And here we are."

The cabbie parked his car in a flat meadow. The sward beneath the cab's wheels rolled down and around two small knots of trees to a series of tall rock fins erupting from the grass.

The groundcar behind them pulled over and stopped, a hundred meters distant.

"The last thing we have to worry about," John said, "is Company security. I work for Director English, and I'm sure he just wants to make sure we don't run into any unpleasant surprises."

Had he been followed into town, the night before? He didn't remember seeing the white groundcar; had he been observed via drone?

Or was Bangerter Cheapside, for instance, in the employ of Company Security Services?

John stepped out of the cab. As his family climbed out to join him, he checked the multitool to make sure he was getting reception, then waved as the cabbie drove away.

They drifted down the grass toward the gray stone. He and Ruth held hands and walked slowly; Sunitha raced from tree to tree to inspect their leaves and bark and occasionally take pictures; Ellie somersaulted, literally rolling down the hill in spurts, punctuated by stretches of rising to her feet and running with all limbs flailing. Ani ran back and forth between the girls, barking and hurling herself beneath their feet.

"As soon as we get to Arrowhawk," John said, "I'll look into how to buy Weave and how to transport it back to Central Transit. There will be other factors and traders who can show me the ropes."

It was a new evolution of a promise he had made to her many times.

She nodded.

"I can buy back your jewels," he said. "The pawnbroker can't sell them for twelve months, so all we have to do is make enough profit in twelve months, and I'll buy the jewels right back."

"At what interest rate?" she asked.

"Technically, the interest rate will depend on the moment when I buy them back," John said. "I'll pay him twelve thousand dollars."

"So," she recapitulated, "you need to take our ten thousand dollars and turn it into twelve thousand dollars *plus* enough additional capital to continue buying and reselling Weave. How much do you estimate that is?"

"The more, the better," he said. "I'll have a better idea of what reasonable numbers are once we get to Arrowhawk and I can talk to the factors and traders."

"Dad-setty! Dad-setty! Look at this!"

But John didn't immediately look at Ellie; his gaze stretched back up the green meadow, to where the white groundcar waited. Two persons had emerged from the car; men, probably, though they wore heavy blue-and-buff coats, and it was hard to be certain. They leaned against the car, watching John and his family, while one of them smoked.

John scanned the air for drones, and didn't see anyway.

"Dad-setty! Dad-setty!"

"John," Ruth asked, "what do those guys want?"

"This is the Company's planet. We're going to have to get used to seeing Company security forces around."

"John, you're an entry-level accountant. Why on Earth would the Company send two security guards to protect you?"

John mumbled wordlessly, asking himself the same question.

"Dad!" Sunitha called. "Pay attention to Ellie, before she explodes!"

John shook off his feelings of unease and turned to face his girls. The fins of gray rock, he now saw, were not ridges all running in one direction, but the walls of buildings. The walls had been constructed of stones, shaped to rectangular pieces of varying size and shape, and then slotted together.

John stopped at the first to run his fingers over the stone. There was no mortar cementing each stone to its neighbors, and no space between the stones; they simply slotted together, as if they had been cast for the purpose in precise molds.

Ruth whistled.

Some of the walls must have been two or three stories tall, at least, to judge from their height. Moving between them, John began to see floors connecting some of them, and the remains of floors that had long since collapsed.

It did indeed seem likely that human hands had shaped these walls.

But the initial settlers from Earth had come here less than a century ago. If the very first members of Homo sapiens to land on Sarovar Alpha had built these buildings, and then immediately abandoned them ... surely the floors would be intact, and the buildings in their entirety would still be standing.

Perhaps the buildings had been destroyed early, and immediately abandoned.

Did something dangerous live in these woods and fields? The taxi driver had as much as said that there were things in the woods that could eat humans. John looked back at the Company security agents. What were they really doing here?

"This was some kind of complex," Ruth said. "A small settlement, maybe."

"Most people build their own houses out of mud and straw and things that don't need to last a thousand years," John said. "Building from stone is a lot more work. It suggests ... what? Wealth? Social organization?"

"A desire for permanence," Ruth suggested. "This looks like a ruined monastery or a temple complex."

"Look, there are ditches lined with stone." John pointed. "Water flowed beneath these buildings. Bringing fresh water in? Washing out sewage?"

"Both?" Ruth suggested.

They still had not reached Ellie, who stood on the other side of a wall from them. They heard her voice get louder as they drew close, and then they rounded the edge of the wall and could see what she saw.

And it took John's breath away.

Murals.

The space where they stood must once have been the inside of a building, and the wall before them had been covered with murals. White plaster had been painted with a series of images that rose ten meters in the air, and that still existed because stone slabs that had once been ceiling, or perhaps the floor of a fourth story, leaned upon the wall and upon three nearby stone columns, sheltering the murals from the wind, sun, and rain.

Big chunks were scarred black—burned, John guessed, by something like the energy pistol he carried in his grip bag. No single scene in the complex and fragmentary collection of scenes was unmarred, and as he looked at the murals, it seemed to him that they had been deliberately edited. Bowdlerized. Redacted.

What he could see of the murals was astonishing. Creatures, with spiderlike eyes and six crab-like legs and six crab-like claws were pictured, in a strict two-dimensional view from the side. They each had two legs and claws pointing left and right, and then a third set that pointed legs down and claws up. They interacted in groups. In some scenes, small creatures surrounded a large one. In other scenes, they seemed to march in parade, or dance in circles, or act out scenes in painted forests or on painted mountaintops.

"Those crab-things," Ruth said. "Are they . . . four-sided?"

"Or is that a two-dimensional way to show a three-sided creature?" John asked.

"They're Weavers," Sunitha said. She showed her parents her multitool, which had an image of one of the mural scenes. Beneath, a caption read: *Sarovari Weavers congregate in a damaged scene.*

"Every scene," John said. "Every single scene has had something big burned out of it."

"But what?" Ruth asked.

A roar erupted from the trees below the ruins. John clutched the grip bag tightly, but didn't pull out the pistol. "Girls!" he called.

Sunitha pressed herself against her mother's side.

Ellie . . . where was Ellie?

John heard barking and ran toward it. He didn't pull out the gun because he didn't want to startle the girls if he didn't need to. At the edge of the trees, Ani stood, muscles tensed, barking at something unseen in the forest. Ellie tried to drag Ani away by her collar, but the dog was resisting. John could see the pit bull in Ani's thick chest and narrow hips and snarling jaws.

"Dad." Ellie's voice trembled. "Ani won't come."

"She's protecting you," John said. "You come away from the trees and she will, too."

But Ellie stood as if glued to the ground.

Another roar echoed from the woods, and tree branches shook. John's heart pounded. "Ellie, let's go." He held out a hand, trying to act calm.

She stared into the trees. "Daddy, I see something."

Time was up. John scooped his daughter up onto his shoulder and turned to jog up the hill. "Heel, Ani!"

Ani snarled and barked but didn't heel. She was loyal to her pack, but not always the most obedient dog.

John broke into a run. Behind him he heard another roar, and as he reached the fins of crumbled masonry, he turned to look back. A bearlike creature covered in shaggy gray fur emerged from the trees and swiped at Ani. The dog dodged once, and then again, and nipped at the bear's flanks.

Then the bear stood up, and John saw that it had six legs.

"Ani!" John whistled, and finally the dog disengaged and came trotting up to meet him. John put his right hand into the grip bag and felt the cool butt of the energy pistol. Ruth gathered up the two girls and pulled them behind him, and Ani stood beside him, barking.

The bearlike thing roared again. It stood on four legs, flailing its front two limbs. Then it rose briefly onto his hind pair of legs and raked the air with four claws at once, simultaneously emitting an industrial bellow that made the hair on the back of John's neck stand up.

Then finally it turned and slunk into the woods.

"Time to call the cab back," John said.

When he turned, the white groundcar and the two men in Company jackets were gone.

CHAPTER
SIX

In the morning, the maglev train took them to Arrowhawk.

The train line skirted a body of water that Sunitha told them all, proudly, was really an enormous freshwater lake even though it was named the Bridger Sea, ran through the deep valleys of a tall range of mountains called the Tenzings, crossed a plain of tall grasses dotted with burly, rectangular quadrupeds, and eventually climbed into a low, gnarled range of hills. These mountains, identified by Factor Doctor as the Mallories, were rocky, abounding in cliffs, and visibly very wet; out the windows of the train car, John saw waterfalls, streams, bogs, and ten thousand little lakes. The runoff from the network of fresh water collected in rivers; at first, he saw rivers that drained off the east side of the mountain range, but by the time the train came to its final stop, they had crossed the spine of the mountains and seen rivers flowing westward.

As they rode, John paced and tried not to bend his wrists. Sunitha lectured, informing them that Sarovar Alpha, uniquely among the planets of Sarovar System, was extremely Earth-like in its physical characteristics. An axial tilt of approximately twenty degrees gave the planet two hemispheres with distinct seasons, size and gravity and atmosphere were all virtually identical to Earth's, and even the planet's year consisted of almost exactly three hundred sixty days of twenty-four and a half Earth hours. The most noticeable difference was that Sarovar Alpha had two moons.

"A person might be kidnapped on Earth and wake up on Sarovar and not realize she had been moved," she observed triumphantly.

"If she were kept sedated for six months," Ruth said.

"Five," John murmured.

Ellie then announced, looking up from her multitool, that the creature that had tried to eat her the day before was called Hausman's Bear, and it wasn't really a bear at all, and it supposedly didn't eat humans, but it did eat fish and other small animals, and how much different was she, really, from a fish?

Ani then climbed onto the seat beside Ellie and laid her head on the girl's lap.

In breaks in the conversation, John continued to try to teach himself Sedjem. Languages were not his strength, but he could remember some twenty-odd words, to Sunitha's robust quizzing.

The train guideway ran high above the ground, on thick pylons, no doubt to protect it from interference by random animals. The only sign that they were approaching the post was the appearance of a handful of gravel roads, and then the train pulled to a stop.

Arrowhawk's maglev station squatted fifteen meters above the ground, atop the tallest building in Arrowhawk Post, with the other rooftops of Arrowhawk visible beneath it. The station itself was covered by its own sturdy roof of opaque plastic slabs epoxied together. The train stopped, doors opened on both sides of the car, and Ruth led the family out the right-hand door onto the platform.

The left-hand door exited into space that was stacked high with crates. John lingered behind his family for a moment to watch as men in blue jumpsuits and coveralls went to work; the seats in the train cars flipped up and snapped into place against the walls, freeing up most of the interior of the train into a space big enough to hold two groundcars, and then the men began loading in the crates.

There was no one on the platform to meet them. Ruth stood looking left and right, lips pursed and concern on her face.

John called back to the men loading the train. "I'm looking for Audit Chief Keckley!"

One of them came bounding out of the car. He was broad-shouldered and narrow-hipped, with the build of a natural athlete. He had a thick mustache and a strong jaw, and he pointed at a staircase that descended into the building beneath the platform.

"Audit chief's office is down there, mar! Two flights down. If you don't see Keckley at his desk, he may be out taking his afternoon nap." The man mimed drinking from a bottle. "I'm Jefferson! Are you a new trader?"

Was Jefferson a first name or a last name? John split the difference and gave both. "John Abbott. I'm technically a factor. Really, I'm an accountant."

"Ah yes, we heard you were coming. Keckley's your man. But hey, a factor...that means you should be looking for a trader to work with."

It seemed unlikely that Jefferson could offer him better terms than English had, but John didn't want to alienate anyone. "Yeah," he said.

"Well, I'm not going to pressure you, but what you need to understand up front is that it can be hard to actually get your product shipped, if you're just a trader. Too many Company bigwigs and buyers are trying to ship, and not only do they get priority, they also bribe the captains or the stevedores when they have to. Some of these guys—like Rock over there, that's the long-haired guy stumping around like a pirate and talking to himself—don't even try to ship. Rock is just piling up a hoard of Weave, and he'll take it with him when he goes."

"If he doesn't ship, why is he here? At the train, I mean?"

Jefferson grinned. "On shipping day, it's all hands on deck at Company House. Unless you're out on a wat. The Company's Weave still has to ship, after all."

"Huh."

"Rock's is not a crazy strategy. When a guy's going home, he knows he can actually get on the ship, and even if he can't get any space in the cargo hold, he can at least fill his quarters with Weave to sell."

"But then he can't grow his capital in the meantime," John said. "He can't sell and reinvest, he's just sinking his salary into the asset. He can't make as much."

Jefferson nodded. "There is the so-called country trade. He could be trading his Weave with other traders on the planet, for gemstones or whatever. And of course, Rock gets all his food and drink from the commissary here, so he's not eating up his capital."

And Rock didn't have jewelry to buy back out of pawn.

"Now me," Jefferson continued, "I have a different approach. I have a cousin who's a buyer, and will give me a better price than any of the other buyers at Central Transit. Is it as good as Earth dollars? No, because he needs to make his cut, too. But then he takes the risk, I get paid earlier, and, like you say, I take that capital and reinvest it."

John nodded. "How long does it take you to get paid?"

"I get paid within the week, mar."

At that speed, John might make profit enough to buy back the jewels and capitalize the business faster with Jefferson than with English. "And you need a cut, too."

"Three percent," Jefferson said. "Five if I do the purchasing for you."

"Stop talking about me!" Rock bellowed.

John had other questions, but he didn't want to ask them of Jefferson, or at least, not yet. What did the traders actually give to the Weavers—what did the Company give them, for that matter? If he signed up to trade through Jefferson, then it would be in the man's interest to show John the ropes. Until then, John was, at least theoretically, the competition, and John didn't want to push the relationship too hard, too fast.

"Thanks," he said.

The stairs took John and his family down two flights. At the first landing was a single door labeled COMMS, with a bright yellow fire extinguisher bracketed to the wall beside it. At the second were two doors, with signs that read AUDIT and MEDICAL, with an extinguisher bracketed between them.

Ruth hesitated outside Medical, but then she and the girls followed John into Audit.

Inside Audit was a room with three desks: the largest was relatively neat, bearing short stacks of paper and a couple of ledgers; the second desk was a chaotic mess that could have been generated by the detonation of a bomb, behind which sat a spherical man in blue and buff with three strands of hair pasted to his skull; the smallest desk was empty.

The spherical man looked up. "John Sanjay Abbott."

"Three for three," John said. "How could you tell? My erect, manly posture, and the keen light of intelligence in my eyes?"

"Bug eyes and elephant ears, I saw your photo." The rotund man pointed at Ruth. "But also, you have a wife and kids. Precious few Company employees bring a wife out here from Earth, and fewer bring kids. My name's DeBoe. I'm the other auditor."

"Pleased to meet you. If they don't bring wives, what do they . . . how do they . . . socialize?" John asked, bending his fingers back.

"Oh, here at the post, there are other ways . . ." DeBoe coughed and blushed. "There are children present."

"Understood."

"If there aren't other children, then there aren't really teachers," Ruth said, "as we had imagined there would be."

"There are children," DeBoe said. "Just not very many, and the post itself doesn't provide schooling. But there's a teacher, and . . . I need to check this, don't hold me to it, but I think there's a monthly child benefit paid by the Company that's meant to cover the costs of schooling."

"I have Factor Doctor." Sunitha clutched her multitool to her chest.

DeBoe looked baffled.

"It's the docent program," John explained. "The encyclopedia avatar."

DeBoe chuckled. "Ah, good, and he's a factor. That must be the Company skin. I have keys for you, and the address of your new home." He held up a jangling ring of keys and a card with writing scrawled on it. "Most of those are to your house. The two that don't match are to this building and the warehouse."

"Keys." John took the keys and smiled. "I haven't seen physical keys for a long time."

"Get used to it. The power is not one hundred percent reliable here, so we use old tech to do some things. Including our bookkeeping." He pointed at the messiest desk, with its ledgers. "If you came imagining this would look like a space station, we're going to disappoint you. Arrowhawk Post looks more like something out of *The Last of the Mohicans*."

John paced over to the messy desk to cast an eye over the books. "With six-armed, circular Hurons."

"The good news is, the Weavers want to trade. And also, if you hear any whispering about some dreaded white Weaver, it's drunk nonsense."

"Captain Ahab." John grinned.

DeBoe nodded. "But there are other things out there in the mountains, and we don't have names for half of them."

"We saw a bear with six arms." Ellie's voice was solemn and her eyes were wide open and round.

"We don't have names for sixty percent of them," Sunitha said crisply.

DeBoe shrugged. "If you said eighty percent, I'd have to believe you. Might be ninety percent. How do you know for sure, until you've actually cataloged every species?"

"How do we buy?" John asked. The girls were fidgeting, but Ruth was interested in the answer to this question, too, so he let the girls fidget.

"Well, it's like any other business," DeBoe said. "You can invest money or you can invest sweat. If you invest all the money and all the sweat, you take all the return."

"That sounds like first-day lecture notes." John grinned and folded his fingers back. "Let's say I wanted to invest all the money and all the sweat, what would I actually do?"

"You'd get good at Sedjem. Weavers don't talk much, but when they do, they Sedjem. You'd go with traders to the known and regular markets. You might go out into the forest looking for new Weavers— some people have scored big by taking caravans of trade goods as far as the coast to find new markets. You'd buy trade goods from the Company warehouse—at a markup, but it's reasonable—and you'd sell them at those markets. Then you'd ship them by maglev to Central Transit, and you'd bid in the auction for cargo space on the next starship. You'd have a buyer arranged in advance, or you'd have an agent at the Earth-end to sell for you."

"Otherwise, the Company has a seller at the Earth end?" John asked.

DeBoe nodded. "And then he takes a cut."

"This is complicated," Sunitha said.

"This is boring." Ellie slumped her shoulders and bugged out her eyes. "Daddy, stop talking."

Sunitha was right. John was seeing that his dream of a quick fortune was mutating into a plan of grinding out a fortune over time, hopefully beginning with quick sales to a buyer at Central

Transit to buy the jewelry out of pawn and amass a little capital, and then somehow arranging his own agent, Earthside, for the longer term.

"Sorry," DeBoe said. "The harshest light is sometimes what allows you to see best."

"Yes," Ruth said, "if it doesn't give you a migraine."

They descended another flight of stairs to the ground. Three sets of doors led back into the building, one labeled EXECUTIVE, the second WAREHOUSE, and the third SECURITY. The door into Security was open and two men glared at John wordlessly. Both were balding and wore spectacles. One had oversized shoulders and the other oversized forearms and they both had short legs, as if the anatomy of a gorilla had been divided between them. A fourth set of doors let John and his family outside.

The streets of Arrowhawk Post were paved with gravel. All around the base of the train station was heaped up the ramshackle, three-story building through which they had descended; turning and looking back, John saw the words *Company House* nailed over the door in iron letters. Attached to the side of Company House, and hunkered beneath the maglev line, was a large, windowless building that must be the warehouse.

Most of the other buildings John could see were one story tall, though a few had two stories. Groundcars and cycles crept along the roads, not in large enough numbers to create what John thought of as hazardous traffic, but enough to make it necessary to look both ways before crossing the street. Pivoting to look in all directions, he could see tall gray slabs of plastic standing like a wall all around the post. Beyond, not far away, he saw a cluster of rocky peaks to the north of the post, and another line of mountains to the south. He thought they were all part of the Mallory Mountains, and Arrowhawk sat in something like a wide pass or valley.

A single drone drifted across the street a couple hundred meters from Company House.

The buildings included residences, a hair salon, a general store, and at least two bars.

An eight-wheeled all-terrain vehicle, body segmented into two compartments, rumbled past, grinding its way toward the gate.

John passed each member of his family a housekey. "Grijalva Street," he said. "Is that Spanish?"

"Juan de Grijalva was a conquistador," Sunitha said in her lecture voice. "He got killed by natives."

"I see," John said. "A good omen. There can't be more than ten streets in this town, but let's ask directions."

The general store across from Company House had printed catalog pages stuck up in its street-facing window. The prices on all the items were scratched out in red ink, with new prices written in: a long-handled shovel was not twenty-five dollars, but fifty. John pushed open the clear plastic door to find a room stacked floor-to-ceiling with items of every description, and only a very small stock of each. There was a fan, a box of nails, the long-handled shovel, a barrel of hard biscuits.

A long-faced man with sleepy eyes stood behind a clear plastic counter. He wore green coveralls, and he labored over a stack of paper with a red pen and a multi. He looked up at John.

"You're new," he said.

"John Abbott."

"Trader?"

"Accountant."

"I don't suppose you'll need a calculator, the multitool will do that. Hmm. And you'll need ledgers, but Keckley keeps a stack of those. How about food?"

"Animal crackers?" John suggested.

"I have a one-liter tube and a ten-liter tube."

"I better start with one."

"You get better pricing with ten. Twenty bucks."

"Ten liters it is." The girls would eat them. John spooled out a twenty-dollar bill. "I'm looking for Grijalva Street."

"Back side of the block." The shopkeeper handed over a clear plastic barrel full of animal crackers. John looked them over and was disappointed to see that they were all familiar Earth animals. "What number?"

John checked the card. "Seventeen."

"Ah, one of the khats. I should have guessed. Back of the block, and that way." He pointed with his left arm.

John emerged to find his daughters and Ani following a small creature down the street with great interest. The creature was the size of an insect, but it was furred. Despite its dimensions, it repeatedly looked up and hissed loudly; Ani batted it from side to side with her paws, a playful gesture that suggested she would soon eat the varmint.

"You know, we haven't learned what might be poisonous here," John said. "If Ani eats it. Or venomous, if it bites her."

"You can't take away her fun, Dad-setty."

"I can trade her fun, though. Ani!" John whistled and held out a rhinoceros cracker. Ani took the cracker and followed him as he trooped around the block toward Grijalva Street. "We live in a khat," he told the girls.

Sunitha frowned. "That's a fortress."

"Oh, good," John said. "I hope it has cannons."

Grijalva Street ended against the eastern stockade wall. The last two blocks of it were occupied by walled houses. Here there was almost no traffic, though there were a few groundcars parked in front of the houses. As he fumbled with the unfamiliarity of a metal key at the three-meter-tall gate for foot traffic, John looked over the top of the wall and saw the second story of a house. It was made of plastic, and prefabricated, but the manufacturers had colored and stressed the plastic to make it look like weathered stone.

"The whole house?" Ellie was suspicious. "I don't have to share?"

"Of course, you have to share." John opened the gate. "There are five of us here."

The girls rushed inside, swarming first to a pond in the corner of the enclosure, then to a thick tree with many low branches, then to a bramble with fat berries hanging below the leaves, and finally up two steps to the broad porch and the front door. A second, wider gate through the khat's enclosure led to a parking space beside the house, though there was no vehicle there.

Ruth threaded an arm through John's elbow. For the first time in weeks, her muscles didn't feel tensed and her voice sounded pleased. "Do you think it's furnished?"

CHAPTER SEVEN

John was at his desk in the morning when Keckley came in; he'd simply sat down at the empty one and made himself at home. The audit chief of Arrowhawk Post had meaty shoulders and arms and a fire-eating expression on his goateed face; if John hadn't known who he was, he would have taken the man for Security, or a stevedore.

John hadn't been certain which of the blue and buff clothing English had delivered to his hotel room in Henry Hudson Post was appropriate for daily use, so he'd chosen a casual jacket, worn over his own trousers and a polo shirt. Just in case, he'd tucked Director English's encryption plug into the pocket.

He was relieved to see Keckley wearing a very similar jacket.

"John—"

"I know who you are, dammit." Keckley flung himself into the chair behind his desk, leaned back, and closed his eyes. "Don't fool yourself that you're going to earn a promotion by the power of sheer enthusiasm and go-getterness. I *hate* those people."

"Understood," John said. "So I'll aim for . . . what? Grumpy? Dour? Intractable?"

"Competent," Keckley said. "Be competent, and I'll keep paying you. If you can also be *fast*, I may actually give you a raise. So far, DeBoe has just managed to be competent, and *that* by the skin of his teeth."

"One way to be fast is to get an early start."

"Touché." Keckley sighed, sat up, and opened his eyes. "What are you looking at, then?"

"I started with the most recent balance sheet," John said. "Just checking it against journal entries."

"Ticking and tying." Keckley laughed. "Just like school, eh?"

John nodded.

"Tell me," Keckley said, "at NYU, did they ever have you confirm your inventory by walking through the warehouse and physically counting everything?"

"No," John admitted. "NYU is a school, so it doesn't have a warehouse."

"Good. Then you can feel like you're learning something this afternoon, while you're doing it here."

"It might be easier if I had a little more familiarity with Weave and with our packaging," John suggested.

"True," Keckley agreed. "But you'll learn that stuff. And you're overlooking the most important reason why you should have the task."

"Which is?"

"It's a crap job," Keckley said, "and you're the junior guy."

"I don't feel enthusiastic or go-getterish about that," John said, "but I'll do the work competently."

"Perfect."

"I'm looking at paper ledgers," John said. "I understand power isn't always dependable here, so the paper books are primary."

"All true," Keckley said. "But we transmit our monthly figures over the network, so of course we have electronic books, too. I'll get that application downloaded into your multi by lunch. There's also the post utility app. It has messaging, scheduling, news feed, a chatroom. Don't abuse it. I'll get that to you, as well."

"Assuming power holds out."

"You're a fast learner."

"That's what they tell me."

"I *hate* fast learners."

"But learning fast is how I become competent."

"Carry on."

The accounting app and the utility app both downloaded into John's multitool well before midday, and he switched from ticking and tying the balance sheet to examining costs. The accounting app connected him to the Depository records of the post, so he could see amounts and also confirm payments.

The salaries all looked in order. For a moment, the payments to traders looked strange, until he realized that there were two components: a stipend paid monthly, and other payments that fluctuated in time and amount.

Keckley had disappeared by then, but DeBoe was sitting at his desk across the office.

"DeBoe," John said, "can I ask you to explain something?"

"Send me a screenshot," DeBoe mumbled.

A few seconds later, DeBoe sipped coffee from a printed cup and examined the image John had sent, while John squatted beside his desk and looked on.

"Those irregular payments—is that the traders, trading for their own accounts?" John asked.

"Uh, no. Unless for some reason the Company got involved in a specific transaction, those deals should basically be invisible to us. You'd have to look at the trader's own Depository Account records to see him getting a payment from his Earthside agent, or from the Central Transit buyer, or whatever. You have to remember that 'trader' means two different things."

"Uh, okay."

"You're a factor, right? Me, too. And someday, I might become a trader, but that just means I'll be allowed to buy and sell Weave, and whatever other commodities I want—but don't get too excited, around Arrowhawk Post it's all Weave—for my own account, right?"

"Correct," John said.

"So factor is my rank and auditor is my job, but in the future maybe trader will be my rank and auditor will still be my job."

"I'm in exactly the same boat."

"Good. Fun bit of trivia for you that might not be obvious from your contract. There's a rank lower than factor. Those people aren't even allowed to buy and sell through a trader, they're just barred from trading in any of the commodities indicated in the Barred Goods Annex to the Code of Conduct. Employees for hire, and that's it."

John nodded. "They call them 'writers.' Poor bastards. Who are they?"

"Not people who write, as it turns out. Or at least, not anymore. The security guards. Porters, and so on."

"I see."

"But some of the men at the post have trader as their job, too. Trader is their rank, meaning they can buy and sell for their own account, and trader is their job, meaning they can buy Weave—and other commodities, where there are others—for the Company's account."

John stared at the image. "And they must get paid a commission of some kind."

"They do. Two percent. In order not to pay them too badly in arrears, the Company pays the commission weekly, and assumes the sale price of the Weave is the most recent posted price from New York City, as communicated by the most recently arrived starship captain."

"That's not really great price data," John said. "The market could have entirely collapsed, and we wouldn't know it until the next starship arrived."

"The price of living behind a wormhole." DeBoe shrugged. "And another reason why the traders are happy to get paid at the most recent price, rather than take the risk that the market has collapsed."

"Of course, if the market goes up rather than crashing, the traders lose out on the upside."

"And historically the market has always gone up." DeBoe shrugged again. "But one day, it will go the other direction, and it will be the Company, rather than its traders, to eat the loss. Unless, of course, the Company changes its compensation policies at that time. Which it will. The Planetary Board may sometimes be slow to act, but the Executive Committee is not."

John went back to his seat, musing. The ledger numbers matched up with the bank transfers, so that all seemed in order.

The traders were all clearly making much more money than he would make, so that seemed...obnoxious. But maybe he could become a trader for the Company; of course, he'd have to learn the business, first.

He didn't mean to skip lunch, he was just too excited to remember that it was time to eat, and he rushed off to the warehouse with a photograph of the physical inventory ledger page on his multi. DeBoe raised a hand and mumbled as he left; Keckley still hadn't returned.

In the stairwell, he bumped into a woman. She had a very straight face and piercing eyes under hair black as pitch. She wore a blue tunic and buff trousers, with a short gold cape around her shoulders.

"Post Chief Carlton?" John asked, extending a hand.

"Hinkley." The woman laughed, a short, stabbing sound. "Surgeon. Which makes me the *real* factor doctor of the post." She pointed at the door to Medical. "We're neighbors."

"John Abbott," John said. "Dr. Hinkley, we've just arrived on the planet."

"Yes, I understand."

"Are there . . . inoculations my family should have? Or other precautions against local disease?"

"No." Hinkley frowned. "Why do you ask?"

"We heard there were . . . Sarovari diseases to worry about."

"Hmm." She peered at him closely. "Listen, this may be none of my business, but have you ever heard of Marfan's Syndrome?"

John felt vaguely embarrassed, as if he had been caught in public in his underwear. "I have it."

"Ah, good. So you know. What are you doing about it?"

"Making regular appointments with my physician," John said slowly, "so she can keep an eye on any symptoms I may develop, and treat them."

"When shall we schedule your first appointment?" Hinkley asked.

"Let me get settled in first. I have a lot going on right now. I guess you must have a lot of free time, at a small post like this."

"I have some flexibility." Hinkley winked. "Carry on." The doctor turned and entered the Medical office.

John continued on his way.

The warehouse was a single floor as tall as a two-story building and stacked floor to ceiling over every available square meter with heavy shelving. There were bay doors in the eastern wall through which vehicles could enter and leave, and three trucks of different sizes and configurations stood squeezed uncomfortably between the shelving. The trucks had big knobby wheels, and the two larger vehicles had segmented bodies, dividing the trucks into fore and aft compartments. A set of scales large enough to hold any of the trucks occupied the space immediately beside the bay doors. Stairs wound up beside the south wall, apparently to the ceiling—did they open on the maglev platform? Or onto a roof below the platform?

The Weave was packed in crates, standing neatly organized on shelves that reached ten meters up. The movable stairs for accessing those shelves were wheeled and had a hand brake, so, all by himself in the warehouse, John could slowly move around the entire space and examine every crate.

The Weave was a standard width, about two meters, and it was measured in meters of length. Working without break and under the dim warehouse lights, augmented from time to time by the light of his multitool, John was able to confirm that the numbers of crates on the shelves and the listed contents of the crates were consistent with what was listed in the post's inventory.

One hundred twelve bales of Weave.

Seventy-five boxes of trade goods, which consisted of various kinds of manufactured tools and canned food.

He found that all the crates were electronically sealed, but that the possession of the accounting app on his multi allowed him to open them. Ideally, he'd have liked to look inside every crate. Given his time constraints, he opened one in every ten, in each case checking the actual contents against those listed on the crates themselves and against the written inventory. He checked Weave and also trade goods.

All consistent, all in order.

The Weave itself was the raw product, undyed. It was shimmering, elastic, and beautiful. It was also, John had read, resistant to flame and puncturing, and when it got stressed, it was self-healing—something about the Sarovari Weavers' process allowed them to create a fabric that regenerated. Weave that had healed from being stressed was stronger than before, which meant that Weave became sturdier over time, rather than becoming frail.

The fabric's beauty made it in demand for fashion reasons. Its toughness meant it was often a component in the armor worn by law enforcement agencies, other first responders, and even soldiers.

No one had yet been able to replicate the Weavers' feat with a competing product. One day someone would do so, and then the price of Weave would collapse.

So, on top of all the other considerations for his new business, John had to keep an eye on the inevitable exit. Into what investments would he spread his capital, as soon as he had enough cash to diversify?

Other posts on Sarovar Alpha collected other products: gemstones, woods, food, some animals. There would be investments to make, when the time came. He might have to transfer away from Arrowhawk Post to make them.

When he had put in an eleven-hour day, John returned to the office. A torrent of rain hammered Company House, drumming on the windows and making the bones of the building creak. Keckley had returned and gone again—a meeting with Post Chief Carlton, DeBoe said. DeBoe in turn was stuffing himself into a clear plastic rain jacket, and only urged John to lock up before disappearing into the storm.

John locked up, bought four rain jackets at the general store across the street, looked at a solar power unit as well, but decided he should consult with Ruth on a purchase that big, and then jogged home.

A line of people waited outside his gate when he reached the khat.

They stood in ponchos and coats, or under umbrellas. John noted, flicking rain from his face with one hand, that the street was fifteen centimeters lower than his own yard, so water seeped out underneath his gate and into the street, where it sank into the gravel.

As he approached, the line of people turned to look at him and began shouting, all at once. "Hey mar, you reddy work? You reddy kat?" "Big par, I clean!" "I guard khat, mar, you mo!" "Nefer bak! Nefer bak!"

John couldn't remember his Sedjem fast enough to interpret any of the individual sentences, much less reply to them, but he understood that the people wanted work. He looked up toward the house and saw Ruth standing in a second-story window, barely visible over the wall. Her arms were crossed over her chest and she was watching him.

He raised the raincoats to show her and waved. She shook her head, laughed, and pointed at the gate.

"Okay, okay," John called, "let me in! I live here." He decided to try a little Sedjem. "I am mar. I mar here!"

The crowd mobbed him, hands supplicating.

"We may need help," John said to them. He tried to think of useful Sedjem words, and couldn't. "I don't know if I'm going to hire anyone tomorrow. I definitely can't hire anyone tonight, and I can't hire anyone until I can get into my house and talk to my wife!"

The crowd closed in around him more.

John heard a sharp whistle. He turned his head to follow the sound and saw a man thirty meters down the street. He wore a tunic and loose, knee-length pants, both the color of faded roses. His long hair was plastered to the side of his head and neck, even though he stood under a pink frilly parasol, its loops and fringes battered by the rain. His skin was tan, with a hint of Mediterranean olive, and he beckoned John to come to him, then pointed at the khat wall next to him.

"Let me in my house!" John cried. The crowd surged forward.

"Mr. Abbott!" the man with the parasol yelled.

John tried to drag himself from the crowd and found that two men had taken hold of him physically, one grasping him by each elbow. He yanked and hurled himself backward, and then the pink parasol was there. Rolled up like a thick, wet club, it crashed down on one man's neck, knocking him sideways, and then poked the other in the face, and then John was free.

"There is an alley!" the man with the parasol barked.

John ran. The raincoats felt suddenly very heavy, and even though the drained gravel road provided good footing, he felt as if he were slogging through mud. The crowd shouted more Sedjem at him, and when he got to where the parasol man had been standing, he saw the alley.

It ran between two khat walls, and seemed to go right through the block. It was ungraveled, and the muddy lane was broken up by tree roots, puddles, and the occasional chest-sized rock.

He ran.

His heart beat loud in his ears. Exercise wasn't bad for him, he reminded himself. He was a regular jogger. An elevated heartbeat because he was running wouldn't cause his heart to separate from the tissues around it and kill him.

Getting hit might do the trick. Getting dragged to the ground and trampled was a bad choice for any man, and maybe an especially bad choice for John. But running wouldn't hurt him.

Almost certainly.

"Left, Mr. Abbott!" he heard the voice behind him shout.

The alley split abruptly, left and right. Following the parasol man's instructions, John turned left. The man with the parasol was right behind him, and the crowd was several steps farther back.

John had run twenty meters when the parasol man shouted, "This is your home, Mr. Abbott. Over the wall to your left!"

But the wall was three meters tall, and John was standing in mud. He jumped, and jumped again, gamely, but couldn't grab the top of the wall.

Then the parasol man was there. "Quickly now, on my back!" The man crouched, offering his shoulders to John. John wanted to demur and back away, but the crowd was too close.

He stepped onto parasol man's shoulders, smearing the pink fabric with mud, then dragged himself up and over the wall.

On the far side was a small shed, standing in the back corner of his enclosure. John dropped the raincoats in a heap. Then he crouched and offered a hand to the parasol man, who was standing up as the crowd reached him.

"No, thank you, Mr. Abbott!" he said. "I will see you again later, perhaps at your office!"

John had to strain to hear the man over the shouted pleading for jobs.

"Perhaps tonight!" John said. "I thought I might go out and get a drink, maybe meet some of the traders!"

"Ah-ha! In that case!" The parasol man took something from a pocket and tucked it beneath the plastic nipple at the end of his parasol. Stretching the soggy sunshade out like a limb extender, he handed the object up to John.

It was a business card. FAISAL HADDAD, it read. KNOWLEDGE-SETTY, INTERPRETER (SEDJEM, ENGLISH, FRENCH, ARABIC, HEBREW), GUIDE, ACQUIROR. It had a number and an ethernet address.

CHAPTER EIGHT

John toweled off his face and hands and feet from the rain and moved to flop onto the foam sofa. He stopped when he saw that it was covered with short, spiky, red-brown hairs. "Ani's shedding, I see."

"Give her a couple of weeks, and she'll be a different color." Ruth handed John coffee and they moved to the kitchen table.

The khat had turned out to be lightly furnished with a few tables and chairs, with a box full of inflatable foam sofas, beds, and chairs. There was no printer-disposal unit, but a set of printed cups and utensils for eight places, and a small cupboard full of actual linens— plain, but serviceable.

Including cloth towels.

It all felt so twenty-first century. Or maybe even twentieth.

"I'm sure we can get a printer in the house," John said. He'd lost count of how many times he'd already said that.

Ruth sipped her coffee. "No rush. As far as I'm concerned, disposable towels and plates come after getting the business started."

"And redeeming your jewelry."

Ruth shrugged.

"What else?" John asked. "What's our list?"

"Material things?" Ruth shook her head. "I don't need toys. I'd like to find a community to be part of here. Friends for the children."

"School. Church."

"Whatever we can find." Ruth nodded. "Or build, if we have to."

"That's the girl I married." John held his hand out and Ruth squeezed it.

He heard giggling from the girls' room, and the voices of a flick.

"You know," John said, "if I'd joined the Space Force, we might have been living out in orbit around Jupiter, in Zero-G, sleeping strapped into hammocks."

"I knew you'd never fly for the Space Force," Ruth told him.

"Not up to the standards of my dad and his brothers, eh?"

"That's not it," she said. "I just knew. As long as I've known you, I've known you'd end up walking your own path. And here we are." She took a sip. "Much better than the Space Force. For one thing, Zero-G is bad for the physical development of children."

"If you end up teaching here, our arrival would be Arrowhawk Post's biggest stroke of luck in its history." Ruth had taught in New York, until she'd given birth to Sunitha and they had decided they'd rather have their children raised by their own mother than Ruth's salary.

"What if I took up preaching?" she asked.

"Or preaching," he agreed. "People would love you."

"You had a long day at work." Ruth pulled wet hair away from John's forehead.

John nodded and looked down at his coffee.

"You're not done," she said.

John nodded. "I think eventually this job will have reasonable hours. But for now, I need to invest some time in figuring out how things work. And especially, I need to invest time in learning how to buy and ship Weave, to get our business started."

"Does that mean going back to the office tonight?" she asked.

"It means going to meet traders." He felt embarrassed. "Do you want to come with me?"

She shook her head quickly. "There's no one else to watch the girls."

"There's Ani."

She laughed softly. "Go and do what you think you need to do, John. Just remember that you should invest time in the children, too."

"And in you," he said. "I remember. And I will."

The bar was called the Commissar's Daughter. Its front door looked like the entrance to a hole-in-the-wall kiosk business, sandwiched between a motor vehicle repair shop and a nameless gambling den. The smell of marijuana wafted from the gambling den; the air from the Commissar's Daughter smelled like cheap gin and sour sweat.

After a few paces, though, the bar's entrance widened and its floor sank. Its common room was high-ceilinged and roomy, if dimly lit. John sipped a beer—glass bottle, no label—and slowly cracked his way through a bowl of peanuts at a small, square table. He raised his hand in greeting when Faisal arrived.

The interpreter sat down lightly, staying on the edge of his seat and smiling. "Thank you for calling me, Mr. Abbott." Seeing the man more calmly now, John noted delicate, playful eyebrows, high cheekbones, and full lips that constantly hinted at a smile.

"I have many questions," John said. "But the first is, what are you drinking?"

"My father did not approve of alcohol," Faisal said, "but my mother was a Jew who was fond of the occasional beverage, and Moses taught us that we must honor both our father and our mother, if we wish to live a long life. Lord of Lights, but that beer looks very good."

John signaled to the waitress to bring a second beer.

"So, a lot of people tried to get me to hire them this afternoon," John said.

Faisal pursed his lips. "People are not always very sophisticated, Mr. Abbott, especially country-setties in need of work. They saw the khat being cleaned out, and then the lights came on last night, so they knew there was a new Company man in town. They hoped you might be an executive or a successful trader, rather than, say, an auditor."

"How did you know I was an auditor?"

Faisal's beer arrived and he cracked off the metal top on the table's edge. "I observed you. I saw you going into Keckley's office, and then counting boxes in the warehouse."

"You were in Company House?"

"Company House has windows, and I have binoculars."

John grunted. "There can't be very much need for Hebrew-language interpretation services in Arrowhawk Post."

"All of my services are niche," Faisal admitted. "Which is why I have to advertise them all on the card. I cannot afford to lose a single customer."

"So you found out I was an auditor," John said. "Why would you think an auditor needed your services?" Did Faisal know why John had been assigned to Arrowhawk? Or did he know of corruption at the post?

Faisal shrugged. "One never knows who will need my services. They are so exotic. But you *did* call me tonight."

John laughed. "Okay. So tell me what your fees are."

"It depends on what you need translated, or done, or acquired. If you need an old engine part, and I have to spend several days traveling to Nyoot Ipetsoot or Nyoot Waaset to find it, that will cost you. I charge for my time and trouble. If you need me to help you through a five-minute conversation, it won't cost you much."

"Nyoot Ipsetsoot?" John asked. "Nyoot Waaset?"

"Country-setty villages," Faisal explained. "Not especially close."

"You helped me this afternoon," John said.

"That was not a paid service," Faisal said. "That was helping my fellow man. You will notice that *human stepladder* is not listed as a professional service on my card. But, if you are more cynically inclined, you can say that I helped you as an act of marketing."

"And you're answering my questions now."

"You have given me a beer. And peanuts." Faisal took a nut, as if to demonstrate the point. "And I am going to answer your questions this evening, to show you my value, so you should ask the best questions you can. And after tonight, if you need me to come up with additional answers or objects or people, we will discuss the price, in advance, if at all possible."

"Fair enough." John finished his beer and signaled to the waitress for two more. "Who are the country-setties?"

Faisal nodded. "Traveling through the wormhole is expensive, so sometimes people get stranded on this side because they cannot afford the fare to Earth. Take your wife and children, if you will forgive the presumption. If you die, what happens to them?"

"I have life insurance," John said.

"Is it enough to pay their fare back to Earth?"

"Maybe not. So maybe if I die, they wind up here. Ruth takes a job locally."

"And if there is no work in the post, maybe she goes to Henry Hudson, or maybe she goes out into the countryside, into one of the country-setty villages, to find work there."

"They're farmers? The country-setties?"

"They also hunt. And they have craftsmen, and teachers, and priests, and all the other occupations that spring up in human settlements."

"Accountants?"

"Perhaps not yet. There are three country-setty villages within a long day's walk of Arrowhawk Post. Nyoot Wawat, Nyoot Abedjoo, and Nyoot Zenenoot."

"Does 'nyoot' mean village?" John had already forgotten the village names.

"Or town. Or post. A country-setty might refer to this place as Nyoot Arrowhawk. Also, 'nyoot' is the Sedjem word for a Weaver nest."

"And some of those people come in to work at the post."

"Yes. A menial sweeping khats and making beds earns enough to be respected and prosperous in his nyoot."

"I don't make enough to hire a whole staff," John said. "Yet." And, for the moment, any surplus cash he earned needed to be saved up for investment, or to pay down debt.

"Hang a sign on your gate," Faisal said. "Make it very simple, few words. I would suggest 'no work.' 'Nee kat' would be the Sedjem phrase, or 'nee kat ees,' if you want to be really emphatic."

John nodded.

"When you do hire someone, make certain it is someone whom you trust. Earth lost its last frontiers a long time ago, but out here, there is nothing but frontier. Take care of your children."

"Sedjem," John said. "Where do all the . . . non-English . . . words come from? Are they Weaver words?"

"Lord of Lights, I have accidentally given you the impression that I am an academic."

John laughed. "I withdraw the question."

"You wished to meet traders?" Faisal prodded.

"Yes. I want to understand how to trade in Weave, and I think I need them to take me out on an expedition."

Faisal nodded.

"Do the country-setties buy and sell Weave?" John asked.

"Very few. Weave is expensive. And mostly, the Weavers want the kinds of trade goods that the Company brings to Sarovar: canned food, plastics, forged metal tools." Faisal leaned in close. "I know for a fact that some traders have purchased Weave using knives. I have heard it *said* that traders have purchased Weave with firearms."

He leaned back, took the second beer from the waitress, and had a sip.

John frowned. He hadn't seen any firearms in the crates of trade goods he'd opened. Trading weapons to the Weavers seemed like a bad idea. Perhaps, after all, the rumor was false. Or perhaps he should check more of the crates.

"So country-setties can't compete in that market," John said. "But . . . who would the Weavers need firearms to fight?"

Faisal shrugged. "Each other? The traders call the places they live 'nests,' but for all we know, the Weavers call them 'kingdoms.' The Weavers are sentient and have language, so they probably also have politics. Or do they need guns to fight the country-setties? Or predators in the forest? Or do we run the risk, as we arm them to buy up their single export, that one day they turn those weapons on us?"

"I don't like the thought of that at all." John stared glumly at his beer.

"Well, perhaps it isn't true." Faisal grinned. "Perhaps the Weavers only have knives, and they use them to eat with. Perhaps, even if an uprising of the Weavers should happen, it would not be your problem or mine."

"I'm here with my wife and two children." John frowned. "So it *is* my problem."

"So you need to get rich, Mr. Abbott," Faisal said. "Make your fortune and get out of here, before the tensions inherent in this place crush you."

"You can call me John."

"No, I cannot. You are a client. Even if, so far, you are only paying in beer."

"And peanuts."

"So, I brought you here because this is the bar where the traders come to get drunk. The home-brewed liquor is acceptable, and for traders who are flush from recent wins, there is even Earth-brew for sale. At ridiculous prices, of course. I know a factor who paid for his journey to Sarovar by packing his cabin full of booze on the journey here and selling it on arrival. Now, at that table in the corner, there are four men. I don't know whether you recognize any of them, but they are traders."

John turned to look. "I recognize Jefferson." The other faces were strangers, but they all wore blue and buff—jackets and kilts.

"Ah, Jefferson," Faisal said. "The handsome one. He appears ready to ride off to rescue the princess this very minute, does he not?"

At a separate table, though, in a different corner of the bar, John saw the trader called Rock. He was bearded and both beard and long hair were streaked with gray, and he reminded John of trappers and frontiersmen in old flicks. Rock sat with a woman in a cotton dress, eating bread rolls and plates of stew and drinking from wide-mouthed clay cups.

"One last piece of information," Faisal said. "Call it advice, even. Carry a gun. If you do not feel comfortable doing that in the post, at least do it when you leave. Sarovar Gamma, I have heard, is a world of luxury cruises and rejuvenation treatments, but Sarovar Alpha is a dangerous place."

John nodded. "We ran into one of Hausman's Bears."

"Hmm?" Faisal asked.

"A six-legged bear," John said. "We saw one back at Henry Hudson."

"A country-setty would call such a creature a 'shay.' It is possible, Mr. Abbott," Faisal said as he stood to go, "that in order to win the traders' respect, you might have to get roaring drunk. Just once."

"I'll call you," John said.

Faisal left.

John approached Rock. Jefferson had been more forthcoming in their previous conversation, but John felt daunted at the thought of tackling conversation with four traders all at once.

The woman with Rock had straight, black hair that fell down to her shoulders but was cut short over her caramel-colored forehead. She and Rock were laughing as John approached, holding his half-full beer bottle.

"Rock, isn't it?" John asked. "I'm John Abbott. This is a very lovely lady you're with."

Rock's face curled instantly into a fierce snarl. "What do you think, I'm with some coochie-setty, and you can just come muscle your way in and talk to her, because you're a big Company man?"

"Whoa." John took a step back and raised his hands in a gesture of innocence. "I was just being polite, making conversation. If I said something offensive, I take it back."

"*You* are offensive! I didn't come forty light-years from Earth so every pencil-necked geek in the system could interrupt my dinner!"

"Listen, I . . . can I buy you a drink?"

"Get the hell out of here, you stupid desk jockey!" Rock barked.

John stumbled away, heart thumping.

Someone unseen caught his elbow and he yanked it away. Spinning, he raised his fist to punch his assailant . . . but it was Jefferson.

"Easy," the mustached trader said. "Man, if you're this feisty when you've had one beer, what are you like when you've had a fifth of gin?"

John took a deep breath. "I've had one and a half beers, technically."

"Hey, come sit with us," Jefferson said. "Hams, in Sedjem. Rock is champion asshole of the system, I apologize on his behalf." Jefferson ushered John toward his table and grabbed the passing waitress by the arm. "Let me get my friend's tab," he said, "and bring us another bottle."

Chairs were scooted a few more centimeters from the table and another seat was dragged across the concrete floor for John. He waved at the three men he didn't know. "John Abbott," he said, "accountant."

"Gonzalez," said a portly trader. "Jefferson here was telling us that you've signed up to trade Weave under his account. He probably told you that five percent was a good deal, didn't he?"

"Takahashi," the second trader said. He had long black hair tied into a neat queue at the back of his neck. "The problem with Gonzalez is that he's going to try to offer to do the same work for a mere seven percent."

"Hager," the third trader introduced himself. His face was merry and youthful, though his beard was streaked with gray. "And the problem with Takahashi is that he'll tell you four percent, but he's such a poor trader that all he ever ends up with is the scraps, and so he gets bad pricing Earthside, and you'll have half as much money."

"And the problem with Hager," Jefferson said, "is that he has so much of his own money to invest, he can never be bothered to actually invest yours."

"Not my fault you guys spend all your money on drugs and women." Hager sipped clear alcohol from a glass.

The waitress deposited a tall, square bottle on the table, and a printed tumbler in front of John. John poured himself a drink.

"I guess there's no help for it," he said. "I'm going to have to ask you to submit written competitive bids."

"Boo!" they shouted, and: "Bean counter!"

John took a drink, and they all drank with him. He already had a slight buzz from the beer, but the clear alcohol was much stronger, and burned going down. It had a faint taste of black licorice.

"I want to come out and observe," he said. "I want to see how it really works."

"So you can see which of us to invest with," Takahashi suggested.

"Yes." John smiled.

"No," Jefferson said, "you idiot. It's because he wants to make trader someday, but to do that, he needs to know how the trades actually happen. Abbott here wants in on the action."

"It's the best reason to come to Sarovar," John said.

"You mean, you didn't come for the liquor?" Gonzalez asked.

John sipped more of the clear liquor. It burned less, this time. Gonzalez drank with him.

"That, too," he said.

"Or the women?" Takahashi asked.

Raucous laughter.

"I'm married," John said. "Fortunately. Or the ladies of Arrowhawk Post would really have to watch out."

They laughed again, and Jefferson poured John another drink.

"What's this?" he asked.

"It's distilled from a local weed," Takahashi said. "Tastes like anus."

"Anise," Gonzalez corrected him.

"I stand by what I said." Takahashi belched.

"You'll hear this stuff called hanket-vodka," Jefferson said. "Though that's a stupid name—"

"Because hanket is beer." John knew that one. He took another drink. Was he drinking too fast? The goal wasn't to get hammered, the goal was to find his way in with the traders. But they laughed and clapped him on the back, and drank with him, so it seemed to be working.

"Look at that, the man can already sedjem a bit." John lost track of which trader was speaking.

"It's possible," John said, "that I might just be fasting a little too drink."

CHAPTER NINE

John strode from the Commissar's Daughter, singing.

What shall we do with a drunken sailor?
What shall we do with a drunken sailor?
What shall we do with a drunken sailor?
What shall we do with a drunken sailor?

It seemed to him that there was another line, a line in which you were supposed to answer the question about what to do with the sailor in question, but John couldn't remember it for the life of him.

"What shall we do with a drunken sailor?" he tried again.

He had a bottle in his hand. He inspected the bottle further and was disappointed to learn that it was empty. He thought it might be a beer bottle, but it was of no use to him now. He tossed the bottle in the general direction of a heap of trash.

"What shall we do with a drunken sailor!" he shouted at the trash. "No, really, I want you to tell me!"

"Go home, Abbott!" someone shouted, and pushed him.

"I have to sober up, first!" he shouted back. "Ruth might kill me!"

Ruth had never been drunk a day in her life. Not that she was opposed to alcohol as such—her family had been Catholic, and wine was part of their thing. And it wasn't that John was much of a drinker, either, but Ruth never lost control. Not of herself, not ever of the girls.

Not of John.

"That's not fair," he said to himself. "That's judgmental."

He was leaning on something; what was it? A plastic wall? Was this his khat, had he made it home? Nyoot khat. Staggering back two steps from the plastic, he looked up to try to take it all in at a glance, and found it was not a khat enclosure wall. This was a building, at least two stories, though he had a hard time counting, but he saw the tarpaper on top of the building, gray in the dim white light of the . . . wherever the white light came from.

Was it day? He shaded his eyes. No, the light came from the tops of poles. Streetlights.

"What shall we do with a drunken sailor?" John took a deep breath and started marching for home. He walked a block, then another, crossed graveled streets, shook a fist at a car that honked at him, and then he was standing beside a tall gray wall. Another house? Trying to see the top, he fell. Lying sprawled on the damp gravel, he could see that this was the stockade wall.

"Something really bad," he mumbled, climbing to his feet. "We'll do something really bad to the sailor. We'll carpet bomb the bastard. He got sick, he riled up the natives, we'll carpet bomb him."

He had gone the wrong way. John turned around and marched in the other direction. A passing cycle struck him in the shoulder, spinning him completely around. John kept doggedly going.

"We'll take all his money. Then he'll be our slave, and we can make him work in a real shithole. Make him solve riddles in a squalid dump and have to suck up to macho salesmen. Stupid sailor. What shall we do with a drunken sailor?"

"Shut up!" Something struck John in the side of the head and he fell.

Patting around on the gravel, he found a boot. It was old and tattered, but still heavy. Someone had thrown a boot at him.

So that was the answer, then. You threw a boot at the drunken sailor.

John vomited.

With his stomach emptied, he felt a little better. Shaky, but his vision seemed to stabilize. He climbed to his feet again. He wished he had a loaf of bread to gnaw on, but even better would have been directions.

"A loaf of waham."

No, that wasn't right? Hanket?

"But Arrowhawk is small," he told himself. "There aren't that many directions to go in, and not that far to go."

He picked a direction that seemed familiar, and started walking.

We'll give him a raise until he's sober!
We'll give him a raise until he's sober!
We'll give him a raise until he's sober!
We'll give him a raise until he's sober!

That seemed right, or at least close. Only there was something about keelhauling. And the captain's daughter, wasn't she in there?

"What about the Commissar's Daughter?" He laughed at his own joke. Only he wasn't back at the Commissar's Daughter, so where was he?

Words swam in front of his eyes.

"Company House. Company House! Hell and donuts, I'm back at Henry Hudson Post!"

Something struck the back of his head and knocked him down. "Stop throwing boots!" he yelled. He tried to roll over and find the person who had hit him with the boot, or find the boot, and he couldn't find either.

But then there was a man there, two men. And they were both kicking John. He couldn't see them clearly; all three of them were covered by the shadow of the maglev station overhead.

"Hey!" He lunged at one of his attackers, and got himself wrapped around the man's knees. John leaned heavily into his hold, trying to drag the man down. He'd wrestled a little bit in high school, but that had been years ago, before John's big growth spurts, and he was too sober to remember the fancier moves.

No, too drunk.

He tried to drag the man down with his weight, but he was getting punched in the head, and hit with a stick.

Bang! Bang!

John saw two quick flashes of light, and they burned his eyes. Then he fell to the ground. He heard feet running away.

"What shall we do with a coward?" he yodeled. "Keelhaul the Commissar's Daughter!"

"Mr. Abbott." A shadow loomed over John, blocking out all the light.

"Ruth, I'm sorry, I know it's late."

"You are quite drunk."

"Yeah, but I did it for the family. I had to drink, to impress the traders. That's what Fossil told me. Faucet. Forceps."

"Faisal."

"Fffffffffffffffffffffffff. And I think he was right. But I'm really late, and it's really drunk."

"Let's get some water into you," Ruth said. "I'd give you coffee if I had any, but you can get that at home. Let's at least dilute the alcohol in your stomach."

She handed him a water bottle and he drank. "Thank you."

John handed the bottle back, belched, and threw up again.

"Well, that will help, too. Mr. Abbott, I am going to lift you onto my shoulder, and then you and I are going to walk together back to your khat. If you can stand on your own feet, that will be helpful."

"I walked here, didn't I?"

"More or less."

"You're not Ruth, are you?"

"On the count of three, Mr. Abbott, here we go. One, two, three."

The person hoisted and John stood. He lurched and almost fell over his helper, but then he caught his balance.

"Thank you," he said.

"You are welcome, Mr. Abbott."

"Only one person in the whole universe calls me Mr. Abbott," John said. "Unfortunately, I can't remember who that is."

"Faisal Haddad," the person said.

"You are Faisal."

"Yes."

"You recommended that I get drunk."

"I said it might be necessary. And that is why I waited around the Commissar's Daughter to see how it turned out. And I am glad I did."

John walked several wobbly steps and then got command of his legs. His mouth was a sand pit and his head hurt. He detached himself from the other man, rested his hands on his knees for a minute, and took deep breaths.

"How do I look?" John asked.

"You are a handsome fellow, and very charming. But I try not to mix business with pleasure."

"Someone attacked me."

"Yes, I caught the tail end of that."

"You shot them."

"I shot *at* them. If I had shot them, we would be looting the bodies right now."

John chuckled. "Thank you. Did you see who they might be?"

"Unfortunately, it is dark under the train. I saw that there were two of them."

"I really want more of that liquor," John said, "but water would probably be better."

"I am all out of that, too," Faisal said. "But we are going to pass a pump in a moment. The water is excellent—we basically live on top of a watershed, surrounded by lakes and marshes, and the water table is right beneath our feet. If you had a peg leg, you would drill a well with every step."

"A peg leg." John giggled.

"Yes, you are still drunk. Here's the pump."

They stood in a small square where two streets crossed. In the center was a concrete pad, and in the middle of the pad, surrounded by waist-high steel railings, was a post that terminated in a hinged handle and a spout. John staggered to the pump and pulled the handle up.

Nothing happened.

"You have to get the water started. Look." Faisal pumped the handle up and down several times, and then water burst from the pump's mouth in a strong stream.

"What is this, the middle ages?" John cupped his hands in the flow, and the water ricocheted off his palms and sprayed him in the face. He laughed, and it felt good, so he stuck his head entirely under the water. Trickles running around his head sneaked into the corners of his mouth, he lapped at water that sloshed down into his palms, and he started to feel a little more sober.

Sober enough to realize that he was drunk.

"Well, I have to go home," he said. "I'm a little unsteady; would you mind accompanying me, Mr. Haddad?"

"No," Faisal said. "You are Mr. Abbott, I'm Faisal."

"That's bullshit." John shut off the pump. "Either it's Faisal and John, or it's Haddad and Abbott, you pick which. Or else I will never hire you."

It was hard to focus on the other man's face, but John thought he saw a smile. "I guess you are going to have to call me Mr. Haddad, then."

"You find things, Mr. Haddad," John said. "How much will it cost for you to find my house?"

"I will do that as a kindness."

"That's bullshit again. You're a professional, and you saved my bacon." John was pretty sure he was sober enough to make this decision. "I'll pay you fifty bucks."

"Deal." Faisal pointed. "It is this way."

"I knew that." John dug into his wallet and, with a little help, counted out fifty dollars. Then he started walking and quickly found he was taking giant steps. He shortened his stride, but then Faisal seemed to pull out ahead of him. Finally, John gave up and accepted the fact that Faisal would yo-yo past and then wait for him to catch up.

Eventually, he recognized his khat and gate.

"Thank you, Mr. Haddad."

"We are going inside, Mr. Abbott. Do you wish to let me open the gate with your key?"

"I can do it." Only he couldn't, not after three tries. Picking the keys off the ground after dropping them, he finally gave them to Faisal.

Faisal opened the gate, shut it behind them, and then shuffled up the front walk with John. John did his best to walk with a straight spine and shoulders held back, and a relaxed smile on his face.

Ani was lying on the porch; she raised her muzzle, sniffed the air, and whimpered.

"You have trained your dog to distrust strangers?" Faisal suggested.

"I think she's smelling the booze," John said.

The door opened. The front room of the house was dark, and Ruth stood in the doorway. "*I* certainly smell the booze."

"I did tell you I was going out to meet traders," John reminded her.

She said nothing. Her eyes were hard and small.

John felt punched in the stomach. "Are you . . . I did this for us!"

"Did you?" Ruth's voice was cold.

"This is my fault," Faisal said. "Please forgive me, Mrs. Abbott. My name is Faisal Haddad, and I met with your husband to help him collect information about how to trade for your family account in Weave. The Company and its traders are all very tight-lipped about the process, and I understand that your husband and you wish to augment your salary."

"Who are you?" Ruth asked.

"I live here," Faisal said. "I undertake odd jobs. I am an interpreter, and a guide, and sometimes even a private investigator."

"He saved my life tonight." John leaned against the doorframe.

"I am the one who suggested to your husband that the way to make friends with the traders was to be willing to drink with them. Just once, naturally. Mr. Abbott resisted, but I am very persuasive, and he is committed to making a good life for the family."

"Just once," Ruth said.

John lurched through the doorway and she let him. He felt his head getting light, so he lay down on the foam sofa in the front parlor. He felt the dog's hair pricking the skin of his neck. "And then he saved my life!" he called to Ruth.

Faisal sounded very far away. "He was getting mugged, and I chased the thugs off. No big deal."

"I can't believe there are muggers in Arrowhawk Post." Ruth also sounded distant. And tiny.

"Well, Lord of Lights, it is a wilderness trading post, not a picnic. Sadly, I did not get a good look at any of the attackers. These belong to Mr. Abbott."

"John's got an energy pistol. This is a revolver."

"Yes, I sold him this one. It is a reliable gun. He should not walk at night without protection, and neither should you. Also, do not leave the post unarmed. Have you considered hiring a guard? If you are only going to employ one person at this time, that is the hire you should make. Before a gardener or a housekeeper."

"Before a teacher?"

"Maybe after a teacher. But some people will take you for a rich woman, and try to take advantage . . ."

CHAPTER
TEN

"Faisal was certainly full of advice," Ruth said.

John cracked an eye open. "Ack." His head throbbed and his mouth felt dry as sand. He lay on the inflated foam couch on the ground floor of the khat. "I'm sorry."

"I'm pretty sure he's also homosexual," Ruth added.

"He *did* tell me I was handsome."

"So he has bad taste."

"As bad as yours."

"There's coffee and eggs," Ruth said. "And water."

"You know I'm not a drinker," John said.

"He suggested we hire a guard," Ruth continued.

"I think I remember that."

"It sounds like a good idea to me. It sounds even better in light of the fact that someone mugged you last night. Faisal said he could recommend someone."

"I think he probably can." John sat up.

"Do you trust Faisal?"

John leaned forward and covered his face. The light was blinding. "I committed to calling him Mr. Haddad, because he wouldn't stop calling me Mr. Abbott."

"You're going to be a very strange CEO, someday."

"I don't need to be a CEO," John said. "I just want my family to be protected."

"Which brings us back to the guard. I only wonder if it's possible that Faisal hired someone to beat you up, so that he could then talk us into hiring someone as a guard."

"That would be devious," John said. "Hard to imagine a job would be worth that much effort."

"Unless we hired his cousin, say, and the cousin helped him burgle us."

"Haddad rescued me last night," John said. "I've only known him for a few hours, but yes, everything I know about him tells me he's a professional and a straight shooter. He helped me over the wall when that crowd was at the gate. Also, he was right about the drinking."

"He said you just had to do it once."

"Yes, and tonight I've been invited to go out trading. They call it a wat; I'm going on a wat to a place they call Mouse Rock. I haven't committed to any of the traders' accounts, so that leaves me free to do business under Director English." He thought about that. "Which is very likely still the best option. But probably only if I get myself out on the trading expeditions and do the buying myself. Otherwise, I need one of them to buy for me, and he won't do it unless he can also sell, and take a bite out of me on both ends."

"So you'll be late tonight?"

"I think I'll be out all night." John stood, stretched, and found his way to the table where coffee and eggs awaited him. There was also thick white toast running golden with melted butter, and he ate that first. "I'll withdraw some of our cash to buy trade goods, so don't be surprised to see that notification."

"How much?"

John considered. "On the one hand, I'd like to push forward as quickly as possible with trading. The sooner we buy, the sooner we sell, the sooner we get back the jewelry. On the other hand, I guess I don't totally know what to expect, and I don't want to do anything stupid. Maybe a third? Maybe half? Is it my imagination, or is there less dog hair on the floor? Did we get a cleaning drone, or did Ani stop shedding?"

"Ani's still shedding," Ruth said. "And there's no cleaning drone to be had in Arrowhawk Post. I looked. We got a broom, and Sunitha has taken to sweeping the house twice a day."

"Lecturing on cleanliness in a fake English accent?"

"She did herself, I didn't even have to ask her. So I'm not looking a gift horse in the mouth."

John nodded.

"Which gun are you taking?" Ruth asked.

John then vaguely remembered Faisal leaving a weapon. "Whichever you don't want."

"I'll have the guard," she said. "Faisal is coming by in a few minutes to help me find one. You can take both, if you want."

"And a teacher?"

"We found a school. The girls are there now."

"Ugh, I need to get into the office." John slurped down the eggs, leaving the coffee to cool while he headed to the shower. "I will look into Faisal this morning, see if I can find anything else out. I'll send you what I learn." He considered. "Two weapons seems like overkill. I'll take the wheelgun."

"I thought you'd say that. No guarantee you'll be able to recharge the energy pistol outside the post, anyway. The gun's sitting by the front door, waiting for you."

John showered, drinking a bottle of water while cool jets scoured his skin, and then dressed. Per his dimly recalled conversation with Jefferson and the others, he packed a blue-and-buff jumpsuit and toiletries in a grip bag, then kissed Ruth goodbye. He examined the pistol—it was a .475 Webley, well maintained, with a synthetic grip—and carefully loaded it before throwing the weapon and plastic ammunition case into the bag. Then he gave Ani a good scratching all around her neck and ears, and went in to Company House.

At the bottom of the steps, three men trickled from the Security door, two of them the men John had seen in that office before. They wore blue-and-buff jackets and blue trousers, and each had a pistol in a chest holster. The man with massive shoulders held up a hand to stop him.

"John Abbott," John said. "I work here. Just arrived."

"Moore," said the one with big shoulders.

"Payne," said the one with big forearms.

John would have laughed if his head hadn't hurt so much. "Really? More pain, huh?"

"What's so funny?" the third asked. He had disheveled blond hair and the distracted expression of a musician during performance.

"I hope your name is Please," John said. "Or Full."

"I'm Korsgaard. I'm chief."

"Right. Sorry, can I go up to my office? I sit with Keckley."

"Your face is cut," Moore said. "Who did that?"

"I just had an accident last night," John said. "I got a little drunk, I walked into a few walls and even a floor or two. You know how it is."

"No, I don't," Payne said.

"Can I come in?" John asked. "Or does having my face a little smashed up mean I have to work from home?"

"Do you want to file a report?" Korsgaard asked.

"No." Nor did he want to explain the reasons why he didn't want to file one.

"It's easier for us to do our work when all the right reports have been filed," Korsgaard said.

"I understand," John said. "But there's no work here to be done. Except my accounting work. Which is waiting for me upstairs."

Korsgaard nodded slowly. "But in general, you understand the point. Reporting is very important to me. And to everyone else, if you want to stay safe here in Company House."

John agreed that reporting was important, and they let him past.

Three men in kilts and tunics, one wearing a turban, sat on the floor outside the Medical office. From inside, John heard two voices, the Surgeon's and the voice of another woman, murmuring.

The man with the turban nodded at John.

As John entered Audit, DeBoe looked up and gave him a discreet wave. Keckley was reading something on his multitool and didn't look up.

"I got your tick-and-tie corrections," the audit chief said. "You think any of that rises to the level of material and needs to be flagged for Henry Hudson?"

"We must have a monthly file where we note adjustments and corrections, right?" John asked. "None of it's a big deal."

"The reconciliations file. I'll note it. And if your sampling is anything to go by, you probably counted all our Weave inventory."

John frowned, then thought through the implications of Keckley's words. "So when my multi opens one of the crates, your multitool gives you a notification."

"We're all about transparency and accuracy," Keckley said.

"The warehouse count and the journal entries matched," John said. "My sampling of the crates in the warehouse revealed no inconsistencies."

"Thank Jeebus," Keckley said. "I've just been bluffing my way through this job for years, guessing what the numbers should be. It's a relief to hear I guessed right."

John felt himself shrink—but then Keckley grinned at him.

"I still hate go-getters," the audit chief said, "but you seem all right."

"I'm planning on going out with the traders tonight," John said.

"Ah, good. Mouse Rock. That'll be an overnight trip, so you'll leave early this afternoon and be gone tomorrow."

"I thought it would be good for me to see how the buying is actually done," John said. "You know, and then the shipping, too. So I better understand our revenues and our costs."

Keckley fixed him with a gimlet eye. "And have you accepted someone's offer to trade under his account?"

"Uh, no."

Keckley chuckled. "I'm no fool. Maybe you're not, either. Good, go to Mouse Rock. Did they tell you what trade goods to bring?"

"Iron tools," John said.

"You know, the Company doesn't extend credit to you to buy those," Keckley told him.

"I have money."

"You are, however, welcome to use any empty crates, so long as you bring them back. So I would suggest that you go make your purchases now—the multi will process it, if you input your Depository account details. The trading expeditions leave from this building, because they drive a Company truck, and if they're going to Mouse Rock, they'll check out shortly after lunch."

John nodded at the hallway. "The, uh, people outside?"

"Hinkley treats the locals in her spare time. Seems alright, doesn't it?" Keckley raised both his eyebrows.

"It seems more than alright."

John went to the warehouse to get trade goods.

The crates opened to his multi; scanning any item with the multitool showed its cost to the Company, under one setting, and its price to him, under another. The costs were higher than what he was used to paying in New York, which suggested that some of the cost of transporting the goods to Sarovar System had been allocated to the trade goods themselves. Given that trade goods came on the same ships as passengers, and that he as a passenger had had to pay an additional wormhole transit fee for his passage, based on the energy spent in the journey, John wondered whether the starship traffic itself might be profitable for the Company. He had assumed that the starships basically operated to cover their own costs, or maybe even ran at a loss, and then the Company made its profit on trade . . . but maybe that wasn't entirely true. The Company was making revenue on its markup as John packed three crates full of trade goods—three thousand dollars' worth—but also covered some of its transit costs.

The thought of the Company earning revenue reconnected John to some of the accounting he had been looking at the day before. His head still hurt and his eyes felt as if they were full of sand, but he remembered that traders were said to earn two percent commissions on all the Weave they bought, based on the sale price of Weave current at the time of purchase.

Why did that make sense? If each trader had access to unlimited trade goods when trading for the Company's account, it didn't. It incentivized traders to overpay. But if each trader had an allotment of trade goods—perhaps an allotment that varied by seniority, or rose over time in response to good results—then that incentivized each trader to get as much Weave as he possibly could for his allotment. Was that how the system worked?

He needed to find out the answer to that question.

And, he realized, those payments ought to reconcile to revenue. Knowing the prices on the basis of which the commissions were paid, he could calculate volume. So all he had to do was find out the rate at which revenue was allocated to the post, and, assuming it was tied to volume, he had a check on the revenue amount.

The amount paid in commissions to traders had to line up with the amount of Weave being shipped to Central Transit.

Revenue had to be tied to the post's volume. What else would even make sense?

Unsure which of the trucks they'd take, he stacked his three sealed crates in the corner of the warehouse and went back into the office.

Keckley had left.

"Where does he spend his time," John asked DeBoe, "when he's not here?"

DeBoe shrugged. "I don't follow him around, but he has meetings with traders, meetings with the post chief, meetings with the security chief, calls with Henry Hudson, calls with the audit chiefs of other posts . . . and naps, and snacks, and sometimes he likes to do a little drinking in the afternoon."

John nodded, unsure how scandalized he should be.

"Hey," DeBoe said, "as vices go, they're pretty tame."

"I thought I might look at revenue," John said. "I've got an hour or two."

"You're a lively one," DeBoe said.

First, though, John looked through the Post's records for mentions of Faisal Haddad. He found no employment records or other records of payment, or any other mention in the records he could figure out how to search. Then he called down to Security.

"Payne here."

"I'm interested in finding out everything the Post Security records can tell me about someone," John said. "A specific person. And then anything you or your colleagues might know about him, as well."

Faisal had never had a conflict with Post Security, it turned out. He'd never been detained or questioned. Payne offered the thought that Faisal was a peaceable country-setty who seemed to make a living by running errands.

John forwarded Ruth the information via the ethernet.

Then he turned his attention to the post's revenues. John found the right ledger and opened to the appropriate section of the multitool. Immediately, he noticed that Total Revenues was the sum of two lines: Date-of-Shipping Revenue and Prior Period Adjustments.

"Oh boy," he said. "Prior Period Adjustments?"

DeBoe chuckled. "Date-of-Shipping Revenue is Weave volume shipped during the month, multiplied by the then-most-recent Earth prices."

"Okay," John said. "It fluctuates because of seasonality?"

"Trade slows down in winter and there is a huge uptick in spring. It also fluctuates because the availability of the train to Central Transit is not constant."

"Because of power outages?"

"Or breakdown of the train or the line, or the train is elsewhere on the rails, or weather. We recognize revenue when we ship to Central Transit."

"Not when it arrives?"

"When the train rolls out of Arrowhawk."

"So what is Prior Period Adjustments?" John asked.

"That number is sent back to us by Henry Hudson. It's the difference between the price at which we shipped and the price actually paid on Earth, multiplied by our volume. Basically, once we know the actual price, we go back and adjust our revenue to match."

John thought about that. "Do you track cash flows?"

"Revenue is not cash in," DeBoe said. "We get transmitted cash from Henry Hudson like we get shipped trade goods, as we need them. We don't produce a cash flows statement, but I manage treasury. You've already been looking at some of my data."

John found the T-account for inventory and the historical prices table. "So I can reconcile shipments to revenue to price, for starters."

"Mmm," DeBoe said.

John had worked through the most recent eighteen months of inventory and revenue, confirming that Director English was indeed correct, in at least this much: revenue had dropped in the last six months at Arrowhawk Post. Then there was a knock at the door.

Jefferson stood there, grinning. "Hey, trader," he said. "Don't want to be late."

John hadn't even reached commissions yet. He took a few quick photos of ledger pages and took up his grip bag. "My trade goods are on the floor of the warehouse."

"Wrong," Jefferson said, "they're on the truck. Which is where your ass should be, if you want to buy any Weave tomorrow morning."

"Oops." John hoofed it quickly across the office and down the stairs.

One of the trucks sat in the open bay doors of the warehouse, its engine idling. John climbed up the ladder into the first of the truck's two body segments, flinging his grip bag in ahead of him.

He didn't recognize the driver, a bushy-haired, sallow-faced man who flashed a completely horizontal smile, showing large, white teeth.

"John Abbott," John said.

"The new guy. I'm Sam Chen."

John nodded and picked up his bag. Jefferson climbed in behind him.

"Up top," Jefferson said. "You always want to be up top, unless it's raining, because the views are better. But since this is your first trip, you really want to be up top. Get a sense of the lay of the land."

John climbed up another ladder. He couldn't stand there without risking hitting his head on the top of the loading door. Instead, he sat, in one of six bucket seats with hip belts. He strapped himself in.

"You're a seatbelt kind of guy," Jefferson said.

"There's a reason I became an accountant."

Jefferson chuckled. "Hey, what happened to your face?"

Was there any point in telling Jefferson he'd been attacked? "I walked into a door."

"What, over and over again?"

"Just once," John lied. "But it was the khat door. Very heavy."

Two minutes later, the truck rolled out.

He heard Chen talking over comms with the gatehouse as the truck rumbled toward the slabs of gray plastic, and then the gatehouse opened. Takahashi, Hager, and Gonzalez were on the truck, along with two other traders John didn't recognize. Rock was absent.

The post's gate faced west, along a smooth gravel road that slowly drifted north. Once the truck had exited the post, however, it turned right, circling around the walls and then crawling eastward, paralleling the maglev line and leaving the roads entirely. In front of the truck, John saw nothing that resembled road—just grass and scrub trees in a long meadow stretching away into indistinctness.

Behind the truck, he saw two deep ruts filled with water.

Jefferson saw him looking. "That looks like grass down there, but if you walked on this path we're following, you'd be up to your ankles in water at every step, and sometimes you'd fall in much deeper than that."

"Pools covered by the grass, so you can't see them?"

"Pools, yes, but really caves, formed by the collapse of the stone. We call them 'cenotes.'"

"Why doesn't the truck fall in?"

"Sometimes it does. But this is why our larger trucks have front and back halves, and each half has its own engine. If the front of this truck fell into a cenote, the back half would pull it out. Of course, Sam knows the route we're taking very well, and there are also charts of it programmed into the truck's computer, so there's no real chance of that happening on this trip."

"Unless we wander off the track."

"Or a new cenote opens under our wheels."

"Is this why all the vehicles are wheeled?" John asked. "I haven't seen a hovercar yet."

"Hovercars can't get themselves out of the cenotes at all," Jefferson said. "And they don't do well on rough terrain generally. The Company has actual aircraft, of course, but trucks are much cheaper for most purposes."

John nodded, fell silent, and watched the mountains. In a few minutes, Chen turned north, driving along the edge of a low rock ridge, and toward the open mouth of a valley ahead of them. Out of habit, John raised his multi, thinking maybe he'd take a look at those revenue and commission numbers now.

"Put away the multitool and look at the scenery," Jefferson said. "Or I will punch you in the face."

John put away the multi, and his fingers bumped the encryption plug in his jacket pocket. At some point, he was going to have to report back to Director English. But first he had to have something to say.

CHAPTER ELEVEN

"It might as well be Earth." John examined the surrounding landscape as the truck rolled on.

"Well, yeah," Jefferson said. "Surely you read all the astrophysics stuff. It's an Earth knock-off. Twins."

"What are the odds?" John mused.

"Given an infinite universe? One hundred percent."

"But the odds that two so similar planets are connected by a wormhole?" John pressed.

Jefferson shrugged. "There's still a lot we don't know about wormholes."

"Different constellations." Gonzalez had joined them and leaned back against the edge of the truck, fingers interlaced behind his head. "I mean, if you're one of those guys who can look at the night sky in Nevada and pick out Orion, the Big Dipper, and so on, you won't see any of that here."

"I *am* that guy," John said. "I mean, just a little. So are there different constellations here? There must be."

"I don't think the Company has a recognized list," Jefferson said. "You could ask the Weavers what they see when they look at the stars."

"Or the country-setties," Gonzalez added.

John nodded. "I wasn't thinking about the stars. But I mean, Sarovar looks about like our sun, Sol. Maybe a shade darker and a shade larger, but that might just be a trick of my imagination, since I know it's a slightly older star."

"Yes," Jefferson said. "And Sarovar Alpha has a similar axial tilt to Earth's, so you have similar seasons."

"Two moons is an interesting difference," John said, "though I haven't really taken the time to observe them yet." And suddenly, he felt stupid that he'd been on the planet a week and hadn't yet looked at the night sky.

"Makes the tides funky," Gonzalez said. "I understand that the high and low tides where the two moons coincide can be really dramatic. Might make for interesting times at the Company kelp farms. Cochin and Moluccas Posts."

"But what I really was thinking about," John said, "was the plants. Look at those. Aren't they conifers? I mean, I'm no botanist, but those look like pine trees, don't they?" He pointed.

"You're going to see animals that remind you of Earth critters, too," Jefferson said. "Some of them you look at and you think, am I really just on Earth, and not many light-years away on a different planet? Marmots and chipmunks and so on."

"Beavers," Gonzalez added. "Butterflies."

"But then you'll see a thing that looks like an elk, but has curling horns like a bighorn sheep." Jefferson shrugged.

"What's the Sedjem word for it?"

"Ba," Gonzalez said, "believe it or not. Like, what a sheep says."

"Parallel evolution, I guess?" John scanned the trees, hoping to see an elk with curling horns. "On an Earthlike world, Earthlike creatures must emerge? There must be botanists and zoologists and others looking at these things."

"The Company does employ biologists," Jefferson said. "And they're still counting species. But I don't think they're publishing very much about them on Earth."

"They're not," John agreed. "Why is that?"

"Because that information may have commercial value," Jefferson said. "So the Company isn't going to release it to the academics until they're sure they're not giving away trade secrets. And when they do release it, the data will be sold, or it will be in the control of academics whose careers the Company wants to advance."

"Surely, there's some way the Company could both disseminate the information earlier, and still benefit from it," John said.

"Like what?" Gonzalez asked. "A section of Sarovari creatures in the Bronx Zoo?"

"Maybe." John shrugged. "Or let documentary flickmakers buy licenses to come here and record? That way, our collective knowledge could advance faster. Or even regular flicks. Adventure flicks featuring six-armed bears. Shay."

"Maybe," Jefferson conceded. "I have to tell you, I think that dissemination of pure knowledge to the public, for the public good, may not be high on the list of the Company's priorities. When *you're* sitting on the Planetary Board, or the Board of Directors, you can make it your personal crusade."

"It's interesting that Congress didn't make this sort of thing a condition of the Sarovar Company getting its charter," John said. "I mean, why not trade the monopoly for information?"

Jefferson and Gonzalez both stared at him.

"Congress traded the monopoly for some pretty fat tax revenues," Gonzalez said.

"Funding, you may recall, some pretty fat social safety net benefits," Jefferson pointed out.

"And some pretty fat Congressmen." Gonzalez raised his eyebrows.

"Hey, not my call," John said. "I'm just thinking out loud. I guess really I'm just seeing all this stuff, and thinking how much people on Earth would love to see it. Look at that bird, for instance—it looks just like a bluebird."

"It *is* a bluebird," Jefferson said. "If it has a name, it's probably the Sarovari Bluebird, or maybe it's named after some dead Company director—Johnson's Bluebird, or whatever. But if a bunch of schoolkids saw what we're seeing right now, they'd think they were just seeing images from Colorado."

"What about . . ." John hesitated . . . "—diseases?"

Jefferson laughed and clapped him on the shoulder. "Ah yes, the rumors of dreaded Sarovari plagues. I heard those too, back on Earth."

"There's nothing to the rumors, then?" John asked.

The traders all laughed.

"Oh, speaking of the famous ba." Gonzalez twisted in his seat to look forward.

John turned to look, just as the truck shuddered to a halt. The marshy meadow stretched out ahead of them like a road, and a herd of quadrupeds blocked their path. John wasn't entirely sure what elk looked like, but these creatures looked like deer, only taller and more muscular. They had long snouts that reminded John of battered leather shoes. And, as promised, they had the backward-curling horns of bighorn sheep.

"Ba," John said.

The beasts looked at the truck and bellowed. Two of the largest turned and stalked toward the vehicle. Chen shifted into reverse and backed up a few meters.

"Uh-oh," Jefferson said. "Are those big fellas in heat?"

"We might be able to know that," John said, "if only biologists were allowed to come here and do research."

One of the big ones sprang forward, head lowered. His horns crashed against the plastic windshield of the truck with a resounding crack.

The truck lurched backward. The second bull raced forward, not to be left out, and butted the truck. The impact was so forceful that the whole vehicle shook, and John felt it in his seat in the second segment.

Other bulls trotted forward. The two who had already attacked now stood their ground, snorting and glaring at the truck, but the new arrivals galloped past them, running for the Company traders.

"Gonzalez," Jefferson said.

"I'm on it." Gonzalez lifted up two of the seats, revealed a long rifle with a scope and a loaded magazine in a shallow compartment. He picked up the weapon, slotted in the magazine, and posted himself at the rear of the truck.

The truck's engine groaned as Chen threw it sideways. The back of the vehicle cracked two conifers, shaking green needles down into the compartment. An elk struck the side of the truck before Sam got it back into gear and lurched forward again.

John considered pulling his Webley from the grip bag, but thought it wasn't a big enough caliber to be helpful.

Ba chased them and Gonzalez leaned over the back of the truck, sighting at them through the rifle's scope. The big creatures fell behind, though, and after a couple of minutes, Gonzalez put the rifle away.

"That was close." John picked up needles from the compartment floor. "Fir."

"What?" Gonzalez asked.

"On Earth, at least, spruce needles are square, fir needles are flat, and pine needles come in pairs. Actually, sometimes more than pairs, but if you say pine needles come in clusters, you lose the alliteration."

"That's where all this is coming from?" Jefferson shook his head. "You're a closet botanist?"

"No," John said. "My dad was in the military, and so were his brothers. For a long time, I thought I'd be a pilot, so I learned the stuff they knew—survival skills, scout lore, boiling water, finding north, all that kind of stuff." He considered. "Does Sarovar Alpha have a magnetic pole?"

"And you can fly aircraft?" Jefferson asked.

"Nothing fancy," John said. "But I have my pilot license."

"And then you became an accountant," Gonzalez said.

"Flat feet," John lied.

"Next, you'll become a trader." Jefferson grinned, but his smile was strained.

"You know," John said, "if we flew aircraft out, rather than driving these trucks, the ba wouldn't be a problem."

The truck shook violently. John was slammed against the truck's frame and fell to the floor, alongside Jefferson. Gonzalez disappeared from his view. He heard shouts of surprise and then screaming.

"What just happened?" John staggered to his feet and cast his eyes about, to see that the front half of the truck had sunk into the meadow. One of the traders he didn't know lay on the ground immediately adjacent to the truck, with one leg stuck under a tire, shrieking.

Gonzalez lay on the ground, too, but he was rolling over, trying to stand.

"Cenote." Jefferson's voice was grim. "This is the real danger of the elk—they forced us off a path we knew was secure. Dammit."

John was dropping down the ladder while Jefferson was still talking. "First-aid kit!" he yelled, then unlatched the door and dropped to the clearing outside.

The ground was marshy and thick with two kinds of vegetation: a thin, scrubby grass, and an inwardly curling leaf that reminded

John of the ear of a cow or goat. Both were pale green, and water flowed across the ground, so that the entire meadow seemed to be one wide, shallow stream.

Gonzalez was limping, but he was on his feet. Hager joined them, jumping down from the truck clutching a white plastic box with a red cross on the front of it.

"Be careful around the truck tires," Hager warned. "The roof of the cenote may not be done collapsing, and you might fall through. Some of those caves are deep."

The trapped man had stopped screaming. John checked, and found a pulse and breathing; he'd passed out.

"Get me a rope!" he yelled, and then, besieged suddenly by mental images of himself getting trampled by Sarovari Bighorn Elk, he added, "Post a guard! Someone watch out for animals!"

He saw Jefferson atop the truck, pulling the rifle out, and then he had no more attention to pay to that part of the scene. When Takahashi brought down a nylon cord, he lay beside the injured man to be able to loop the rope beneath his armpits and tie it in a bowline.

"I don't think pilots tie knots," Hager said. "That's sailor stuff, there."

"I have uncles who are marines and special forces," John grunted. He knotted a second bowline in the rope, close to the first, and crawled into it, holding on to the unconscious man. Tossing the line back to Takahashi, he said, "Wrap that around the thickest tree trunk over there. Both you guys, get dug in and anchor us."

Sam Chen, watching from the front of the truck, nodded. "You want me to back up?"

John saw that someone had run a cable from a winch at the back of the truck, attaching it to a boulder the size of a garden shed, squatting at the edge of the meadow.

"Yes," he said. "Slowly. If you spin the wheels, I worry you might rip his leg off."

Chen took his seat again. He had a gentle touch with the truck's controls, despite all the lurching of the recent minutes; the truck's tires rotated slowly backward, most of the pulling being done by the winch, and the vehicle eased away, freeing the trapped man.

John breathed a sigh of relief.

He gathered the injured trader into his arms to drag him back.

The wounded man cried out in pain, even in his sleep; his foot was crushed, and a parabola of blood leaked from the maimed leg into the flowing water of the meadow.

He heard the sound of falling water, and saw a black pit whose opening was the size of a small table, a depression into which the meadow's water dropped.

John heard the sudden crack of the rifle.

He looked up and saw Jefferson, standing atop the truck with the rifle pressed against his shoulder and his cheek. Turning, pulling the injured man with him, he saw the bighorned ba again, galloping toward the truck across the meadow.

Jefferson fired again, and this time one of the elk dropped.

Then the ground beneath John gave way.

He only fell a couple of meters, and then his bowline caught him up under his armpits. The force of the fall ripped the injured man from his grasp, but the other bowline secured him, and they bobbed together in a void, with no walls or floor, and water sloshing all about them.

He heard the distant crash as the ground that had given way beneath him slammed to the bottom of the cenote.

He heard several more shots. He looked up in time to see two ba leap over the new pit in quick succession. From this vantage point, they looked, if anything, even bigger.

Then he began to rise from the pit.

Cold water sluiced over him at the lip of the opening. He used one hand to guide his own ascent over the grass and mud, and the other to bring up the wounded man with him, pulling him between his knees and then dragging him onto the wet meadow.

Gonzalez grabbed him and the wounded man and dragged them both away.

"He needs help," John said. "Look at that foot."

Takahashi and Hager joined them, and the four of them lifted the injured man into the truck. There, John tied off the wound with a tourniquet.

Meanwhile, Chen was on the comms, barking coordinates and demanding immediate medical help.

It was only fifteen minutes later that a helicopter appeared, coming low above the trees from the south and west.

"Where is Arrowhawk Post's helipad?" John asked.

"On top of the maglev platform," Jefferson said.

John felt like a fool for not having noticed it.

When the aircraft landed, the surgeon, Dr. Hinkley, jumped out. She was dressed in a blue-and-buff jumpsuit like the traders', with the addition of a red cross on the breast.

"That's the post medic," Takahashi said. "Dr. Hinkley."

"We met," John said. "I thought her title was surgeon."

"It is," Gonzalez said.

Hinkley checked John's work on the injured ankle, pronounced it good, and clapped John on the shoulder by way of rough congratulations. "Don't forget to come see me," she called to John as she climbed back into the chopper.

Then the traders bundled the injured man into a plastic pod bolted to the underside of the helicopter and it took off. John didn't see a pilot in the aircraft, and Hinkley didn't touch any visible controls—someone must be operating the craft remotely.

Once the helicopter was gone, John noticed that his hands were shaking. He took deep breaths and leaned against a tree to steady himself. It certainly *smelled* like a fir tree.

The ba had disappeared, other than two that lay dead on the meadow floor.

"Do we go back?" John asked Takahashi.

"I came here to trade," Takahashi said. "I intend to trade."

The other traders nodded.

John took a deep breath and climbed back into the truck.

"The marked route is clear now, Sam," Jefferson called to the driver of the truck. Then he and John and Gonzalez again took their seats at the back of the truck.

Chen turned the truck around in a tight circle and headed to rejoin the route they had been on before the Sarovari elk had driven them from it.

"The reason we don't bring aircraft trading," Jefferson said, sighing heavily, "is that it frightens away the Weavers."

"I hope this isn't a wasted trip," Gonzalez said.

CHAPTER TWELVE

"It gets its name from its shape," Gonzalez said.

John squinted at Mouse Rock in the early evening sun. It was a wide, flat shelf of gray stone, with a bouquet of rounded and oblong boulders heaped together in its center.

"That's supposed to look like a mouse?" he asked.

"Not like a real mouse. Like the head of a cartoon mouse."

"Oh, right." Now John saw two rounded ears, a depression that modestly impersonated an eye socket, and an upturned boulder resembling a rodent's snout; a grape-shaped stone at the tip of the snout suggested a nose.

Chen braked the truck in a meadow on one side of Mouse Rock. John followed Jefferson and Gonzalez down the ladder and out. The air was cooling as the sun went down, so John wore his light Company jacket—blue and buff. He put his revolver in one deep pocket of the jacket, and his box of shells in the other.

"Do we set up camp and get ready to trade in the morning?" he asked Takahashi.

"The Weavers trade at night," Takahashi said. "We have a wat here on the first night of every full phase of the larger moon, Yah."

"Assuming it isn't raining," Hager said. "The Weavers don't come out in the rain."

"And other scheduled wats?" John asked.

Takahashi nodded. "At other locations, with other communities of the Weavers." He shrugged. "Though we often don't know exactly where the Weaver nests are. And many of us have our own scheduled wats that we've found or negotiated. And we go on longer journeys to find and fix new wats, or to trade on the road."

The others were carrying their crates of trade goods out to the flat stone of Mouse Rock, so John did the same. It took him two trips. Again following the lead of the traders, he set his crates together with their tops removed and their contents clearly visible, a couple of meters distant from the crates of any other trader. Retreating from the rock, he brought the lids with him.

Then he helped carry out the crates of trade goods that were being offered for the Company's account. These were all placed, together and open, on the far side of the individual traders' goods. The traders carried the lids away and placed them in the truck.

Jefferson took a small bullhorn from the truck and stood on Mouse Rock. Turning, he repeated several times into the amplifier the same message: "We yoot for wat, we got inoo. You got shesroo? We yoot for wat."

He put the amplifier back in the truck.

The traders gathered in the meadow to one side of Mouse Rock, beside their vehicle. Mouse Rock stood on a raised, grassy ridge, so the ground was soft earth, but not swamp. Hager, who had been the first to finish setting out trade goods, emerged from the truck carrying a set of light poles. He stood them in a ring around the truck, pushing the spikes at their nether tips down into the earth and then turning their dials at eye level. The white bulb at the top of each light pole shone with strong white light, illuminating the traders and their truck, and casting strong, clear light over the field of trade goods.

Takahashi then climbed back onto the top of the truck. John didn't see him with a rifle, but he assumed the trader was stationed up there to be able to shoot, if need be. Sam Chen slung a hammock between the two walls of his cockpit, climbed in, and began watching something on his multi.

Gonzalez brought out beers.

John sipped his, resolved to make the one beer last through the night.

"Does it ever happen," he asked the assembled group, "that we set up like this and the Weavers don't show up?"

"Yes," Hager said. "Reasonably often."

"Sometimes a really productive wat just dries up," Gonzalez added. "You never find out why. Maybe the Weavers moved on. Maybe they lost a fight with another band of Weavers and were all killed. Maybe disease got them. Maybe they got tired of trading with you. Who knows?"

Maybe they lost a fight. John remembered the rumor Faisal had reported, about weapons being traded for Weave.

"What do they do with the trade goods?" John asked.

Jefferson took a long swig from his bottle and looked closely at John. "What would you do with a bunch of awls, chisels, needles, pots, pliers, nails, and so on?"

"Make things," John said. "Make houses. Maybe make the machines I used to create Weave."

Jefferson nodded.

"We won't be stood up tonight, though." Hager pointed toward the open space on the far side of Mouse Rock.

Shadows moved across the meadow. At first, John thought he was seeing indistinct blobs drift forward toward the rock, but then he realized that he was seeing piles of fabric heaped up into bales, and that the force generating the motion was the creature beneath, and carrying, each bale. They crawled up onto the ridge from the forest on the other side; they seemed to move by spinning, but the spinning motion advanced them.

The creatures reached Mouse Rock and set down their bales. John tried to count, but they were too much in shadow, and too low. When they set the Weave down, though, he could see them: in mass, each Weaver was larger than John, but their organization was entirely different. They were a meter tall, and two meters across, and they looked like red hockey pucks. They moved by rotating, and they had three big legs, emerging from their bodies spaced equally around the puck. The legs moved in and out, rising and extending like the legs of a spider or a crab. Between each pair of legs, John saw a pair of crab-like pincers and a glittering row of four eyes, the two in the center larger and raised above the joints of the pincers.

These were the creatures John had seen in the scorched murals at the Stone Gardens, outside Henry Hudson Post.

The Weavers.

"Are they always this color?" he murmured.

Hager heard him and laughed. "Except for the famous White Weaver of Arrowhawk. He's three times the size of the others, and eats human children."

"Really?" John asked. "Not really."

Hager laughed.

The Weavers piled up bales of Weave, then retreated into the meadow on the far side of Mouse Rock.

John followed the traders, other than Takahashi, onto the flat stone. Takahashi stayed atop the truck. John couldn't count the Weavers in the darkness, but he could make out thirty stacks of Weave. The trade goods, the inoo, were all one side of the stone shelf, and the Weave, the shesroo, was on the other.

"How do we make an offer?" John asked.

"Like any other negotiation," Jefferson said. "We suggest a deal, and we have a fallback position in mind. Move all the Weave to our side of the rock."

John and the other traders moved the Weave; it took a few minutes, and despite the crisp chill of the night air, John broke into a sweat.

"Okay," Jefferson said, "now we move the Company goods over onto the Weavers' side. Company goods only!"

John helped move the crates. Then the traders retreated from Mouse Rock, into their ring of light poles. John watched as the Weavers came out again. They looked like spinning crabs as they crawled over the pile of trade goods, lifting them with their pincers and holding them to their glittering eyes for examination. They struck tools together, brandished them in the air, and even tapped them on the rock.

The Weavers carefully gathered up all the crates of trade goods on the shelf and moved them all onto their side of the negotiating ground. They came back, slowly scooped up half the Weave as well, and laid that down on their side of the stone shelf.

Then they crawled back out onto the meadow to wait again.

"We're getting half the Weave for all the tools." John didn't know whether that was a good deal, but he thought it was. And there would be some mechanism for allocating that Weave among the traders and the Company's account, but if he ended up with two or three bales for himself, well, that wasn't a fortune, but it easily made back his investment and a quick profit, resold at Central Transit.

"We'll do a little better," Hager said.

The traders walked out onto the stone shelf again. "Everyone, take back one crate of your own goods," Jefferson said. "Leave all the Company goods."

John dutifully picked up one of his crates and carried it back to the near side of the shelf. He imagined doing this on his own; he'd want to be protected. Maybe he could hire Faisal to come be security for him while he traded with the Weavers.

"Okay, now bring all the Weave back over," Jefferson announced.

The traders obeyed. Then they returned to the circle of lights.

"Now we're offering most of the trade goods for all of the Weave," John murmured, thinking out loud. "Including all the Company's. As we're required to do."

Jefferson clapped him on the shoulder. "You're getting it. Of course, if you stay an accountant, and get promoted from factor to trader, you won't always have any obligation to trade Company goods first. Makes it simpler. You could find a Weaver nest, set up a monthly or quarterly trade, and just do it all yourself. Once you've built up enough capital and experience by trading with me."

"With us." Hager's beard wagged. "He hasn't chosen a trader yet."

"I'm still considering," John told them. "But what's a good deal?"

Gonzalez chuckled. "That's the best part. If we came away with one bolt of Weave, we'd make a profit. Anything we get above that is gravy."

"He's exaggerating," Jefferson said. "But not by much."

The Weavers returned, crawling over Mouse Rock. They collected all the trade goods, dragging them over to their side of the stone shelf.

"The funny thing about commerce," John said, "is that the same might be true for them. We think we're trading our crap for their things of value, but they might think the reverse is true. If they don't have access to iron, for instance, we might be seriously empowering the Weavers nests we deal with by rapidly advancing their technology levels and material culture."

Hager and Jefferson looked at each other.

"So philosophical," Gonzalez said. "I want to have your baby."

"Okay, okay." John laughed. But his words were true, and they left a lingering question in his mind: Did the Weavers think they were driving a hard bargain? Did they think they were being cheated? Did they, perhaps, believe they were cheating the off-worlders, getting valuable tools for fabric they regarded as plentiful, cheap, or of little value?

They were clearly intelligent, and not merely semi-sentient, whatever he and Ruth had heard in New York.

The Weavers dragged over more bales from their side of the shelf to the traders' side. Then most of them retreated, remaining on the stone shelf, but scuttling to its far end.

Two of them remained at the edge of the shelf nearest the traders. One raised itself, changing the arc of its legs to elevate its body off the rock, and then called out, in a voice that sounded pained, rough, and awkward, but which unmistakably cried out: "Iker inoo!"

John tapped open the Sedjem app on his multitool. Inoo was trade goods, and iker? He looked it up: *good, excellent.*

Then the Weavers retreated, crawling off the shelf entirely and back onto the meadow grass on the far side.

Jefferson led the traders back onto the rock. All the trade goods were now with the Weavers, and perhaps eighty percent of the Weave was with the traders. "I think this is it, gentlemen. Any objections?"

"This is it," Gonzalez agreed.

Hager nodded.

The men gathered up the bales of Weave, carrying it back into the truck. Then they stood in the meadow and watched as the Weavers gathered up the trade goods. Now they pulled them from the crates, wrapping the tools into the folds of the Weave bales that remained to them, and then lifting the Weave-wrapped trade goods over their heads.

John took two steps forward, impulsively.

"Iker shesroo!" he called.

"Get your ass back here, Abbott," Jefferson growled. "You're breaking protocol and you might make them angry."

John stayed where he was. Several of the Weavers pivoted, stopped and spun slightly closer to him, as if watching him.

"Iker shesroo!" he said again.

"Iker inoo," grunted one of the Weavers. The sound might have been produced by grinding rocks together.

The Weavers took their bales and left Mouse Rock.

"You're lucky," Hager said to John. "That might have gone badly wrong."

"They complimented us," John said. "Our trading was all symmetrical, we take an action, then they take an equal and opposite actions. It seemed . . . symmetrical to tell them we liked their fabric."

"They know we like their fabric," Gonzalez said. "We keep coming back."

"Then why did they tell us they liked our chisels and hammers?" John pressed.

"You got lucky," Jefferson said. "You didn't upset them. If you're going to come out again, though, you'll button your lip."

"Understood," John muttered.

They collected the empty crates and loaded Weave into them. Jefferson synched up their multitools, divided the result into the number of bales they'd collected, and allocated bales to each trader and to the Company.

John came away with two crates full of Sarovari Weave. The Company came away with eighteen.

On some level, the result left him very happy.

But his thoughts were elsewhere as he sealed up his crates using his multi and stowed them in the truck. What was happening on this planet that the Company traders weren't seeing? What was the effect of the commerce on the Weaver nests that did trade with the Sarovar Company, and those that didn't?

And where did Sedjem come from? It couldn't possibly be from the Weavers—their speech had been slow, halting, and forced, as if they were making sounds that were unnatural or even painful for them.

So that meant there was some third species out there, whose words, like inoo and shesroo and wat, had been borrowed into English to create the trade patois. Who where they, and where? Could those be the Riders Sunitha had lectured him about, after hearing of them from Factor Doctor? But weren't they native to the southern continent, Bonaparte?

If the Weavers here could speak Sedjem, didn't that suggest that this third species was somewhere reasonably close? And sentient, obviously. Perhaps it was a species that was very common, and located all around the planet.

But if it was a common species, it was one John hadn't seen. Or didn't realize he'd seen. Might the words have been drawn from a language spoken by the ba? Or the shay? Or by the giraffe-like things he had observed near Henry Hudson?

The sun came us as John was chewing on these thoughts. He climbed back into the truck, Takahashi woke Sam Chen from his nap, and they headed back to Arrowhawk Post.

CHAPTER THIRTEEN

"Really, though," Ellie said, "the kids wanted to see Ani." She looked glum and stared at the gravel under her feet.

John walked Sunitha and Ellie to school. Clouds intermittently blocked what would have been a warm morning sun.

"I see," John said. "Would it help if I crawled around on all fours and barked?"

"Yes." Ellie sulked.

"Ani doesn't crawl," Sunitha told him in her English voice. "You'll have to be on your fingertips and toes."

"You're right. I'll scamper on all fours, and then lie down and roll onto my back to encourage the children to scratch my belly. Good thing I'm so flexible."

"The problem with bringing pets to school," Sunitha said, "is that once one child does it, everyone wants to do it, and some children have snakes." She tilted her head back as if looking down her nose at the world.

"Poor Ani," John said. "I'm sure she's thoroughly bored of the khat and would love to come to school with you."

Ellie harrumphed.

"This is school," Sunitha said.

The schoolhouse was a one-room building, rectangular and utilitarian, with a slightly peaked roof to shed rain. The building's plastic walls were printed to have a grain and a brown tint that resembled wood. Short steps ran up from the gravel street to wide double doors.

John followed his daughters inside.

"Ah, Mr. Abbott!" The teacher was a thin woman, nearly as tall as John, with a tight smile and surprisingly beefy knuckles.

"Mrs. Jenkins." John shook the teacher's hand. "I'm here to be show and tell."

"Well, there's an element of that," Mrs. Jenkins said. "But it might make more sense to think of it as a kind of Careers Day presentation. The parents of the various children have a wide range of vocations. You're not the only parent who works for the Sarovar Company, of course, but you're the only accountant."

"Oh, the children are in for some rare thrills today." John grinned.

She leaned in conspiratorially. "Although I think Ellie had promised some of the other children that you would bring the dog. Ani?"

John looked at his younger daughter, who stood shaking water off her raincoat over a floor grate beside the door. Her little face was marred by a deep frown. "Animoosh. Ani for short. It's a Chippewa word. Is she having trouble fitting in?"

"All children do, at first."

John kicked himself for not bringing the dog.

"I feel I must tell you," Mrs. Jenkins said, "that your girls are precocious. Quite precocious."

John nodded. "I know them."

"In a big Earth city, any decent school would have accelerated classes, or would have the ability to advance the girls into a class with their intellectual peers. Here,"—Mrs. Jenkins shrugged—"we're in a single room."

"Hopefully the docent will help supplement what you can do in school." John smiled, trying to be encouraging. "We try to teach them to be self-directed learners."

Mrs. Jenkins nodded. "I can introduce you to the class, if you like."

John had an idea. "I'll introduce myself."

He stood at the back of the room for ten minutes while the class assembled. His girls hung their raincoats, names neatly lettered inside the collars and visible through the transparent plastic, on pegs on the back wall. They put their lunches under the hinged plastic slabs that served as desktops and plugged their multitools into the power sockets. Other children arrived and worked their way through the same ritual. John was amused that a few children took multitools from a shelf at the front of the class, and a few had shiny new multitools, which they pulled from matte black cases, and ostentatiously didn't plug in.

School—was it the same everywhere you went?

"Good morning, class," Mrs. Jenkins said. "In a few minutes we'll get to our geology discussion, but first, we have a special visitor." She extended a welcoming hand to John. "Would you like to introduce yourself?"

Children tracked John's approach to the front with their eyes over their shoulders. A few whispered to their neighbors.

"Good morning," John said. He barked, as if due to an uncontrollable tic, and stretched his neck. "My name is Ani. That's short for Animoosh, which, in a very old American language, means dog. Yes, I'm a dog named Dog. Many of you have probably already guessed by the shape of my muzzle, but I am part Labrador. I'm also part pit bull, but the thing that may be puzzling you is my reddish-brown coat."

The children stared. Ellie's frown was gone, replaced by an uncertain look.

"I am, you see, a genetically modified dog. My coat changes colors with the seasons. In winter, I'm white, in spring a chocolate brown, and in summer, a tawny golden color. This is my autumn coat. You're thinking, but it isn't autumn."

"No," a boy in the front row said. He was wide-hipped and narrow-shouldered, with very long fingers, thick, spiky hair, and an East Asian complexion. "I am thinking, shouldn't you turn green in the spring?"

Oh good, at least one of them was quick-witted. "Yes, you're correct, the reason my coat changes colors is to provide camouflage throughout the year. I too have wondered why green isn't the spring shade. Shame—I would love to have been able to photosynthesize!"

Most of the class laughed.

Ellie laughed with them, and John smiled at her.

"But now," the Asian boy said, "tell us why you're the wrong color?"

John rubbed his fingers together. "It was spaceflight, you see. The scientists who created my breed foresaw me changing colors with the seasons, but didn't think about what would happen if I were to take a long-distance spaceflight."

"Say, from Earth to Sarovar?" the boy asked.

"Aboard the Company starship *Oberon*." John nodded. "Tell me your name."

"Gary Chen."

Sam Chen's son? "Very good, Gary. My coat changes color with the changing of the light. So right now I'm shedding like crazy because I'm changing color."

"Did your family have you custom-built?" asked a child with a spherical head.

"No, I was a rescue. But my breed was created for hunting, so I'm a good tracker and I change color. I don't change very quickly, or night would make me turn black; it takes a few weeks. And, as you all know, it takes months to get from Earth to Sarovar. There's the shuttle to orbit, and then the flight to Jupiter, and then you generally have to wait for the wormhole to be opened. It's months passing through the wormhole, and then you have to come in through Sarovar System and land. And it turns out that the photoreceptors in my body interpreted the artificial light aboard the starship as the light of autumn, so I went from chocolate brown straight to rust, without the intervening gold. And now, just in the last two days, I'm beginning to turn back to brown."

"Neb nee rach that," said a different child. This was a boy with a delicate jaw and thin eyebrows under dark brown hair.

"How would you say that in English?" Mrs. Jenkins prodded gently.

"Not everyone knows," the boy said.

"Knows what?" John asked.

"That it takes months to get here from Earth."

"Oh." John considered. "Are you a country-setty, then?"

Mrs. Jenkins coughed sharply.

Had he been rude? John tried again. "I mean, were you born here?"

The boy nodded.

"What's your name?" John asked. He thought of his Sedjem word lists. "What you ren?"

"Pianki."

"Ah." John nodded. "Well, you're very lucky, Pianki, because this is a beautiful place to be from. And you have so much water! I got back yesterday from a trading wat. Not only did we see some beautiful creatures, like ba, but we also saw a cenote. And when I say saw, I mean that I fell into it, so I was lucky that I was tied to a rope at the time."

The children's eyes had gotten round.

Other than Gary Chen's. Gary folded his arms across his chest. "What's a color-changing dog like you doing going to a wat? I didn't know they let dogs be traders."

John chuckled. "In fact, they don't, which is why I have come to Sarovar as an accountant."

"A bean counter," Gary said.

"Why do you count beans?" Pianki asked slowly.

"I don't actually count beans," John said. "That's an old expression that's used to make fun of accountants. We even use it ourselves! I count bales of Weave, and truck tires, and screwdrivers, and buildings, and employees, and dollars."

"Why would anyone want to make fun of accountants?" another girl asked.

"People are afraid of our power," John said. "You see, in any business, the mightiest people are the accountants."

"That's not true," Gary said.

John nodded solemnly. "Oh, yes it is. Let's think about this. If you were running a business, what kinds of questions would you want to have answered?"

"Can I pay myself a big bonus?" Gary suggested.

"You see, you have to ask the accountant that," John said. "Are my prices high enough and my costs low enough that I can afford to pay myself a fat bonus and stay in business? The accountant knows!"

"Can I hire more people?" Pianki asked.

"Better ask the accountant!" John said.

"Can I invest in a school?" Mrs. Jenkins offered.

"Oh good," John said, "now you're asking questions about the future. Do I think, if I build a better school, it will be worth it? Will the school pay for itself by generating smarter workers? How long before the school pays for itself? Those are questions for the accountant."

"This is kind of boring." Gary smirked. "Tell us how you fell into a cenote. I guess you forgot to count the cenotes first."

"Actually," John said, "the man who was driving the truck didn't see the cenote coming, and he drove right into it."

Gary shut his mouth.

"But it wasn't on purpose," John said. "And he did a good job backing the truck out of the hole."

"But wait," Pianki said. He frowned, as if struggling with unfamiliar words. "Are you saying a . . . business can't do *anything* without an . . . accountant?"

"The business can make any decision it wants," John said, "even without an accountant. But it's the accountant who measures and tells the business whether it is being successful, and helps the business plan to be successful in the future."

"But the post chief makes the decisions." This observation came from a squarish child with pigtails and skin the color of a coconut husk. She had one of the brand-new, high-end multitools.

"She does," John agreed. "But if Post Chief Carlton doesn't talk to Audit Chief Keckley first, she's making decisions blind. So most post chiefs, or CEOs, or other senior business leaders, get very comfortable with the language of accounting, so they can understand the guidance their accountants are giving them."

"You're not Audit Chief Keckley," Gary said. "You're a dog named Animoosh."

"Actually, I'm an auditor named John Abbott," John said. "Auditor is what the Company calls its accountants who work on their financial accounts. Audit Chief Keckley is the senior accountant here at Arrowhawk Post."

"What else do accountants do in the Company?" Pianki asked. "Besides the financial accounts?"

"There are tax accountants," John said. "And accountants in compliance. And there are accountants attached to other functional groups, or to business units, to do specialized work. There's also Internal Audit, which are accountants who investigate crime. Kind of accountant-detectives."

There was a brief pause. John had run out of things to say. He was also pretty sure that most of what he'd said, after he stopped pretending he was a dog, had gone right over the children's heads. He wished he had prepared better.

"What questions do you have for Mr. Abbott, class?" Mrs. Jenkins asked.

"Is it fun, being an accountant?" Pianki wanted to know.

"Yes," John said. "It's an adventure. Every day, you're solving mysteries and you're trying to keep the train on its track. A lot of people depend on you to get the answers right, or they'll lose their jobs. It feels good to be necessary."

"Do accountants get paid a lot of money?" the square child asked.

"Accountants get paid pretty well," John said. "That's because you have to have special training, so not everyone can do the job. When you do something that not just anyone can do, you get paid more."

"That's not true," Gary said. "My dad said any dumbass could do a better job than the post chief does, and she gets paid most of all."

"Hey!" the square child shouted.

Uh-oh. John raised his voice and stepped forward, putting himself between the kids. "Salespeople get paid a lot, but usually only if they are successful. This makes them work harder to sell more. That's because nothing else can happen without sales. At the Company, we call our salespeople 'traders.'"

"What about the owners of the Company?" Pianki asked. "Do they get paid a lot?"

"Our owners are called 'shareholders,'" John said, "and I don't think any of them live on Sarovar Alpha."

"Maybe Sarovar Gamma." Pigtails nodded smugly. "I've been to Sarovar Gamma. You could have ice cream for every meal, if you wanted it, and swim all day."

The children gasped.

"Unless they're also working as employees of the company," John continued, "owners don't get paid salaries. Instead, they get money if the company they own can generate extra cash. That gets paid out to them as a dividend."

"So how *much* do they get?" Gary persisted.

"When the business fails, the owner loses money. But if the business does well, and especially if it does really well, the owner gets all of the extra value. We'd call that the upside. And one of the really great things the Sarovar Company does is it lets all its employees trade for their own account. That means that every employee here can start his or her own business, buying and selling Weave. Every employee becomes the owner of his own business, and can get the upside. So one of the best-known facts about the Sarovar Company is that any employee can get rich, trading for his own account."

Pianki frowned. "Not *any* employee."

John hesitated. "You're right. Most of the employees."

"My uncle is a bak for the Company, mar," Pianki said. "He's a cleaning-setty. He can't trade in shesroo."

What was a bak, again? He'd heard the word. John nodded. "Yes, I misspoke, I apologize."

Pianki nodded. "And he knows where dashroo nyoots are, too, and he could trade with them, except the Company won't ship any Weave."

"How does he know it won't?" John asked. "Has he tried?"

"He tried," Pianki said. "They put him in jail for a week."

John felt ill. "I'm sorry if I said anything offensive."

Pianki stacked his fists and rested his chin on top of them, frowning.

"Besides," the square child said, "what do you know? You're just a dog."

John chuckled. "Well, thank you very much for having me. Are there any other questions?"

There weren't.

"I would really rather have seen the dog," Gary said. "Before it turns brown, especially. It would be cool to see a red dog in the spring."

"I'm sorry," John said, "we weren't quite sure how Ani would react to a crowd. But if you're friends with my girls, you can come by the khat and play with Ani. She's pretty good at fetch."

"She's even better at eating snacks," Ellie said. The faces of several of the younger children around her brightened.

"Ani sounds like a very interesting dog," Mrs. Jenkins said. "Maybe you can bring her on our next field trip."

Ellie's face burst into a smile so big, it looked as if her head might explode.

"That sounds like fun," John said. "Where are you going?"

"Outside the post," she answered, "to look at a cenote for our geology unit."

"I see," John said. "I'll try to come."

CHAPTER FOURTEEN

DeBoe was working at his desk when John reached the office.

John sat. He was still dragging from the physical exertion and the sleep deprivation of the wat, and now his heart also felt heavy.

"DeBoe," he said. "What happens to someone who tries to ship Weave, who isn't a trader?"

"I don't see how they'd get their Weave onto a ship," DeBoe said. "Do you mean smuggling?"

"I guess so."

DeBoe set down the ledger he was poring over. "Well, that would be a Code of Conduct violation. No different from theft of services, back on Earth."

John sighed.

"You don't want everyone to be able to ship," DeBoe said. "The more plentiful Weave is, the more the price comes down."

"That's true." John considered this. Was DeBoe saying that the Company deliberately propped up prices by limiting who could sell?

"The market here is for skilled employees," DeBoe said. "If you need to attract someone with a set of skills—say, in law, or accounting, or engineering, or whatever—and you also have to compensate that person for taking the risk and being willing to come here, what do you do?"

"You pay them more."

DeBoe nodded. "And one way to pay them more is to let them take advantage of Company opportunities. Let them trade for their own accounts."

"You're saying that some labor doesn't need to be compensated like that."

"Correct." DeBoe sucked on a tooth. "If we hire someone in a menial position . . ."

"Say, a cleaner."

"A cleaner, then. That's a good example. We don't have to attract special talent, so we don't pay extra. Cleaners aren't factors. Or traders, obviously."

"And we don't attract cleaners from Earth. We hire the locals. That's true for all of our writer-grade employees, I think."

DeBoe nodded.

"So, the Company is lucky that there were human colonists here when the system was handed over to the Company."

"*You* are lucky," DeBoe said. "That means the Company doesn't need to pay too much for *other* jobs, but it *does* need to pay a lot to attract you."

"I guess that's right." John felt deeply conflicted.

"Only you weren't lucky," DeBoe said. "You took advantage of the market by being smart. Price is the signal of supply and demand, you saw that the price of an accountant on Sarovar Alpha was high, and you took advantage by developing the skills for that job. You might not have fully thought through all the reasons why the Company makes so many men's fortunes, but very few people Earthside have anything like a clear picture of Sarovar."

John nodded slowly.

"Do you feel guilty?" DeBoe asked.

John rubbed his eyes with the butts of his hands. "No, I . . . I'm just still new. Still trying to figure things out."

"Well, if you decided it wasn't for you, and went home . . . let's just say you wouldn't be the first."

"Of course not. I suppose a Sarovari could study accounting and then underbid me for my job," John suggested.

"Yes," DeBoe said, "but to do that, a country-setty would have to get something reasonably close to the education you got, at least in the actual accounting portion of your education. I don't think that's available on this planet. Although, think about this: a country-setty's best chance for any education at all, as far as I can tell, is to attend school on a Company post."

John considered. "And the word 'country-setty'...is that offensive?"

DeBoe laughed. "Dear God, you've been talking to Jenkins."

"She just...she looked mortified when I said it this morning."

"She's very sensitive. But she's wrong to imagine that everyone else is as sensitive as she is. 'Setty' itself is a country-setty word."

Pianki *had* referred to his uncle as a cleaning-setty. And Faisal had called himself a knowledge-setty, and neither had seemed to feel demeaned by the terms. "I might start calling myself a 'numbers-setty.'"

"You do that," DeBoe said. "But first, go upstairs and call English."

John froze. "The Comms office?"

"You generally don't need it, and can just use your multi for any calls you make. But English likes people to call him from Comms. Sometimes he likes you to have access to Comms data or the post computer, but I think he also just likes the privacy. Tell Stohel you need the comms panel to talk to English and he'll get out of your way."

The encryption plug was in John's pocket; he worried it with his fingers as he climbed the stairs to Comms.

Stohel was a short man with a thick neck, heavy jowls, and nervous fingers. He stepped aside immediately at the mention of English's name and left the room in John's sole possession, shutting the door behind him. Out the windows of the Comms room, and only a meter or so overhead, John saw the underside of the maglev line. A column supporting the maglev guideway dropped down onto the corner of the warehouse rooftop; the pillar had ladder rungs bolted to it, maybe for emergency or maintenance access.

He had great views out the windows, too, of the rocky peaks south and north of the post, and of the gray scudding sheets of storm that were scrolling in from the west.

The comms unit was a fairly obvious one, but it took John a few minutes to find the socket for the encryption plug. Once he'd nestled that into place, in a subtle socket below the lip of the panel, the words ENCRYPTION PROPOSED appeared on the unit's screen.

He entered the address for Director English's comms unit and waited. After a few seconds, the words changed to ENCRYPTION ACCEPTED, and English's face appeared on the screen.

"You're alone?" the director asked.

John nodded. "I hadn't reached out to you because I haven't come to any conclusions yet."

"But you're much too smart to not know *anything*."

"I can see that post revenue declined," John said, "you're right. But trade seems to be booming. And I've audited the inventory in the warehouse, so if bales are being diverted out of what is due to the Company, they don't appear to be stored in the warehouse."

"That's a start," English said.

"And I've been out to observe traders on a wat," John said. "My observation is limited to one session, and they knew they were being watched, but the traders on the wat all subordinated their own trading to the Company's."

"This all sounds good," English said. "You're getting your arms around how the post and the trade work, and how the accounting is done."

John nodded.

"None of that precludes the possibility that bales of Weave are being skimmed," English said.

"I am going to check trader commissions against reported volumes," John said.

English pursed his lips. "Do that. And keep looking. And I assume you went not only to observe, but to buy."

John hesitated.

"Let's not be coy," English said. "You purchased inoo from the warehouse."

"Right. And I bought bales. I'm only trying to figure out whether it makes more sense for me to trade with one of the traders here."

"I'd be astonished if any of them could offer you better terms than I did."

"They didn't. Only, I want to get on their good sides."

"You don't understand salespeople, John. As long as you say maybe, maybe, maybe to them, you're a prospect, and will be treated with great solicitude. The minute you sign up to trade with one of them, the deal has been done, and you're behind them. Even the one you signed with, but especially the others. Tactically, you should tell them all that I've ordered you to trade through me for the time being, but in the future, you'll switch to one of them."

"That does make some sense." It felt a little devious, though.

English shrugged. "Do what you wish. If you want to trade through my account, someone at the post will show you how to package the Weave and send it on the train."

English's transmission ended abruptly. John took the encryption plug and drifted down the stairs.

He felt confused, in his thoughts as well as in his heart. To straighten himself out, he sat down to look at the revenue numbers. Picking out exactly which shipments were connected with which commission payments should have been easy—in the detail, there should have been explicit records connecting the amounts. There were not.

He tried for an easier test, plotting out commission payments over the last year against volumes of Company-owned Weave over the last year. As he had seen before, volumes had dropped.

Commissions had gone up.

"Have we raised trader commissions in the last twelve months?" he asked.

"What the hell are you looking at?" The voice was Keckley's; John looked up to find DeBoe gone and Keckley in his desk, wrestling with his multitool.

"Uh, sorry. Just P&L data, trying to make sure I understand our figures. Looks to me like revenue has declined, but the commissions we pay to traders has gone up."

Keckley grunted. "That's probably a mistake. Something else has bled into the commissions journal account on accident. I'll look at it and see what it might have been. We need to get you onto a higher-value task."

"I could keep looking at this," John offered.

"I've got a bigger project. You went out on the wat the other day."

"I did."

"What did you think of the truck?"

"It seemed in good working order, no problem."

"That truck was fully depreciated two years ago."

"You must have a really good maintenance program."

Keckley shrugged. "No better than anyone else's. I think the depreciation period is too short on the trucks."

John furrowed his brow. "Does each post get to choose depreciation periods?"

"No. But the Company has set the depreciation schedules too short, which means that our annual depreciation expense is too high."

"It feels like this is a . . . policy question," John said.

"Yes. What we need is a white paper. And I think you're going to need to personally test the trucks, and probably talk to all the engineers you can find, to get the paper together."

"This is going to keep me away from the post accounts," John said.

"I regret that," Keckley said. "On the other hand, if you can cut our depreciation expense by twenty-five percent, you'll be the hero of every post chief and audit chief in the system."

John hesitated, unsure what to say.

"Believe me, you'll like being the Hero of Arrowhawk and the Depreciation Wizard when it comes time to apply for some open audit chief position," Keckley said. "The number of accountants in this Company who ever manage to get a Company-wide reputation can be counted on the fingers of one hand. Promotions and transfers, anything you want, the skids will be greased."

"Well, I do like the sound of Depreciation Wizard," John said.

"Good. You know your stuff, it seems, but I'd suggest you start by getting familiar with our depreciation accounts. And maybe tomorrow, you can start looking at the trucks themselves."

"We must have literature from the manufacturers," John said.

"There are no manufacturers," Keckley said. "The Company Frankensteins them together in the larger posts, out of parts of other factory-produced vehicles. Ours were knocked together in Henry Hudson. There's an old leaflet around somewhere with operating instructions and a replacement parts guide, and I think the depreciation schedule is printed in the back of that. But if that doesn't give you enough data, you can call the guys who make them. Or train right back to Henry Hudson and take them out for lunch."

John nodded. "I guess I'm going to ship the bales I bought to Director English. He offered to let me trade through him at really good pricing."

Keckley harrumphed, an approving sound. "He'll get priority shipping, too, so you'll get paid first. There's a multi app that will allow you to seal and mark crates appropriately. The train's in town the day after tomorrow, and I'll show you how to use the app. Or if I'm not around, ask any of the traders."

"Thank you." John cracked open the ledgers again. "I guess I'll get to looking at the depreciation accounts."

"That trader you pulled out of the cenote," Keckley said.

"Is he going to be alright?" John asked.

"Hinkley got him to Henry Hudson in time, and they've grafted a new foot on. Looks like he'll walk again."

"Glad to hear it."

"That's another way to get a Company-wide reputation," Keckley said. "Save a few traders' lives."

"Anyone would have done it."

Keckley snorted and looked John in the eye. "What I'm saying, Abbott, is keep it up."

John dug into the accounts. They were strictly banal—marching columns of straight-line addition, showing the trucks and buildings of the post being spread over time to line up with revenue. He noted useful lives and a few ratios, and then it was time to go.

Keckley was gone and DeBoe hadn't reappeared, so John locked up the office. Shrugging into his jacket, he felt reassured by the weight of the pistol and bullets in its pockets, but he was reminded that Ruth hadn't yet hired a guard for the family khat. He should check in with Faisal.

It occurred to him that the post's security personnel might be another source of recommendations, so he stopped at their open doorway on the way out. Korsgaard sat at a desk alone in the small room, and looked up when John knocked.

"Korsgaard," John said.

"Security Chief Korsgaard," the blond man said, "if you were wondering."

"Chief," John said, "I'd like to hire someone to be a security guard at my khat."

Korsgaard nodded approvingly. "Get someone you trust."

"That's why I thought I'd ask you for a recommendation."

"The post employs a militia," Korsgaard said. "Strictly part-time, and what they mostly do is drill. They're called the Arrowhawk Post Irregulars. Occasionally, they've had to deal with a wild animal issue or a lost child. These people are country-setties, you understand? But they're the ones I trust."

"Can I get a list of the Irregulars?"

Korsgaard nodded again. "I'll send it to your multi."

John hesitated. "Also . . . I talked to Payne earlier about this. Do you know Faisal Haddad? He's a country-setty."

"He's a weird languages-setty," Korsgaard said. "I like Hebrew as much as the next fellow, but who needs to speak it out here?"

John laughed. "Yeah, he's offered to do some jobs for me."

"Meaning you want him to find something. Like what, a black market printer-disposal unit?"

John hesitated. "Something like that."

"He's done a lot of that kind of thing for Company personnel over the years," Korsgaard said. "I think he knows people at Henry Hudson. I've never heard anyone say he ripped them off, if that's what you're asking."

"That's what I'm asking."

The street was wet and the sky clouded as John emerged from beneath the maglev line. He dodged a truck crossing the gravel and trudged toward home.

His job, he now saw clearly, was the product of monopoly. This was always the case with the professions; the whole reason to have a bar exam or medical licensing was to restrict the number of professionals, and keep prices up. But the Company's position seemed . . . a little worse than that, somehow. Local people weren't being allowed to benefit from local resources.

Other than by having schools, maybe. They were boxed out of the good jobs, and could only work part-time, as an Irregular, or as menials for people who were getting rich off the resources of their world.

Including John. He groaned.

What should he do about that fact?

Well, he could give Mrs. Jenkins good gifts on holidays. Or gratuities, if that was acceptable. He could make sure to pay his khat guard really well, when he got one. He could engage Faisal.

It was a start.

But eventually, in the long term . . . what?

School. Maybe he could start an accounting school, to let kids like Pianki have access to Company jobs. If the Company didn't pay a local accountant a risk premium for moving to Sarovar, that local accountant could underbid an Earth accountant and still get paid great money.

Or maybe he could take a portion of his trading profits and donate them to the country-setties, somehow. Endow a library. Pay for education. Something.

He sighed, turning onto his own street, and then froze.

Two blocks past his khat, parked on the side of the gravel street, sat a white groundcar. It was an inconspicuous make and model, so much so that John couldn't place it.

But he was sure he hadn't seen it there before.

It might be the same make and model car he had seen at the Stone Gardens, outside Henry Hudson Post.

He set a consistent pace, and avoided looking at the groundcar, as he headed home.

CHAPTER FIFTEEN

"We hired a khat guard today," Ruth said over dinner.

John took a bite, wondering what the meat was.

"His name is Nermer," Sunitha said in her faux accent. "He's a country-setty, and he also worked for the Company for twenty years. He's been a guide and a wat-guard."

"Also," Ruth added, "he's a member of the Arrowhawk Post Irregulars. I gather that's sort of a militia unit."

John nodded. "Does he drive a white groundcar, by any chance?"

Ruth shot him a curious look. "He rides a donkey, actually."

John nodded, trying to focus on his family's words. In his head, he was turning over the fact that Keckley had just assigned him to study depreciation. The least likely of any of the Company's accounts to show evidence of theft.

Keckley was sidelining him.

It didn't mean Keckley was guilty, but English had thought he might be.

And John still hadn't met the post chief.

Working on depreciation meant that John couldn't use his time at the office to look at what English wanted. And he had a question that he wanted answered, which would require him to go count inventory again.

He'd have to do it at night.

Really, he should do it tonight.

"Did you hear me, John?" Ruth asked.

John swallowed. Whatever he was eating, he was pretty sure the chunks of red meat weren't beef. "He rides a donkey. That's pretty great. Maybe the girls could take a ride, once in a while. Or he can tell us where to buy our own donkey. Or maybe we can just rent one. Also, I'll double-check with the security people at Company House, make sure they don't have anything bad to say about him. About Nermal."

"Nermer. You missed the part where I said he was going to come live with us."

"Oh. I did. I'm sorry, I just . . . I'm distracted." John set down his fork. "Nermer's going to come live with us. Does that mean I give up my office?" It wasn't much of an office, just a narrow room upstairs with a folding table for a desk, but John liked the idea of having a private place.

"The shed out back," Ruth said. "It isn't actually a shed. It has three small rooms, including a little latrine. He'll live there. That's apparently the ordinary way this is done. And we have a couple of unused foam inflatables."

John nodded. "That sounds reasonable. Good work. When does he move in? Or is he there already? Of course not, you would have invited him to dinner if he was here."

"He'll be in tomorrow. He's getting a few possessions together. Including weapons."

"Speaking of weapons, we should teach the girls to shoot, and get them some target practice." John took a small mouthful of meat and its red, tomato-like sauce, so he could keep talking as he chewed. There were capers in the sauce, or something like capers. "Maybe we could go for a little hike outside the post."

"Yes!" Sunitha said.

"I'm sure I can get a small-caliber rifle here in town," John said. "Something appropriate."

Ruth nodded. Her family didn't have the military background John's did, but she came from stubbornly independent minority religious stock. Minority religious folk only tended to retain their independence when they were armed and vigilant, and Ruth's family certainly was. One of the favorite family tales, which John had heard recounted over repeated Christmas dinners, was the one in which Uncle Christopher had delivered a homily and blessed the eucharist with a pistol strapped to each hip and a pump-action shotgun tucked away in the sacristy.

"I'm not too jubilee?" Ellie asked.

"You're pretty juvenile," John said. "You both are. But you're really smart. And you won't always be little, so I want to make sure you know how guns work now, so you don't lose your head around them when you're older. We'll learn safety rules, and just take a few shots."

Ruth nodded.

"Is this beef?" John took another bite.

"You're distracted about work," Ruth said. "Are you going back in tonight?"

"I got assigned a new project," John said, mopping the last of the tomato sauce up with a heel of bread. "To clear the decks for it, I should really finish some of my old projects, first."

"Old projects?" Sunitha asked. "You haven't been here a week."

"My boss, Director English, sent me here with some questions to try to answer." He hesitated. English had insisted on discretion. "I didn't bore you with it because it's accounting stuff. I should probably go in tonight and try to make progress on that. Finish it, if possible." He had no plan to go back to the office; he wanted to go to the warehouse. He felt very conflicted, not telling Ruth the entire story. "We'll ship our Weave the day after tomorrow to Central Transit."

"You've moved fast," Ruth said. "Good job."

"When do we get paid for it?" Ellie asked.

"I still have to decide that part." John met Ruth's eyes. "We can get paid earlier and a known, certain amount, if we agree to take less. Or we take the risk and gut out the wait and probably make more."

"I'm not married to getting the jewels back," Ruth said. "I'm married to you."

John smiled. "It's true that, sooner or later, the market for Weave will cool down. Maybe we should ship all the way to Earth."

"You look at the numbers."

John stood and carried his plate and utensils into the kitchen. He rinsed them off and set them in the sink; a black market printer-disposal unit would certainly simplify kitchen work. "I'll look at the numbers. And I'll be back in a few hours." He bent to kiss Ruth and whispered into her ear, "You know where the energy pistol is?"

She nodded. "One more thing. I want to get back to church with the girls."

"Of course," John said. "Is there a U.C. church in town?"

"There isn't *any* church in town. Is there a post chaplain?"

"I don't think so," he said.

"Hmm."

He took his jacket from the peg near the door, feeling the weapon of the pistol and ammunition in its pockets, and shrugged into it. He waved goodbye at the exit.

"It wasn't beef!" Ruth called out as he shut the door behind him.

John climbed up Nermer's hut, looked both ways, and then dropped into the alley. He walked along it the opposite direction from Company House, angling back to reach Grijalva Street where it ended in the stockade wall.

The white groundcar was still there. It was parked on the gravel, facing John's house.

Facing a lot of houses, though.

And it was a very ordinary-looking groundcar. There was no reason to think it was the same car he had seen at the Stone Gardens.

He wished he'd left his family on Earth.

John crossed the street and passed through another alley between two khat enclosures, heading for the looming shadow of the maglev line. The shops and eateries and bars of the post didn't stay open all night, as some did at Henry Hudson, but they were still open now, the bright lettering of their signs casting cold, wet shadows across the gravel.

There was a light on in Security, and Moore sat in the office, looking at his multi. John let himself into the warehouse through the bay doors, shutting them behind him. The Company had taken eighteen bales of Weave at the Mouse Rock wat. On his previous count, the Company had had one hundred twelve bales in the warehouse. Nothing had shipped in the meantime. There should now be one hundred thirty bales of Weave.

Easy math, an easy check.

He left the lights off, and operated by the light of his multi. It took him less than half an hour to examine all the crates under Company seal and count their totals: one hundred twenty-eight bales.

Two had gone missing.

Sitting in the warehouse with the lights turned off, to avoid attracting attention, John examined the accounts on his multitool. One hundred twenty-eight bales in inventory. Only sixteen bales had been checked in from the Mouse Rock wat.

Was it possible John had miscounted?

The bale count from the wat was signed by Jefferson.

Jefferson was stealing Weave.

Jefferson could have hidden the stolen Weave anywhere, including the khat where he lived. But it was worth checking the warehouse. John searched the trucks first, using the light of his multi, and found nothing.

Then he scanned the traders' crates until he found Jefferson's. His multitool wouldn't open these crates, but they were electronically marked for their contents. His multi wouldn't personally read the creates, but his accounting app could.

Eleven crates. The number of crates alone suggested that Jefferson had been trading for a long time and was successful at it. The contents were identified as trade goods, an enumerated list of shovels and hammers and similar tools. But the list looked rather short, to be filling eleven crates.

John placed the crates on the floor scale. They were heavy, so he had to carry them one at a time, grunting. In his multitool, he found the standard dimensions of the crates, including weight. He also found the weight of each tool Jefferson had purchased—confirmed by cross-checking against the post's inventory accounts—and he added those weights together, comparing them to the weight that showed up on the scales.

Almost two hundred kilograms' difference.

His back and shoulders ached. There was two hundred kilograms of *something* in those crates that was not identified on the labels.

John shuffled the crates back into place, thinking. He could break a crate open. But the logs would show that he was the one who had opened the warehouse, or at least, his multi had done it. If he found something that clearly confirmed Jefferson's guilt, that might end his investigation and satisfy English.

But what if something other than stolen Weave was in the crates? Weave was light; he didn't think you could add two hundred kilos of weight, even if you stuffed every one of the eleven crates full of Weave.

And there must be some Weave in there, anyway, because

Jefferson, too, had taken a personal allotment at Mouse Rock. Since his personal allotments were not part of Company records, how could John confirm that any Weave he found in the crates was stolen, anyway? He could work up some kind of notional dollar cost of Weave for each of Jefferson's recent wats, based on how many bales the Company brought back and how many trade goods it delivered, and then look at how much trade goods Jefferson had acquired... his head was spinning at the problem already, and that was before he took into account that theft of bales—which he now knew was happening—would throw his numbers off, anyway.

"Dammit," he growled, perched on one of Jefferson's crates.

The warehouse didn't have audio or video security recordings, as far as he knew. He could find out whether those existed—he'd have to be careful that Keckley didn't hear what he was looking into. And if they didn't, he could install something.

Or did he need video recording on the trucks, so that when Jefferson drove out on wat and he opened his crates, John could see what was inside?

Maybe he could get Faisal to help him.

John heard footsteps outside the warehouse entry door. He froze, waiting for them to pass, but then he heard the rasp of a key in the lock.

He had every right to be in the warehouse, but the fact that he was in here with the lights off would strike anyone coming in as strange, and probably suspicious.

John quickly climbed into one of the trucks.

The warehouse door opened, and he heard voices.

"This is heavy," one man grunted. He sounded like Gonzalez.

"It will turn into many dollars in your account," Jefferson said.

The men's footsteps sounded as if they were shuffling. John climbed carefully up the ladder into the truck's upper compartment. He was frightened to look over, so he turned on his camera's multitool function and raised just the corner of the multi over the railing. The images picked up by the multi's photoreceptors showed on its screen, turning the multi into a tiny periscope.

Jefferson and Gonzalez carried two crates. They grunted, dragged their feet, and slouched over to the pile of Jefferson's crates, then set the crates down on top of the pile.

Weave just wasn't that heavy. This was more unaccounted-for . . . whatever it was.

"You sure they're still buying?" Gonzalez asked.

Jefferson slapped Gonzalez on the arm. "Yes, man. But you're right, we need to make our noob while the market's hot, because the market is going to go away."

Gonzalez ran his hands through his hair. "This particular market is going to go away in a very ugly fashion, mar."

"Six months, I'm done," Jefferson said. "At the higher volumes and with our higher cut. How about you?"

"I could be done in six," Gonzalez said. "Eight for sure."

"I'll make sure you're a rich man within six. You're coming to Bourbon Lake, right?"

"Is it just you and me?"

Jefferson chuckled. "It's a small nyoot. Wouldn't do to bring too many traders . . . or too much Company Weave."

They headed for the door.

"Six months," Gonzalez agreed. "Jesus, I want off this planet."

"Before it blows."

Jefferson turned out the lights and shut the warehouse door.

What did the two traders fear? And why did they want to go out to the Bourbon Lake wat alone? Would that mean that they didn't take a driver, either?

John opened the regional map on the multi and searched for the name 'Bourbon,' then, for good measure, 'Whisky' and 'Whiskey' and half a dozen other names for spirituous liquors. Nothing.

The surface features of Sarovar Alpha were meticulously mapped. But only the largest had names applied to them in the app.

There were records of trading wats in the account books, though, and they had names. He searched for 'Bourbon' there and found monthly trips. They were four-day rather than two-day, and each trip was linked to a notes file that gave some detail. No map. The first trip had been Jefferson alone with a driver named Steve Diamond. A notation in the file read, 'Diamond dead, fell off a cliff.'

Subsequent trips had involved Jefferson only, and then Jefferson and Gonzalez.

So Jefferson must drive a truck. Maybe the smaller one?

And the presence of cliffs implied that Bourbon Lake was in

mountains. John pulled up the map again and looked. How far would a truck go in two days, where there were no roads, and terrain was mountainous? Seven hundred kilometers? A thousand?

And within a thousand kilometers of Arrowhawk Post, there were thousands of little lakes.

John sighed.

Was the Weave market about to blow up? What did the traders know that he didn't? Had he brought his family here at the worst possible time, sinking them all into debt just as the ability to pay off that debt and make a fortune evaporated?

When he was certain the two traders had gone, John let himself out and crept across the street. Sheltering in a shadowed nook between two businesses with dark windows, he pulled out his multi and called Faisal Haddad.

CHAPTER SIXTEEN

Faisal answered promptly. Asking no questions, he arrived five minutes later. Rain was just beginning to fall, and he handed John a clear rain jacket, then opened his parasol above his own head.

"What does the parasol mean, by the way?" John asked.

"Branding does not have to mean anything," Faisal said. "Sometimes it is just the way you remember something. 'Which one was the delicious cookie? Ah yes, the ones shaped like animals.'"

"Specifically, the one shaped like a rhinoceros. I see you've met my daughters."

Faisal tipped his head. "During the process of recruiting Nermer."

"How well do you know this guy?"

"He has a good reputation," Faisal said. "He has worked at the post since I was a boy. He's patient, he's been in fights as one of the Arrowhawk Post Irregulars, he's been wounded. He's dependable, and a family man."

"I like someone with skin in the game," John.

"Oh good," Faisal said. "Then you must like yourself an awful lot."

John found that funny, but a little too painful to laugh at. "I need help, but I'm not even sure exactly what the help I need is."

"Tell me," Faisal said, "and I shall propose a solution, and tell you the price."

John explained about the unknown, heavy contents of Jefferson's crates, and his ignorance and curiosity about Jefferson's wats to Bourbon Lake, including the death of the driver who had accompanied him the first time. Faisal watched him closely with narrowed eyes.

"Are you with the Company's Security Services, Mr. Abbott?" he asked, when John had finished.

John laughed, but cringed. "No, I . . . I wish I were. If I were, I think I would know what to do here. Or I would have tools. Or I could arrest Jefferson and interrogate him."

Faisal took a deep breath. "You want to know what Jefferson is doing. And specifically, what is in those crates, and if have they something to do with his somewhat off-the-record trips to Bourbon Lake."

"Correct. Suggestions?"

Faisal began ticking off fingers. "I could break into the warehouse and open the crates. We would need to do something about the security team, and if there's any record that you've been nosing around his files, you might end up a suspect, but we could see what's in the crates tonight. Or we could grab Jefferson and beat him up. I could round up a few country-setties who'd be willing to do that. If he figures out it was you, you could be in for some hot water."

"No. Something more subtle."

"Subtle." Faisal ticked off his third finger. "I could follow Jefferson. I can probably get away with it here at the post. He drinks a lot, and if I hire someone to spell me off, we could stay incognito. If he gets in a truck to drive off to some mountain wat, though, it will be hard to follow him without being seen. That brings me to this finger, which is I could follow his truck using a remote drone."

"Can you get a drone here with that long a range?" John asked.

"That is the question. I could probably call Henry Hudson and have something delivered here. It might take a few days to arrive."

John shook his head. "The trucks might go tomorrow."

"Understood. So here is my last suggestion: we attach a simple tracker to one of the crates. Ideally, one that you think is carrying his mystery cargo."

"The last two crates," John said.

Faisal shrugged. "We then see easily on the map where he goes to. Yes, a thousand kilometers will be no problem. If he goes too far underground or underwater, we will lose the signal, but it does not seem like that is a likely risk. Then later you can go there yourself, or I can go, or we can send a drone or call in the Company."

"This sounds great," John said. "What will you charge?"

"A hundred sars," Faisal said. "Plus expenses."

"That seems cheap."

"It is. Even if expenses might add up to another couple hundred bucks. You have your multi?"

John pulled the device out.

"Okay, open the PersonnelTracker app. That's the one you use to keep track of your kids."

"How do you—? Ruth must have mentioned it. But Ruth is much better with this application than I am."

"Ruth mentioned it," Faisal agreed. "*Add Friend*, then choose *Search by Multi ID Number*, then punch in the number I show you."

John entered the number. On the map that showed the locations of Ruth's, Sunitha's, and Ellie's phones as a tight cluster a few minutes' walk away, a new icon appeared, this one right next to John's own symbol. His family's icons were the letters *R, S,* and *E* in blue circles; the new icon appeared as the letter *F*.

"That's not your multi number," John said.

"It is my spare," Faisal told him, showing him the second device. "You might be surprised how often it is convenient to have a second multi. Now keep watching your screen."

Faisal turned off the spare multi, but the icon stayed steady on John's screen.

Then Faisal opened up the back of the multi's shell and removed a small chip.

"That's the subscriber chip," John said.

Faisal nodded. "It is what your phone, and mine, are both following. It won't run out of power and its signal should reach us from halfway around the planet."

Faisal stepped into the little general store that was the only shop still open at this hour. He emerged with two tiny vials, one full of high-strength contact adhesive, and the other containing nail polish. "It is not quite Company blue, Mr. Abbott," he said, showing John the color, "but I think we will get away with it."

"If they find the chip, will they trace it back to you?"

"They will trace it to a prepaid cash account in the name of Faroukh Katz. Purchased from a bodega in Henry Hudson Post."

❖❖❖

Moore was no longer sitting in Security, but an examination of Company House's windows found him climbing the stairs to the third floor. John let them back into the warehouse through the bay doors. There he lifted one of the two most recently arrived crates up onto the stack, leaving a corner exposed. Faisal lay on his side and reached up, first to glue the subscriber chip into a depression on the underside of the crate, and then to paint over the chip with blue nail polish.

Then he helped John resettle the crate into place. "A hundred bucks," he said, "plus five for the glue and polish."

"Hey, you could still use that nail polish." John grinned. "Just kidding." He gave Faisal two hundred dollars in cash. "What about the chip?"

Faisal looked at the cash. "Oh, this will cover the chip."

"Do I need to pay you a retainer, or something?" John asked. "So that you agree not to work for either of those guys in the meantime?"

"First of all," Faisal said, "I offered my services to every trader that came here. Other than one or two, who wanted to know where to find prostitutes, the only information they ever asked me for was, 'Tell me where to find untapped Weaver nyoots.' When I explained I couldn't help them, they always told me to go away."

John frowned. "You helped two of them to find prostitutes?"

"No, I told those two to go away as well. The country-setties have enough difficulty negotiating life with the post and traders without prostitution getting into the mix. The same goes for drugs, but I do not think you are the kind of man who would ask me for drugs."

"It's hard to imagine," John agreed.

"Second, I have an ethical code."

"Like, from a bar association or a medical board?"

"I do not require a guild to tell me what is right and wrong behavior," Faisal said, "with respect to my clients or with respect to any other person. I will not cheat you, Mr. Abbott, I will not double-cross you, I will not take work that will conflict with what you want. And if something does conflict, I will tell you as soon as I possibly can, and I will extricate myself from the conflict."

"I'm sold," John said. "I'm also exhausted, so I'm going to go home."

"Shall I accompany you?"

"The crowd of job-seekers has dissipated," John said. "Possibly because they heard we hired Nermer."

They stepped outside, and found that the rain had also stopped. John gave Faisal back the rain jacket. They shook hands and John headed home.

He retraced his steps along the stockade wall and through alleys, finally reaching Grijalva Street and hiding in the shadow of a tangled thicket of short trees to survey the gravel. No sign of the white groundcar, which probably meant that it simply belonged to someone in the post, and John would see it around again. The khat in front of which the car had been parked was as long front-to-back as John's, but was narrower; its lights were dark now, and from where he stood, John couldn't see into the enclosure.

He pulled up PersonnelTracker on his multi. He was reassured to see his location, his family's—very close, with Grijalva Street appearing as a gray stripe separating them—and the stationery F that told him the location of Jefferson's marked, heavy crate, with its mysterious contents.

He put away the multi and was about to walk the block to his gate when he realized there was a man standing in front of it.

Nermer? But he was supposed to come tomorrow. Faisal? Had the interpreter remembered some issue he wished to discuss with John, and intercepted him here to have the conversation before John went to bed?

John pulled up his multi again, looked through the video lens, and zoomed in.

It was hard to see the face of this man because he stood in shadow, but he wore a blue-and-buff coat.

John hesitated, disliking all his options. After considering, he took the Webley from his pocket and checked its chambers. He liked the heft of the gun, and the barrel wasn't so long that it would get in the way, either.

Holding the loaded pistol in his pocket, he walked casually to the front door of his own khat.

The man turned to face him as he approached. He had a flat face, thick eyebrows, and a bulbous nose. A horizontal scar cut across his lower lip. He wore a blue-and-buff frock coat, but John didn't see any other insignia. A broad blue hat shadowed his eyes. "John Abbott."

"What do you want?"

The man chuckled. "That's exactly what I've come to tell you. Only first, I thought I should tell you a few things about myself."

"I don't care to know anything about you," John said. "You're on my property. Buzz off."

"You're on Company property," the stranger said. "You have no right to tell me to leave. You can defend yourself with whatever it is that's bulging in your right pocket, but if you attack me, you'll find that I'm a very competent combatant."

John sized the man up visually. Was this one of the people who had beaten him up the other night? His memories were far too cloudy to tell.

"I'll call my boss," John said.

"Do you mean Keckley?" the man asked. "Or your *real* boss, Director English?"

John's blood froze. The stranger chuckled again, a heavy wheeze rounding out the edges of his laughter.

"John Abbott," the stranger said again. "Accounting. NYU. Marfan's Syndrome, or you'd have been a pilot? Space Force, John? Was the family disappointed when you didn't make the cut?"

"What do you want?"

"Two daughters and a wife, Ruth." The stranger gestured at the khat. "They're all asleep, in there. Safe for now. Your wife's much better looking than you are, you bug-eyed bastard. No offense. But she must really be betting on you becoming a big earner someday."

"She likes my sense of humor," John said. "But she knows when not to push it too far."

The stranger laughed. "I like you, John. I like that you slipped out without us noticing. My partner is around the other side, waiting for you back there. I bet that you'd walk up to the front gate, though, and I was right. I've been reading your file, you see. You're not devious. You're smart as hell, but you're not cunning. And that might be the problem here."

"That I failed to creep back into my own house?"

"You're here to do a job," the man said. "You're here to catch a thief. Director English is really counting on you."

"If I don't do my job, you'll beat me up?" John asked.

"If you don't do your job, you'll end up swabbing out toilets back in Henry Hudson like the lowest country-setty on Sarovar Alpha."

"That was you at the Stone Gardens," John said, "and your partner."

And after the Commissar's Daughter?

"You can call me Diaz," the man told him. "My partner is Choat."

"Those names won't be in the Company databases," John said.

"I'm not in the databases under any name."

"You came here to scare me," John said.

Diaz looked both ways along Grijalva Street and took a step closer to John. "I came here to tell you that you're being watched. Now, this could play out in a lot of ways. Maybe you'll need help, and I'll be there to back you up. Or maybe, other things could happen."

John nodded. "I have Marfan's Syndrome—that doesn't make me a weakling. I'm an accountant, and not a commando like my uncles—don't therefore mistake me for a coward. And if you ever again utter words that imply a threat against my wife or my daughters, or my dog, or my employees, or anyone else under my care . . . I will kill you."

Diaz pursed his lips and nodded.

"Now, you make whatever report you have to," John said. "But step aside. I'm going into my house."

Diaz glared for a few seconds, then stepped to his left. "I'm just here to let you know."

"You're here to try to bully me," John said. "And you failed."

He let himself into the khat and then locked the gate behind him. His heart was pounding and he was sweating, despite the cool evening. The lights were out in the house; John let himself in a side door, then sat in the kitchen and listened to the house in the darkness. It was still a new place to him, but he could hear the breathing of his family, and the soft hiss of air moving through the plastic vents, and the rumble beneath the sleeping breath of the dog. He heard a power generator hum almost imperceptibly, and the whisper of sheets as Ruth rolled over in bed.

He heard no intruders.

Jefferson was crooked, he was confident. Had he sent Diaz and Choat to make John stand down?

Was it possible English had sent them? The director's insistence on extreme discretion made his actions seem dishonest. On the other hand, Diaz knew that English has sent John, so maybe the demand for confidentiality had been intended to prevent exactly this sort of interference—maybe Diaz's appearance validated English's instructions.

John's instinct was to call Internal Audit. English had said he preferred to have his own person, John, investigate at Arrowhawk. But this wasn't about investigating corruption anymore, it was about investigating Diaz's implied threats.

He wished now that he had taken a picture of Diaz with his multi. Then at least he could have forwarded that to Internal Audit. There was a confidential reporting line, wasn't there? He'd use that, next time.

He sighed.

John had come to feel conflicted about the wealth opportunities of Weave, shutting out as it did the planet's country-setties, its pre-Company settlers. Carrying out his mission seemed fraught with moral and actual peril, promotion looked distasteful, wealth looked repugnant, there was no way to get back to Earth now, and his family was counting on him to make this great journey of a lifetime, this commitment to the Sarovar Company, a success.

What had he done?

CHAPTER SEVENTEEN

John was in the office the next day, reading through a stack of cheaply printed user's manuals and replacement part guides to the trucks in the post's warehouse. The different types of truck didn't quite amount to models, since they hadn't been given names, but only vehicle identification numbers, and they didn't have a manufacturer—they were bolted together by Company engineers in Henry Hudson Post. It had taken John two hours to confirm, one laborious line at a time, that the Arrowhawk-1 and the Arrowhawk-3 were, in fact, identical vehicles. Or, at least, they had identical manuals. The parts were all common Earth-available vehicle parts, other than the chassis, for which each vehicle's manual specified material, dimensions, and manufacturing process.

John had gone to Mouse Rock in Arrowhawk-3. Arrowhawk-2 was a single-segment vehicle.

To take breaks, John paced back and forth across Audit. While pacing, he confirmed from the personnel records he could access on his multi that Nermer was a member in good standing of the Post Irregulars, and had been for years. He also confirmed that the post did not have a chaplain. Henry Hudson Post had a chaplain, but that seemed awfully far away. He also stretched his wrists and fingers a lot.

Keckley and DeBoe were both out.

John would require another day of poring over the manuals before he even had all the data, but he was already scratching his head about how to set a depreciation schedule for a fleet of vehicles, each one of which was manufactured from scratch.

He'd need more data. He saw himself riding the maglev around Wellesley, collecting manuals and taking rides in a hodgepodge of hand-built Company trucks.

He hadn't taken any theory of accounting classes, and he wasn't entirely sure what the goal of a new depreciation allowance should even be, other than to align with revenue. Maybe he needed to collect data on the average lives of all the Company's homemade vehicles and simply set a schedule accordingly. If half lived beyond the end of their schedule and half broke down sooner, that should be alright, shouldn't it?

Maybe the task that Keckley had assigned him was a useless waste of time and energy.

While he was eating lunch, which was a sandwich of cured meat on a chewy flatbread, John checked PersonnelTracker. The F on the multi's display was no longer in the post. Tapping it with a fingertip, he was able to get distance and direction and speed data—the crate was traveling away from him, north and west, at about thirty kilometers per hour, which was a reasonably brisk pace for a truck not traveling on roads.

He dropped down into the warehouse to see which of the trucks was missing, smiling and nodding at another small knot of patients waiting to see the Surgeon. The smallest truck was gone; Arrowhawk-2, just big enough for three passengers, at most. He checked the personnel schedules, and found that all the drivers were currently assigned to be at the post.

When John came back up to the office, Rock was standing there.

John hadn't realized how tall the trader was. Standing close to the man, he realized that Rock was taller than his own one hundred ninety centimeters, and might even top two hundred. He stomped rather than stepping, and he hunched forward like a bear nosing after prey.

"Rock," John said. "I'm very sorry we got off on the wrong foot. I'm afraid it's my fault, I may not have seemed as respectful to your lady companion as I should have."

"Wife," Rock growled.

"Oh, lovely," John said. "I'm also married. My wife's name is Ruth."

Rock fixed him with a baleful eye and said nothing.

"We should get drinks sometime," John said, his voice faltering. "Or something."

"Where did they go?" Rock asked.

"Where did what go?" John pointed uncertainly at the manuals strewn across his desk. "Are you looking for information about... are you looking for these?"

"Jefferson and Gonzalez," Rock said.

John hesitated, reluctant to share too much information. "I've just been down in the warehouse and one of the trucks is gone. Let's check the schedule." There was a ledger the traders used to reserve the trucks for their wats, weeks and sometimes months in advance. Wats that somehow didn't show up on the post utility app were still supposed to be in the ledger.

"The schedule's missing." Rock pointed at a gap in the shelved books.

John looked at the gap; Rock was right, the schedule was out of its place. He dug through the shelves, found nothing, searched Keckley's archaeological tell of a working space, and then dove into the papers on his own desk. He'd accidentally picked up the schedule with ledgers he'd been reading. Rock leaned over his shoulder—an impressive feat in and of itself—and they flipped through the pages together.

"There it is," John said. "Bourbon. Is that a wat?" Why would Jefferson and Gonzalez write down where they were going, if it was a secret? But they had to write something down, to be able to check out a truck, and if no one else knew where Bourbon Lake was, the word was as good as a code name.

Rock snapped his teeth and stalked from the office. As the trader descended the stairs toward the ground, John quietly moved into the stairwell and looked out the window at the street below. He called Faisal Haddad on his multi.

"I need you to tail someone," he said when Faisal picked up.

"Twenty dollars an hour."

"The trader Rock," John said. "He's just coming out of Company House right now."

John watched Rock grind his way through the post and across the street, and just before he lost sight of the trader, Faisal slipped from a sidestreet behind a stubby gray truck to pick up the trail. John reshelved the schedule and returned to his truck manuals.

Rock didn't seem to be part of Jefferson's circle of traders. But what was their relationship, then? There was some connection, because Rock had come seeking information about Jefferson...or Gonzalez, or both. He hadn't seemed happy at the news of their destination, but he hadn't seemed unhappy, either. He just seemed to be a snarling beast.

Like he always did.

John kept working.

Keckley returned from lunch and muscled through half a ledger book in two hours, head down like a burrowing animal. "Post chief is taking us out to lunch day after tomorrow," he grunted as he shrugged into his rain jacket and headed for the door.

"Am I included in us?" John asked.

"No reason to tell you otherwise. You own a tie?"

"One," John said.

"Don't wear it. Post chief likes us to look rugged. If you have, say, a badger hat, you could wear that."

John laughed. "A badger hat! What kind of idiot do you take me for?"

Keckley giggled. "Just testing you. But don't wear your tie. She hates a kiss-ass." He left.

John's multi hummed; Faisal. John answered.

"I would give you a verbal report," Faisal said, "but it might be better if you came and saw for yourself."

John locked the office and left. The rain had just stopped. Following Faisal's directions, he found himself in the northwest quarter of the post, at the end of an alley, which he escaped by climbing up a pile of construction materials—plastic slabs and spars and rolls of some synthetic fabric—onto the top of a building.

Faisal lay on his belly on the wet rooftop, peering over the edge. He beckoned to John to get down and come closer, so John lowered himself onto his stomach, too, and crawled.

At the edge he peered down into the street and saw a truck parked on a quiet gravel side street. It wasn't one of the Company's vehicles, but was something similarly cobbled together and brandless, only smaller and more battered. A tarpaulin covered a stack of something in the back of the truck.

"What am I looking at?" John asked.

"Just wait," Faisal said. "I am pretty sure he has one more load."

A few moments later, Rock emerged from the wooden door of the adjacent building. He carried a green plastic crate with two handles, and he waddled as if it were a heavy burden. He lifted the tarpaulin and pushed the green crate in among other identical green crates, and alongside a stack of long, gray-plastic crates.

All the crates were unmarked.

Rock ran several elastic cords over the stacks, binding them in place to hooks in the sides of the truck bed.

The woman John had seen at the bar—Rock's wife—appeared in the doorway, and they kissed. Then Rock got into the truck.

"I don't understand," John said. He and Faisal both pulled back from the edge.

"Guns," Faisal said.

"What do you mean, guns?"

"Rifles and ammo boxes," Faisal said. "For a man whose family is supposed to be all military, you do not have a lot of imagination."

"I can imagine a lot of other things that could be in those boxes besides rifles and bullets."

"But not Weave, right?"

John nodded slowly. "Not likely. Not in the form in which I've seen it."

"And those are not the crates the Company uses to ship trade goods," Faisal said. "And why would you ever shape a box like that, long and awkward, unless it had to be that shape to accommodate what was inside?"

John was about to suggest flagpoles or short broomsticks, but he realized the suggestions sounded stupid.

"It's too bad we don't have a subscriber chip on Rock's truck," John murmured.

Faisal chuckled slowly and slapped John on the shoulder. "It is too bad you do not have any faith in me, you big, dumb accountant."

"That doesn't sound right."

"It does not." Faisal frowned. "You big, dumb outsider . . . does that sound better?"

"Okay, I'm a big, dumb outsider." John grinned. "I'm a big, dumb, happy outsider if you're telling me that you already put a chip on that truck, too."

"Get ready to punch in an ID number," Faisal said.

John took the number and entered it into PersonnelTracker, and a K appeared on his screen. As Rock drove away, the K drifted away from John on the display.

"What would Rock want with guns?" John asked. "Is he going to rob Jefferson and Gonzalez?"

"This is a small post," Faisal said. "It seems like that would be ... hard to get away with."

"He was worked up about those two leaving," John thought out loud. "We can see if he follows them."

"And do what?" Faisal asked. "Even if the little K catches up to the little F, if they are somewhere out in the mountains, we will have no idea what is going on."

Faisal was right. John chewed on the possibilities, including on his need to figure out who was stealing Weave. Could this be connected to the post's loss of revenue that English had sent John to investigate?

"I need to go home and see my girls," John said. "Can you get us a vehicle?"

"I have an ATV," Faisal said. "I will rent it to you. If I come along, no extra charge, because it means I can take care of the vehicle."

"How much do I owe you now?"

"I have a running tab."

"I'm sure you do, Mr. Haddad." John stood and headed back for the ground. "Meet me at my house in an hour?"

Walking home, John reviewed the PersonnelTracker historical feed on his multi. Scrolling forward and backward through it, he found the path of the F perplexing. It had driven straight out away from the post, then turned, driven behind what appeared on the display to be a ridge, and driven back. Now it was stationary, nearly due north of the post, somewhere up in the Mallories.

Equally surprising was the trajectory of the K, which was driving in a straight line toward where the F rested. It had miles to go before they met, but Rock appeared to be driving in a beeline to intercept the other traders.

John zoomed in on the map and saw a small lake. Like most of the other features on the map, it had no name—could it be Bourbon Lake? And if so, then why had the two traders traveled there by such an indirect route? And why schedule four days, for a trip that clearly could have been two?

It suggested deception. It suggested that Jefferson and Gonzalez didn't want other traders to know where Bourbon Lake was.

John sighed. The traders were like salesmen in other industries: competitive, elbow-throwing, hard-driving. If they had a great source of Weave at a good rate, they had every incentive to keep it hidden from the other traders, and even from the Company. Salespeople could be the death of a business, because they were in a position to keep business to themselves, and away from the corporation—and when they left, customers could leave with them.

Would those instincts lead the two traders to steal from the Company, too?

But the PersonnelTracker data also suggested that Rock knew exactly where Bourbon Lake was. So maybe it wasn't as secret a location as John had imagined. And Rock was rushing to get there, with a truck that might be full of guns.

And what were his intentions?

And was the Company truck also full of guns? Was that what was weighting down Jefferson's crates?

He let himself in and found a man in the khat.

He was short and thin, but he had large, heavy-knuckled hands. He wore a tunic and kilt, his head was wrapped in an undyed turban, almost completely covering his white, curly hair, and he leaned on a thick staff. He stood halfway between the gate and the front door of the house.

"I hope you're Nermer," John.

"You are Master John," Nermer said. "I have seen images."

John offered to shake Nermer's hand, but Nermer retreated a half step and bowed. "You had better go up to the house, Master John. You are late, and dinner in the warmer becomes dry."

John sat to eat noodles and large shrimp with Ruth, who had waited for him. The girls were doing homework—math and science, based on what John heard of Factor Doctor's lectures, one striking his right ear and one his left.

"Thank you," John said. "Nermer checks out, from the Company records. Good reviews, seems responsible. An unlikely burglar, if you're still thinking about that."

"He calls me Mistress Ruth," she told him, swallowing a curried shrimp. "That's an improvement. It was Mistress Abbott when we started."

"I have to go out again tonight." John wanted to explain to her what was going on, but he understood so little of it himself, and anything he could say would make his decisions sound foolish. "It's a thing Director English asked me to look at."

"That's how you'll get promotions," Ruth said. "And how you'll get us back to Henry Hudson Post."

"Speaking of Henry Hudson." He cleared his throat. "I think it might be good if you took the girls back to Henry Hudson for a week or two. Things are . . . I just worry about you all, with my working late hours all the time."

"We have Nermer now."

John nodded. "That's a good start. But maybe for just two weeks—"

"No."

Ruth's eyes flashed like police lights.

"But—"

"No!" She clearly had more to say, so John waited. "I have declared tomorrow to be Sunday."

"Uh . . . what?"

"The Company has created a completely boring calendar for this place," Ruth said slowly. "Thirty-day months, numbered rather than named, and the thirty days also numbered. No weeks. No real weekends."

"That sounds efficient," John said. He hated to admit that he hadn't really taken the time to look at the calendar.

"There's no Sunday. The girls have no school tomorrow, so I have declared tomorrow to be the first Sunday."

"You found a church."

"No. I'm making one. I sent an invitation with the girls to give to every child in school, and Mrs. Jenkins let me post a notice. Tomorrow, here, I will preach."

John controlled his breath, and did not sigh.

"Among other things," she added, "Ellie has a couple of friends who are coming."

He nodded. "I'm very impressed."

"I respect your work," she said. "I know you will respect mine."

"Thanks for being understanding." He laid his hand on the table, palm up, and she curled a fist up inside his fingers.

"We're making an investment together," she said. "I feel bad, though. You might miss some really good years with the girls."

"That happens. And I will make it up to them."

"They certainly think so."

"Does that . . . uh-oh. What did I promise?"

"You promised to take Ani on a field trip with them."

The field trip. He nodded. "Ellie will like that."

John finished his dinner, took a heavier coat, and went out to meet Faisal.

CHAPTER EIGHTEEN

Faisal's ATV was a black four-knobby-wheeled recreational vehicle with no protection from the elements. It had one saddlelike seat, but it was long enough for two to share, and behind the saddle bulked a storage compartment.

Faisal slapped the compartment. "I have food and blankets."

John settled himself behind Faisal on the seat. "Nuclear power cell, right? We're not going to run out of petrochemical fuel and be stranded?"

"Nuclear power." Faisal accelerated away from the Abbot khat and toward the stockade wall surrounding Arrowhawk Post. "The gate does close at night," he mentioned as they drove through it, "but only for about six hours. And there are still Company Security personnel on guard when it's shut. One of the men from Company House plus some Irregulars."

John turned and shot a look back through the open gate at the mention of Security Services, expecting to see men in blue-and-buff coats, or Diaz and Choat in their white groundcar. He saw neither.

Though if he was following Rock and Jefferson with a simple component taken from a common electronic tool available at several different vendors even in this tiny post, might Diaz not be following him, but perhaps using some more sophisticated tool?

Well, John was doing nothing wrong. Diaz had been threatening, but it remained the case that John worked for Director English, and if he did what English asked him, and committed no crimes, then John should be fine.

Although...had John already committed crimes? He, or Faisal on his behalf, had planted tracking devices on two Company employees.

"Mr. Abbott."

"Yes?"

"Your multi is the one that can track our Mr. Rock, not mine. May I affix your multitool in this bracket, so I can look at it while I drive?"

John handed over the multi. Faisal pushed it into the firm grip of a rubber-lined, indented panel, and then whistled.

"Rock is going right for our tagged crate," he said.

"Can you get there?"

"Easily. I can go the way Rock probably went, there is a pass." Faisal turned in a slow circle, arcing away from the post's gate across wet meadows. Ahead, in the darkness of late evening, John saw rocky ridges bulking against the night sky and blocking out the stars. "You have brought your pistol, of course. I am also armed."

"We're not going to go charging into any firefights, though."

"No. But we are chasing a truck full of guns toward crates full of we do not know what."

"Could be guns," John said.

"My point exactly."

The meadows and scrubby forests around Arrowhawk Post soon gave way to thicker forest, trees clinging to gnarled tussocks and humps of dirt and rising above boggy grassland. Narrow, winding rivulets of water cut unpredictable grooves across the meadows; Faisal's ATV was going fast enough that it simply jumped over many of those, and when they crossed streams too broad to simply jump, the ATV hit the bottom, threw water in all directions, and then ground out the far side with its oversized tires.

John didn't like the thought that cenotes might be beneath his feet, and might crack open at any moment. He told himself that it couldn't happen, because the ATV didn't weigh nearly as much as a Company truck.

He looked over Faisal's shoulder and saw that the two dots had nearly converged, and both were stationary. He was tempted to ask Faisal to stop and zoom in, thinking that at a closer resolution, he'd get a better sense what kind of encounter was unfolding, or was about to unfold. But he didn't think Faisal could drive if he had to zoom in on the *F* and the *K*, and he didn't want to distract the driver.

But Rock hadn't gone that far; he was only some fifty kilometers from the post, and John and Faisal closed the gap quickly. Faisal drove with intense concentration, leaning over the handlebars of the ATV as if he personally wanted to dive into every thicket or roll across every rock. He followed rocky ground and low ridges where he could, but mostly he cut a straight line, up between knuckles of rock that shone gray under the light of moon and stars, into an earthy saddle. John's fear of cenotes relaxed, and the earth drained, the bogs giving way to dirt meadows, lanced and evacuated of their water by broad streambeds.

They crossed the height of the pass into a high basin. Faisal slowed down and took to pausing to examine the terrain before him visually.

"Do you know this valley?" John asked.

"I have never been here. I am too much of a city person to spend time out in the sticks on purpose. Arrowhawk Post is already much smaller than I prefer. Really, Henry Hudson is smaller than I would like, and I have never been anywhere bigger than Henry Hudson."

"What are you looking for?"

"A different road from the one the others took. Here, look, we are close enough now that we are zoomed in to the best resolution we can get from Company landsats, and what do we see?"

"A lake. Jefferson and Gonzalez are stopped on one side, and Rock is on the other."

"Right. What don't we see?"

"Uh . . . help me out."

"No names," Faisal said. "Nothing other than the facts of physical geography. This place has been scanned by satellites, but the multi doesn't know anything else about it."

"I think the traders are hiding it," John said. "Jefferson got here by a roundabout path."

Faisal scrolled back through the historical data. "I see. Secret because . . . illicit activity?"

John nodded slowly. "At the least, they're trying to keep this location hidden. I had thought, maybe because it was good pickings. But maybe it's something more off-book than that."

"Could be both." Faisal nodded. "Okay, so, I want to get close enough to observe. I have a directional microphone and binoculars in the trunk, and I'm thinking that if we get down to the top of that cliff, there, at the edge of the lake . . . we should be able to observe both of them. Do you see any trails?"

"The scan isn't going to help," John said. He climbed off the ATV and waded into waist-high undergrowth. "We can do this on foot. We throw some branches over the ATV and hike down."

"That is two kilometers," Faisal complained.

"Yes. Are your feet broken?"

"They will be. Have I explained that I am more of a city person?" But Faisal put the ATV behind a screen of trees and removed two shoulder packs from the storage compartment, handing one to John. "I have the surveillance equipment."

They hid the ATV and began climbing down. They clambered slowly across a wide slope of scree, angling down toward a lake that John saw as a silver button in a sea of green. On John's multi, their journey looked like two kilometers, but it took them over an hour. John occasionally checked his screen to confirm that the icons marked *F* and *K* hadn't moved; they were still.

John imagined predators. He was tempted to pull up Factor Doctor on his multitool and ask it what animals there were out here that might eat humans. He imagined sabertoothed-cats and furred venomous snakes and carnivorous tree-dwelling apes, but he resisted the urge to stop and do research, and nothing ambushed them.

They reached the brow of a cliff. A flat slab of rock fifteen meters wide and six deep made a good place for them to stop. John drank a little water and looked through binoculars while Faisal assembled the microphone. It was conical, wrapped in wire mesh, and had a dish behind it like the flared neck ruff of a venomous lizard; the whole thing was mounted on a bulky handgun.

"I can think of lots of places where you'd get binoculars, Mr. Haddad," John said. "Where did you get the listening gear?"

"My secret underworld sources that I am sworn not to reveal."

"Really?"

"No, Mr. Abbott. I had a friend make it. The parts are common enough. And look how bulky and awkward it is. I am certain your Security Services have much more sophisticated and discreet equipment."

John flinched and looked back up toward where they'd hidden the ATV. He imagined Diaz and Choat hiding behind bushes, training such listening devices on him as they spoke.

He swallowed his fears and looked first for Jefferson and Gonzalez. Their truck was easy to find—it sat in an open meadow at the edge of the lake. Its headlights were off, but its cabin lights were on. Light leaked out the front windshield, illuminating a stretch of muddy, rocky beach. Light also bled upward, through the rooftop compartment, creating a column of dull yellow that climbed into the night sky.

He couldn't see the two traders, either through the windshield or on top. Might they be already trading? But probably not. If they booked four days of the truck's time and they had a trading wat in the middle, that wat would be the second night of the trip. Still, John spent ten minutes combing the valley visually, looking for a meadow or a shelf of stone or any open place that might be suitable for trading. He looked for crates of trade goods, or for traders themselves, tramping about in the wild grass.

He found none of those things.

"Do you want to listen?" Faisal asked.

John put an offered earbud into his ear, took the bulky microphone, and pointed it at the truck. He heard terse, clipped conversation: *Tell me what you know. I'd rather die.* He frowned.

"You may be hearing a police drama," Faisal suggested.

"They're watching flicks," John said.

"I think you can also hear the scrape of eating utensils," Faisal added. "I believe I heard the rush of the vacuum toilet a minute ago."

"We may have to sit here through tomorrow night," John said. "It could become very boring."

"I brought blankets, food, and water." Faisal smiled. "And I bill by the hour."

John handed back the microphone and began searching the other end of the lake. It was much harder, and he wouldn't have succeeded without PersonnelTracker. Rock's truck was dark, and there was no movement in its vicinity.

"Rock drove down into the valley without lights."

"An impressive feat of driving," Faisal said. "Or he knew where he was going."

"It has to be the latter, doesn't it?" John said. "He's been here before. And not only did he want to intercept Jefferson and Gonzalez, he wanted to surprise them. Right?"

"To what end?" Faisal asked.

A bright orange stab of flame caught John unawares, and a split second later, he heard a loud *Boom!* He fumbled with the binoculars but caught them, and then looked with his natural eyes just in time for a second explosion, at the Company truck.

Boom!

But the truck itself hadn't exploded. It had toppled sideways and one of its tires was torn off.

"They are still alive," Faisal reported. "They are cursing. A lot. I think they are getting guns."

"We're too far to get there in time to help them." John was glued to the binoculars, searching the darkness around the truck. He couldn't make out Faisal's muttered response.

Gonzalez emerged from the truck first. He came out of the rooftop compartment, now lying on its side against the earth. He moved hunkered down in a squatting stance, and he carried a rifle. John didn't see what Gonzalez was looking at, but the trader came out shooting. The muzzle flash of his shots stabbed the night repeatedly.

And then, from the darkness, there came answering flashes.

Gonzalez pressed himself against the compartment wall and fired back.

"He is calling for Jefferson," Faisal said. "This is hurting my ears."

The truck door opened. It now faced skyward, and Jefferson slithered out. He didn't have a rifle. John thought he could hear Gonzalez shouting, even without the microphone.

"Who's shooting?" John asked. "It has to be someone connected with Rock."

"Maybe Rock came to rescue Jefferson."

"I didn't get the sense they were friendly, did you?"

"I hate to tell you this, Mr. Abbott," Faisal said, "but, as Company employees go, your friendliness makes you far and away the exception, rather than the rule."

Jefferson didn't return fire. He dropped over the edge of the truck and sprinted. The light was all on the other side of the vehicle, including the light of the firefight, but John saw well enough to see the trader rush down to the lake and throw himself into the water.

"Jefferson is in the water," John said. "We can rescue him."

"You think long and hard about that," Faisal said. "I want to hear your considered opinion on the subject."

Gonzalez fell.

Shapes advanced out of the darkness, approaching the flipped truck. For a moment, they struck John as specters, but as they came into the light, he saw that they were humans. They wore tunics and kilts and turbans.

"Lord of Lights," Faisal said. "Are those country-setties?"

"They are. And look," John said, "that's Rock."

The country-setties dragged Gonzalez away from the truck and then several of them swarmed inside. Gonzalez was waving his arms and talking.

"'You can't do this,'" Faisal said, passing on what he heard. "'This is murder.' And now Rock: 'You only call it murder when the people who get killed are people you like.' Gonzalez: 'That's just life, you son of a bitch, grow up.'"

John was watching through the binoculars as Rock pulled a pistol, pressed it to Gonzalez's forehead, and pulled the trigger.

Gonzalez fell.

"Mr. Abbott," Faisal said slowly, "what are we tangled up in here?"

Flashes of gunfire still snapped here and there in the darkness beyond the downed truck. Some of the country-setties, armed with rifles, began investigating the lakeshore. John looked, but couldn't find Jefferson. Country-setties dragged Company crates from the truck and smashed them open; inside were guns and ammunition.

"I have no idea," he said. "I think, for starters, that the Company doesn't know what Jefferson and Gonzalez are really doing here. And so, whatever made Rock come attack them, the Company doesn't know that, either." Did that mean this whole encounter had nothing whatsoever to do with skimmed bales of Weave, and John could and should just walk away from it?

He doubted that.

"What will Jefferson say when he gets back to the post?" Faisal asked.

John groaned. "Clearly, we can't rescue him. But if he makes it back, I bet he describes an accident. Gonzalez died somehow, but it wasn't Jefferson's fault, and it won't be because there was a firefight with country-setties."

"And what about when investigators come to look for the truck?" Faisal asked.

As if in answer, the truck exploded.

Rock and the country-setties with him disappeared in the darkness. They carried no lights, so John quickly lost track of where they went, but they didn't head back to Rock's truck.

"Rock can't risk an investigation either, apparently," John said. "If Jefferson's alive, he saw that. He'll say the truck exploded while he was outside, and Gonzalez died in the blast."

"We cannot accidentally run into Jefferson here, if he swims across the lake."

"No." John stood. His limbs were shaking. "We need to get back."

CHAPTER NINETEEN

John slept poorly, tossing and turning. Fortunately, Ruth was a sound sleeper, and in the morning, she was up before him, and brought him coffee.

"Ugh." He sipped the black restorative and took slow breaths, waiting for it to take effect.

"You didn't go to the office last night," she said.

"How could you tell?"

"You wore boots. They're filthy, and you smell like sweat and pine trees."

"I have this project for English," John said. "He gave it to me when we were at Henry Hudson. It's kind of a compliance or an Internal Audit-type affair, and it's required me to do some strange things."

"Anything you want to talk about?" she asked.

John shrugged. "It's complicated. And I think it will be over soon."

"'Internal Audit' sounds . . . maybe dangerous. Like maybe you're policing the traders."

John remembered Gonzalez, falling to the ground with Rock's bullet in his head, and Jefferson, jumping into Bourbon Lake.

"That's not entirely wrong," he said. "I guess that's why English wanted the new guy. So it would be an outsider poking around, and not someone who was already friends with everyone. I did suggest you take the girls—"

"Stop."

John nodded his surrender.

"Just be careful, John," Ruth told him. "Sometimes, the outsider poking around is the guy who gets hurt."

"I have to go into the office today," he said. "Today we ship, it's all hands on deck. I'm going to miss your preaching."

"Just don't miss the train," she said.

"Please record it," he suggested.

She smiled.

With coffee and a little bread in his belly, John shaved, showered, and dressed, and then walked to the office. There was no sign of the white groundcar from Henry Hudson—what would Diaz and Choat make of Gonzalez's death, if they knew? Was he their ally? What if English's reaction to the information was to inform the two men from Security Services?

John was about to find out.

He was supposed to ship Weave later this morning, and he intended to address it to Director English, for sale on Earth. This was his big play; sending his first shipment all the way meant it had just barely time to get sold and return to him with the maximum possible profit, before his deadline for redeeming Ruth's jewels had passed. With his second purchase of Weave, he could sell to the broker at Central Transit, if he wanted; he'd make smaller profits, but still have the money in time, maybe, to get the gems out of pawn. So John had enough time, just barely, to swing for the fences and still leave himself time to get some base hits.

But John couldn't very well send the Weave to English before he informed him of the prior night's events.

John could see the maglev train sitting at the station above Company House, ready for loading, when he arrived.

Stohel hadn't yet arrived at his station, but John's key opened the Comms office and he plugged in the encryption bolt. It took him nearly five minutes of signaling to get a response.

"I had a visitor," English said, when he appeared.

John scratched his scalp, suddenly acutely uncomfortable. "I'm not quite sure how you're going to hear this, but one of the traders here is dead, and I wanted to tell you how it happened."

"You killed a trader?" English's face showed no expression. "Did you have to kill someone because he was stealing?"

"It wasn't like that." John had tried to sort the information into concise blocks on his ride back from Bourbon Lake the previous night, and in his walk to Company House this morning, but the pieces suddenly sprang apart, like magnets pressed together on the wrong sides. "I've been investigating. For sure, someone has taken Weave out of the Company's share. Trying to figure out who did that has taken me out on a wat, and then also for . . . other trips outside the post."

"I've heard," English said.

John felt a chill at the base of his spine. What had English heard, and from whom? "Last night, two traders, named Gonzalez and Jefferson, were out alone with a small truck on a wat. They took some pains to hide where they were going. And they carried along with them, I think, several crates of firearms."

English leaned into the camera. "Fascinating."

"I don't know for sure what the firearms were for."

"Surely, they expected to trade them," English said. "Is the connection with the skimming that the traders stole Company Weave and used it to buy guns to resell?"

John hadn't thought through the connection yet. "Maybe. Although, these are guys that get their own Weave on a regular basis, so they could have used that."

"Unless the opportunity was too big for their own resources," English said. "And if the opportunity was going away, and they needed to take advantage of it now, and they didn't have enough Weave themselves . . . maybe they stole from me. From the Company."

That made a certain sense. "They did seem to think that the opportunity was going away." What was it they had said to each other? "That things were going to blow up."

"So that leaves two big questions," English said. "Where were they getting weapons? And who were they arming?"

"Yes," John agreed. "But what I wanted to tell you is that I followed those traders last night."

"Enterprising fellow," English said. "I knew I picked the right man."

"They were camped," John said. "I would have guessed they were waiting for a wat. And they were attacked."

English thumped the counter before him with a fist.

"The attackers appeared to be locals," John said. "Country-setties. And there was another trader with them, a man named Rock."

"And one of the traders got killed."

"Rock shot Gonzalez through the head," John said. "Jefferson jumped into a lake and swam away. I think it's likely he escaped, though he may have drowned, or been caught by his assailants."

"Country-setties." English leaned back and steepled his fingers before him. "So tell me what you're thinking."

"I'm thinking Gonzalez and Jefferson were selling arms to the country-setties," John said. "And maybe Rock came in and undercut them on price. Or he armed the country-setties first, and then together they stole the weapons Gonzalez and Jefferson had brought to the gun-wat."

Gun-wat. He had just invented the term, and he liked it.

"And do you have any idea how things are going to 'blow up,' exactly?"

John exhaled and considered. "My ideas are pretty grim. It seems likely to me that, if the country-setties are getting armed, it's so they can attack the post."

"There are other possibilities. Maybe they're at war with another group of country-setties."

"That would still be pretty grim."

"For those at war, yes. For the Company, less so. Or maybe the country-setties have other enemies. Maybe they wish to protect themselves against wild animals. We haven't come close to mapping out all the species on this planet, and many of them are dangerous."

"They were willing to kill traders."

"You said Rock killed the other trader, didn't you? So the attack might be something incidental, something personal. Maybe Jefferson and Gonzalez offended the country-setties, or offended Rock."

That rang true, given Rock's touchiness about his wife. "Rock seems . . . he seems a little bit like one of the country-setties."

English nodded. "Some traders do that. Sometimes, the *best* traders go that way. To get the most accurate information, they get close to the locals, only in getting close to the locals, they become less and less Company men, and more and more . . . country-setties."

"I think I can figure out the scale of the stolen Weave," John said. "That's just math, I can compare commissions paid to Company Weave shipped. But I'm not sure I can account for every bale."

"Every bale, no," English said. "But I'd like to account for every thief. Do you have any reason to think that Gonzalez and Jefferson alone were responsible for all the missing bales?"

"I have no reason to think one way or the other on that issue." John considered. "I can see if there appear to have been any missing bales from wats where neither of those two was present."

English nodded. "Though presumably they could have stolen bales out of the warehouse even when they weren't on the wat."

"Maybe." John rubbed his temples.

"We also want to know which of the post's administrative staff may have been involved," English said. "The Post Chief or the Audit Chief . . . or others."

"Right." John sighed. "More investigation it is. One more thing. Do you know Security agents going by the name Diaz and Choat?"

English frowned. "I don't. Are they involved in all this mess?"

"It seems like it." John shook his head. "Diaz threatened me. It seemed that he knew what I was up to. And he wanted to scare me off."

English was looking away from his camera and working something with his hands. "I don't see their names, but that only makes sense. Did you get pictures of them?"

"I will, next time I see them."

"Get those to me next time," English said. "I'll look at them and share them with Internal Audit. In the meantime, be very careful."

John nodded and signed off.

A soft bell heard throughout Company House, and a groan as the building settled under new weight, announced the arrival of the train. John made his way to the warehouse. He checked his crates, then labeled them with his multi as addressed to Director English, Henry Hudson Post, for forwarding to auction on Earth. He strapped the crates into a pull-buggy with elastic bands and then dragged them up the stairs to the maglev platform.

Rock was strapping crates into place. The grizzled trader looked fatigued but also manic, his hands shaking and slipping with the strap buckles.

John warily found one of the securing bolts in the floor, near where Rock was working, and made his own crates secure. It was less a matter, he now knew, of securing the crates in case of a crash, and more a matter of fixing the crates in place via the shipping app on his multi, so that they wouldn't be opened or removed until they reached their destination.

Which, in John's case, was Central Transit.

Other traders set to work securing their crates of Weave. John knew Takahashi and Hager, both of whom looked completely unaware that anything unusual might have happened the night before, but there were traders he didn't recognize. And, under DeBoe's direction, Company porters set to work bolting down the Company's own crates of Weave.

"Good morning," John said, trying not to sound annoyingly cheerful or loud, securing his Weave.

His family's future. His girls' educations, or their down payments, when they eventually bought houses. His own debt. He took great care that the details in the app were correct, because the shipment was much more to John than just some Weave. It was more than money, it was what the money could buy.

"I may have been hard on you," Rock said. "Before."

"It's okay," John said. "This is an isolating place, and you work long hours. People get stressed, I understand."

Rock nodded and offered his hand.

John took the handshake, and saw again in his mind's eye Gonzalez dropping dead on the grass beside Bourbon Lake.

"How long have you been in Sarovar?" John asked.

"Twelve years," Rock said.

"Wow, I bet you've seen some things." John grinned, then felt embarrassed. "I mean, I feel like *I've* seen some things, and I've been here a week. Just the ba alone were worth the price of admission, and outside of Henry Hudson we saw a shay."

"I've been to Sarovar Beta." Rock nodded. "That's all mining. Earned a reward junket to Sarovar Gamma early on, for tripling my quota, but I never did take it."

"Not interested in massage parlors and rejuvenation clinics?" John grinned.

"I traded it." Rock cleared his throat, suddenly emotional. "For a hospital stay and treatment by Company doctors."

"You got sick and the Company didn't automatically treat you?" John frowned.

"Wasn't me that got sick."

John thought about that for a moment.

"The country-setties aren't what you think," Rock said.

John swallowed. How much did Rock know? "No?"

"They're just as human as you or I. They have just as much culture as you or I. They're just as smart, their lives are worth just as much."

"Of course," John said.

"I'm not the only offworlder who ever married a country-setty, either. Hell, we're all offworlders originally."

"Your wife seems lovely. What's her name?"

Rock hesitated. "Nefreet."

"My wife is Ruth. We have two daughters."

"Don't be an asshole, is all," Rock said. "So many of these guys get here and all they can think to do is be assholes."

"So many guys on Earth, all they can think of is to be assholes."

"That's right." Rock guffawed.

"Maybe you and I can get a drink sometime."

"I doubt it." Rock snorted and left.

John sighed and massaged the back of his neck.

"Don't worry about him," Takahashi said. "He went a little native."

"No, he didn't," Hager said. "He was always a jerk."

"Jefferson and Gonzalez are out on a wat, aren't they?" John asked.

Takahashi patted a stack of crates near him. "You're worried to make sure they ship. Good man. I have them covered, right here."

"All hands on deck." John nodded, carefully controlling his tongue so as not to let anything slip.

"Are we getting lunch today?" he asked.

"With Post Chief Carlton." Hager nodded. "This is a good thing. Carlton likes the best wines, and there's a restaurant in town that stocks them, just for her. We'll get a big table and we'll get good hooch and we'll eat prawns and steak until we burst."

"Cow-steak?" John asked. "Actual beef? Or are you talking about lab-grown beef?"

"In a stew, you can't trust a menu that says beef," Takahashi said. "Not around here. Too many other cheaper quadrupeds that might end up in the pot instead. You'll get the synthetic meats at a restaurant in Henry Hudson, but around here you'll just get ba. But the Company has ranches for Earth-style cattle and sheep. There's a herd that runs on the Mallories south of here, and Company cowboys who run them."

"Company cowboys?" John grinned.

"Honest to God. They ride horses, have bandanas over their faces, even have the big hats. Beef is rare enough and pricy enough that you don't want to feed it to just anyone . . . but for Post Chief Carlton, when she's buying lunch on the Company tab, no meat is too good for the table."

"But what should I know about her?" John asked.

"You know Keckley, right?" Hager asked. "You ever try to butter up Keckley?"

"Bad idea," John said. "He wants results."

The two traders nodded. "Carlton is the same," Takahashi said. "Only Keckley just expects that you should get results, because that's your job, you have the privilege of being here, and what else are you going to do? Carlton wants to rain encouragement down on you to get results."

"Encouragement," Hager said. "And good wine."

CHAPTER
TWENTY

"The restaurant is called the Tiger," Keckley said. He and John stepped out from beneath the maglev line and into the rain; beneath his see-through plastic raincoat, true to his word, Keckley was not wearing a tie. He was wearing a blue-and-buff jacket and kilt that both looked suspiciously dressy. The jacket wasn't his casual Company jacket, but a heavier version, with brass buttons and squared shoulders.

"Tiger?" John had his necktie in his pocket, where it made a conspicuous bulge. "Does that mean there are tigers in these hills, too?"

"There are big cats," Keckley said. "Or big, catlike things. There's a beast called a hatty. But no, it's just a name. Tiger of Mysore, actually. But there's only one restaurant called the Tiger in town, and its signboard is just a picture of a tiger, anyway."

They stepped around a pair of country-setty women, dickering over the price of a shawl.

"That's it." Keckley waved with an arm at a storefront ahead of them. A fading orange plastic tiger prowled atop four pillars, rain slashing off its muzzle. The pillars were painted a vivid fuchsia, the lintel across the top of them was black. The carpet beckoning prospective eaters inside was saffron yellow.

"Mysore." John frowned. "I feel like I should know where that is."

"I feel like you should, too, John *Sanjay*. Mysore was a kingdom of early modern India. In the south. The Tiger of Mysore was not

169

actually a tiger, but a king. Fought a series of wars against the British . . . against the East India Company. He had Napoleon for an ally. Loved rockets. About the same time as the American Revolution. I've always liked history."

"I'm more of a flicks guy, myself," John said. "After sixteen hours of looking at columns of numbers, I'm ready to laugh at some actors. Once in a great while, I'll watch a documentary. Maybe I should see a documentary on the Tiger of Mysore."

"The trick is to arrange someone else to pull the sixteen-hour shifts for you." Keckley turned and grinned, standing in the Tiger's entrance. "Seniority, my son. Grind out the hours now, and in a few years, you, too, will be reading all the history you want."

"Oh, good."

They stepped through the pillars and into an entrance hall. A hostess in a bright yellow saree stood at a reservation book and smiled at them. Dancing figures painted gold lined the hallway as columns.

"We're with Carlton," Keckley said.

She led them away from the general dining room toward a doorway filled with strings of beads.

"I rather had the impression that all the people around here were either Company employees or country-setties," Abbott murmured to Keckley. "So I'm surprised there's an Indian restaurant."

"Sure." Keckley's voice was loud in the small passage. "But the country-setties come from somewhere. Mostly India, Southeast Asia, East Africa, and Australia, as it happens." He tapped a finger to his temple. "History."

"And they kept their cultures. At least some of them did." John didn't know why he felt surprised. Faisal had cracked a joke about being from Muslim and Jewish parents. But perhaps he just hadn't thought of Faisal as a country-setty. He had assumed his sometime hireling's parents were or had been Company employees.

"At least, they kept their cultures enough to be able to draw on them for their businesses." Keckley handed his raincoat to the hostess, pulled out a chair, and sat.

The back room was large, and dominated by a rectangular table in the center. On two walls, windows carefully shrouded behind pale yellow curtains let in light and the crashing sound of rain, but no images of the street outside. A wide strip of floorspace around the table gave servers room to maneuver. Plates, utensils, and menus were arranged neatly around the table's edge.

John handed off his rain coat, keeping the light jacket with the Webley in the pocket. The places were set with a full array of silverware and a range of glasses, from extremely narrow champagne flutes to broad tumblers. He sat and took up the menu.

"Whoa," he said.

"Get the steak," Keckley said.

"But there's also shawarma," John said. "And biryani."

"Get what you want." Keckley grunted. "There's no pleasing some people."

At the thought of prawn biryani and lamb rogan josh—even if it might be something-like-prawn biryani and ba rogan josh—John's mouth began to water.

"Chief Carlton." Keckley stood.

John stood, dropping the menu. Carlton had a narrow, thin-lipped mouth and one eyebrow permanently cocked above the other. Her graying hair was cropped short around her squarish head and her cheeks were gaunt, but there was a twinkle in her eyes.

"The new guy," she said, extending a hand to John. "I hear Keckley hates you."

"Uh . . ." John turned to look helplessly at his boss.

"Means you're a go-getter, I like it." Carlton shook his hand. "Someone's going to have to replace Keckley when he dies of terminal grouchiness."

"I've tried assigning him the most boring work," Keckley said. "Legendarily boring. I'm talking accounting tasks so dull, the mere mention of them has killed people. He just won't quit."

"That's the spirit!" Carlton pumped a victorious fist in the air.

Carlton came at the head of a rush of people John recognized as traders. Takahashi was there, and Hager, and another half dozen whose names he heard in quick succession without being sure which name went with which face: Rogers, Grandi, Tasto, Benson, Singh, and Kowalski. DeBoe was there, and Sam Chen, along with two other drivers. Rock came in last, looking at his feet. The traders all crowded forward and seated themselves, hurling raincoats, ponchos, and umbrellas onto the soon-tottering hostess. John sat, then added his voice to a chorus calling for beer.

"Notice anything?" Keckley asked John.

John looked around the table and shrugged.

"No one's looking at the menu," Keckley said. "You know why?"

"They're getting steak," John guessed.

"Just because something is your call," Keckley told him, "doesn't mean there isn't a right answer."

With pitchers of beer came out two bottles of red wine and a bottle of scotch, all of which reached the table and then stayed there. John stuck to his guns and ordered lamb rogan josh and prawn biryani.

Rock, he noted, ordered fish.

Most of the traders ordered steak.

Bread—both naan and crusty white bread—came immediately. To John's surprise, Chief Carlton spoke right across Keckley and kept asking him questions.

"You have two children, don't you, John?"

"Two girls. Eight and five."

She nodded. "My daughter knows them from school. She says you have a dog, too. You're so young. How on Earth are you old enough to have an eight-year-old daughter?"

"Uh, well . . ."

"She's not asking about the mechanics, John," Keckley said. "She's just saying you have ambition."

John laughed. "I guess I just committed at a young age."

"You find the right person, no point waiting?" Carlton tore bread open and smeared butter on it.

"I'm not sure I believe in the *right* person." John shrugged. "That's the kind of language my wife would use. But I found an *excellent* person, and she thought I was the right person. I didn't see how I could possibly do any better by waiting."

"Still feel that way?" Carlton asked.

John nodded. "And I stand a decent chance of becoming a grandfather in my forties."

Someone across the table whistled. John smiled at Rock, who was staring at him.

"I like commitment," Carlton said. "Also, I like leverage. Get started early, get productive early. Focus now, earn rewards later on. Do everything with your whole ass. Also, I like a man who has to worry about his family. Keeps him honest, I think."

There was scattered laughter around the table.

"What are you laughing at, you tramps?" Keckley snarled.

John nodded. "I agree."

"Your wife's a churchgoer, is she?" Carlton asked. "I got a flyer about a church service."

"We all are. She and the girls more than me."

"Keep it up." She wagged a finger at him. "This is how you become audit chief and then post chief one day. More babies, more commitment, more accounting work. What was it you said you had him doing, Keckley?"

"Depreciation schedules."

Chief Carlton feigned instant death, to another round of laughter, then drank red wine with a handful of raisins and buttered bread. She lowered her voice slightly. "Dr. Hinkley says you have Marfan's Syndrome. Is this something I need to worry about?"

John picked up his champagne flute. "Practically speaking, all it means is this. How many fingers do you think you could put into your champagne flute at once? Touching the bottom, that is."

"Three," Carlton said immediately.

John nodded. "Try it."

Carlton furrowed her brow, made the attempt, and then announced the result. "Two. It's just too narrow, and I can't fold my fingers over enough."

"Watch this." Folding his fingers together into their narrowest formation, John inserted them all into the flute at the same time, all the way to the bottom. "That's Marfan's Syndrome. That and my silly-looking ears."

Carlton laughed. "Good." She clapped John's forearm. "And that's not a bad party trick, either. Bring it out again at Christmas, maybe."

Then she moved on to harassing the trader named Rogers, who was a woman with long fingers and an angular face, and who had apparently gotten especially good pricing on Weave at a wat she had returned from the previous evening.

Entrees had just hit the table when Jefferson walked in the door. He was dirty and the stench of sweat roiled the air about him.

Chief Carlton frowned over a glass of wine. "Early isn't good," she said. "You shouldn't be back for three days. What went wrong?" Her voice had an edge that was anxious, but not harsh.

"Gonzalez is dead," Jefferson said. He didn't look at Rock. Did he know the other trader had been there, and had pulled the trigger?

Rock, in turn, didn't flinch. A large baked fish was laid in front of him, and he began peeling back the skin.

"What happened?" Carlton gestured to Tasto and Grandi, who poured Jefferson a beer and dragged a chair to the table for him.

"Must have been a defective fuel cell." Jefferson slowly turned his head to face Rock, and then said with deliberate slowness, "The truck blew up."

"Solves the depreciation problem for that one," Keckley muttered behind his hand to John.

"Good thing you weren't in the truck." Rock stripped a forkful of pink flesh from the fish and popped it into his mouth.

"Is that all you have to say for Gonzalez, Rock?" Jefferson snarled. "One of ours just died!"

Rock swallowed his fish, then raised his glass of beer. "To Gonzalez!"

John's hand shook as he raised his own glass to join in the toast.

"You want more eulogy than that, you'll have to give it yourself," Rock said after a swallow of beer. "I didn't really know the guy. He was one of yours."

The revolver in John's jacket pocket felt very heavy. He noticed that Rock's right hand was beneath the table, and that he toasted with his left. Given the angle of Rock's shoulders, he could easily be aiming a pistol at Jefferson, out of sight.

"Gonzalez," John said. "I didn't know him very long, but he dragged me out of a cenote."

"Barlow, too," someone muttered.

"Yes," John agreed. "And he shot one of those bighorn elk, that ba, took it down in one shot, when it was chasing us in the truck." A sound like a grim mutter ran through the traders.

"Thing was as big as a bus," Hager added. "That was a good shot."

John groped for something to say that might add a note of levity. "And I'll say this for him, too. He knew the difference between anise seed and anus."

"Most likely due to his well-known expertise in buttholes," Takahashi said. "To Gonzalez!"

"Gonzalez!" They all drank.

John was careful to sip only lightly from his glass, and to keep an eye on Jefferson and Rock.

Jefferson glared daggers at Rock. He knew Rock had shot Gonzalez, and wanted Rock to know he knew.

Did he also know why? Was this a long-running hostility, or had Rock surprised the traders? Carlton's face, on the other hand, bore no indication that John could read that she was aware of anything other than what had been said openly.

More rowdy toasts were offered up to Gonzalez.

"We'll have to check his file," Keckley murmured over his beer to John. "See who we might have to notify."

"Where to send his last paycheck to, and so on?" John asked.

"Not just the paycheck," Keckley said. "All his accounts. Data. Physical possessions might need to be shipped to someone, or we may have to liquidate assets here. If he has a will on file with the Company, we might need to send last messages for him. It's a lot of work when a man dies forty light-years from home."

Chief Carlton pushed her steak over to Jefferson and ordered another for herself as he tucked in. "Where did the truck blow up?"

Jefferson hesitated. "We lost our way," he said. "We were having trouble with the cell from the start, and after a delay while we attempted to fix it, we tried to make up lost time by driving after dark."

"Dangerous," Takahashi said. "Cenotes. Wild animals. Rough terrain."

Jefferson nodded, swallowing steak. "And somehow we ended up going north when we should have gone east. We had stopped the truck and I was outside looking around, trying to figure out where we had ended up, when the truck suddenly exploded."

He had to explain why he wasn't farther away, given the four days for which he'd scheduled the truck. It was a good lie. John might have believed him if he hadn't already known the truth.

"Trade goods all aboard?" Keckley asked.

"Everything but the clothes on my back," Jefferson said.

"More write-offs." Keckley grunted. "This is not going to be a good quarter for us. Relatively speaking."

Carlton raised a hand to stop the audit chief's grumbling.

"I walked back," Jefferson said. "I followed the truck's tracks; I guess I got lucky. I just arrived at the post now, and I remembered there was going to be this lunch, so I walked straight here."

Rock left shortly thereafter.

John felt conspicuous for the remainder of the meal, but he remained where he was, drank more toasts to Gonzalez when called upon, and watched Post Chief Carlton sign for the meal on the restaurant's multitool with big, looping characters. Then he left with Keckley.

"I could have dressed up a little more," he said to his boss.

"Just a bit," Keckley admitted.

They walked back to the office to begin working out the administrative consequences of the trader's death.

CHAPTER TWENTY-ONE

"Yay! Dad-setty's coming to school!" Ellie hugged John's leg yet again. "And Ani-setty, too!"

"I think we can just call her Ani," John said.

"Ani's coming!" Ellie ran out of the front room of the house, doing yet another lap of the building.

John put on his jacket, filling the pockets with the pistol and ammunition. Ruth shrugged into a long coat.

"You're coming, too?" John asked.

"You object?"

"I'm pleased." He kissed her. "Maybe you'd like to take the pistol."

"I'm heeled." She patted the hip of her coat.

"Are these shoulder bags for us?" John pointed at four bags of ascending size, lined up by the door.

"We're supposed to bring lunch," Ruth said.

John picked up the largest pack. "That's a big lunch."

"It may have a few other things in it."

"Snacks?"

"Water purifiers, blankets, flares, spare energy cells for all our multis, a knife, a first-aid kit." Ruth picked up her bag. "And snacks."

"Energy cells? How many years is this field trip supposed to last?"

"You never know."

Nermer let the family out the front gate. The sun shone clear and cold, but a dampness on the breeze blowing in from the west hinted at rain later. Ani clung to Ruth's heels, head swinging easily back and forth and she snuffled the spring air. The rust-red of her space travel-induced coat had almost completely dulled to a chocolate brown.

"Dad," Sunitha said, "you missed church."

"Mom talked about compunction," Ellie said.

"Compassion." Sunitha practically sneered at her little sister.

"Sorry." John held out his hand, but she didn't take it. "I had work."

"Work isn't everything," Sunitha said. "You can't neglect your responsibilities. That isn't like you, Father."

"I'm coming on a field trip, aren't I?"

That mollified her somewhat, but she still didn't take his hand. John exchanged glances with Ruth, who shrugged.

They walked without talking for a few minutes. Other than the scrape of shoes on gravel, and Ani's panting, the only sound was an aimless tune Ellie was humming.

"Cenotes are caused by water flowing through limestone," Sunitha said as they approached the school. Her mood seemed to pick up as she dropped into her false accent. "Over time, they erode open pockets inside the stone, which develop into cave systems. They become cenotes when they dig up close to the surface and then the ceiling collapses, turning one of the chambers of the cave system into a well."

"I actually have personal experience of that," John said.

"We know," Sunitha said. "That's the second reason Mrs. Jenkins thought you ought to come."

"What's the first?"

"Ani, of course!" Ellie cried. "Here, Ani! Touch! Touch!" She held out her hand, palm down for the dog to touch it, and ran ahead. Ani loped easily after her, raising her head to bump her nose to Ellie's hand.

A truck waited in front of the schoolhouse. It might have been made by the same engineers in Henry Hudson who had bolted together the Company's vehicles; it had a long body in three segments, and treads running over four wheels on each side of each segment. Sam Chen sat at the controls, gnawing at a ration bar.

Just behind Chen, a ladder led up to a hatch in the ceiling.

The truck was already half-full of children. John recognized many faces from his visit to the post school. Pianki was among them, as well as a girl who was several years older than Pianki and sat holding his hand.

Ruth led the girls to the open seats immediately behind the driver's nook, and John followed.

"Chen," he said, nodding.

"Don't worry," Chen said. "We aren't going far, and it's a known, sturdy road."

"Good." John nodded. "This is a heavy truck, and I'd hate to have it fall down a hole."

Mrs. Jenkins arrived, said good morning, and proceeded to check names off a list on her multitool.

Ani laid her head on one of John's feet. John wrapped an arm around Ruth and dozed while they waited for the rest of the children to arrive. They came without parents, in ones and twos, from all directions.

John was tired. He had spent the previous afternoon looking into Gonzalez's file, to see what there was to do about the dead man's estate. Mercifully, it was simple: all material goods were to be auctioned off, and all his money was then to be forwarded to an Earth account, with a notification to a lawyer in Santa Fe. If there was a complex will, or a family to deal with, it was the lawyer's problem.

John had taken an inventory of Gonzalez's material possessions and photographed them with his multitool. There had been nothing shocking—such as, for instance, crates full of guns and ammunition. Gonzalez had had a personal sidearm that hadn't gone with him out to Bourbon Lake, but otherwise, there was a short stack of battered paperback spy novels, clothing, and an array of tools.

John took out his multitool. The traders were bidding on all the items on the post utility app, so he tuned in to watch the auction. It must be some form of gallantry or generosity—did the traders know something John didn't, about who would ultimately get this money?—but they were bidding up some of the items outrageously. Tasto had bid fifty bucks on the reprint of some old thriller, and Grandi thought the semiautomatic pistol was worth five hundred.

Should he bid? He looked for bids from Keckley and DeBoe and saw none, but Carlton had bid on a few things, and John wanted to ingratiate himself with the traders, for more than one reason.

He bid twenty dollars on a novel called *The Day of the Jackal*. Tasto promptly kicked the bid to twenty-five.

"Okay, everyone's here, and we're ready to begin," Mrs. Jenkins said. "Yesterday in class, we all chose a buddy. My buddy is going to be Aliska. Does everyone remember who their buddy is?" As the children all recalled and found their buddies, Mrs. Jenkins leaned over to Ruth and John. "You two can be buddies, if you like."

"Why don't you be buddies with Ellie?" Ruth suggested to John. "Sunitha and I can be together."

"Okay," John said, "but we get Ani."

Ellie waved her fists in victory. "We get Ani!"

Mrs. Jenkins returned to her instructions. John nodded at the girls, encouraging them to listen, but he himself was paying more attention to the auction. He bid thirty bucks, and Tasto bid thirty-five.

John didn't think he wanted to actually read these novels, but now something inside him really hungered to win the auction. He bid fifty-five dollars on *Tinker, Tailor, Soldier, Spy*.

The instructions over, Mrs. Jenkins took her seat and Sam started the truck. The children promptly came up to a boil of activity as games and conversations broke out. A minority stared at John and Ruth, and another group of kids tried to summon Ani to them by waving what looked like a short meat stick at her. Ani sniffed and lowered her head. Ellie crossed the bumping floor to where the children interested in her dog sat and held down her hand.

"Touch," Ellie said. Ani pushed herself off the floor and loped over to her littlest pack member.

"If you get her fat," John said, "you'll be the one who has to carry her."

"It's just a little dried lamb," Pianki said.

"I'm sure she'll love it," Ruth said. "Just give her a little, as a treat."

Tasto bumped his bids on the two novels to sixty and forty dollars. Then, as if to goad John, he bid twenty dollars on a book called *The Bourne Identity*.

"I don't even like spy novels," John said. "Why couldn't Gonzalez have had a bunch of comedy flicks?"

Ruth looked over his shoulder. "Is this work?"

The truck left Arrowhawk Post and turned northward, leaving the gravel road.

Where did the roads go to? No one seemed to use them.

John sighed. "Sort of." He hadn't told her anything of what he'd witnessed at Bourbon Lake, but had reported Jefferson's appearance at lunch and his version of events. "The guy who died. Traders are buying his stuff, so that the heirs, whoever they are, just get cash. It's . . . uh, I guess they're bidding stupid amounts on what is basically junk, to show respect for the dead guy."

"*You* are bidding stupid amounts," Ruth said. "To show the other traders that you are one of them."

John nodded.

"Don't bid anything *too* stupid."

Was seventy-five dollars too stupid for a twentieth-century spy novel? Probably. But was it too much to bid if it got John invited to another wat?

He upped his bids, and bid on the Bourne novel, too.

He looked up from his multi and saw something flicker through the back window of the bus. He only saw it for a moment, but it dipped down into view and then rose again out of sight. And it didn't move like a bird.

It moved like a drone.

John looked to Ruth and Mrs. Jenkins, but neither gave any indication that she had seen what he had.

And then he saw it again. Four rotary blades and a smooth black body the size of a large bird.

And something hung beneath the drone. It might be a camera, or it might be a weapon. An explosive, or a projectile, for instance. Or it might be all of the above.

John considered his options. He didn't want to spook anyone, including especially Mrs. Jenkins, so he had to be careful what questions he even asked. On the other hand, he knew that Rock, for one, was perfectly capable of killing, and Jefferson certainly seemed to have reached a similar state of hostility.

If either man knew that John had been at Bourbon Lake, might he have sent a drone to kill him? John could message for help with his multi, but how long would it take for help to arrive?

"Mrs. Jenkins," John said casually, "does the school have any kind of surveillance on the truck?"

"You grossly overestimate the resources of the school," she said.

"There's no school district, no tax base. There's a school board of three people, a truck and a building, and me. The lessons are published by the Company and made available to the entire planet for free, to anyone with a multitool. Mr. Chen is volunteering his time."

John nodded. "What if I couldn't come along on a field trip, but I want to keep any eye on the girls? Could I put a camera in the truck?"

"You mean tape a multi to the wall?"

John shrugged. "Or fly a drone alongside to watch."

"I don't see how I could stop you," she said. "No parent has ever done that, though. We don't see that many drones around Arrowhawk Post."

"The kids are obviously in good hands." John smiled. "I just like to think through how things work."

"It's the accountant in you."

"Probably." John pointed at the ladder. "You know, in the Company trucks, there are observation compartments on top. I'm guessing from that ladder that there must be a deck on top of this truck, too."

Mrs. Jenkins nodded. "I sometimes let the children go up there when the truck is stationary, but not while it's moving. If they fell off, there'd be hell to pay, and since you know kids, you know that, sooner or later, one would fall off."

"Leap off," John said, "on purpose."

He kept a casual smile on his face, even when he saw the drone dip into sight a third time.

"Listen, I don't want to cause you any trouble, but I'm new here and learning the geography still. Would you mind if I just went up top for a little while to watch from there? I wouldn't bring my daughters, just me." John smiled his most winning smile.

Mrs. Jenkins sighed, looked at Ani, who was patiently accepting the pawing of eight different children at once, and nodded.

"Honey, can I borrow your *coat*?" John asked Ruth. "It gets cold up there when the trucks are in motion."

Ruth narrowed her eyes. John was slender and could wear her coat, though the sleeves and body would be very short on him, but he never did. Did his emphasis on the word 'coat' let her know what he was doing?

She nodded and handed him the coat. He felt the bulk of the energy pistol inside and nodded.

First, he stepped to Sam Chen's shoulder to hold a huddled conference with the driver. "Sam, there's a drone following us, and I think it might be armed."

Display screens showed three different rear-facing views on the panel in front of Sam, and he looked down at them now. "Yes, there is."

"See that bulge?" John pointed. "That might be a gun or a bomb, don't you think?"

"Or a camera," Sam said.

"Can you think of any legitimate reason for someone to be following this truck with even a camera?" John asked. "Because Mrs. Jenkins doesn't know of one."

Sam shook his head.

"Keep the truck as steady as you can." John clapped Sam on the shoulder.

Then he put on Ruth's coat, smiled at her, and climbed the ladder. Halfway up, with his body obscuring the view of the children and Mrs. Jenkins, he pulled the energy pistol from the coat pocket and adjusted its settings—safety off, widest beam selected. The hatch opened with a gentle pneumatic hiss, admitting John onto the wind-whipped observation platform.

They had left the valley in which Arrowhawk Post was located and were winding through wet green hills. John could see the drone plainly; it flew directly behind the truck. If John was the specific target and the drone had come to kill him, he had just offered himself to it, so he couldn't afford to wait.

He stepped away from the drone, toward the front of the truck, raised the energy pistol, and fired.

Stepping back would give him the widest possible beam at the distance of the drone. He needed the energy pistol, because there was no way he could hit just a tiny target with the revolver, especially not from the top of a moving truck.

He scored a hit. He could tell that he hit the drone because its paint bubbled and because he saw red reflected back at him from a glass surface that must be the eye of a camera.

But the drone didn't explode.

Instead, it charged him.

John ducked. The drone missed him, slammed into the wall of the truck and then zoomed away sideways, rising.

John ejected the spent energy cell and inserted a new one. The drone swung away from the truck and then lunged back toward it, but its movements were broad and awkward.

Had John damaged its photoelectronics? Maybe the wide beam had been too diffuse to destroy the drone, but had blinded it.

He narrowed the beam on the energy pistol slightly.

The drone swept past the truck, left to right, and then right to left. Then it fell back, dropping into a constant position again, hovering behind and above the school vehicle.

John still had the pistol set on a relatively wide beam, and the truck was steady. He hit the drone again, and this time it burst into flame.

It charged John one last time. He ducked and it raced ahead, passing the truck entirely and slamming to rest in the watery seep of the meadow through which the truck rumbled. John swapped out the spent cell for his last fresh one and watched the downed drone carefully until it was far behind.

He took off the coat, replaced the energy pistol in the pocket, and climbed down.

"Did you see what you hoped to see?" Mrs. Jenkins asked.

"That was very helpful, thank you." He nodded.

But he'd lost the bidding for every one of Gonzalez's spy novels.

CHAPTER
TWENTY-TWO

You'll tell me what happened later? Ruth messaged John over their multitools.

A drone was following the truck, John messaged back. *It might have been harmless, but it might have had a weapon. I destroyed it.*

Ruth looked unsettled, but put away her multi.

Sam parked the truck. John looked out the windows, and as far as he could tell, the truck sat in one of a chain of meadows like dozens of others he had now seen on Sarovar Alpha. Evergreens ringed the meadows, and a stream flowed across one of them. No sign of a cenote.

Ani came padding back to the front of the truck from the rear segment, where kids had been slipping her scraps of meat and trying to avoid John's glare. Her tail wagged. John scratched the dog behind the ears and stood.

Mrs. Jenkins exited the truck first. "Buddies!" she cried, holding up her own hand clasped with Aliska's by way of example.

Ruth leaned in to whisper to John. "Why would you see a drone and assume it might be armed, and in need of destruction?"

"I didn't assume," John murmured. "I looked at it, and it appeared that it might have a weapon. I figured, the worst case if I destroyed it was I would have to replace someone's drone."

"Why would someone want to kill anyone here?" Ruth asked. "Does this have to do with the trader who died?"

"Maybe," John said. He took a deep breath. "I don't know. I'll tell you what I know tonight. Or when we're somewhere without kids to overhear."

They exited the truck last, pulling on raincoats against cold wet sheets that had just begun to fall and shouldering their packs. John held Ellie's hand; Ani sat beside Ellie, as instructed, and looked around, ears cocked forward.

"The cenote we're about to enter," Mrs. Jenkins said, "is just on the other side of those trees. I've been bringing school children here for ten years. It was a cousin of Pianki's, in fact, who told me about the cenote in the first place. We come here because it's accessible on foot, and also very impressive to see. Follow me, stick with your buddy, and be careful."

"Do you live near here?" Sunitha asked Pianki.

The little boy nodded. "My village is called Nyoot Abedjoo."

"There's a lot of water down in the cenote right now," Mrs. Jenkins said. "Ideally, we'd come here in high summer, when it's driest, but the truth is it's never really dry down in these caves."

"It freezes in the winter," Pianki said. "Neferooee the caves! The caves are really beautiful then. But slippery."

"We're going to explore the cenote a little bit," Mrs. Jenkins said, "but only a little. We'll go into four chambers, because all of them have had their ceilings collapse, and are open to the sky. That means there's light inside there. The cenotes connect to many other chambers, a long network of caverns that has not been mapped. Since there's no light, and since there are other dangers—such as slippery footing, and deep, cold pools—we won't go into that part of the cenote."

"What about animals?" Gary Chen asked. "Like bears? Or lions?"

"There are hatties in some of the cenotes," Pianki said. "And hefaoo."

"Hefaoo are snakes," Mrs. Jenkins said in response to looks of puzzlement on some children's face. "But a hatty is a folkloric creature."

"I don't know what a 'folkloric' is," Pianki said. "A hatty is like . . ." He pointed at Ani. "Four legs. But much bigger than a tchezmoo. Bigger than Ani."

The word 'hatty' tugged at something in John's memory. What was a hatty?

"'Folkloric' means that a thing only exists in stories," Mrs. Jenkins said.

"Hatties are real," Pianki insisted. "They eat our animals, and sometimes when they bother us too much, we throw sheep down into the cenotes to keep the hatties away."

Mrs. Jenkins smiled and nodded, unconvinced. "Here's the entrance. Walk slowly!"

A hole yawned in the meadow. Water poured slowly down into the pit on three sides, sliding along dangling lengths of grass and dark green creepers. The fourth side was a tumble of boulders that created something approximating a staircase. Mrs. Jenkins climbed down this rough slope first.

"Have you ever seen a hatty?" Sunitha asked Pianki.

The boy shook his head. "But my uncle and my sister have both seen them."

"Then how can you be sure they're real?" she asked.

"There's a dead hatty's head on my uncle's wall," Pianki said. "He saw it when it was alive, and he killed it. And there's a rood on my mother's floor."

"Rood?" Sunitha asked.

Pianki ran his fingers along his forearm. "Skin. Animal skin."

Sunitha harrumphed. "A pelt."

John counted as people climbed down into the cenote. Twenty children, four adults, and one dog. He saw the square-faced girl with pigtails, and realized who she must be.

"Is your last name Carlton?" he asked her.

"My mom is your boss," she said, and then she and her buddy rattled down into the cenote.

John and Ellie climbed down last with Ani leaping about their ankles, and the rain let up as they descended. They shucked off their raincoats and packed them away into their shoulder bags.

The cenote was larger than it seemed from above. The vegetation was different from what grew on the surface; it was a brighter green, and it consisted of ferns and mosses rather than the weedy yellow grass and the cow's ear-shaped leaf that grew everywhere around Arrowhawk Post. Pools of limpid water flowed around an archipelago of boulders on the cenote floor. Water flowed out of the cenote into the dark open mouth of a cave, and into the cenote from another cave opening, deep within which, however, John saw the gray, rainy gleam of daylight.

"Those seeps you see coming out of the rock are the flows of water that create the cenotes," Mrs. Jenkins was saying. "That's potable water. You can drink it because the rock itself has filtered out impurities. And the rock is . . . ?"

"Limestone, of course," Sunitha said in her accent.

Mrs. Jenkins continued, "This plant here is very similar structurally to an Earth plant called watercress, and is even more dense in nutrition. The cenote cress, together with the fish that live in the pools, provide enough nutrition that a person could live down in these cenotes and never starve."

"Might drown, though," Sam Chen said.

"In the spring, lots of water flows through these chambers." Mrs. Jenkins pointed at high shelves up underneath the lip over which water flowed down into the open hole. "If you look at that ledge, though, you'll find that it's dry. These cenotes have been very little explored, but they've been examined enough to know that ledges like those are very common."

"My people used to live down here," Pianki said. "For a very long time. There are also hefaoo you can eat."

Several other children shushed or booed Pianki.

"You already told us there are snakes down here," Mrs. Jenkins said. "Thank you."

"And hatties," Pianki said. "But you don't eat hatties. Hatties eat *you.*"

"When did your family live in the cenotes?" Mrs. Jenkins asked. "It stays cool down here all year round. Once you get back in the caves, the temperature is constant. Out in this open bowl, it will freeze in the winter, but inside the caves, it will feel warm in the winter and cool in the summer. Did you stay down here in a bad winter? Or a really hot summer?"

"Hundreds of years ago," Pianki said. "Nobody I knew was alive."

"I see." Mrs. Jenkins's smile was flat.

John smiled at Pianki. The boy was a little confused about dates, but there was no reason not to be encouraging to him.

"They left pictures," Pianki added.

Mrs. Jenkins took a deep breath. "Let's go look at the other roofless chambers."

She led the class along a gray stone shelf that ran beside the stream, marching up against the direction of the flowing water. "Keep tight hold of your buddy!" she called. "And step carefully, because the rock can be slippery!"

John looked down at his feet. In the stream to his left, something glinted as it moved. He couldn't tell whether it might be snakes or fish, but he thought he saw something more than mere reflection of light; blue-white spots moving in the stream seemed to glow.

Ani splashed into the water and the lights scattered.

In the second sinkhole, the stream split around a tall, angular boulder. From the right, a trickle of water flowed out of a black crack in the wall. Mrs. Jenkins kept walking to the left, where the ledge of water continued to creep above the flowing brook.

The bottom of the third sinkhole was flat. The ledge ended, and the stream flowed across the entire floor of the pit. From the upstream end of the pit, the water poured out of a broad passageway, with enough room overhead that a human, even a child, could wade up into the darkness.

There were definitely luminescent blue dots moving around up there.

Mrs. Jenkins pointed out a different opening in the rock wall. Beyond lay another sinkhole, and the class and the adults stepped through. Here, no stream flowed. Water poured down the sides of the sinkhole from the wet meadow above, dripping along grass and roots and creepers. It all pooled at the bottom of the sinkhole and then trickled through the opening, sluicing down to join the stream.

"Like an oxbow lake, maybe?" Ruth asked. "The river used to flow through here, but it doesn't anymore?"

John nodded.

Mrs. Jenkins rewarded Ruth with a broad smile. "You could be a geology teacher, if you ever wanted to give up the pulpit. Fair play and compassion, such elegant sentiments."

"Love," Ruth said. "It's simple, but not easy."

"I hope you recorded that," John said.

"I did as you asked."

Ani snuffled at the ground. She was an athletic dog, and something had her fascinated; in a single leap, with a little scrabbling on the hind end, she climbed to the top of a two-meter-tall boulder. From there she leaped up onto a ledge beneath the lip of the sinkhole.

John could hear her sniffing.

"Ani!" he called, but she ignored him.

"She probably found a dead thing." Sunitha's voice was sour with condemnation.

"Maybe she found a friend," Ellie said. "Like a butterfly."

"Ah, a friend to *eat*," Sunitha said.

"There's an easier climb up around that side." Mrs. Jenkins pointed.

John clambered up to the ledge. Ani was sniffing at withered, gray, objects shaped like sausage links and strung together in a pile half the size of the dog.

Pianki and Sunitha both scrambled up behind John, as John was pulling Ani away from the gray mound.

"It's poop," Sunitha announced.

"It's hatty-poop," Pianki said.

Sunitha frowned. "How do you know?"

"It's not hatty-poop," Mrs. Jenkins told them. "It's probably from a ba or from beavers that took shelter down here."

"You can tell by the shape," Pianki said.

Sunitha examined the droppings as John pulled his dog back down off the ledge. "Don't plant eaters have spherical poop?" she asked. "Horse, deer, cows, rabbits."

"Wombats have square poops," Gary said.

"Well, it's not square," Sunitha told him. "It's shaped like sausage links. Like a dog's poop, or a cat's."

"Or a human's," John pointed out.

"There are no wombats on Sarovar Alpha," Gary said.

"That would have to have come from the biggest human who ever lived," Sunitha said.

"It came from a hatty." Pianki looked pale.

John helped both children down, reuniting them with their buddies. "Okay, well, there's no hatty here now, and no wild animal is going to attack a group of twenty-four humans and a dog, and if any animal is that stupid, then I have things to chase the animal away."

"Like what?" Gary asked.

"What do I have, honey?" John asked Ruth.

"Bear spray," she said. "And flares. Both should work really well against a hatty."

"A bear is like a shay," Pianki said. "Bears are big, like hatties. Does the spray make bears disappear?"

"It makes their eyes sting," Ruth said, "and then they run away."

"I don't know whether stinging eyes will be enough to make a hatty run away," Pianki said. "Maybe you should use the flares first."

Ani growled.

"Shh, Ani, there are no hatties," Ruth said.

Ani growled again. She backed away from the stone wall, toward the passage connecting the third and fourth sinkholes.

"Ani," John said, "sit."

She barked.

John looked up at the lip of the sinkhole. "There is, after all, a monster pile of poop left by some kind of creature up there. Maybe it's coming back to its den."

"Children," Mrs. Jenkins called, "come back with me into the other sinkhole."

The children hesitated for a moment, then scrambled out of the pit. Buddies became separated, breath came fast and ragged, and a few of the smaller ones started to whimper. John backed into the passageway last. He dug into his backpack and pulled the bear spray out of its holster. The bright orange printing on the pine-green can promised 10-METER RANGE AND 10-SECOND DISSIPATION; he held it in his left hand, and in his right, he took the Webley.

Ani barked louder.

Whatever it was, John decided that he didn't need to see it. "Heel!" he called to Ani, and then he and Ruth pulled back into the third sinkhole.

John looked up as he stepped into the sinkhole, casting his eyes toward the passage back through to the second. Lights shone in the sinkhole—for a moment, he thought he saw the blue luminescent dots that had been swimming in the stream, now bobbing at the height of a human belt buckle, but then he realized that the lights could only mean people.

He relaxed. Ani was barking because strangers were approaching, and she was surprised. Probably these were just country-setties, coming here to enjoy the cenotes like the schoolchildren were. Or maybe they came to fish in the deeper pools that Mrs. Jenkins had said were here.

"Hello!" he called out.

He heard clicking in return.

Maybe, it occurred to him, the lights were made by the same people who had sent the drone. And maybe they were upset. "Get the children inside the cave!" he snapped.

Mrs. Jenkins and Sam Chen complied instantly, dragged the kids splashing into the open cave mouth. Ani splashed in the stream, tail down, growling and snapping at the advancing lights.

The first person emerged from the tunnel, and it wasn't a human at all. It was a Sarovari Weaver, and it held an automatic rifle in its hands. Pointing the rifle forward, it began to spray bullets in short bursts in John's direction.

John raised both the pistol and the bear spray. He sprayed the first Weaver in one of its three faces and it shrieked, hurling itself into the stream. He kept spraying, stepping forward toward the tunnel from which the Weavers emerged, spraying and now also firing the pistol.

He didn't like fighting. John's instinct was always to talk.

But the Weavers were armed and attacking, and he was no idiot.

A flare hissed past him, a tiny ball of orange fire. It struck a Weaver and embedded itself in the creature's carapace. The Weaver wailed and fell to the ground, trembling. Its companions stumbled over it, trying to shoot at John and Ruth.

"Their aim is terrible!" Ruth had the energy pistol out now, but wasn't aiming at a target.

"There are enough of them that it won't matter!" John shouted. "Take cover in the cave!"

As he bellowed the words, he realized what Ani must have been barking at. Splashing across the water and spinning to look behind him, he raised his eyes, and saw three Weavers reach the lip of the sinkhole above him.

Bang! Bang! Bang!

John had been kicked out of the Academy on a bum medical exam, but growing up in a family of shooters meant he had a reasonably good aim, and the Weavers were not small targets. He hit each once, and then he and Ruth dove into the cave, splashing in water up to their thighs, with Ani swimming at their side.

CHAPTER TWENTY-THREE

"Mrs. Jenkins!" John snapped. "Get the kids as far back into the cave as possible!"

She didn't answer, but he heard splashing and scrabbling sounds that suggested she was complying.

It was the Weavers, after all. Jefferson and Gonzalez had been selling guns to the Weavers. Then what was Rock's role? A coconspirator who fell out?

"Sam!" John continued. "Get help!" This was what the Arrowhawk Post Irregulars were for, after all.

"There's no signal," Sam Chen said. "But I have a pistol. Ten-millimeter Kupari, and a spare magazine."

The driver crept to the front of the cave and crouched low in the cold water, so that only his head and hands emerged.

"I don't have a signal, either," Ruth said.

"It can't be the cave, can it?" Sam asked. "We're right here in the opening."

"Maybe a satellite is down." The flat tone of Ruth's voice hinted that maybe she didn't think it was a coincidence that their multitools couldn't connect to the network.

"Can we address the bigger issue?" Sam asked. "Why are there Weavers with guns?"

John sighed, rummaging through his pack. The Weavers were milling at the far side of the sinkhole, careful not to expose themselves. "Because some of the traders have been selling them weapons."

"Sweet Jesus," Sam said. "Jesus, that's a terrible idea."

"It's a terrible idea in the long term," John agreed, "for lots of people—for the Company, for the country-setties, for everyone who wants to try to live on this planet. But in the short term, it can make some traders a lot of money."

"Is this . . . Gonzalez, was he selling the Weavers guns?"

"I think so," John said.

"This is what you weren't telling me?" Ruth asked. "This is why you've been working late nights?"

"It's my job," John said. "And I was told to keep it a secret. English asked me to look into some accounting irregularities, and . . . well, this is where it led."

"Into a cold, wet hole in the ground!" Ruth shouted. "With three-sided crabs armed with automatic rifles, penning us in!"

John hung his head. "Yes."

Ruth laughed manically, then cut herself short. She took a deep breath. "And do the Weavers have drones, too? Was that who was following us earlier? So they could just drone a bomb on over here and blow us up."

"For sure, if a drone comes flying this way, shoot it," John said. "But there's another possibility: maybe the Weavers have human allies."

"Human allies?" Sam asked. "Allies against whom?"

John chewed over what he knew. "Some Arrowhawk traders supplied arms to the Weavers. Or to some set of Weavers. Specifically, a nest of Weavers around Bourbon Lake."

"You're thinking Gonzalez and Jefferson, then," Sam said.

"At least," John agreed. "And maybe at least one trader was supplying the local humans with weapons."

"The local humans?" Ruth asked.

"Country-setties," John said.

"That's not a good idea, either," Sam said. "Long term, either the Weavers or the country-setties could decide they've had enough of Arrowhawk Post and the Company, and come in shooting."

"I didn't say it was a good idea," John said.

"Who was arming whom first?" Ruth asked.

His promise to Director English to be discreet was out the window now. "If I had to, I'd guess that Jefferson and Gonzalez, and maybe others, started selling weapons to Weavers because they found they could get a lot more Weave for an automatic rifle than they could for a hammer. And then the . . . other side stepped in to help the country-setties arm themselves, for defense against the Weavers."

"Jesus," Sam said. "It was Rock."

"He's not the only trader who feels empathy for the country-setties," John said.

"He's not," Sam agreed. "*I* feel empathy for them. But his wife is one of them, and if my wife's people were threatened by armed aliens, I sure as hell would find a way to get them weapons." Sam lowered his voice. "John, I'm pretty sure Rock has a kid in the school."

John sighed. "Yeah. One step leads pretty inevitably to the next."

"And if the Company finds out," Sam said, "what's the inevitable step?"

John didn't want to think about it.

Carpet bombing was a possibility, English had said.

"Where are they buying these weapons?" Ruth asked. "Isn't it possible that the Company already knows about this? That the Company is profiting from the sale of arms to the natives?"

"Possible," John said, "but I haven't seen anything in the books that makes me think that's happening. Mind you, I've spent so much time counting inventory and going out on a wat and doing other things, maybe I just haven't looked at the right ledgers yet."

Maybe there was an arms-dealing subsidiary, with its own accounts? Or the arms sales were on Henry Hudson's books?

Or maybe the Company was profiting, but it was all kept off the accounts? In theory, Congress had the power to audit the Company's books, and might demand an accounting for the Company's revenues.

"I have no idea where they're buying them," he added.

"How much of this do you know, and how much do you guess?" Ruth asked.

"I know Jefferson and Gonzalez were taking weapons out to a wat whose location they were very discreet about. And I know that Rock and a bunch of country-setties with rifles and explosives ambushed them, and killed Gonzalez. Jefferson escaped by swimming across a lake. And I know that we're trapped by armed Weavers. Much of the rest is guessing."

"Speaking of armed Weavers . . ." Sam said.

Gunfire rang out, loud and echoing in the sinkhole. Bullets struck the cave wall in the darkness behind John. "Keep the kids back!" he yelled.

Under the covering fire, four Weavers charged them. They kicked up water as they spun their way forward, looking like giant red pucks in a game of field hockey played in the rain. With guns.

Ruth pressed close against John and fired the energy pistol. On a medium-beam setting, she hit the two Weavers at the front of the charging squad. The ones following struck their comrades and were flung sideways by their own impetus.

John fired six shots with the Webley, bringing the rest of the charge to a halt, then pressed himself back against the cave wall for cover.

"That's your last charged energy cell," he said as he reloaded.

"Here, take my pistol," Sam said to Ruth. "I can patch my multi's cell into the pistol, it'll be good for two or three shots."

"What? How do you know how to do that?" John asked.

"I'm an engineer," Sam said. "You think the Company ships people out here whose only skill is to drive trucks?"

"We have four spare multi batteries," Ruth said. "There in John's pack."

Ruth took John's shoulder bag, and she and Sam retreated into the cave. Fully reloaded, John peered out of the cave mouth. He was rewarded with a wild spray of bullets, but he also got a glimpse of what faced them outside: twenty Weavers, maybe more. There were Weavers hunkered down in both tunnels that led to other sinkholes, and along the lip of the sinkhole, above. And if he'd had any hopes that he might rush out and grab the rifles from the fallen attackers, they were now dashed; the Weavers had crept forward and dragged back to their lines the bodies of their fallen comrades, along with their weapons.

John checked his multi: no network.

The Weavers hadn't done that. Someone had shut the network down, and that someone was human.

The fact that Sam could convert multitool energy cells for use in the pistol evened the odds somewhat. Not all the kids had multis, but assuming that half of them did, together with Ruth's spare cells, the pistol would have twenty-plus shots. Probably thirty-plus.

But there might be more Weavers than John could see.

And he couldn't afford to lose any of the children, so there was no question of breaking out and making a run for it. If the class rushed across the sinkhole taking fire from above, it would be a massacre.

Ani, crouching on a knob of rock beside John, growled.

"Yes, girl," John said. "Good girl, yes."

Ani barked and leaped into the water. She swam forward, and John saw what she had been warning him about, and he had missed.

There were Weavers in the stream, swimming his way.

They were fully submerged, and they clung to the bottom of the stream to avoid floating, but they carried firearms.

If John shot at them, his bullets would ricochet off the water. If they shot at him, the water would slow and probably stop their bullets. He needed a spear.

What he got was a dog. Ani hurled herself on the first Weaver, grabbed one of its pincers in her jaws, and tore it right from the Weaver's body. She dug at one row of its eyes, too, until it rose from the stream, shrieking, and John put three slugs in its side.

John got one good look at the Weaver before the water current flushed it out of his sight. Something was wrong with its shell. Beyond the damage John had done, the carapace was spotted with black splotches, and riven with cracks that spread from the dark patches. More than anything else, the smears looked like black mold.

Like the black mold that had afflicted the old brownstone in Crown Heights that John and Ruth had rented during his first year at NYU. The black mold that the landlord had refused to acknowledge, and that John had had to fix himself, working at nights while the family slept, ripping open the walls with a crowbar, dousing the mold with vinegar, and then plastering the holes shut again.

He gagged at the memory, and at the sight of the mold-encrusted Weaver.

Gunfire erupted from above, bullets striking the Weaver and the water around it. Blood churned in the water.

"Ani, heel!" John shouted.

Ani thrashed back through the stream and into the passage opening. She was bleeding from her flank, but her movement wasn't impeded.

Ruth reappeared at John's side. "Let's give this a try," she said.

"They're in the water," he told her.

Ruth dialed the pistol to a tight beam. She fired once, then again, then a third time, but the third bolt of light was paler, and then the trigger clicked without effect.

John scratched Ani's neck with his left hand and risked a glance out. Two more dead Weavers floated in the water, their flesh burned and blistering, their carapaces cracked. A third dragged itself away with a single leg, its other legs still and useless. John thought he saw mold on the survivor.

"Sam!" Ruth called out.

Sam grabbed the energy pistol and began patching another cell into it.

"I need to learn how you're doing that," John said.

"I'll show you, once we have good light."

"Do you want to hold the gun, or take a look at the dog?" John asked Ruth. "Ani got hurt."

"Good girl," Ruth said, probing at Ani's injury. "Good girl, yes."

"She saw them coming when I didn't," John said. "Or smelled them or heard them, probably."

"She just got grazed, it's not bad." Ruth quickly shaved around Ani's wound and applied tape. "Well, I know who's getting a treat once we get home."

"Damn," John said. "*I* was hoping for a treat."

"*You* might still have some explaining to do."

"*Then* treat?"

"Depends on the explanation."

"Ugh, you guys are gross." Sam handed Ruth the energy pistol. "Here you go."

"How are the kids?" John asked.

"They're so far back, I can't see them," Sam said. "The cave goes around a couple of bends, and they're past that."

"That should protect them from ricochets," Ruth said.

"Just what I was thinking," John agreed. "Not too crazy about the idea of hatties, though."

"Probably just something like a bear," Ruth said.

"Correct," John said. "Our kids are back there in a wet cave, possibly with something like a bear."

SPLASH!

Water rose in a wave and struck John and the others in the face, soaking them. Before John could catch his breath, there came a second enormous splash, and then a third.

"Boulders," Sam said. "They're dropping rocks from above."

"They'll dam the stream," Ruth said.

The water was already beginning to rise. More rocks fell in.

"I can't get out to shoot at the ones who are doing this," John said.

"They'll force us out," Sam said. "Or drown us."

"Are there markers in the backpack?" John asked Ruth.

"Luminescent," she said. "Waterproof."

"Good. If the tunnel forks, you can mark your trail. Leave the multitool energy cells and the energy pistol with us." John handed the shoulder bag to his wife. "But take this revolver and the bullets, just in case there are hatties."

"I'll go upstream, look for a way out." Ruth nodded.

"Keep an eye open for the possibility of *making* a way out," John said. "A really high roof might mean the surface is close, and we can use the energy pistol to open a hole. Take Ani. She might smell hatties coming. Or she might help you find your way to daylight."

"How long are you going to stay here?"

"Sam and I will stay to try to slow down the building of the dam. I just want to keep the water from rising as long as I possibly can, and keep the Weavers off your back. Who knows how long it will take us to find a way out?"

"Who knows if there's even a way out at all?" she countered.

"Well, if you want to pray," John said, "I'm certainly not going to object."

Ruth sloshed her way upstream, singing an old Lutheran hymn about mighty fortresses.

John set the energy pistol to the tightest beam it could produce. He blasted away the largest rock in the Weavers' dam, releasing a flood of water around his thighs but also prompting gunfire from outside. A ricocheting bullet struck him in the leg, but its force was mostly spent, and it only stung him.

Sam returned fire.

John picked the largest remaining boulder and blasted it to bits. A third shot sputtered and died, so he swapped pistols with Sam for a reload.

He heard clicking sounds outside, and then Weavers swarmed toward the entrance. John fired, killing two in the mouth of the cave before the others retreated. The dead Weavers clutched spears, rather than firearms.

"They're sentient," John said. "They've figured out we get two to three shots and then have to reload."

"Maybe it makes sense to let them dam us in," Sam said. "I think I'd rather take my chances with the water than with the Weavers."

"We need time, though," John said. More rocks fell from above, splashing them with water and damming the stream again. "And I'd rather fight them here than in the darkness."

He blasted open the dam again.

Sam reloaded.

John shot three Weavers who tried to swarm in through the opening.

"This is the last spare energy cell." Sam handed the energy pistol to John and took his gun back. "After this, we have to start opening up our multitools."

"Okay," John said. "We start the retreat."

Rocks fell again, and he and Sam turned and hurried up the stream.

CHAPTER
TWENTY-FOUR

John shone the light of his multi ahead of them as they clambered over rocks covered with a wide, thin sheet of flowing water, and into another large chamber, this one without an opening to the sky. Turning, he flashed the light behind them, looking and listening for any sign of the Weavers.

"A second dog," he muttered. "Of all the things in the world I could have right now, I'd give a lot to have a clone of Ani."

"Can the Weavers see in the dark?" Sam asked. "How good is their sense of smell?"

"I was just about to ask you the same thing."

They hurried on. They exited the chamber through a narrow crack, which required them to press their arms and knees against one wall and their backs against the other and move like crabs, sideways. Beneath his feet, John saw flowing water of unknown depth, with glowing blue dots floating lazily within it.

The water was rising.

The next chamber was the biggest they had been in thus far, and its center was a raised plateau, around which two streams flowed to converge and then exit through the wall. John searched and found a big silver X marked on the wall near where one stream entered the chamber. Before leaving the room, he scampered up on top of the plateau.

"What are you doing?" Sam called, heading straight for the exit.

"There might not be a better place to place an ambush."

"Yeah, but if you wait to set an ambush, you're letting them catch up."

Sam was probably right. Still, John shone the light of his multitool around the top of the plateau. It was twenty by thirty paces, roughly rectangular . . . and there were ruined buildings all across its top.

John knelt to get a better look. The walls that remained were of stone, waist high. The rocks were fitted together so tightly that John sometimes had to put his eye right next to them to be certain there were two stones, after all. The walls had once been higher; tumbled stones lay on the floor of the chamber, scattered about.

"John!" Sam called. "I'm not waiting!"

John turned to leave, but a flash of white caught his eye. Looking back, he saw that the walls inside the structures were plastered.

Like the Stone Gardens.

Sam harrumphed and left. The hair on the back of John's neck prickled as he considered the possibility that a swarm of Weavers was just outside the chamber and about to enter, but he didn't hear anything, so he took a deep breath and walked the length of the plateau, shining his light in and around the ruins.

He found two skeletons.

All flesh on the bones was gone. He saw strips of what had once been some kind of fabric about the pelvis and thighs of both skeletons—kilts? Or trousers? One wore a leather skullcap. The other had a scythe in its hands.

John had no background in archaeology, and he knew his history mostly from watching historical action-adventure flicks. But a scythe and a skullcap? He grabbed them both, tucking the skullcap into a pocket.

"Help!"

John paused. Had he heard a voice? It had been faint, if he had.

"Help!"

"Hello?" John walked back the way he'd come across the plateau. The hair on his neck stood up. Could there be creatures in this cave that mimicked a human voice? Predators, even?

"Help!"

He was certain he heard it the third time, and it came from the stream Ruth and her group had not marked. He set the scythe down to free his hand. Then John edged his way around a puddling stalagmite until he stood in the stream. Water splashed over his legs and he shone the light of his multi up into the crack from which the water emerged.

"Who's there?" he called.

He saw a flash of brown skin in the light. "It's me! Janae!"

John didn't recognize the name, but he knew the voice: Post Chief Carlton's daughter.

"This is John Abbott! Can you get down?"

"I'm stuck! Can you come get me?"

Forcing himself not to imagine Weavers at his back, John climbed up into the water. It splashed all around him and made his handholds and footholds slippery, but a minute of determined climbing brought him to the girl. He shone his multi's light on her to see what was wrong.

Janae's face was wound tight into an expression of fear. "My foot is caught."

John plunged his hands into the cold water. The girl's ankle was trapped between two rocks, and he struggled to pry them apart. At first, they didn't budge, but with his long, narrow fingers, he was able to sink his grip deep around the stone on two sides and try again.

"I was in the front," Janae said. Her voice sounded higher-pitched than before, and words poured out of her like automatic fire. "And then they said to go the other way, and my buddy went, but I was stuck and no one noticed." She clutched John's shoulder. "Can you help me? Please help me!"

The stone moved and Janae was free.

"Quickly!" John said. "But carefully!"

He shone his light on the descent and Janae let herself down and began crossing the plateau. John's own climb down was more reckless, little better than a jump. He skittered across the stalagmite, grabbed Janae by the hand, and listened.

Was that the scraping sound of something approaching over the rocks? Weaver claws?

He grabbed the scythe in the hand that still held his multi, took Janae's hand with his other, and headed upstream after the others. Turning his multitool light on, but only dimly, and holding up the hand with the scythe and multi in front of his head in case the ceiling abruptly lowered, he scampered out of the chamber.

The run felt hours long, but could not have lasted more than a minute. Rock walls loomed up and disappeared again, stalactites stabbed at his head, and boulders and rivulets tried to trip. Through it all, he dragged Janae Carlton and tried to protect his head.

"Ow!"

John ran into Sam, not seeing him in the gloom.

"Where'd you get the knife?" the engineer asked. "And why are you trying to chop my head off? Hey, you found a kid!"

"Her name is Janae. And it's not a knife, it's a scythe. Look." John pointed out the blade that curved back.

"Yeah, but it's not on a pole. Look at the handle. And see how it's sharp down here? This is like what the Gurkhas fight with."

"It's not a kukri," John said.

"But it's *like* a kukri."

"Why are you stopped?"

"Turn off your light."

John turned off the beam, and saw. There was light in this chamber, and it came from above. It was a dim illumination, and it took John's eyes a moment to adjust. The bluish glow filtering down from the top of the chamber was daylight, and at the top of the chamber, ten meters above John's head, it lit a broad dirt shelf. The floor of the shelf sloped and twisted, and became a corkscrew slide packed hard with pebbles, steep but traversable, that descended to the water's edge.

The lower part of the chamber was wide but short. The water here sprang from the chamber wall as if through a spout.

The road didn't go on; it went up and out.

The rest of the children and Mrs. Jenkins were stretched in a winding line, up and around the dirt corkscrew, stopped just below the dirt ledge. Ruth stood at their head, and she held the revolver in her hand. She, and Sunitha and Ellie directly behind her, were perhaps six meters from daylight, and Ani crouched beside her.

But between them and the exit crouched a lion.

"Hatty," John heard Pianki chattering. "Hatty, hatty, hatty."

The lion was bigger than Earth-lions John had seen; it had the general dimensions of a bull. Its hide wasn't tawny, but dark brown, with a deep reddish note in its mane and in the hair at the tip of its tail. Its snout was longer than a lion's should be, giving its head a canine, Greyhound-ish look, and it had teeth too big for its mouth—they jutted up and down, like the teeth on a wild boar, or on a saber-toothed tiger.

"Hatty!" Pianki was nearly shrieking. One of the older girls wrapped her arms around him and put her hand over his mouth.

There were three more of them, approximately the same size and description, though they lacked the thick red mane. The four beasts curled languidly together on the dirt slope.

"I could shoot that thing," Sam murmured.

"You have eight bullets," John said. "Ruth has six. I have two shots with the energy pistol. You feel confident we can kill all four of those animals?"

"You feel confident we can sneak out past them without a fight?" Sam countered.

"I don't feel confident about anything right now," John admitted.

He heard definite clicking noises behind him. He pushed Janae toward the other children.

"Weavers coming!" he called to Ruth. "We're going to have to shoot. Can you back away? Maybe the hatty will calm down."

Ruth eased backward two slow steps, Ani growling at her heels. "Maybe the hatty will get angrier," she replied.

John kept his eye on the hatties. "Give 'em hell, Sam."

Sam leaned around the rock and unloaded his magazine into the passageway. The boom of the pistol was loud in the chamber, and the muzzle flash was bright.

RRROOOOOOOOOOOAARRRRRRRR!

The hatty opened its mouth, showing an enormous maw with a bright red tongue and gums. Ruth took two more steps back, but didn't run. Ani growled, her tail so low it brushed the ground.

Sunitha rummaged around inside one of the shoulder bags, looking for something.

The other three hatties stood, all growling.

Sam reloaded.

An answering torrent of bullets poured out of the passage. The schoolchildren crouched on the corkscrew, making themselves tiny and hunkering beneath schoolbags and wadded-up raincoats. Mrs. Jenkins was saying encouraging things to them. Ellie started to sing.

"I might stop volunteering for school outings," Sam said.

"I don't think we can hold the Weavers here," John called.

"Collapse the passageway!" Ruth called. "Cave it in!"

"You brace yourself!" John's heart didn't feel like it was beating at all. "That monster might jump!"

Ruth eased back another step and crouched. She was holding Ani back now, and shushing her, but she had the pistol out front, squarely aimed at the hatty's face. If that beast ate John's wife, it was going to get a serious punch to the snout first.

Whatever Sunitha had been looking for, she found. She held it, trembling, crouched in the shadow behind her mother.

"Get ready to jump back," John advised Sam.

Bullets rang sporadically out of the passage, but the clattering of Weavers' legs on stone sounded like hail now.

"Wait," Sam said.

He leaned in front of the passage and fired three quick shots into it, then pulled back.

In answer, the clattering of feet stopped, and an eruption of bullets vomited forth.

John stepped to the side and fired into the height of the passage. He targeted the loose fill around a heavy boulder, blasting it to dirt-vapor and gravel with one shot. The light and heat in the enclosed space were intense, and the hatty reacted, roaring again.

Ani burst into loud barking.

John felt his limbs shake and his heart hammer. Was it possible his heart could beat so fast from sheer adrenalin that it would derail itself, detach from the rest of his chest and kill him? That wasn't a risk doctors had warned him about, but in this moment, it seemed possible.

The boulder fell with a heavy *CRUNCH*. Dust exploded out sideways and up, and John suddenly struggled to breathe. Sam leaned around the passage opening and fired again, now over the top of the fallen boulder and down, into a newly appeared, narrower tunnel mouth.

The answering fire struck Sam and knocked him down.

"Dad!" Gary Chen broke ranks and ran down the corkscrew.

"Again!" Sam yelled.

The big hatty roared.

John fired, and then fired his third shot, pale and weak, both at a dagger of stone that hung over the opening of the tunnel. With an immense *GROAN*, the rock swung one way, then the other. A Weaver emerged from the opening beneath, a rifle in its forward pincers, and the rock plummeted, smashing the Weaver to jelly and plugging the hole.

The level of the water around John's legs had already risen ten centimeters.

"Stay away from the hatties!" he called. "The water will rise, and we'll just float out with the water. Those things are like cats, they won't want to stay in here and get wet!"

But all four hatties were advancing on Ruth.

John dragged Sam out of the water and handed him to Gary. "Just help your dad walk," he told the boy. "We're getting out of here."

Ruth backed away, pulling the dog with her. "For about one minute there," she called, "I thought we were just going to walk right out past some sleeping cats."

"What happened?" John asked.

"The big one wasn't sleeping."

John was acutely conscious of the fact that his energy pistol was spent. He thought Sam might have an empty magazine, too. "The hatties have to smell the water," he said. "Let them smell the water and get uncomfortable and leave on their own."

"And if they wait by the entrance to try to fish us out as we float past?" Mrs. Jenkins's voice shook.

"Then we shoot them," John said, trying to keep his voice as calm as he could.

The water reached the bottom of the corkscrew. "Can everyone swim?" Sam asked.

The kids all nodded or said yes. This was good, though they all had shoes and coats on, which was not ideal swimming garb. But above all, what the children needed right now was a tonic against fear.

"Good." John pushed Sam and Gary ahead of him, leaving himself as the bottom person on the corkscrew. "We're just going to swim right on out of here, and then boy oh boy, are you all going to have an adventure story to tell your families."

Mrs. Jenkins's laugh sounded like a squeal of pain, and she covered her mouth with both hands.

The water rose. John let himself float, half-supporting his weight with a hand gripping the chamber wall. Sam and Gary were overtaken by the rising water, too—Sam's breathing was hard and fast, and the sound of it made John wince in pain.

The red-maned hatty took a step toward Ruth and roared again. John smelled the monster's breath now, and it stank of meat and blood. The other three beasts paced left and right behind it, tails switching, muzzles twitching as they sniffed the air.

Had John made a mistake?

Ani barked and lunged forward.

The red-maned hatty opened its mouth and roared, and Ruth fired the revolver into its open maw.

She got off three quick shots, and John was pretty certain they all hit. The hatty staggered back, swiping with a paw that missed Ruth, but knocked Ani off the corkscrew. The dog fell, plunging into the water beside John, and he scooped her up.

The other three hatties leaped forward, and Sunitha fired a flare at them.

The orange firebolt struck one of the hatties in her flank. The beast leaped sideways, yowled, rolled, knocked over another hatty, and then bolted out of the cave.

Sunitha launched another flare. This one didn't hit any of the hatties, but struck the back of the cave wall above the dirt shelf and hung there, burning. The remaining two unmaned hatties fled.

Ruth stepped forward, pressed the muzzle of the revolver against the maned hatty's head, and fired her remaining three shots. The creature jerked spastically and then lay still.

"Go!" John cried.

Ruth led them to daylight. Her first steps were slow, as she reloaded the Webley, but then she picked up speed. Ani climbed over and crawled under the line of children to get to the front, and went at Ruth's side. Behind her, pushed and harangued by Mrs. Jenkins, came the class of children.

Finally, Sam and Gary Chen, and John.

"Without you, we'd be dead," John told Sam.

"Without Ruth, we'd be dead," he answered. "Without the dog, we'd be dead. Without you, we'd be dead. Without Gary, *I'd* be dead." He tousled his son's hair. "We're all heroes."

They sloshed their way up the corkscrew.

"We can't go back to the truck," John said, as he reached the huddle of children in the mouth of the cave. "I think it's probably two long days of marching before we get back to Arrowhawk Post."

He checked his multi; still no network.

"Nyoot Abedjoo is a lot closer than the post," Pianki said.

Three other children were nodding.

John took a deep breath. "Your village it is. Ruth—do you want to take the front with Ani? I just need to pull a bullet out of Sam here, and then he and I can bring up the rear."

CHAPTER
TWENTY-FIVE

"But greater than these is love," Ruth said. John was listening to the recording of her sermon on his multi as he trudged along. He could listen and still watch the woods around them for signs of Weavers or other threats.

It had been a good sermon, and John regretted he hadn't seen it in person. She was winding up now. "The love of the good Samaritan may be beyond you and me—that's the love of Jesus. But you and I are called at least to show the love of the innkeeper, and to care for the wounded whom the great good Samaritan entrusts to our care."

"Is it my imagination," Sam asked, "or is that kukri made of bronze?"

John raised the curved weapon to look at it. The metal was furred green and white, and he hadn't thought about what that meant—he'd been too busy keeping an eye over his shoulder for possible Weaver attack.

"Uh . . . or copper, right?" he said.

"Weird, isn't it?" Sam asked.

"I guess I hadn't thought about it." John considered. "Maybe Pianki's great-great-grandfathers, or whoever the first settlers were, were light on metals."

"So they learned how to mine and smelt copper?" Sam frowned. His expressions and movements since John had patched the two bullet holes in his body were light-headed, a little whimsical. Ruth had given him something from the first-aid kit, and John thought it might have been an opioid. "They came on a starship. I think it would be easier to salvage bits of the ship. Must have been tons—literally, tons—of interior metal as well as the hull. Learning how to smelt copper, or worse, copper and tin both so you could make bronze, so you could make this seems . . . frivolous. Like an act of art."

"Maybe that's exactly what this is." John hefted the weapon. "Or maybe it's a mistake to think this was made by humans. Maybe it was made by the Weavers."

"That handle is a good fit for a human hand," Sam said. "I don't think it's a good fit for a Weaver claw."

"Then maybe it wasn't made by humans or Weavers," John suggested. "Maybe it was made by some species that has hands like humans do. There are Sarovari creatures that are analogous to lions, and to elk. Maybe there are Sarovari primates. The Riders I've heard about, what do they look like?"

"Sarovari indigenes who smelt metal and make swords? That's what you're saying?"

"I guess that's what I'm suggesting."

"Maybe that's it." Sam nodded. "I just don't feel very reassured at the thought."

The skeletons by which John had found the curved sword had certainly looked human, but maybe in life they had had green skin, or fur covering their faces. Or maybe those skeletons had been human, but they had been the skeletons of people who had found an older artifact, the curved bronze sword made by an unknown Sarovari primate.

Sarovari Man, John thought. Homo Sarovaricus.

He knew that the United Congregations, like most other Earth religion practitioners, had adapted their theology to the idea of other intelligent species in the cosmos. It would be hard not to, with Zaphon and Illig merchants and diplomats present and visible in Earth's capitals. But how would Uncle Christopher react to the discovery of a cousin of humanity on an alien world? He should ask Ruth what she thought.

Or was it possible that Pianki's ancestors had been on Sarovar Alpha longer than three or four generations? That they had lived in caves hundreds of years ago, as Pianki himself had said?

John shook his head. He had other things to worry about right now.

They had hiked steadily uphill since agreeing to follow Pianki to his village. John had regularly checked his multi, and never yet seen the network reappear.

Now they were climbing up to an elevated zone surrounded by three gray stone crags. The lower part of the slope they ascended was thick with evergreens, but halfway up, the trees disappeared.

The slope was still covered by stumps, so someone had cleared its upper reaches deliberately. At the top of the hill was a stockade wall, similar to the enclosure that surrounded Arrowhawk Post, but not nearly as tall, and made of timbers. A wooden blockhouse with a plank roof stood at the end of the path, its gate closed, and two men stood on the wall beside the blockhouse. They leaned on spears and watched the party approach.

Pianki ran forward, waving his arms, and the gate was opened.

John hiked the last sixty meters looking backward, sweeping the trees a final time with his eyes to be certain that they hadn't been followed by Weavers. Ani trotted back to join him from the front of the procession, and they were ushered inside the stockade.

The settlement was built around a crystal-clear lake, fed by a spring and by two different melting snowpacks on the crags. 'Village' was too humble a word for the community, which had packed-gravel roads, groundcars and trucks. The stockade, taking advantage of the natural rock walls of the high valley in which it sat, enclosed not only the lake and a small town, but many acres of vegetable garden and a sheep pasture. Two of the town's gates, John now saw, were narrow, permitting foot traffic or beasts of burden, but the third gate was larger; a smooth gravel road emerged from it and descended the hill, running south and west in the direction of Arrowhawk, and just inside the gate was a packed gravel field where several trucks stood.

People in kilts and turbans ran to meet them as they came through the blockhouse gate. There was surprise on their faces as they gathered several children out of the class. Pianki ran into the arms of a woman who looked familiar to John. Then the people of Nyoot Abedjoo began interrogating Mrs. Jenkins.

In the absence of the children, John would have liked to give a simple, coordinated and rehearsed story about a broken-down truck, to avoid panicking anyone. But there was no way that twenty school-aged children would all keep secret the fact of having been attacked by Weavers with rifles. So instead, they had agreed that John would explain first what had happened.

John had voted that Ruth or Mrs. Jenkins should explain, but he had been outvoted.

As he stepped forward to relieve Mrs. Jenkins and recount why they were delivering children home directly from this field trip, though, Sam Chen collapsed.

Two men picked Sam up and carried him deeper into Nyoot Abedjoo.

John followed the two men to a square wooden building down by the lake and the crowd followed. They bubbled with questions, but John waved them off. In front of the square building, two men with bandaged limbs sat on woven chairs playing a boardgame that involved moving pawns around a three-by-ten grid. A cross stood outside the building, but inside, visible through large windows, were four rooms, three with a simple bed each. The fourth had a medical diagnostic scanner, an old multipurpose unit John had seen before in an aging hospital in lower Manhattan, a printer, and a pharmasynthesizer.

The local children were whisked out of sight. The rest of the children, and Mrs. Jenkins and Ruth with them, were plied with hot drink and cookies. Ani was given a bowl of meat, and John found himself finally surrounded and trapped by men and women with questioning eyes.

"We had an incident," John said. "No one died. The only serious injuries were sustained by Sam, the man you've . . . whom you are very kindly treating. And my dog."

He got a mix of responses back, some of which were blank stares. He tried to remember his Sedjem.

"Nee moot ra," he said, digging deep into his memory of Sedjem words. "Hatty nee semamoo." *Semamoo* meant *kill*, didn't it? "Neb ank." *Everyone is alive.*

"You tell us what did *not* happen," said a man with no eyebrows and skin that was so tan, it was almost orange.

"He calms us," a woman with short hair and multiple rings in each ear said. "He puts us at ease."

"I know my granddaughter is not dead," Orange Man snapped. "Perhaps now I can know what happened."

"Dashroo aha." John knew the voice even before he saw Rock muscle his way through the crowd. "Weavers attacked. Weavers with guns." He looked John in the eye. "Tell me if it isn't true."

"It's true. Mat poo." John wasn't sure whether to feel apprehensive about Rock's presence—the man had killed Gonzalez!—or relieved that Rock lifted from him the burden of persuading these people of a strange and shocking thing.

"Is it revenge?" Orange Man asked. "For our raid?"

"Maybe," Rock said. "Though attacking children is an evil revenge for the death of a criminal."

"I was there," John blurted out. The villagers stared at him, and he felt he was revealing a secret, but if Rock was talking openly about Gonzalez's death, then the people of Nyoot Abedjoo must know about it.

They must have been the armed country-setties who had fired on the two traders.

"Where?" Rock narrowed his eyes.

"Bourbon Lake," John said. "I saw...how Gonzalez died."

"Good." Rock spat. "And today, you saw *why* he died."

John hung his head. "I didn't want to have this conversation under false pretenses."

"I kind of like you, Abbott," Rock growled. "I think you might be an honest man."

"On my good days," John said, "I think I might be, too. You're willing to have this conversation...openly?" He gestured at the crowd of men and women surrounding them.

Rock nodded, and the crowd rumbled in satisfaction.

"I'm not sure I understand why Jefferson and Gonzalez thought to start selling weapons to the Weavers," John said. "And I don't know why they thought they could get away with it."

"They thought they could get away with it because they're traders," Rock said. "Have you not seen who's in charge in Arrowhawk Post?"

"But they had such a good thing going," John said. "Why not just trade a few years, make the money you need, and then go home? Why ruin the trade for everyone after you, for a little extra profit?"

"I see why you're an honest man," Rock said. "You're naïve."

"That's not fair."

"Not fair, but true. I'm an honest man, too, John Abbott, but I'm an honest man for a different reason—I simply don't give a damn anymore. At least, not about the things that the Company and all its traders think I'm supposed to care about. I'll tell you why Jefferson and Gonzalez and the others are doing what they're doing."

"I'm listening." Did this conversation ultimately connect with the missing bales of Weave, the stolen revenue?

The villagers continued to show John a mix of facial expressions. Some still stared without comprehension, but others looked angry or anxious.

"Aristotle taught us that there are four ways to answer the question why," Rock said.

John blinked. "Aristotle?"

"The Greek philosopher."

"Yeah. Uh, go on." He had not expected the conversation to take this turn. What had Rock done for a living, before becoming a Company trader?

"Formal, final, material, and efficient. Or in other words: in what shape, to what end, made of what stuff, and caused by what cause."

John thought he was following. "Okay."

"The form is an old one, that plays out around the knees of any Imperial power. Corruption among the servants of the Empire and ambition among the leaders of the conquered leads to a wicked bargain. Money and the pleasures of the flesh are swapped for power and the ability to kill."

"I'm following you, except with the Imperial part," John said.

"May your naiveté be a shield to you," Rock said.

The crowd watched and listened to Rock intently, nodding.

John's shoulders felt heavy. "Go on."

"The material is the rotten stuff of mankind. Few are the men who can be persuaded to care beyond their own insatiable desires, and those few never, ever go into sales."

"Believe me," John said, "we accountants are in it for our own self-interest, too."

"The efficient cause is that the Weavers approached Jefferson and Gonzalez and asked. I believe they had been observing humankind, and had seen weapons in use against wild animals—such as the hatties you met today, perhaps. Having lost too many battles against the long spears of the country-setties over the centuries, they saw an opportunity to become better-armed than their rivals."

"Decades," John said. "Not centuries. Right?"

Although the bronze kukri suggested it might indeed be centuries.

"Centuries," muttered a one-eyed man wearing an undyed kilt and turban.

Rock ignored John's question. "I would like to think that it's just bad luck that the Weavers approached two eminently corruptible traders. But as I said, humankind is rotten. Whoever the Weavers approached would have reacted the same."

"You don't mean that," John said. "If you'd been approached, you would have said no. Because . . . Nefreet. Because . . ." He waved his arms, trying to encompass the village.

Rock looked at his feet. "No, John. If I were approached *now*, I would say no. In fact, I am doing what I can to fight against Jefferson and the others. But if I'd been approached before I knew Nefreet . . . I know my own heart well enough. It's to my eternal shame that I say that I think I'd have taken the deal."

John felt tired, his limbs heavy. He could hardly process the fact that he was having this conversation with a man he had taken to be little better than a bear. "There's a fourth one. What's the fourth one? The goal?"

"The final cause," Rock said. "The object or purpose for which a thing exists or for which an event takes place. From the point of view of Jefferson and his ilk, the final cause is mere wealth. Wealth, with no desire to leave anything behind for others. From the point of view of the Weavers, though, the object was to get rid of the competition."

"The country-setties with their long spears," John said. "And maybe also one day the post itself?"

"Maybe."

"Arming the country-setties . . . I'm not saying I disagree." The puddle of faces surrounding John grew abruptly cold, and John felt his spine grow stiff. "No, I'm in favor of people being empowered to defend themselves. But long term . . . armed mutual hostility at best gets you détente. It's not enough."

"There's no taking the weapons back," Rock said. "If these people disarmed, they'd only put themselves at the mercy of their enemies. No sense in that."

"I agree with that. Genie's out of the bottle. And look, this is none of my business, I'm new here, and I get to live a sheltered life in the post."

"For now," Rock said.

John nodded. "And I'm naïve, fine. But the thing is, people might leave each other alone when they're both equally armed, but that's a situation just waiting for an imbalance to materialize and trigger a war. People embrace peace when they have something in common."

Rock stared. "You've *seen* the Weavers, right?"

"I know they look strange." John nodded. "And I find them . . . terrifying. At least when they're shooting at me." He turned to face the largest group of people. "What happened today is that we were in a cenote, in a cave, for school. And Weavers with guns attacked. We don't know why. We escaped through the cave, thanks to Mrs. Jenkins and Sam Chen and Ruth, and we had to frighten away some hatties on the way out. There is more detail, but that's the whole story." He pivoted back to Rock. "I'm just saying . . . trade, man. You can dislike traders all you like, and you're not wrong in any of the things you say. But it's the traders who bring peace in the long term."

"If they're properly controlled and supervised," Rock said. "Maybe."

"Lack of supervision might be one problem," John said. "But another problem is that we have a situation with huge imbalances to begin with. One side has firearms and starships. The other side weaves cloth."

Rock snorted.

And Rock was right to be skeptical, wasn't he? The Company deliberately created the imbalances with its monopolies, just as John's own accounting profession kept its wages up by creating monopolies.

"Eventually, free trade—*true* free trade—will even out those imbalances." John said the words with confidence and he even meant them, but in his mind's eye he was seeing what the evening out of imbalances would really mean. The arming of all the Weavers, so that no one was at a disadvantage in trying to project force? The Company's admittance of competing trading companies into the

Sarovar System? Maybe the liberation of the wormhole itself, or the creation of some economically feasible alternative?

"Naïve."

"An optimist," John said. "And look, in our lifetimes, you and I are not going to see a universe in which the imbalances are evened out. In fact, maybe there is no such universe.

"Maybe by the time we figure out how to even out imbalances between Weavers and . . ."—the word 'country-setties' suddenly gave him pause—"Sarovar's humans, new imbalances will arise. Fine. This is why it's important that we teach people to be kind, and generous to the poor, and to play fair." He pointed to the lakeshore, where Ruth and Mrs. Jenkins were leading some kind of game with the children. "My wife's religious. I'm not, not so much. But what she's passing on to my kids, and to the kids she's playing games with, about compassion and love and fair play, is very important. It's important enough that I'll put up with all the God stuff that comes wrapped around it. Without those ideas, free trade is a jungle. With those ideas, free trade is peace."

Rock narrowed his eyes. "I think there's something you should see."

CHAPTER
TWENTY-SIX

Rock led John to one of the three rocky bluffs overlooking the town. The crowd didn't follow.

A curled finger of rock descended from the crag and snaked out toward the edge of the cultivated land in this spot, and a young woman sat on a rock at the end of the curl, rubbing the ears and neck of a black-and-white spaniel.

"Rock," John said as they approached the woman, "do you have children?"

"Yes," Rock said.

They reached the young woman and the dog, and Rock nodded to her. "Ronit," he said, "we mo. Just a short time." *Mo* meant *look*.

Ronit scratched her cheek with her thumb and nodded.

Inside the curl of rock, a crack in the face of the bluff descended steeply into the earth and became a cave. John followed Rock, and when the darkness swallowed them, both men turned on the lights of their multitools. John didn't feel completely at ease going into the darkness with the trader who had killed Gonzalez, but he had Sam Chen's pistol in his pocket. He forced himself to avoid patting it for reassurance.

He clutched the bronze weapon and his multi in his left hand, because he had to use his right to steady himself as he went down. The gray stone of this cavern was damp to the touch in places, but didn't flow with water like the caves at lower elevation. The air was close and humid. The crack tumbled down through a ragged zigzag passage, and then opened into the top of a chamber. The rock here was mottled with white spots. Scarred with the marks of picks, an artificial ledge had been hewn into the rock to permit passage across the top of the cave.

Rock walked several steps out onto the ledge and stopped. John joined him. Both men were too tall to stand on the shelf in comfort. John hunkered over, trying not to straighten his posture and accidentally knock himself into the abyss. Rock stood in a slouch that seemed practiced and relaxed.

Shining his multi's light down, John thought he saw the cavern floor, a sandy bar some fifteen meters below.

"We don't need to go any farther," Rock said.

"If there's a better stopping place . . ." John said.

"You need to see this." Rock drew a long knife; John retreated half a step, deeply aware of the fall to his left, his hunched stance, and the fact that it would take him several seconds to grab the Kupari and shoot, if Rock wanted to attack. John held the scythe, but he had no confidence that he knew how to fight with it.

But Rock applied the tip of his blade to a white spot on the cavern wall. Touching it to the very center of the dot, he pressed gently, and a shimmering silver ooze trickled out.

"Okay," John said, bending his wrists back and forth. "What is that?"

"That," Rock told him, "is Sarovari Weave."

"It looks like pus."

"It does. But you can dry it, and then spin it into fine thread, and then weave it."

"Is that . . . is that a mineral secretion of these caves? Or am I seeing the root of some kind of plant that extends really deep into the rock?"

Rock pressed the tip of his blade against the rock at the edge of the dot. Working slowly and methodically, he edged around the dot's outside, pushing the steel beneath the white material. Disconnected from the stone, the white material curled inward, and when he had worked his way entirely around the dot, he tucked his knife under the curling white mass and tugged.

The white mass came away from the wall. Behind the fist-like curling clump, a stem extended into the stone. Rock pulled, removing the white thing. The stem became more slender, and as it was removed from the stone, it suddenly twitched, and then curved one way, then the other, like a snake held in midair.

John discovered that he was holding his breath. He inhaled, put his hand against the stone to steady himself, and found he was resting his hand on a white dot. The dot was noticeably warmer than the stone around it, and he pulled his hand immediately away.

Rock finished pulling the stream from the rock. The slender white thing moved in a probing fashion, pushing its tip forward and swinging it around, then pulling back again. When it probed toward John, he saw that at its tip was an opening, circular. Like the mouth of a lamprey, only instead of visible teeth, it had something like gums, and they were as white as the rest of the creature.

Most of the creature. Around the circular mouth-like opening, the thing had a ring of red beads that might have been eyes.

"This is the thing that makes Sarovari Weave," John said.

"Really, this is the thing that makes Sarovari Thread. The Weavers turn that thread into Weave."

"What do they eat?"

Rock grunted. "Not really sure which end of this thing is the head and which end is its ass. It seems to get some nutrients out of the limestone, because if you try to put it into any other substance, it withers and dies. But it also gets nutrients out of the cave. The flat visible part seems to absorb moisture, and nutrients that are in the moisture, and . . . here, let me see." Rock backed away a step along the ledge, scanning the rock wall. "Look at this one."

John looked. A beetle-like insect sat still on one of the white dots. It wasn't dead, because it had antennae that wiggled back and forth, but when Rock touched it with the top of his knife, it didn't retreat.

"It's stuck to the . . . cave snake," John said.

"We call them Spinners," Rock said. "I don't think they have another name. I don't think the Company officially knows they exist at all. And yes. It's being slowly digested. Come back in a week, and you won't see a bug here at all."

John pulled his hand away from the wall and glared in suspicion at the white dots near him.

"They're harmless to humans," Rock said. "You're just too big. Apparently, the Spinners choose when to release the chemicals that trap and dissolve their prey, and they know the difference between a bug and, say, a dog."

"So they eat insects," John said.

"And lizards. And the Spinners can live underwater, thrive underwater, in fact, and they eat fish and amphibians. And very small mammals, little mice and such. Small snakes."

"You've cultivated these. You put them here deliberately."

"Not me. But my wife's people, yes."

Rock held the Spinner near the hole from which he'd pulled it. The questing tip of the white creature found the opening and began to ease itself inside.

"And your wife's people can do the weaving, too?"

"Their thread is not as fine as what the Weavers produce. The Weavers have some technique, or some tool, the country-setties don't have. Which means that the Weave the humans make is a little rougher, not as beautiful."

"But it still has the other properties?" John asked.

"Tough as hell. Elastic. Self-healing." Rock nodded. "Yes. And the country-setties are much better at caring for the Spinners than the Weavers are. I think it might be because we have fingers. But I've seen a Spinner cave run by Weavers, and the population wasn't nearly as dense as what you're seeing here. And this is far from the densest population, even in this village."

John was rethinking many of his wrong assumptions about the economy of Sarovari Weave. "So you could bring it to market now."

"I'd call it Sarovari Rough. We'd sell it cheaper than the Sarovari Fine, and in bigger bulk."

John thought through the consequences. "Industrial purchasers would buy from you. Uses in manufacturing, construction."

"Armor," Rock said. "Even some clothing. Any use where you didn't need a superfine weave and a superhigh thread count, you could buy from us, cheaper."

"Which means less demand for Sarovari Fine."

"The Weavers would sell less, and so would all the traders who trade with them," Rock said.

"At the current high price points," John said. "But the Weavers could keep selling as much as they do now, by dropping their price. Consumers would benefit. The country-setties would benefit."

"The Weavers would lose."

"This is why the Weavers wanted weapons," John said. "Because they know the country-setties have the ability to move in and soften their market."

"Bear in mind that we are talking about *some* Weavers," Rock reminded him, "and *some* country-setties. But yes."

"Do the Weavers understand economics?" John wondered out loud. "Are they thinking through price points and demand, or do they just not want anyone else to sell Weave?"

"That's a subtlety that doesn't really make a difference when the issue is a Weaver with an automatic rifle, crawling through your village at night and shooting people."

"So you armed the country-setties," John said.

"The ones I'm close to," Rock admitted. "And their kin."

"And you intercepted Jefferson and Gonzalez at Bourbon Lake."

"Trying to shut off the flow of guns to the Weavers. And bear in mind, you're oversimplifying. The Weavers who traded for weapons with the Arrowhawk traders are using those weapons to oppress other Weavers, too."

"Stopping anyone else who sells Weave. Do they take the Spinners from the Weavers they kill?"

"I don't know." Rock shrugged. "Or are they just deliberately restricting supply, so they can get the largest number of screwdrivers and hammers for their Weave?"

"Screwdrivers, hammers, and guns," John said.

"Welcome to Sarovar," Rock said.

"Where do the guns come from?" John asked.

Rock took a deep breath and sighed. "I think you ought to consider the possibility that you don't really want to know that information."

The Spinner had entirely returned into its hole in the wall. The curled white fingers of its fist-like protuberance were beginning to straighten out.

Rock still held the knife in his hand.

"I'm new here," John said. "Just out of school. I'm in debt, and I don't even have the money to get back to Earth. I'm committed, me and my family both. And Director English sent me here to find out why revenues of the post are down. If I can't find the answer for him, and it means that I get fired, or can never get a promotion, or I'm not allowed to trade . . . then I've sunk the ship, and my entire family on it."

"And do you know the answer?" Rock asked.

"I *think* I do," John said. "I can't prove it, but I think Jefferson and whoever else is in on it with him have been stealing Weave from the Company take to buy more guns. They're accelerating the problem of guns among the Weavers, but they're also accelerating their own wealth, getting closer to the day when they retire rich."

"So turn Jefferson in," Rock said. "While you're at it, turn in Tasto and Grandi. Gonzalez, you don't have to worry about anymore. Turn them in and let English sort them out."

"Maybe." John considered. "But when I gave him a partial answer before, he sent me back to finish the work. I don't think English is the kind of boss who wants to work *with* me. I think he wants me to bring him a completed solution. Were you embezzling Weave, too?"

Rock shook his head. "I used my own take to buy guns for my people. Also medical supplies and sometimes other things. The country-setties can benefit from the Company's presence even when it doesn't mean to help them. Told other traders I was selling in the country trade instead of shipping home."

"So Jefferson and the others thought you were saving up Weave and other Sarovari commodities to bring home with you."

"I think Jefferson knows the truth now. If I tell you who sold me the guns," Rock said, "and you turn them in, and English investigates, it could get back to those people that I gave them up. And they're the kind of people who have lots of guns, and are engaged in an illegal trade, and don't want to get caught. Which means that, if I tell you who sells to me, then I'm putting my family at risk—Nefreet, but also my children, and this entire village."

John nodded. "That's true."

"And those same people, by the way, know who you are and they know your family. So you get to share the delightful risk with me."

"How do they know who I am?"

"You idiot," Rock growled, "you're a Company man. You live in a big khat, you work in Company House, you're still wearing shoes from Earth. The country-setties who cleaned out your house to make it ready for you knew you were coming, and they told the whole post.

How do you think there was a line of people around your khat the day you arrived, asking for jobs? You can't hide, Abbott. Not here. You stick out like ten sore thumbs and a giraffe."

"You're not offering me any solutions," John said.

"I'm not sure there are any. Not good ones, anyway."

"Your solution is war," John told him. "You keep buying guns yourself and you stop the enemy Weavers from buying guns, and then when you feel comfortable in your advantage, you attack."

"Wrong," Rock said. "War is here. War is a fact. My solution is to win the war."

"I want to figure out a solution in which there is no war," John said. "No threat to your family, and no threat to mine. But I can't even think through the possibilities unless you're willing to tell me who it is that sells you guns."

Rock nodded slowly. "It's men from Company Security Services."

John frowned. "Korsgaard?"

"Two agents out of Henry Hudson Post who often work Arrowhawk. They call themselves Diaz and Choat, but those aren't their real names."

John felt dizzy. He steadied himself against the rock wall. "I need to think."

"Let's get fresh air," Rock suggested.

They threaded their way back along the ledge, up the zigzag, and out into the open air. Rain struck John's face as he passed Ronit and her guard dog. It was cold but not refreshing. He felt numb.

Reflexively, he checked his phone, and found he had a network connection again. "Who do you think shorted out the network?"

Rock shrugged. "Can't have been the Weavers. Jefferson and his friends?"

"Or Diaz and Choat? Which means they might be afraid that I'm going to upset their trade."

Rock sighed. "If so, I'll hear about it. They've been happy to sell to me and Jefferson both. But if they think I'm helping you shut down their business, that will change really fast."

"If two agents are willing to sell arms to the locals, maybe they aren't the only ones. Maybe the entire security service is selling guns."

"The Company couldn't be that stupid," Rock said. "The Company has to think about the long term. Individual traders or cops might be happy to shit in the pond, because they plan to leave it, but the Company can't deliberately arm forces that might drive it off the planet."

"I don't know," John murmured. "Maybe the Company is happy to sell rifles, knowing it can drop bombs from orbit if it has to."

"No easy solutions," Rock said. "You could join me. Help me win this war."

"I don't think I can," John said. "I don't think you and I together can do it. I think I need to take this to Director English."

CHAPTER TWENTY-SEVEN

John called Faisal Haddad to ask for a ride. Several of the children called their parents, too.

John and Ruth walked once around the lake while waiting for the transportation to appear, and John explained everything he could remember keeping secret from his wife to this point. Ruth asked a few questions, and John answered them, and then John explained what he planned to do.

"Obviously," Ruth said, "the girls and I will stay here while you contact Director English, just in case these security service agents decide they want to stop you by kidnapping us."

She had anticipated his next words. "If that's okay with you," John said.

"It sounds like going back to Henry Hudson would only have put us in the sights of the corrupt security men," she mused.

When the parents of the children who lived in the post arrived, John took them aside. He explained that Weavers had attacked the school field trip, and that they had weapons. He told them that this was a problem he was working with Company leadership to solve—but that, just in case, it was probably a good idea to keep the children home for a few days and see what shook out.

They asked questions, and John mostly didn't know or didn't feel free to tell the answers, and then the post families left. Sam and Gary Chen stayed at the village; Gary looked shaken up, and Sam said he thought a day of fooling around in the lake might help him relax. He took back his Kupari. John and Faisal mounted up on Faisal's ATV. John had the Webley and bullets.

Faisal exited the stockade through the wide gate and onto the smooth gravel road.

"Did the people of Nyoot Abedjoo grade this road?" John asked as they descended the hill.

"The Company did," Faisal said. "There was an existing track, and the Company improved it."

"The Company doesn't trade with the country-setties." But could it? Should it?

"But many of them are employees," Faisal pointed out.

John explained the situation as they traveled. "You'd better drop me off," he said as he finished, "in case there's trouble."

"I will watch the door to Company House," Faisal countered, "so whatever trouble there is does not catch you by surprise."

The sun set as they approached Arrowhawk Post, throwing vermilion streaks across the meadows and deep blue shadows into the woods. The Irregulars at the gate waved them in, and Faisal took John first to his house, to leave the corroded bronze knife and skullcap. Then he dropped John off two short blocks from Company House.

"I will be watching," he promised.

The doors were locked and Company House was dark other than the Security office. Payne slumped in a seat at his desk, dozing. Working the metal key, John stared up at the haphazardly stacked headquarters of the post and thought about all the secrets it contained. Secrets of theft and bloodshed. He sighed.

He locked the door behind him and left the lights off. Climbing the stairs in the darkness by sense of touch and pure spatial memory, he paused at the accounting desk. Commissions were too high for revenue. That meant that whoever was doing the calculations knew about the stolen Weave and went ahead and counted it anyway. That could only have been done by very few people. In particular, it could have been done by Keckley.

Why had it been done that way, in any case? It was a trail that didn't need to be left. Jefferson and his coconspirators could have pulled Company Weave out at the beginning, and simply paid traders less commission, and the clue wouldn't have been left at all. Maybe they couldn't do that because not all the traders were in on their scheme—Rock had named only four of them. If every trader coming back from the wat was calculating his own commission, the way to keep skimming hidden from those men was to pay the commission they expected, and then take some of the Weave.

Or maybe it was just greed, and Jefferson hadn't been able to resist double-dipping—insisting on his full commission even as he was stealing from the Company.

In either case, the only way this embezzlement remained unnoticed was with the cooperation of Audit Chief Keckley. And how had Keckley prevented the Company's auditors from noticing? Some note of explanation in the accounts that were transmitted to Henry Hudson, maybe?

John sat at the comms panel, inserted his encryption plug, and attempted to contact Director English. The blue glow of the panel's lights on the plastic of the windows warned him that, despite his precautions, he was not invisible here. He wished there were curtains he could draw. He took out the Webley, checked to be certain it was loaded, and laid it on the comms panel.

Director English appeared. He wore a dark blue suit that looked to John like evening wear. "John."

"I've got more information," John said. "It might not be enough to make arrests on, but I think it's at least enough for you to investigate."

English looked about him. Behind the director, John saw velvet curtains and dark wooden panels. Was that jazz music he heard?

"Hold on," English said. "Give me five minutes, and I'll call you back."

The line went empty again.

Five minutes. That might give John time to do a little research. He pulled up the accounting tools on his multi and looked for quarterly packets transmitted to Henry Hudson. He had access, and it took him only two minutes to do the math to verify that, in the two most recent quarters at least, the commissions paid by Arrowhawk Post were calculated on higher revenue numbers than had been recognized.

Skimming.

But what about an explanation? John found a note documenting that commission payments had been authorized at a higher rate than standard due to exceptional performance. Was that, after all, the explanation? Had John chased a mirage? Only he had chased it into a gun-smuggling arms race, so it hadn't been entirely a will o' the wisp.

Something about the note nagged at John. What was it? It seemed in order, formally correct. It answered John's question, so it was on point.

And the note bore Post Chief Carlton's signature.

Only John had seen the chief's signature at the Tiger of Mysore, and the signature on the note didn't match it. That was what was wrong. Carlton's signature was a series of loops, bold and graceful. The signature on the note tried to loop, but its curves were cramped and angular.

Someone had forged the signature. Had English noticed, too?

English reappeared on the comms unit. A marble wall and ferns now appeared behind him. "Go on."

John set his multi down on the console. "You'll recall a trader died."

"Gonzalez," English said.

"Gonzalez was one of four men who were stealing Weave from the Company. That's why the post's revenues have been down. And maybe you already noticed this, but the post was paying commissions on the higher numbers, the Weave take before the embezzlement. I suspect this was done to keep honest traders in the dark."

"So not all the traders were in on this?"

"As far as I know, Gonzalez, Jefferson, and probably Tasto and Grandi. They were embezzling so they could have more cash to invest in a . . . side hustle."

English's eyes narrowed. "What kind of side hustle?"

"They've been buying weapons from a couple of men in Security Services. Diaz and Choat. And selling them to the Weavers."

"The two men who threatened you?"

John nodded.

"You can prove this?"

"I have a witness," John said. "I suspect that more audit work will turn up more evidence. For instance, those four traders have been doing something with the extra Weave they made on the side. Likely, the wormhole's shipping records will show that they've shipped much more than any of the other traders, or sold more to the Central Transit Broker. Or if neither of those is true, maybe we'll find they all have crates of Weave in a warehouse somewhere." There would be a trail of some kind.

"Very good." English steepled his fingers. "So that's the next avenue of your investigation."

"I'm very happy to do that," John said. "But Diaz and Choat... you know they've already threatened my family. And the situation here at the post, with the Weavers in the area being armed, it's ... precarious." He did not say, *This is really not what they taught me to do at NYU.*

"You want me to find and remove Diaz and Choat," English said. "Do you have pictures of them?"

"That's what I want," John agreed. "I haven't got pictures."

English nodded, frowning. "And what do you expect me to do about the armed Weavers?"

John sighed. He hated to suggest that the solution was more weapons, but it was hard to see any way around that. "Can you strengthen the gate guards, at least? Maybe have a squad of the Post Irregulars accompany every trading wat?"

Or he could ask Carlton. Maybe the post chief would be relieved her daughter was safe, and provide what John asked. Unless, of course, she was in on the fraud.

But if she were part of the scam, the signature on the note about the disparity between revenue and compensation should have been genuine. Didn't the forged signature suggest Carlton was innocent?

English nodded. "Hold on. I'm at a Company ball, so this is a little awkward. But give me some time to investigate a few of these things, and I'll call you back." He ended the call.

The connection terminated. John looked up from the comms unit, and found himself looking down the barrel of a shotgun.

DeBoe was on the other end of it.

"Hey," John said. "Easy, I'm not trespassing."

"You're definitely poking around where you don't belong." DeBoe's mouth was flat, his eyes tight.

John's heart sank. "The quarterly accounts. You transmit them." It wasn't Keckley covering for the corrupt traders, after all.

"You wouldn't know that from the files themselves," DeBoe said.

"You'd have to check the comms records. But sooner or later, you'd have checked. You might even be doing it tonight."

"No," John said. "I was telling English what I knew."

"Don't think you can frighten me," DeBoe said.

"Did they cut you in for some of the stolen Weave?" John asked. "Or would that look too strange? Maybe they just paid you in cash."

"Goodbye." DeBoe raised the shotgun to his shoulder.

"Stop." Faisal Haddad stepped from the shadows of the stairwell. He pressed something to DeBoe's temple, but John could see that it was only the mouth of a flask. "Lower the gun."

DeBoe spun with the shotgun.

Faisal threw himself sideways.

John grabbed his revolver off the comms desk, aimed for the center of DeBoe's mass, and pulled the trigger. The weapons went off simultaneously. The plastic in the windows of the door into the Comms room cracked with the impact of DeBoe's shotgun, but didn't break. John's shot hit DeBoe in the shoulder rather than in the chest, because he'd been turning.

DeBoe dropped his shotgun and fell to the ground.

Faisal grabbed the weapon and pumped the action to chamber another round.

"The white groundcar," he said. "It was arriving as I entered the building."

"Diaz and Choat." DeBoe clutched the bleeding wound in his shoulder. "You can't leave me here."

"Suddenly you're my problem?" John shook his head.

Maybe Payne would slow Diaz and Choat down. Maybe Payne would help them.

"They'll kill me," DeBoe said. "Please."

Faisal stepped into the stairwell. "Footsteps," he hissed. He tiptoed to the edge of the stairs and fired a blast down with the shotgun.

Gunfire rattled in response. The shots came not from the stairwell, though, but from outside.

"What's that?" John asked.

The other two men shrugged.

"We can't go down the stairs," John said.

"We can get down to the warehouse roof from here," DeBoe said. "Just open that window, and it's only a three-meter drop."

"You're going to tell me everything," John said.

DeBoe's face was pale. He nodded.

John grabbed the encryption bolt and pushed open the window. Faisal dropped the shotgun first and then lowered himself. With only one arm, DeBoe had a harder time, but managed to fall onto the warehouse roof without breaking a leg, and then John went last. It was awkward, but he pulled the window most of the way shut before jumping down to the rooftop.

They stood in the swampy darkness between the Comms office and the nearest column holding up the maglev tracks. The sound of gunfire was louder, and became more constant.

"Where is that coming from?" John asked.

Faisal pointed. "Outside the walls."

The Weavers were attacking Arrowhawk Post.

"There's a trapdoor in the roof." DeBoe pointed. "Hurry, before Diaz and Choat catch up."

"Shh," Faisal said.

John looked up in time to see Diaz approaching the window. He was illuminated from behind, so his face was in shadow, but it might be the best image John would get. He whipped out his multi and took a short moving image. The security agent turned, giving John a reasonably good view of his face before he disappeared back into Comms.

KABOOM!

John turned to see the post's gate in flames. Irregulars in the street fired at the Weavers, who spun forward, trying to get into the post. A shrill klaxon sounded.

"What now?" Faisal asked.

John shook his head, trying to clear it. His family wasn't in the post, but the families of many other people were. He needed a solution, and he needed one that encompassed more than just the embezzlement.

He tried dialing English's number, and got no response.

Maybe English wasn't responding because John wasn't using the encryption device?

John's eyes fell on the ladder rungs on the maglev column.

"We're going up," he said.

"That's stupid," DeBoe said. "That's just for guideway maintenance. What are you going to do, walk to Henry Hudson?"

"You're welcome to stay here." John began climbing.

He cast repeated nervous glances over his shoulder into Comms as he climbed, and saw neither Diaz nor Choat.

At the top of the rungs, a square opening was punched through the concrete of the maglev guideway. John was careful to avoid touching the metal rails, and once he was on firm concrete, he reached a hand down to help DeBoe up the final stretch.

Faisal followed, climbing with one hand and lugging the shotgun with the other.

John sent a simple text message to Director English: *The post is under attack. Diaz and Choat are here. This one is Diaz.* He forwarded the moving image he'd just captured.

"Faisal," John asked. "Do you have family?"

Faisal's hands trembled and he was sweating. "Not in the post."

"I have an idea," John said. "I think we can fix this."

"Good," Faisal said. "If this place is destroyed, I do not have a home on Earth to go back to."

The maglev guideway was a U-shaped concrete trough with a magnetic rail running along the side of each wall. John led the way, running away from Company House. At the point where the maglev guideway crossed over the stockade wall, he leaned against the concrete to look down. There was little gunfire on this side of Arrowhawk—the Weavers seemed to have concentrated their attack on the gate, which was on the west, on the far side of the post. Did that mean the Weavers were few in number? Maybe they were counting on surprise to achieve a victory, or maybe they weren't tactically very sophisticated about their target. Maybe they didn't even want to conquer the post. Or maybe they just wanted to scare the humans inside, into giving them better trade terms, or into withdrawing.

He checked his multi; no answer from English.

A thought struck him, and for a moment his heart seemed to have stopped beating.

He had dialed English from the post's Comms office. English had disconnected, then contacted him again, and then Diaz and Choat had come.

Was it possible that English had *sent* Diaz and Choat?

Hands shaking, he found the confidential reporting line. It wasn't hard, there were links to it in almost every company app. His hands shook because he was going over English's head, potentially. But English wasn't answering.

And might be his enemy.

"Internal Audit," the voice on the other end of the connection said. It sounded human, but was no doubt programmed. "This is the confidential reporting line. You do not have to identify yourself, and will only be contacted if you choose to be. Please tell me the information you wish to share."

"I'm transmitting a moving image," John said. "It's of a man who claims to be an agent of Company Security Services and identifies himself as Diaz. Together with another Security Services agent who identifies himself as Choat, they have sold firearms to traders of Arrowhawk Post for resale to Weavers. In addition, this man Diaz threatened me and my family for investigating his activities. My name is John Abbott, I'm an Auditor at Arrowhawk Post. Please contact me."

"How's that going to help us get off this train track?" DeBoe asked.

"It might not," John admitted. "But if we don't make it off the maglev guideway, it may help someone else ensure that justice is done. And also, sooner or later, it might just bring the cavalry."

But John had no intention of waiting to be rescued.

They kept going. John was gambling that there would be a way down from the tracks, and the gamble paid off. A kilometer and a half beyond the wall, another hole in the floor gave way to rungs leading down. This ladder was blocked by an iron crate with a lock and keypad, but Faisal's shotgun proved an adequate key, and they dropped down into marshy meadow.

"Where are we going?" Faisal asked.

"First," John said, "back to Nyoot Abedjoo."

CHAPTER
TWENTY-EIGHT

They walked through the darkness to reach Nyoot Abedjoo.

John tried three more times to reach Director English on his multi, and got no response.

Internal Audit also didn't call him.

John's legs felt like knots of wood by the time they staggered up the mountain toward the village, but he was in much better shape than DeBoe. The other accountant had fallen four times in the darkness, and each time, John had been progressively more astonished that DeBoe managed to drag himself to his feet and continue. Under the light of moons and stars, John could see that DeBoe's face was white as a sheet, and sweat poured profusely down from his elusive hairline.

At the bottom of the slope below the village, DeBoe finally collapsed and lay still.

Faisal, who hadn't complained once, knelt to check the man's pulse. "He is alive. We should get a healer down here to look at him. I shall stay here and guard him."

DeBoe probably didn't need guarding to be certain he wouldn't run away, but he might need protection from hatties or shay. Or Weavers.

John staggered up to the gate, and it opened for him. At his request, men ran down to collect DeBoe, and Ruth and Rock were summoned to a meeting on the shore of the lake. Two village elders, a woman and a man, joined them, as did Faisal. Without being asked, Sam also showed up.

Sam's presence was good. John could use his skills.

John told the group what he knew, and also what he feared.

Then he explained his plan.

"You're insane," Sam said. "We should all get off this planet, right now."

"Some of us can't," Rock said. "Besides, did you hear him? What if English *is* behind the gunrunning? All English has to do is tell Central Transit not to allow you to board, and you can't leave, either, even if there is a starship leaving right now, with an empty berth. But I don't think this can succeed."

"Okay," John said, "I'm open to other plans. What do you think will work?"

"The Weavers of Bourbon Lake aren't home. We attack them now. Wipe out the nests. Ambush them when they return."

The elders both grunted their approval.

"You're assuming that the nest you're thinking of is the nest the Weavers came from," John said. "But maybe there are more armed Weaver nests than you know. Or more Weavers. I couldn't count the force attacking Arrowhawk Post, but it didn't seem huge. If there are still significant numbers of armed Weavers in the nest we attack, then we're charging to our deaths."

"We can attack the Weavers at Arrowhawk Post, then," Sam said. "If they're laying siege, we attack them from behind. Or we ambush them when they turn and head home."

Rock and the elders nodded.

Looking at the elders' faces, wizened and calm despite the emergency, John suddenly thought he could believe that their people had been on Sarovar Alpha for centuries.

But if so, had they come from Earth?

And how had they got here?

"That's a better plan," John said. "But all you're doing is upping the ante in this war. You killed one of their suppliers, they attack the post. You kill a bunch of their fighters, what's next?"

"We stop them from getting more weapons," Rock said. "We kill Diaz and Choat. Or we arrest them, if you think that's meaningful. And we take the arms from the Weavers we kill, and establish a permanent superiority over them."

"There will be more Diazes and Choats, as long as there's money to be made," John said. "And no superiority is permanent."

"But it might last thirty years," Rock said.

"Which only makes it your children's problem," Ruth pointed out. "John is talking about a permanent solution."

"Long term, at least," John said. "But if we benefit everybody, hopefully we can create something stable and enduring."

"How do you plan to carry this out?" Rock asked.

"You know exactly how it will work," John answered. "We run it like a wat. Like you've done a hundred times."

"Five hundred," Rock said. "More than five hundred."

"Only instead of screwdrivers or guns, we offer them something different."

"Establishing a new wat is a bit different from going to an existing one," Rock said. "They won't be expecting us. They might be nervous and touchy, especially with what's going on at the post. We'll need to bring gifts."

"They *will* be nervous and touchy," John agreed. "So we won't even *try* to trade this time. We'll *just* bring gifts."

"So the worst-case scenario is that the Weavers attack and kill everyone on this expedition, take our wealth, and continue to make war on us."

"That's always the worst case," John said. "We'll bring armed men."

"We'd be taking a lot of risk."

"I'll be right there, taking it with you."

"I don't really have a fitting vehicle," Rock said. "We have beasts we can ride and a few cars, but the only cargo carriers we have are wagons, and they'll move really slowly over to Bourbon Lake."

"Do you want a solution?" John snapped. "Or do you just want to list the problems for me?"

"I know where there's a vehicle," Sam said.

The others all looked at him.

"The school truck," Sam said. "It'll carry a lot of cargo. And it's all-terrain. And it's not that far from here."

"The Weavers might have taken it," Rock said.

"I doubt they've figured out the technology," Sam said. "Especially since I have the key. And lots of the controls are touch-screen, which require you to toggle them with soft tissue, like a fingertip or a padded stylus. I don't think the Weavers will even be able to figure those controls out. And I also doubt they've destroyed the truck. It's pretty rugged, and I left it locked."

"They might be lying in wait," Rock said slowly.

"Sure," Sam said. "There are armed Weavers at the truck, and at the post, and hiding in ambush along the roads to and from the post, and also in their nests, waiting for us. Anywhere else you think there are armed Weavers, waiting to attack? Maybe on our satellites? Central Transit Station? Company House in Henry Hudson Post? In my bed?"

"Point taken." Rock's voice was sour.

"I'll go with you to look at the truck," John said. "And if we don't come back, you're only down two men, you can still launch an attack if you like."

"Down three," Faisal said. "I am coming, too."

"But if we bring the school truck back," John continued, "will you come with us up to Bourbon Lake? To make peace?"

Rock offered his hand and they shook.

"Just in case," John said to the trader, "could I have a bit of metal foil?"

"John," Ruth said. "This is not a great time for it, but your girls could use a hug."

John looked his wife in the eye. She was drawn and lean, as if the recent days had leeched muscle from her body, and she had wrinkles around her eyes he had never noticed before. He took her in his arms and held her.

"I didn't mean *me*," she murmured, but she didn't resist.

The sun was coming up as Ruth led him to a hut beside an open firepit. The building had solar panels on its roof; looking around, John spotted other solar collectors he had missed on his previous visit. What exactly were the lives of the people of Nyoot Abedjoo like? And where had the solar collectors come from—had those, too, been unintended benefits the Company had bestowed on the country-setties?

"Rock got us this house," Ruth said. "He has influence here."

Inside the hut, John's daughters sat on a wide bed, plugged into separate lectures by Factor Doctor. Ellie saw John first and ran to wrap herself around his knee. "Dad-setty, there are so many kids here!" she squealed. "And Ani is famous!"

As if in answer, the dog came bounding in through the door, followed by two smaller dogs in a rowdy game of chase.

The barking alerted Sunitha, who hurled her multi to the mattress and flung herself around John's neck. "I'm so sorry!" She burst into a flood of sudden tears. "I'm so sorry!"

"You have nothing to be sorry about," John said, hugging her back.

"I'm sorry, Dad!" she kept saying through her tears, and, "I know what matters now!"

Was this post-traumatic shock from the encounter with the hatties? John looked at Ruth.

"Several of the village children have had a very rough day," she said softly.

John squeezed his daughters as long as he felt he could, and then peeled them off so he could rejoin Sam and Faisal.

They borrowed three horses from the village to ride to the truck's location. The horses looked just like those John knew from Earth. "Are these indigenous to Sarovar?" he asked Rock. "Or did the Company bring them for their cowboys? Or the pre-Company settlers?"

Who perhaps had arrived centuries ago.

Rock shrugged, tightened the horse's saddle cinch, and handed John the reins.

They rode back toward the sinkholes where they'd left the school truck. It seemed like a hundred years had passed; had that only happened yesterday? John nodded off from time to time, but his horse's gait was measured, and he never fell from the saddle. Sam, who remembered the map well, guided them in consultation with Faisal's multitool.

John had turned his own multi and Sam's multi both off, removing the subscriber chips and wrapping them in a bit of metal foil Rock had given him, for fear that Security Services might use the chips to track their location.

Before deactivating his multitool, John had checked the Weave shipping app. To his surprise, his sole shipment to date was marked SOLD—PRICE CONFIRMATION PENDING. Had English somehow changed his shipment, and sold it to the Central Transit Broker? Or did that designation just mean, really, that the Weave had shipped? Or was there something about the process that John hadn't understood?

On his multi, Faisal got news that the Weavers had been repulsed from the streets of Arrowhawk Post, but were still camped about it in the woods and meadows. Security services were being sent from Henry Hudson to relieve the defenders.

Disabling his multi meant that Internal Audit would be temporarily unable to reach John, of course, but he'd given them the crucial information he had.

The three riders dismounted near the top of a forested hill, to walk through the evergreens and stay lower to the ground. The dirt here was dry, padded with needles, and gnarled with roots and cracked stone. They avoided lingering on the brow of the hill, crossing quickly around to the front of it to stand among pines and look, hopefully unobserved, on the meadows below. The sinkholes appeared as shaded smudges around crescents of gray stone.

"The truck is where we left it," Sam said.

"There are Weavers," Faisal said.

"How can you even tell?" John asked.

Faisal used the photo lens of his multi to zoom in, and then they all saw the Weavers, waiting in a loose circle around the vehicle. Black flecks on the screen suggested that they were armed.

"Well, maybe Rock is right," Sam said. "Maybe there *are* infinite armed Weavers, and all we can do is kill them."

"If there are infinite armed Weavers, we don't stand a chance." John studied the meadows. "Well, Sam, clearly we need you to drive. So, Faisal, either you're the decoy or I am."

"I think being the decoy sounds like the most fun." Faisal grinned. "And I do not even know what the alternative is."

Faisal nudged his horse forward and descended the hill by a different path from John and Sam's, going right where they went left. Without his multi, John had only an approximate sense of time, but he drifted left and circled around, trying to get close to the truck without leaving the cover of the trees.

The signal came that the plan was in motion: a gunshot.

John and Sam stuck to the trees still, creeping forward, and watched to their right. At the meadow's edge, they saw orange gunfire flashing in the early evening gloom, and then Faisal, galloping away from them, toward distant trees.

"Now," Sam said.

They spurred their horses into a gallop. Racing over the marshy grass, John worried about the many things that might go wrong. There could be more Weavers than he'd detected or imagined; indeed, they already knew that was the case, since there were Weavers protecting the truck. Were there so many here that they hadn't all been drawn off by Faisal? Or were they simply canny enough not to fall for the ruse? Or might they have set traps, on or around the vehicle? They had already showed, at the post's gate, that they were masters of the use of explosives, but it needn't be anything that technologically advanced—a simple ditch dug around the truck would stop John. Or worse, a ditch with spikes at the bottom.

He told himself to focus on the prize.

The prize was the front segment of the truck, which faced them. He scanned the grass for signs of the Weavers and saw none. Faisal disappeared from sight, far away, and then John and Sam reached the vehicle. John positioned himself beside the truck's chassis.

Sam took the reins of John's horse and handed him the keys; John had wanted Sam to drive, but Sam didn't think he could climb with his injuries, so John now stood in his horse's saddle, holding himself steady with two hands on the truck. With a short jump, he managed to grab the railing around the roof compartment.

Then he was drawing himself up and Sam was riding away.

John followed Sam's retreat, and noticed that the tall grass moved around the horses' hooves. Weavers? To give Sam cover, and draw the attention of any Weavers, John fired into the grass with his revolver.

He saw two Weavers rise up from the grass and then break away from Sam. One of them was bleeding, which made John uneasy. If he wanted to make peace, he was going to have to stop fighting.

He had really hoped there would be no Weavers still watching over the truck.

Then he ducked, and only just in time. Bullets ricocheted off the chassis of the school truck from several directions. The truck's plastic windows cracked, but didn't break, and John rushed down the trapdoor and into the driver's compartment.

With a turn of Sam's key, the truck started instantly. John looked forward and saw Weavers rushing toward him. They spun in rapid circles to move in a straight line, planting their radially symmetric

legs ahead of them one at a time. Since each held a single rifle in a
pair of pincers, the rifles spun around in a circle.

John could run them over, but he didn't want to. Instead, he
jammed the truck into reverse and stomped on the accelerator. The
truck's big wheels churned up a wave of muddy water before John's
eyes, hurling it across the advancing Weavers.

The Weavers stopped.

John shifted back into forward, swing the wheel hard right and gave
the truck power. Orange flame stabbed from the Weavers' weapons
and a spiderweb of cracks sprang instantly across the plastic of the
truck's windscreen. Beyond the Weavers firing at him, John saw a
second wave of the circular crab-like things, and beyond that wave, a
third. Weavers leaped in front of the truck, but this time John didn't
hesitate to run them over. The plastic wouldn't hold forever, and with
two hard thumps, John was past the Weavers and picking up speed.

Bullets rattled along the side of the truck, cracking more
windowpanes without breaking them. These vehicles might be
cobbled together by engineers out of spare parts, but they were solid.

John was heading north toward the rendezvous point when he
saw Faisal.

He was lying on his back, and Weavers were dragging him. He
was alive, because he was waving his arms and legs, but he was
overwhelmed, and he was bloody.

Alongside Faisal, the Weavers dragged the severed head of a
horse.

They weren't moving fast enough to get in John's way; he could
adjust his course and miss them, moving up into the hills and back
toward the village.

But they weren't *trying* to get in John's way. They stopped and
propped Faisal up, and waited.

John sighed.

And braked, and stopped the truck.

He climbed up the ladder to the rooftop compartment and raised
his hands over his head. "Don't hurt him!" he called. He tried to
think of Sedjem words. "No kill!" What was *kill* again, was it *aha*?
No, that meant *fight*, but maybe it would do. "Nee aha! We want mat!
I nee aha! You nee aha! Mat!" *Semamoo*, that was *kill*. "Nee
semamoo! Nee semamoo!"

"Mat," one of the Weavers groaned. "You hefty."

"Hefty?" Inanely, John fought not to giggle. Soft rain began to fall on him and on the Weavers and Faisal. The Weavers shuddered as the water hit them. "I'm thin."

"You hefty, you nee mat."

"Faisal, can you hear me?" John called. "I don't know that word, is it Sedjem?"

"Hefty." Faisal groaned. "He's saying you are his prisoner."

CHAPTER
TWENTY-NINE

John and Faisal were thrown into a vehicle together. John saw no sign of Sam.

The outside of the vehicle looked like an ice cream cone spackled with sticks and rocks. John was reminded of Earth creatures—crabs, weren't they?—that camouflaged themselves by covering their shells with pebbles and bones and bits of detritus. If this cone were lying on the forest floor, John might mistake it for a thicket, or debris left behind by a flash flood.

Weavers stripped off Faisal's clothing. John flinched and stepped back, but Weavers pinned him in place. They wrapped Weave tightly around Faisal's wounds, stanching the flow of blood.

"Mat," John said. *Peace.* "Want mat. No semamoo."

"Hefty," a crab behind him groaned. *Prisoner.* "Nee sedjem." *Don't talk.*

The wide end of the cone was capped with a covering of Sarovari Weave. At first, John thought the cone was sealed shut, but after a Weaver wrapped a length of Weave tightly around Faisal's wrists and another around his ankles, two of the crab-like creatures shoved Faisal against the end of the cone and he passed right through.

They took John's pistol and the foil-bundled multitools, wrapped his hands and ankles, and shoved him through, as well.

They lay on a pad of Weave, within a cocoon of Weave. John reached up with joined hands and pulled the entrance open a hair, which permitted him to see six Weavers take up lengths of Weave that were attached to the wide end of the cone, like traces at the front of a wagon. Each Weaver wrapped the end of his length of Weave around his circumference, but not entirely. Then they began to run forward in a synchronized fashion. The ones on his right ran forward spinning clockwise, while those on his left ran forward spinning counterclockwise. Each pulled the Weave against his body forward, but also ran with the motion of the vehicle, so that the Weave never wrapped itself around his body, but stayed in place by friction and dragged the cone along.

The cone went from a bumpy amble to a galloping pace that would match that of a horse in the space of a minute.

John wanted to make a joke about rope burns to Faisal, but the fixer was drifting in and out of consciousness.

They weren't going to kill him. Or at least, they weren't going to kill him immediately. If they only wanted him dead, they could have done it when he climbed out of the truck. Was it possible the Weavers had a sense of honor, that they would refrain from killing someone who surrendered?

They had language, after all. They were sentient. They could be bargained with.

Or maybe they wanted something from him. Was it possible that they had lain in wait around the truck specifically for the purpose of taking John prisoner?

Maybe they would trade him for guns.

The cone carried them for several hours, with Faisal poised on the edge of sleep and groaning. Light filtered in through the Weave cap over the broad end of the cone, until suddenly it didn't, and then the cone stopped.

"Out," a voice croaked.

John dragged himself from the cone and stood. He was inside a cave, not unlike the caverns he'd explored with the schoolchildren, only there was no river. The cave was dim but not dark because it had a skylight, a small, circular opening overhead that was covered with a panel of Weave. The cave was also arid, its rocky floor covered with sand. John saw several Weavers spinning as if to sink themselves lower into the sand, and heaping sand on their carapaces with their claws.

The chamber had only one entrance, guarded by two Weavers

with rifles. The six Weavers who had dragged John here stood ranged around him in a semicircle.

"Want mat," John said. "Nee aha, nee semamoo." *No fighting, no killing.* "Want mat. Want sedjem." He didn't know what the word for 'trade' was. "Want wat."

"Want mat, you oor," a Weaver groaned. *Oor* was *small or weak.* The other five Weavers shook and croaked. Was that laughter?

"Want mat," John said firmly. "Always want mat. Mat nefer."

"Nefer mat," the Weaver said.

Nefer mat? John had said *mat nefer,* and the Weaver was correcting his grammar. *Peace is good.*

"Neferooee guns. Guns reddy mat." *Guns are very good. Guns give peace.*

John didn't have nearly the vocabulary he needed for this conversation. "I nee nebba guns." *I don't have guns.*

The Weavers croaked again, and one of them produced John's Webley from a hole in its carapace. "You nebba guns. Waw always nebba guns."

John was not entirely following the conversation. Were *waw* humans? "Nee reddy guns ees," he said. *Nee ees* was an emphatic denial. "Nee ees. Reddy . . . silk." He didn't know how to say what he wanted. He tried pantomiming a rope, but his hand-over-hand gestures didn't even convince himself.

"You nee reddy guns," the Weaver spokesman said. "We reddy you."

"You reddy me who?" John asked.

"We reddy you . . . guns."

The Weavers promptly spun away, ending the conversation and leaving John in the gloom.

His limbs aching from too much walking, riding, and sleep deprivation, John paced around the chamber. A wad of Weave lay piled up to make a sort of cot or mattress, but it didn't seem any thicker than the pad Faisal lay on currently, so John left him where he was.

Trying to appear casual, John examined the sides of the cave, looking for handholds or cracks he could use to climb, but he found none that were big enough to be of any use. He did find a rivulet of water trickling down the wall, and by cupping his hands together and pressing them against the trickle, he was able to collect a mouthful of water, cold and sweet. Otherwise, the cavern was bone-dry.

He could charge the two Weavers at the exit. He had no way to tell whether they were asleep or awake, they held so still. But it was unlikely that he'd catch them both napping, and with their rifles, they'd shoot him full of holes.

The Weaver had said they planned to trade John for guns . . . John thought. Maybe they'd try to trade him to Rock and the country-setties. More likely, that meant they would offer him to Jefferson.

That might be fine. Jefferson had no reason to know that John was anything other than his friend. Unless, of course, Diaz and Choat had told him something. Or English had.

John sighed. Finally, he checked on Faisal to make sure he was sleeping and then lay down on the mattress of folded Weave.

He awoke several times, the first two in complete darkness. The first time, he called out softly to Faisal and heard only silence. The second time, Faisal answered, moaning that he was thirsty. A little bit by memory and a lot by trial and error, John was able to find his way to the trickle of water again and to carry water to Faisal, one cupped double handful at a time.

Faisal mumbled thanks and slept again.

The third time John woke up, illumination again came down through the opening in the ceiling. He heard the patter of rain on the Weave overhead; the fabric held back the water and let in just enough gray light to see. Faisal was sitting up against the wall, beside the trickle of water, with a shawl of Weave wrapped around his shoulders.

"Mr. Abbott," he murmured.

"I'm sorry, Mr. Haddad," John said. "My plan. My fault."

"Good," Faisal said. "So when they want to eat us, you will volunteer to be first."

John was surprised. "The Weavers eat human flesh?"

"I am just saying *if* they do."

John heard a rhythmic thudding. "Does that sound like footsteps to you?"

"I am not going to stand up," Faisal said. "You will have to be the one who shows good manners, Mr. Abbott."

A brighter light shone in the entrance, and John stood.

Two Weavers with rifles spun into the chamber first, and behind them, walking by the glow of a multitool, came Jefferson. The trader crossed the cave, circling around the cone-shaped cart, and stopped, shining his light on John's face and then Faisal's.

He carried a large pistol strapped to his thigh. A ten millimeter, like Sam's.

"You're prisoners," he said.

John cracked a grin. "I was hoping you would get us out. My Sedjem isn't great, but they were telling me they were going to reddy me to someone. Reddy is give, right? So are we going to be released?"

"I don't know, John." Jefferson smiled, but his voice held a note of menace. "I think if I let you go, you're going to tell on me."

It could be a bluff. Maybe Jefferson was testing him to see if he'd admit to knowing anything. "Tell on you for what?"

"*You* tell *me*," Jefferson said. "Tell me what you know, and I'll decide whether I ask the Weavers to release you."

John knew then that Jefferson had no interest in getting John out. His heart fell. He looked at the Weavers—there were four within earshot. If he couldn't persuade Jefferson, maybe he could persuade the aliens, instead.

"Well," he said, speaking slowly, "it's hardly a secret. Everyone knows you've been buying guns from Security Services and selling them to the Weavers of Bourbon Lake. Meanwhile, someone else has been arming the country-setties of Nyoot Abedjoo." There was no reason to throw Rock under the truck, at least not just yet. "That's no big deal. It's written all over the post accounts; Keckley and I were joking about how incompetent DeBoe is at trying to hide your deals. You know there's an accounting trail for the weapons too, right? The Diaz-and-Choat side isn't even discreet."

"If it's all so open," Jefferson said, "who's been arming the country-setties?"

"One of the other traders," John said. "Whoever killed Gonzalez."

"Don't be coy," Jefferson said. "You were there. You saw it. Who killed Gonzalez?"

John hesitated, uncertain.

"It's not a guess," Jefferson said. "The Weavers saw you. They helped me escape, and in the process, they saw the two of you. That's why they attacked the school outing. That's why they attacked the post. They were supposed to kill you, without casting any suspicion on me. Naturally, I paid them."

"The attacks did rather give away the fact that the Weavers are armed."

Jefferson shrugged. "You assure me that everyone knows that, anyway."

Oops. "And you operated the drone that was following the school truck."

"Pity you spotted me. That would have been a neat solution. Tragic accident, schoolchildren dead, we all mourn together."

"Was it you and Gonzalez who beat me up when I was drunk? Or was that Diaz and Choat?"

Jefferson snorted. "I still thought you were an innocent young factor then, and I was trying to win you over. I have no idea who attacked you."

John's mouth was dry. "Well, the other thing that everyone knows is that now the Company is going to have to act. Rumors of Weaver unrest is one thing, the occasional missing trader is the cost of doing business on an alien planet. But when Weavers attack a Company post with firearms and explosives, the Company has to respond." Could the Weavers possibly understand him? Should he be speaking in Sedjem? But Jefferson would notice that.

"The Company will do no such thing," Jefferson said. "The Company will see to its profits."

"Yes, and profits depend on continued trade. And if it looks like the Weavers of Bourbon Lake are threatening trade, because someone made himself rich by arming them, the Company will bomb Bourbon Lake from orbit." Those words would definitely not make sense to the Weavers. "The Company will kill all the Weavers."

"Company nee semamoo dashroo ees," Jefferson said. *The Company definitely won't kill the Weavers.* "Dashroo nebba guns." *The Weavers have guns.*

Uh-oh. Jefferson had cut him off at the pass. "Company nebba more guns," John shot back. "Company nebba bigger guns. Company semamoo Jefferson, semamoo dashroo." He needed a better vocabulary.

He heard a squeaking sound from the Weavers.

"Bluff," Jefferson said. "Nee mat ees." *It's not true.*

"There's another way," John said. "New wats. Nee aha, nee semamoo, mat for neb." *Peace for everyone.* "New wats."

"What wats?" Jefferson sneered. "If Company want semamoo dashroo, dashroo need guns. You reddy guns? Rock reddy guns?"

So he knew who had killed Gonzalez, and who had been giving guns to the country-setties. Maybe the Weavers had told him.

"No need guns," John said. "Need mat." John liked the fact that *mat* was both *peace* and *truth* in Sedjem. He definitely wanted both.

"Guns reddy mat," Jefferson said firmly.

"No," John said, knowing that the constraints of language were forcing him to tell a partial truth. "Guns reddy semamoo. Guns reddy aha. Guns reddy aha with Company. Company nebba big guns, semamoo but nee mo. Wat reddy ank. Wat reddy mat." *Trade gives life. Trade gives peace.*

He wasn't sure that 'wat' really could mean 'trade,' as opposed to a trading mission or a negotiation, but he hoped that the Weavers would understand, anyway.

"Semamoo, nee mo?" groaned one of the Weavers. *They can kill without seeing?*

"Nee mo," John repeated. "Semamoo far away, you sedjem far away?"

"Far away," the Weaver repeated. "Arrowhawk?"

"Far away Henry Hudson." John pointed at the ceiling. "Far away yah! Company semamoo far away yah!" *The Company can kill you from as far away as the moon!* At least, he hoped that was what he was communicating.

One of the Weavers at the exit squealed and wilted, its legs collapsing and its body sinking to rest on the cave floor.

"Don't tell them this bullshit!" Jefferson snapped.

"Jefferson reddy bad guns." John gestured with his arms, trying to show small, large, and the distant moon in turn. "Jefferson reddy guns oor. Company hebba big guns, semamoo far away yah, Weavers nee mo. Just die. Only moot." He wished he knew more words.

The Weavers were all squeaking now.

Jefferson drew his pistol.

Bang! John flinched, but the flash and explosion didn't come from Jefferson, but from one of the Weavers. The Company trader and gunrunner dropped to the cave floor, clutching a wound in his thigh.

A Weaver scooted forward to scoop up his dropped pistol. Jefferson cursed a blue streak of which Uncle Christopher would have approved.

"Listen," John said. "This can be saved. Still can mat. Wat reddy mat."

"Wat reddy mat," the Weaver agreed. "Wat who?"

"Wat me," John said. "Wat setties."

"Setties aa," the Weaver said.

"What's 'aa'?" John asked.

Two Weavers moved forward with a strip of Weave held between them and began wrapping it around Jefferson's injury. "Nee wat setties!" Jefferson growled, grunting in pain. "Nee wat John Abbott ees! Wat Jefferson! Jefferson reddy guns!"

"Guns semamoo," John said. "Wat me reddy mat."

"Setties aa," the Weaver said. "Wat aa. Wat heroo. Wat setties, wat Jefferson, wat John Abbott."

Heroo was *now*.

Did *aa* mean *here*?

"Good," John said. "Wat aa, wat heroo, wat neb."

The two Weavers who had bound Jefferson now hoisted him into the air and carried him out of the chamber. John slipped an arm under Faisal's shoulder and lifted him to his feet.

"You talk as if you were born here, Mr. Abbott," Faisal said.

"It's the adrenaline, Mr. Haddad. I hope I made sense."

"Well, I think you just got the Weavers to the bargaining table. With you and the gunrunner and the setties, whoever they are."

Unfortunately, there was more than one possibility. "Let's hope they're the right setties."

CHAPTER
THIRTY

John helped Faisal walk through the Weaver nest. He tried not to turn his head too far to one side or the other; he wanted to show respect, and not appear to be snooping. His curiosity overwhelmed his self-restraint, though, and he snuck in peeks left and right whenever he thought he could get away with it.

There was light in the nest, though it was dim. It drifted down from gaps overhead, which were always covered with sheets of Weave. Some of the chambers through which they passed seemed entirely sculpted by water, with rounded curves to the walls, and the buds of stalactites and stalagmites showing like dull teeth in open mouths. Elsewhere, the caverns seemed to have been carved by hand—John saw roughly rectangular rooms that no stream would carve, but angles that were still dull and rounded. Elsewhere still, the rooms were cut to crisp edges and tight corners.

It was all very, very dry.

"Tools," Faisal said. "Once the Company arrived and started selling the Weavers chisels, they carved more precisely. These rooms with the straight edges are the newer ones."

John nodded.

That evolution of building techniques and results raised a troubling question in his mind, though. If the Weavers carved only roundly and roughly before they started buying tools from the Company, that meant that the Weavers certainly hadn't been the ones who had built the Stone Gardens, or the ruins in the caves John had seen on the school field trip. In both those places, the stones had been fitted together so close that there was no visible mortar and often no visible seam. That was precision work, tool work, and apparently work that the Weavers didn't and maybe couldn't do with their pincers alone.

So who had made those buildings?

Process of elimination seemed to leave only the country-setties. He'd have to inquire whether they claimed the credit, though, and what tools their grandfathers had had when they first worked the land of Sarovar Alpha. Maybe the precision work at the Stone Gardens and in the sinkhole caves was the result laser-stonecutting.

Although the plasterwork looked older than seventy or eighty years.

And if the first Earth colonists to this planet made the two ruins John had seen, that still did nothing to explain the corroded bronze scythe he had taken from the fieldtrip cenote.

But how could humans have possibly been on Sarovar Alpha prior to, say, the twentieth century? Had some spacefaring race brought them here? Had they evolved here independently? But that didn't seem likely given that, for instance, Nefreet and Rock had children. Had some secret pocket of Earth humans been spacefarers in a past of which John was ignorant?

John saw the natural courses of streams, barreling their way across and around several of the chambers. In many places, new ditches had been cut, to make a stream's channel more direct, or to render a room dry. Again, some channels had a rounded, almost natural appearance, and others had been carved to crisp corners and angles.

"Dry," he murmured.

"What?" Faisal staggered and nearly fell, but John caught him.

"These caves are very dry," John said. "The cell was, too. They only had a tiny trickle of water running through, but that isn't natural. These caves were made by water, and there's water very close to us, in the form of a lake, and the water table can't be that far away."

"You are saying the dashroo don't like water."

The light in the chamber dimmed. John looked up at the Weave covering the skylight above, and saw the sheet tremble and bounce as rain struck it.

"I'm certainly saying it isn't natural," John said. "These caves were sculpted in the first instance by running water, but look how much effort the Weavers have gone to in order to contain the water or keep it away from themselves."

"Hmm," Faisal said.

Some rooms had gained extra upper stories with the addition of catwalks and new openings carved into upper walls. Chambers rescued from the flow of water had sometimes been given additional levels in the downward direction, where the natural floor of the chamber had been sculpted away to a slender span or two of stone, and perhaps a ledge, and the rest of the floor had been carved down another six meters. In several cases, John saw stories both below and above him.

This wasn't a *nest*. It was a Weaver *city*.

Weavers were everywhere. They seemed to rely on the sun's light from overhead; he never saw fire or an artificial illumination, and for all that he saw the evidence of tool use in construction, he didn't see tools, either, and he only saw firearms in the chamber that was his prison cell and in the wide mouth that exited from the caves; there, six Weavers huddled beneath a limestone canopy on a rocky, gritty shelf, looking down at a sandy floor.

Rock stood on that floor, alone. Behind him, John saw the school truck, parked thirty meters away. Several men sat on top of it and John could see Sam Chen in the driver's compartment through the windscreen. None of the men appeared armed.

The Weavers deposited Jefferson on the sand, pushing him into a standing position. Jefferson swayed, unsteady on his feet, but then he took a deep breath, and the blaze of hatred in his eyes seemed to give him strength. He glared at Rock.

"You killed Gonzalez," he growled.

"I'd do it again," Rock said, "if I had the same cause. I was defending my home. I'd kill you for that reason, too."

"Home." Jefferson spat. "Earth is home."

"Earth *should* be your home. A nice, tidy prison cell, in any federal prison you like, back on Earth."

The Weavers with John and Faisal descended a narrow chute of rock and sand. When John reached the sandy floor beneath the overhang, they herded him into standing at the third corner of an irregular triangle defined by him, Rock, and Jefferson. Faisal stood beside John, taking his arm off John's shoulder to balance, swaying slightly, on his own.

"Only one of us committed a crime." Jefferson sneered. "Firearm laws don't apply in Sarovar System."

"I don't have to hide behind the law," Rock said. "What I did was right. And if anyone disagrees, I'd do it again, anyway."

Two Weavers crawled to a fourth point, making a square. One had a deeply mottled carapace, pink and gray; the other was nearly white.

Did that mean these Weavers were *old*? Elders, leaders?

Other Weavers stood in a half circle around one side of the square, making an arc that ran from very close to John, behind the two elder Weavers, to right beside Jefferson. This line of Weavers was armed—some of them had spears and knives, but half had rifles.

John wished he could read the Weavers' moods. They didn't seem to have facial expressions—they had three faces!—but maybe there was something subtle in their coloration, their posture, or their scent that would have given away, if only John had had the right knowledge, whether these Weavers felt excitement, anticipation, amusement, dread, or suspense.

Just beyond the truck and the edge of the stone overhang, rain drummed onto grass. Down a long gentle slope, dotted with evergreens, John saw a body of water. Was this Bourbon Lake?

Or one of the other thousand lakes within a day's drive of Arrowhawk Post?

"I am called Rattat." The voice had the wheezing, rattling quality that gave it away as the voice of a Weaver, but its enunciation was startlingly precise, and its syntax was English, not Sedjem. The voice came from the white Weaver. He dragged a claw along his own shell as he spoke, adding a rasping accent noise.

"I Chatz," groaned the mottled Weaver.

"We are here to hear an offer," Rattat said. "We think it is new and complex, so we do not wish to leave it to the silent stacking and shifting of crates that takes place in a wat." He scratched himself again.

John found his mouth hanging open in astonishment to hear such a long speech in such clear English from a Weaver. He forced himself to nod and act natural.

"Two offers, actually," Rock said. "But there's something we have to show you, for you to understand our offers."

He held forward a cannister; it was labeled as a container for ground coffee, and for a moment, John imagined the trader opening up a coffee trade with the Weavers.

Chatz wheeled across the open space between him and Rock and took the cylinder. Opening it, he pivoted to reveal the contents to all parties; it contained the white slime that Rock said was spun into thread and then woven together to become Sarovari Weave. What John had ineptly called 'silk.'

"Zenef," Chatz said. Then he touched the tip of a pincer to the glistening white of the stuff in the cannister, and reached beneath his carapace . . . to an unseen mouth, perhaps? "Nefer zenef."

"We cultivate the Spinners," Rock said. "We kat zenef. Nefer zenef. We know it's difficult for you to make it."

Chatz held the cannister out to Rattat, who sampled it in the same fashion. "We know you make zenef," Rattat said. "We do not like that fact. Go on."

"Our first offer is this," Rock said. "We'll buy the freedom of John Abbott and Faisal Haddad. We will give you one Company crate full of zenef for each man."

"That is not enough," Rattat said. "This man has killed Weavers."

"Only when attacked," John said. "You attacked a truck full of children, and I defended them."

"This man has killed Weavers," Rattat repeated.

Rock nodded. "Then we will give you two crates of rifles. One to free each man."

"Rock!" John snapped. This was a terrible idea. Rock couldn't possibly like it, because he was offering to arm the Weavers, who were a threat to his own people. "What are you doing?"

"It's your money," Rock said.

"What?"

Jefferson laughed. "This is rich."

"Ruth bought arms with your money," Rock said. "She said she wants a husband more than she wants her mother's jewelry back."

John buried his face in his hands.

"It is not enough," Rattat said. "Either we will make a deal, and this man will go free because we like the deal, or we will not, and he will die."

John's heart sank.

Rock nodded.

"What is your other offer?" Rattat asked.

"Let me make this pitch," John said. He forced himself to stand still, when his natural urge was to pace up and down the chamber, but he couldn't keep from bending his fingers back and forth with nervous energy.

"It's your idea," Rock said. "And your life, apparently."

John took a deep breath. He heard Jefferson chuckling low, and he tried to tune the trader's voice out. "You know the country-setties cultivate zenef."

"Yes," Rattat said.

"I'm not an expert," John said, "but I think it's good zenef."

"It is very good," Rattat admitted. "It is better than the zenef we steal from our neighbors."

John's intuition started making connections. How thin was the ice under his feet?

"You steal from your neighbors because it's so hard to make zenef."

Chatz grunted.

"Yes," Rattat said. "The Spinners like caves that are wet. And, even with the tools we take from the Company, it is laborious to drill holes in the rock for new Spinners. So we cultivate as many as we can, but we find it easier to take the zenef our neighbors grow."

"This is why you wanted weapons," John said, "guns. To take zenef from other Weavers by force."

He felt exhilaration. Maybe the conflict between the Weavers and the country-setties was purely incidental. Maybe it would be easy to reach a deal.

His excitement was brief.

"And to take zenef from the country-setties," Rattat said. "The country-setties have been our enemies for thousands of years."

Thousands of years.

John tried to stay focused.

"The country-setties are good at cultivating the Spinners and at collecting zenef," John said. "The country-setties offer to sell you zenef. They can make it in greater quantities than you can make it. You can stop fighting with your neighbors, and you can stop fighting with the country-setties." He hoped that Rattat was following him. He'd hate to try to say all this in Sedjem.

"Our neighbors may fight us to take our zenef," Rattat pointed out.

"Hire your neighbors to do the work for you," John suggested. "Make your neighbors friends."

"What do the country-setties want in payment?" Rattat asked.

"It would be convenient if you all decided to switch to dollars . . ." John said slowly.

Rattat said nothing.

"You could also pay in Weave," John conceded. "The country-setties can readily sell the Weave."

"We give Weave to the country-setties for zenef, and Weave to the Company for tools and guns," Rattat said.

"You might not need guns," John said.

"We give tools to our neighbors so they will do some of the weaving for us," Rattat continued. "We stop cultivating Spinners, and we weave more than we used to. If our extra capacity and the capacity we buy from our neighbors exceed what the country-setties require, then we sell more Weave."

"You become richer," John said. "You all become richer."

"For thousands of years, my ancestors have dominated the country-setties," Rattat said.

"We all have history," John said.

"They tricked them, enslaved them, and crushed their eventual revolts. I would betray my ancestors if I groveled before a people my ancestors destroyed."

"No one grovels," John said. "Everyone trades freely, everyone gets rich."

He didn't add, *And therefore no one goes to war.*

Except, of course, the people who were hell-bent on going to war, regardless.

"And then again," Rattat continued, "the Weavers of this water have dominated the other Weavers in the area for thousands of years, as well. You call it Bourbon Lake, but the name of this nest is Atela Anta, and it is a proud and ancient name. Why should I beg my neighbor to do work for me, when my grandfather ate my neighbor's grandfather's flesh? You call us 'Weavers' and the country-setties call us 'dashroo,' but we are the Ochatat, the Always Ready. All fear us. You fear us, or you would not be here."

"I think I prefer it when they can only speak Sedjem," Faisal said.

"I invite you to consider your best alternative to the offer," John said. "Without a deal, you fight. You fight your neighbors, you fight the country-setties. Maybe you even have to fight the Company. You trade the amounts you are trading now, and it costs you more and more of your people's blood over time. Your people's wailing fills your ears. Perhaps they tire of you and replace you."

"I can kill the man Rock," Rattat said. "And buy more guns from the man Jefferson. My people are bold and fearless. We can enslave the country-setties and make them cultivate the Spinners, and give us their zenef. We will pay nothing for this. We can enslave our neighbors, too. Already, many of them are our slaves. Our neighbors will weave while we guard over them. We will pay them nothing, as well. The wailing that will fill my ears will come from the country-setties and from the nests of Weavers who are not us. My name is chanted in songs of victory for a thousand years. Is *this* not my best alternative?"

CHAPTER THIRTY-ONE

"I have the next shipment I promised," Jefferson said. "It's inside the post."

"The post is harder to take than you said it would be," Rattat said.

"But it's almost fallen," Jefferson said. "And I'll get the next shipment ordered immediately."

"This is a terrible idea," John said. "The Company can't stand for one of its posts being attacked."

"The Company barely notices what happens at Arrowhawk Post." Jefferson shook his head. "It's fifteen years old, and the Company has never continued the construction of the maglev line beyond as planned. Arrowhawk isn't even on half the Company maps."

John looked at Rock for confirmation, and Rock nodded. "There are other posts that are richer, so Arrowhawk sometimes gets forgotten."

"Doesn't matter," John said. "What can happen at Arrowhawk can happen at Henry Hudson, or at Central Transit. The Company can't let anyone think that it's okay to attack Company posts. And the Company won't risk any lives on it, either, or at least, not any of their own lives. They'll call down an airstrike."

"This is what you were warning your guards of," Rattat said. "An attack from the larger moon. Some thought perhaps you meant that the Company would destroy the moon."

"Maybe not literally the moon." John felt flushed. "But from aircraft, from satellites. Do you know those words?"

"I have seen aircraft," Rattat said. "You are describing a massive attack from the sky."

"Where will this airstrike be targeted?" Jefferson laughed. "There's no map to Antela Anta. There's no indication in the wat records of sales of guns to any Weaver nest. Don't worry, Rattat, there are no tracks that lead to you."

"If not now, then there will be," John said.

"I am unconcerned," Rattat said. "This is a distraction from our negotiation." He made a rattling sound that might have been a laugh, and dragged a claw across his carapace again. "From our wat. Do you have anything else to offer?"

"You imagine that you will simply buy guns and wipe my people out," Rock said.

"Country-setties," Chatz groaned.

"We won't go so easily," Rock said. "We're willing to seek peace and trade, like John Abbott here suggests. But we're also willing to go down fighting, and we'll kill a lot of Weavers, if we go that way."

"We are short-lived," Rattat said. "How old would you guess that I am, John Abbott?"

John shrugged. "Seventy?"

Chatz made a sound like choking.

"Thirty," Rattat said. "Which makes me very old. I am not the oldest member of this nest, but I am the oldest who is still fully functioning. We live short lives, and we reproduce quickly. We do not regard it as a steep price to pay, that a few of us who would live short lives, should live slightly shorter ones."

How was it that this one Weaver was so articulate?

"I regard it as a steep price to pay," John said.

"Then nee semamoo," Chatz said. "Nee aha ees. Surrender."

"We have other tools we can trade," John said. "Farming tools. Vehicles. Like that truck over there."

"The truck goes fast," Rattat admitted, "but it limits the roads you may take. We do not want a truck."

Rattat again settled himself on the sand. He ran the tip of one leg around the edge of his carapace.

"Medicine," John said.

"What medicine do you think I need?" Rattat asked.

"I'm not entirely sure," John said. "But I think the damp affects you. Is it a fungus, or mold, or mildew? Do you know those words? I bet that under your carapace, your flesh must really itch."

"That is simply age," Rattat said.

"I don't think it is," John countered. "I think you know it's not. I think you build your nests to channel water away from your living spaces."

"We can shemi maw," Chintz said.

"Yes, you can swim," John agreed. "I've seen it. You shemi maw nefer. But the damp makes you sick if you spend too long in it. I'll bet wherever you keep your young . . . or your eggs, or whatever it is you have . . . is a very dry place. You must not be from here. You came from a desert place."

"We are conquerors," Rattat said. "Our songs tell us that we come from a stony land, far away."

Did Rattat mean another planet? Or simply a different place on Sarovar Alpha?

"Stony," John said. "And dry."

"What is all this?" Jefferson snorted. "If you need medicine, I'll get you medicine."

But Rattat remained focused on John. "So we are creatures of dry lands, so what?"

"So here, your flesh itches. Your shells rot and break. Do your songs tell you that you used to live longer?"

Rattat said nothing. Chintz made an explosive sound.

"Do your songs say that your ancient heroes had itching flesh and crumbling shells?" John asked.

"Stop asking questions," Rattat said. "You are rude."

"Cultivating Spinners makes it worse," John said. "The Spinners thrive in damp caves, which are bad for your shells. So either you are subject to rot, or you grow weak, undersized Spinners. I bet that's one big reason why you trade for our tools is that you can more quickly hollow out dry spaces inside these caverns."

"We *are* subject to rot," Rattat admitted slowly.

"We can help," John said. He wasn't really sure that they could, but he thought it was likely. If nothing else, he could get, or could make, vinegar, and give that a try. And he preferred taking a chance and attempting to help the Weavers to letting Jefferson have his way.

"The country-setties can't help," Jefferson said. "They have no great medicine. Their best medicines, they buy from the post. I will add medicines into our wat, and I will do it for the same amount of Weave. You will lose nothing."

Rattat was silent for a time. It was difficult to be certain, given that he had three sets of eyes facing three different directions, but John thought the Weaver elder was inspecting him.

"You are wrong, Jefferson," Rattat finally said. "I think that if I take your trade, I will lose something valuable. Something important. Something, above all, unexpected."

"Don't do it," Jefferson said. "I'll bring more guns."

"If you buy zenef from the country-setties," John said, "you can focus on weaving the cloth, and you can make more Weave. You can get out of the damp zenef caves. I'll bring doctors, and we'll examine the plague, and we'll bring medicine to the wat."

"We would become dependent upon you," Rattat said.

"In trade, we all become dependent upon one another," John said. "And we all become richer. But I don't intend to withhold healing, or knowledge. If at all possible, we'll give you the knowledge of how to make the medicine. A gift."

"You do not know that there is a cure," Rattat said. "Perhaps there is not."

"Perhaps there is not," John agreed. "But humans are also subject to funguses, and other kinds of rot that attack the body. We already have many cures. They're cheap, and easily available, and we'll try them first. And if I can't guarantee that there's a cure, I can guarantee that I'll look for one. And if there is no cure, then perhaps there are other things we can do."

"Climate control," Faisal said. "Machines to keep your nests even drier than they are now."

"Engineering," Rock said. "We could help you build houses above the ground, to keep out the damp better. Geology. We can help you find the driest caves, farthest away from the aquifer."

"I can do all these things!" Jefferson cried. "You know me! We're already trading partners! Why disrupt the trade that exists, when I can offer you all the same things?"

"You can offer me all the same things," Rattat said slowly, "and yet you did not. None of these things occurred to you. It only occurred to you to sell me more weapons."

"You *asked* for weapons!" Jefferson's handsome face was twisted. Was he feeling rage? Fear? Both?

"That's the difference between someone who wants to make the sale today and get out," John said, "and a trader who wants partners, who wants to buy and sell for the long term."

Rattat purred. "Or perhaps that is the difference between a mere trader and a friend. We will trade as you suggest, John Abbott."

Jefferson dropped to his knees and screamed.

"The truck is full of zenef," Rock said. "Shall we unload it and stack it here, under the cliff?"

"I got shesroo." Chatz spun back, away from the square and toward the entrance to the nest.

Rock turned to wave at the truck. Sam waved back, and the truck doors opened.

Jefferson sprang to his feet and threw himself at Rock. He had a stone in his hand, and he smashed it against Rock's skull, behind the ear, knocking the other trader down.

John tackled Jefferson. He grabbed the trader's forearm and his neck and pulled him away from Rock with all his weight. Jefferson was a good deal heavier than John, though, and likely wouldn't have budged, except that, at the same time, the Weaver Chatz threw himself against the back of Jefferson's knees.

Jefferson fell.

"Rock!" John stripped the stone from Jefferson and threw it away. The trader was shrieking incoherently, and his violent thrashing threatened to throw John off until Chatz and a second Weaver settled next to him and pinned him with their pincers.

Did John hear barking?

Rock lay still.

Sam came running over from the truck, first-aid kit in his hand. He knelt to examine Rock.

With him arrived Ani, who threw herself on Jefferson, chewing on a pants cuff and snarling.

"I've got this," Sam said to John. "Go unload the truck."

"You're an engineer," John objected.

"And you're an accountant. *Go unload the truck.*"

John looked around at the Weavers. They were still, other than two more who were settling themselves into place to hold Jefferson.

They had all just struck a deal, just opened a new wat, or maybe a series of related wats, and the relationship was still fragile. Jefferson's attack on Rock might have been an act of rage, but if it unsettled the Weavers enough, it also might undo the negotiation.

John nodded.

"I shall help," Faisal said.

"No, you won't," John said. "You're wounded."

He unloaded the zenef. All of it, which made a pillar of cannisters from the ground to the rocky overhang, ten meters in diameter. There were two other men in the truck, country-setties from the village, and they helped. When they had finished, Rock was sitting up, leaning his back against a boulder, and sipping from a flask.

"This is a large quantity of zenef," Rattat said.

Rock groaned. His words sounded slurred, but he managed to speak. "It's all we have. We can produce the same quantity every year, for now. More, as we cultivate more caves with Spinners."

"Nefer this wat," Chatz groaned. "Neferooee this wat!"

"Neferooee this wat!" other Weavers intoned.

"Perhaps you have already caused me to be written into my people's songs," Rattat said. "We do not have enough Weave to pay for this zenef."

"We propose to leave this with you," Rock said. "You can pay us when you have the Weave."

"This is a new way of doing a wat," Rattat observed.

"This is a new way of doing a wat," Rock agreed. "We're going to trust you. We believe you'll pay us."

Rattat emitted a series of whirs and clicks. A cadre of Weavers turned into the entrance of the nest. "We will give you all the Weave we have now, and we will give you the rest of the Weave when we have produced it."

"I will be prepared to buy the Weave you don't give to the village," John said. "But I'll bring medicines sooner than that. In fact, Sam, there must be an antifungal in the first-aid kit, isn't there?"

Sam produced a finger-sized tube and handed it to John. John passed it to Rattat. "This may not work, but please try it and see. If it works, I'll bring more. If it doesn't, I'll bring other remedies." He lowered his voice. "Just in case, maybe try it on someone less valuable than yourself, at first."

Rattat chuckled. "I will, if I can find such a person."

John hesitated. He wanted to show trust, but he was uncertain what the limits of that trust should be. "When I come to buy Weave, what shall I bring to pay for it?"

"This is delicately put," Rattat said. "You wonder whether you should bring guns. You hint that you would be *willing* to bring guns, because you wish to preserve our new wat. But clearly, you would *prefer* to end the process of arming the Ochatat of Antela Anta."

"I would prefer to end the process of arming *everybody*," John said. "I want trade and peace."

"I also wish to preserve our new wat," Rattat said. "Bring tools."

Jefferson grunted beneath the weight of four Weavers and the growling dog.

John looked at the trader, trying to think what to do with him. "Can we take Jefferson?"

"In our old songs," Rattat said, "great events were celebrated with blood sacrifice. Is the founding of this new type of wat not a great event that deserves to be celebrated?"

Ani at that moment managed to get past Jefferson's cuff and sank her teeth into his ankle. He screamed in rage but couldn't move.

"I want to respect your customs," John said gravely. "If our wat is to be successful, the Company must approve of it. I'm tempted to kill Jefferson, but I'm afraid his death might cause the Company to terminate the wat."

"Has he committed crimes against the Company?" Rattat inquired gravely.

"I think he has done things that will get him sent home," John said. "Away from this world, where he will be unable to interfere with our wat."

"That is acceptable."

Chatz handed John a bundle of Weave, containing his pistol and the multitools. Sam tied Jefferson's wrists and ankles and the two country-setties slung him into the back of the vehicle. Faisal and Rock limped to the vehicle, and John, with a little persistence, called Ani to heel. He promised to bring medication as soon as he could, waved farewell, and walked with Sam to the truck, now half full of Weave.

He reinserted his subscriber chip and checked his multi for

messages. He had one, from an unrecognized user, and it made his heart beat faster.

With the text message, was a picture of Ruth and the girls. They were tied up, and sitting in the Comms office of Arrowhawk Post. Pianki and Nefreet were tied up with them.

The message read: *Time for you to get out of our way.*

CHAPTER THIRTY-TWO

"I didn't know Pianki was your son," John said. Although, now that he was thinking back, when the school group had arrived at Nyoot Abedjoo, Pianki had run to Nefreet.

"I said I had children," Rock growled. "Did you want me to point them out to you?"

"Actually, yes, that would have been a normal human thing to do."

"Guess I've never felt the need to be a normal human."

John processed the thought. "Does that mean . . . did you try to help your brother-in-law ship Weave once?"

"When I was first married, and naïve, like you. I promised Nefreet I would try to help her brother. It didn't go well."

"Not naïve," John said. "Decent."

Sam drove the truck. The vehicle's headlights threw long cones of light ahead into the darkness, casting sudden bushes and startled animals alike into stark relief. Sam drove as much by the scanner on the dashboard as by eyesight. John didn't envy him the task, especially at the breakneck pace Sam had set.

Sam worried about his own son.

Rock and John stood in the front segment, like straphangers on a public jet, anxious to get to an appointment and so staring out the front windshield, prepared to jump from the doors the moment they opened. John had his Webley, Rock had an automatic rifle, and a shotgun rested stock-up in a holster underneath the truck's dashboard, beside where Sam worked the truck's pedals with his feet.

Faisal sat on one of the truck's seats, behind them, armed with a pistol.

John looked at his multitool again; no signal.

"Can you check the comms, Sam?" he asked.

"It's on the same network as your multi, Abbott." This was not the first time Sam had given John this reminder, and his voice was terse.

"Maybe my multi is malfunctioning."

Sam touched the appropriate spots on the dashboard. "Arrowhawk Post, this is Sam Chen, do you copy?"

Silence.

"I think it was Diaz and Choat who shut down the network before," Rock suggested. "I'm not sure how, but maybe Security Services has an override protocol that shuts down the satellite feed regionally."

"Or Stohel has it," Sam said, "and they're leaning on him."

"There's a direct physical line to Henry Hudson Post," John said. "It runs from the Comms office, parallel to the maglev platform. Even if the satellites are down, we can reach Henry Hudson."

Though there was no guarantee that anyone other than Director English would be watching from the other side.

"Yes," Faisal agreed. "How convenient for them that they have taken hostages and are sitting in Comms."

Sam drove toward Arrowhawk Post. John knew enough of the topography to recognize that they were now descending into the broad valley in which the post was located, and if they wanted to escape notice, they'd soon need to park and walk the rest of the way. He wished he could contact the post, though he wasn't sure whom he could trust. Carlton? Probably. Keckley? Uncertain. Perhaps the traders Rock hadn't named: Hager and Takahashi and the others. Or perhaps not.

Or Faisal might recommend someone.

"I think that little knoll there," he told Sam. "That's close to the ladder."

Sam stopped the truck and they exited. They didn't bother trying to conceal the bulky vehicle; it would be daylight soon enough, and if anyone was looking, they'd find it.

John went first, up the ladder to the maglev guideway. Had Diaz and Choat figured out his escape route from the post during the

Weaver siege? Hopefully, they assumed he'd climbed down off the Company warehouse and then gone over the wall in some other way, with a ladder, or jumping from the rooftop of a house. If they knew he'd gone by the maglev line, or even if they knew that was a possibility, then they could very easily have booby-trapped this route.

So John went first.

Even in the darkness of night, John saw evidence of the siege as he looked down from the maglev platform. The post's encircling wall was scorched and scarred, and there were large swathes of burnt grass around it. The Weavers had withdrawn now, but the gate was shut, and oscillating lights showed where Arrowhawk Post Irregulars patrolled.

He held his breath, but nothing shocked John, stabbed him, or blew him up, and when he reached the end of the guideway, the opening over the ladder down was unblocked. He lay on his belly and looked through, angling to get a view of Company House.

He could see only through a corner of one window into the Comms office. The light there was on, and he saw a flash of movement as someone walked back and forth past the visible spot. The column beneath him, with its ladder rungs, was in shadow, so unless someone inside Comms was watching specifically, it should be possible to climb down the ladder without attracting attention.

There was no direct way to get up from the warehouse roof into the Comms room. If John descended into the warehouse, maybe he could bring up crates, and stack them to create an improvised staircase, but that was an hour's work.

John lowered his legs down the opening in the platform, groped until he found a ladder rung, and then started his climb down.

"I'll follow," Sam said.

"Let's go one at a time," John suggested. "Maybe less likely to be spotted."

He forced himself to a steady rhythm, feeling the revolver in his holster swinging with the motions of his body. Halfway down the ladder, he turned his shoulders and craned his neck to look into the comms room. He saw Diaz, and a burly man in Company blue and buff who must be Choat. He also saw his wife and daughter, and Pianki and Nefreet, and Stohel, all strapped into chairs in the far corner of the room. When he reached the rooftop, he turned and looked up at the comms center windows. From this angle, he couldn't see the people inside; no one was standing in the windows looking down at him.

He was knocked to the ground from behind.

The rooftop scraped his forehead. The weight of a body dropped beside him, pinning his jacket to the roof, and the revolver with it. A second body hit him, driving a knee into the small of his back. He was pinned in seconds.

"Shh!" someone urged.

And then cold steel pressed against his cheek.

"Who is this?" a voice demanded in a harsh whisper.

Muffled cursing.

A light shone down on John's face. "John Abbott," he said, keeping his voice low. "I work here."

"Dammit, Abbott!" The metal to his face and the knees pushing him down disappeared and John was hoisted to his feet—to find himself facing Keckley. "You don't work on the rooftop, do you?" Keckley whispered. "These guys have guns and short tempers, so you'd better explain yourself."

John held his hands up at his shoulders to show his harmlessness. "They have my wife in there. Also, I have friends up on the maglev platform coming down. Don't shoot them."

His words became heavy in his stomach as it occurred to him that Keckley might very well be on the side of Diaz and Choat, here guarding the rooftop for them.

John had a chance to see who else was with the audit chief. Half of them weren't even Company men—or at least they weren't people John recognized. Maybe they were Irregulars. Takahashi was there, though, along with Payne and Moore, and Nermer. "That isn't half an explanation," Keckley muttered. "Where have you been? Did you know we were under siege here?"

"There's no time." John waved at Faisal to come down. "Look, the men in there call themselves Diaz and Choat. They're Security, or at least they say they are. They work out of Henry Hudson, and they've been selling guns to Jefferson and some of his friends."

"Jesus," Takahashi murmured.

"I contacted Internal Audit about them, but I haven't heard back yet. Jefferson was selling guns to the Weavers on the side, and he was stealing Weave from the Company take to help fund his hustle. Rock started buying guns from the same dealers, to arm the country-setties of the village. The Weavers attacked because Jefferson saw that his deal was coming to an end, and wanted to shut me up."

"This is a cogent explanation," Keckley said, "but it's kind of dense."

"I'm leaving out a lot," John said. "I set up a deal to make peace between the Weavers and the country-setties of Nyoot Abedjoo, and to end the arms trade. If you've noticed the Weavers fall back tonight, that's why. I don't think they'll attack again. And I'm pretty sure Diaz and Choat want me to come up there so they can kill me."

"That sounds about right," Keckley said. "Who else is untrustworthy around here? Who's trading guns?"

"Tasto and Grandi."

Rock reached the rooftop, the last of John's companions.

"Those guys are with Carlton and Korsgaard," Keckley said. "First order of business is to catch those two with their pants down, so we don't get shot in the back."

"Where's Carlton?" John asked. "What's going on here?"

"A fire alarm went off this afternoon," Keckley said. "When it ended, and we tried to go back in, we were shot at. Carlton and Korsgaard and I rounded up the troops, and she's down at the front doors. I brought these men up here to see what we could make out through the windows, and we got here just in time to see you climbing down."

As he spoke, Takahashi was climbing the ladder and peering over toward Comms.

"He's going to see Diaz and Choat," John said. "They have my family and Rock's family tied up. And poor Stohel."

"They must have gone out to the village and grabbed them." Worry shone openly on Rock's face.

"Once we get in there," John said, "we'll reactivate the network, and check on the village."

"I care about the village," Rock said. "I care about Nefreet and Pianki more."

Takahashi came back down the ladder and confirmed what John had said about Comms. Then Keckley grunted out his orders about

Tasto and Grandi, and the men all descended through the warehouse, by its winding metal staircase.

They emerged into the street beneath the maglev station, brightly lit by streetlights. Carlton and Korsgaard crouched across the street from the front door of Company House, behind a stack of sandbags. Dr. Hinkley knelt with them. Tasto and Grandi and other armed men, most not in Company uniform, sheltered behind the brick walls of local businesses or squatted behind improvised barricades, guns in hand.

John and Rock approached Carlton directly, Takahashi and Hager drifting slightly behind. John watched the windows of Company House carefully, especially the windows of the comms office.

"Chief Carlton," John said, in a loud, get-your-attention voice. "I have to tell you about a gunrunning operation that's been going on, right under all our noses."

Whether Tasto and Grandi might have attacked John, or fled, or done anything else, quickly became hypothetical. In the moments during which they were distracted listening to John, Keckley, Sam, Moore, and Payne got behind them and pressed firearms against their backs.

Carlton, to her credit, digested the information quickly. "Tasto and Grandi are in on it?"

"And Jefferson and Gonzalez," Keckley said.

"Gonzalez is dead," Carlton said. "Jefferson?"

"Tied up in a truck a couple of kilometers east of here, under the maglev line," John said.

"And the lunatics up in Comms, shooting at us?" Carlton asked.

"Those are the men who were selling them guns," John said. "Security, from Henry Hudson."

"There's a holding cell in the Security office in Company House," Carlton said. "I'm not real comfortable using it while the top floor of the building is held by mutineers."

"I will get some tape from the shopkeeper," Faisal volunteered. "We can just tie them up here. If it rains on them, it rains."

"That seems like small enough punishment," Carlton agreed.

"We have to be real careful about storming Comms," Keckley said. "The mutineers have hostages."

"They summoned me here," John said. "They want me. I'll go in.

Maybe I can talk them down. Maybe when they know their game is up, they'll surrender. No one wants a trial or messy headlines back on Earth, so maybe they'll get nondisclosure agreements and a one-way ticket back to Earth."

"They summoned me, too," Rock said.

"Or maybe they figure they're better off if they kill you two," Keckley suggested. "Or maybe it's not about them being better off at all, maybe they just resent you for stopping their business, so they want to kill you before they go."

It was a good question. Why did Diaz and Choat want the two men?

"Our families are up there," John said. "If we go in shooting, our families probably die."

"You're going to do what, then?" Keckley's face was red. "Go in reconciling the monthly accounts? Come on, Abbott. This happened on my watch, I should have been paying more attention. It's my responsibility. *I'm* going in."

"I'm going to go in talking," John said. "Maybe they don't know how much has happened. Maybe I can talk them into standing down. Or if someone has to be sacrificed, maybe it can be me."

"I'm coming with you," Rock said.

"I found something." Faisal had emerged from the general goods store. He still moved stiffly, but he moved. He held a thick roll of silver adhesive tape in one hand, and a small plastic case in the other. "It is a radio. I procured two sets. Four buds."

John stared blankly.

Keckley punched him in the shoulder. "Network's out, remember? So we can't use our multitools or the post security systems to listen in on what's happening to you inside. But if these use radio waves, they should still work."

"They use radio waves," Faisal said.

John took one of the buds in his hand. They were made of smooth black plastic, designed to nestle inside the user's ear. "If those guys look inside my ear and see this, the game's over."

"Tape it up under my hair," Rock said.

Faisal attached one of the beads to the base of Rock's skull with a bit of the adhesive tape. With the trader's long hair draped out over the top of the bead, it disappeared entirely.

Carlton and Keckley each took one of the buds. When no one else reached for the fourth, John handed it to Faisal. Then he and Rock both passed their firearms to the fixer, and John cleared his throat.

"Let's go get our families out," he said.

CHAPTER
THIRTY-THREE

John pulled open the front door to Company House and called up the stairs. "Diaz! Choat! This is John Abbott!"

"Show yourself," Diaz's voice called back. "And do like it a smart guy who wants his family to live."

John raised his hands over his head and stepped through the doors. He turned and looked up the stairs; two flights up, at the level of the comms center, Diaz stood with an automatic rifle in his hands, watching John.

John took a step toward the stairs and slipped. He managed to catch his balance, just as he noticed that the puddle that had nearly dropped him on his face was reddish brown and sticky.

He felt ill. At least there were no corpses.

"Don't tell me you showed up without the trader!" Diaz barked.

John cautioned Rock with a raised hand; the trader waited outside. "He's here," John called. "Listen, I need to update you on some new arrangements."

"Where's Jefferson?" Diaz called.

"He's here! He . . . won't be joining us."

Diaz laughed. "So you have him tied up. Good. He deserved it. And I take it you've tied up the Italians, too, Tasto and Grandi?"

Diaz sounded altogether too happy that his former customers were now prisoners. "You don't need to worry about them," John suggested. "The arms trade is over."

Diaz shrugged. "It's never *over*."

"No more traders will buy from you here," John said.

"You the post chief, all of a sudden?" Diaz pressed him.

"Carlton knows now. So does Keckley. Everyone knows. You're not going to sell any more guns here. But the biggest reason you won't sell any more guns is that the Weavers won't buy them from you."

"You're really confident about that," Diaz said.

"Like I said. New arrangements."

"And did you include *every* local Weaver nest in these arrangements?"

John's heart stopped beating.

"I thought not." Diaz laughed. "So Jefferson's old clients have agreed to stop buying arms, and so have Rock's. But that leaves a lot of other Weaver nests, and human villages, too, comparatively defenseless. How long before some enterprising young trader offers to level the playing field by arming the unarmed? Assuming I don't decide to cut out the middleman and do it myself, that is."

"What would it take to get you to walk away?" John asked.

"You mean money?" Diaz laughed. "I've made millions of dollars selling arms to your locals here. But my share is the smallest part."

"You mean English," John said. "You mean English is earning a cut, too, and the only way to stop the sale is to buy off you and English both." It was a guess, but why else would English not have called him back? Why had Diaz and Choat showed up at Arrowhawk Company House just as John was talking to the director? How had they been following John from the beginning, in Henry Hudson Post, if English hadn't turned them on to him? He took a deep breath. "I'll cut a deal with English separately. But I want to get your assurance, and Choat's, that you guys are out of the trade. You take your money and retire. What's that going to take?"

"You're not fully understanding me." Diaz grinned. "Yes, English makes a cut. More fundamentally than that, I have orders from English, and you're telling me not just to drop a lucrative trade, but to disobey instructions from my boss."

English was guilty.

John felt vindicated and frightened at the same time. But then a doubt nagged him. If English was behind the arms trade, why send John to Arrowhawk Post to investigate it?

"Criminal orders," John said.

"Are they?" Diaz frowned. "What's criminal, exactly, in Sarovar System? There are the bylaws and the Code of Conduct, but U.S. federal law mostly doesn't apply, and zero state statutes matter. There's no statute against smuggling, or the unlicensed selling of firearms to the locals. What criminal law? Are you talking about the legal traditions of the country-setties?"

"The wasting of Company assets, and the personal expropriation of Company assets, are violations of the Code of Conduct," John said. "The Code also mandates treating the locals with scrupulous respect in accordance with the highest standards of commercial behavior."

"I never rip off my clients," Diaz said. "And I sell the arms that the director tells me to. If there's any wasting of Company resources, seems to me that it's happening above my pay grade."

A soft, bell-like sound rang throughout Company House. The maglev was arriving, and John didn't remember that a train was due. The discrepancy made him feel uncomfortable.

"All that aside," John said, "you know you've done wrong. What will it cost? How much do I have to pay you to go home?"

"All that aside," Diaz said, "go to hell. Now get up here, immediately, and bring Rock with you, or we start by shooting the children."

Rock raised his hands and passed through the doors. John let them swing shut behind the trader; the thud of their closing sounded final.

They trudged up the stairs.

If Diaz planned to get rid of them, why hadn't he shot them already?

"You can't kill us," John said. "Too many people know."

"I'm not going to kill anyone," Diaz said. "I'm just going to leave, and I don't want you messing that up."

"On the train," John said.

"Fastest way back to civilization." Diaz grinned. "Who knows, maybe I'll end up doing exactly what you want, Abbott. Maybe Director English will give me an NDA and a pension and send me to live on the beach somewhere."

John and Rock reached the third floor. They were one flight below the maglev platform, and standing beside the open doors of the comms office. Ruth had her jaw set in a determined line, but the girls looked scared. Pianki looked nervous, too, but Nefreet's face blazed with wrath.

John got his first look at Choat, standing in the corner. The man was burly, with a nearly spherical head that was completely shaved. He squinted, and his lips were pursed as if he wanted a kiss. He held a large-caliber pistol in one hand, and idly pointed it first at one prisoner, and then at another.

Stohel leaned forward, straining against the tape that bound him into the chair. "The airstrike can still be recalled!" he snapped. "Please, there's not much time!"

Airstrike?

English had said that the post could be carpet bombed, as a last resort.

"No," John murmured.

"Is there enough time for the train to depart?" Choat's face bore a thoughtful expression.

"Maybe twenty minutes," Stohel said. "Let me at the comms panel and I can recall the strike in five seconds!"

"Twenty minutes will do." Choat raised his pistol and emptied the magazine into Stohel's chest. The sudden bang and the bright flash shook John, and instilled into his heart the cold sensation that death stalked him in Company House.

Stohel slumped forward, blood spilling down his blue-and-buff Company jumpsuit.

"You're evil," Ruth said.

"You noticed," Diaz shot back. "Don't forget it."

"You heard the man." Choat turned to John and smiled. "Twenty minutes. So here's the deal: Diaz and I leave on that train in ten minutes. If you aren't back here by then, we still leave, but first we kill your families. Clear enough?"

"Clear." Rock's voice was thick, as if he were struggling with great emotion.

"You want us to take a message or something?" John asked.

"You're going to go down into the warehouse," Choat said. "Twice each. And each time, you're going to haul up a crate of Weave. Two of you, two trips, that's four crates total. And I wouldn't waste any time trying to talk to Carlton across the street there . . . you're down to nine minutes already."

John pulled Rock with him; the trader looked on the verge of starting a brawl. John dragged him down the stairs, three and four steps at a time. They passed through the doors from Company House into the warehouse on the ground floor, and John said, "Maybe someone can intercept the train. What about the helicopter?"

"Stohel pilots the helicopter from comms," Rock said grimly, lifting his first crate of the Company's Weave. "He's dead."

John grabbed a crate also. He was talking to Rock, but he was talking for the benefit of those listening in. "Choat shot and killed Stohel." He risked a glance across the street as he charged up the stairs and saw Carlton, deep in a furious conversation with Takahashi. Dr. Hinkley leaned forward as if on an invisible leash, anxious to run up and into the building.

They heard the train arrive, a squeal that quickly stilled to silence, and the creaking sound of Company House settling under the maglev's weight. They hurried back to the stairs.

Choat stood at the platform, beckoning John and Rock up. At his direction, they dropped the two crates on the train compartment floor and turned to race back down for two more.

Something bright yellow caught John's eye as he ran, and he risked a glance over his shoulder to confirm what he thought he saw: fire extinguishers. A stack of fire extinguishers stood on the maglev platform, behind Choat.

Running down the stairs, he looked for the extinguishers that had once been bracketed into the walls at each level—gone.

"Fire," he said, talking to the back of Rock's head as they grabbed two more crates in the warehouse. "They've removed the extinguishers, they're going to start a fire."

They climbed again, John's heart thudding violently in his chest. He and Rock heaved the crates onto the train, and then Diaz grabbed Rock and pressed a gun to his head. "Back into Comms," he said. "You can wait for help there."

Diaz took Rock back down the stairs. How many minutes had passed? Eight? Was there really a drone bomber squadron on its way to wipe out Arrowhawk Post?

John didn't move to get a clear look, but out of the corners of his eyes he saw bustle in the street below, and he heard the grinding of wheels in the gravel. That bustle and noise might be consistent with evacuation.

"You too, you goofy-looking bastard." Choat pressed his pistol to John's belly and pushed John down the stairs into Comms. There, Diaz tied Rock into one chair and Choat tied John into another. Then Diaz exited.

John was strapped firmly to the chair, each ankle bound to a leg of the black plastic chair. His hands were tied behind the seat back, which would have been awkward for a shorter man, a man with shorter limbs, or a less flexible man. But John's Marfan's Syndrome meant that his joints were all very flexible, and being tied into the chair didn't even give him discomfort.

And he was tied with a thin synthetic line; it cut into his flesh, but it wasn't adhesive.

"So," Choat said, "here's the situation. One of you men is obviously wearing a listening device. Maybe you both are. Let's be one hundred percent clear about the situation, to anyone who is listening. If you're not already running away from Arrowhawk Post at a very fast clip, you're going to die, by Company airstrike, called in response to the post being overrun by local Weavers. How sad that none of you can use the network to contact Henry Hudson to tell them that the Weavers have retreated. My partner is making certain at this moment that you won't be coming up the stairs. And just in case, we've booby-trapped the windows. Run now, and maybe you will live."

John looked to the windows and saw that grenades had been wired into the latches. It wasn't a perfect booby trap, but it didn't have to be perfect—it only had to slow Carlton and her people down a few minutes.

He heard a *bang* and then a *whoosh* in the staircase, and then he smelled smoke.

Ruth began to sing.

Nearer, my God, to thee
Nearer to thee
E'en though it be a cross
That raises me

By the time she reached the chorus, both girls had joined her. Pianki and Nefreet looked startled, but Pianki sang some of the words.

But if Ruth thought she would inspire Diaz and Choat to show mercy, she was mistaken. Instead, they grabbed John's chair; Diaz stopped and gripped the front two legs, and Choat seized the back of the seat. They tilted him backward and lifted.

"I'd rather die with my family," John said.

He rotated his right wrist. He could turn it at unnatural angles, and he did so now, forcing it inward. He also collapsed his fingers together, narrowing his hand as tightly as he had ever done at college parties.

"You'll die," Diaz said. "But English wants to talk to you first. At a special little house he keeps in Henry Hudson."

Choat retreated into the stairwell and up the stairs toward the train. Over Diaz's shoulder, John saw that the bottom of the stairwell was full of fire. Black smoke raced up the ceiling above him.

John narrowed his hand even more. The cord helped; he could feel his thumb lying tighter and tighter against his palm as he forced it flat. The muscles of his hand weren't really designed to do this work, so he pressed against the cords and against the wrist of his other hand.

He felt his thumb dislocate and he gasped in pain.

Ruth stopped singing. There were tears on her cheeks.

"Oh, good," Diaz said. "I like it when they cry."

John slipped his right hand free of the cords. Pain lanced from his thumb up his forearm; he had imagined that he'd grab Choat's gun from its holster, but he couldn't see himself even holding the weapon, much less firing it.

But, with his right hand pulled out, the cords went slack and fell entirely away from his left. He would be noticed immediately, and had to act.

Stretching to his full height, he shot his left hand back. The elastic connective tissue in his shoulder meant that he could reach at an extreme angle, an angle that surprised Choat, eliciting curses from him as John twisted his wrist around to wrap his fingers around the firearm's grip and pulled the pistol free.

It was a semiautomatic, a ten-millimeter Kupari like Sam Chen's.

The Finns, Uncle Christopher had often preached, made guns that packed a punch. Diaz looked up just as John racked the slide with his crippled right hand. He wasn't ambidextrous, he'd never practiced shooting with his left hand, other than for the sheer novelty of it— but the pistol was thirty centimeters from Diaz's chest.

Choat dropped the chair.

As John fell, he squeezed the trigger. It occurred to him that Diaz had to be wearing a shirt of Weave, at least to cover his vitals, so he adjusted his aim at the last moment, pointing the muzzle of the pistol at the security man's exposed neck. The smell of chemical propellant and the echoing booms of the explosions filled the angled, smoky space of the staircase, and then Diaz let go of the chair legs. He stumbled back, red blossoms bursting from his shoulder and cheek, and disappeared from John's view.

John's head cracked against the cement of the stairs. His eyes stung from the various kinds of smoke and his vision jarred and slid sideways. He felt his heart leap once within his chest, tremendously, and then he bounced sideways, rolling down the hard steps.

Toward the fire.

CHAPTER
THIRTY-FOUR

John flung his arms out, left and right, trying to flatten himself into a shape that wouldn't roll. The result was a tremendous thud as he landed on his back, and then a clattering sound as he skidded down the steps headfirst—but stopped short of the flame.

He was close enough that his forehead and the tops of his ears felt scorched.

And he had kept hold of the pistol. He wasn't sure how many bullets he had, and he couldn't see straight, and he didn't know where Choat was.

Or was Choat the one he'd shot?

"John!" He heard Ruth yell.

He jammed the pistol down among the ropes, alongside his ankle, and squeezed the trigger. *Bang!* He felt the powder burn on his flesh, and it worked as a tonic, focusing his attention and forcing his vision into line.

He saw Choat crashing down the stairs toward him.

John's shot burned his ankle, but it also freed that leg from the ropes. He was only attached to the chair by the rope around his right calf. As Choat lunged to grab him, John threw himself sideways and turned, raising the bound leg and the chair with it, and jamming them both into Choat's gut.

Choat sat down hard on the stairs with a choked bellow. Diaz was stirring, moving slowly, but reaching for his pistol. John aimed at Choat and squeezed the trigger three times.

The gun fired twice, both misses, and then the magazine was empty.

John kicked, trying to yank his leg from the chair. The cord that tied him was sagging loose, but not loose enough for him to extract himself or stand up before Choat was up again and on him.

Choat grabbed the chair and yanked it. The chair came free and tumbled to the edge of the fire, but John also slid along the steps, coming to rest with Choat crouched over him, his face a round mask of rage made orange and yellow by the flames.

Choat punched John in the face, and then again, and again.

"The train."

John was dazed, but he could tell this was Diaz speaking. Diaz was standing, holding his wounds, and pulling Choat away from John.

"I'll tell English he died," Choat growled.

"No," Diaz said. "Get him on the train, alive."

Choat grumbled, but he scooped John up and slung him across his shoulders in a fireman's carry. As he landed along Choat's neck, John slapped his good hand forward, grabbing Choat's belt and his empty holster. He tucked his head down against his own chest as he pulled, dragging himself off-center.

Choat's knees buckled, he staggered, and they fell together, landing on the edge of the flames.

Choat screamed. Diaz stumped away.

John's chest ached. Was he dying, at this moment, of a heart attack? He dragged himself to his feet and picked up the chair. It was made of hard black plastic, but it was upholstered with a soft Company blue cushion, and the cushion was on fire.

Choat rose to his knees, and John hit him in the face with the chair. Choat fell.

How much time until the airstrike? John had no sense of whether minutes had passed in the stairwell, or hours, or seconds. At some point, if he delayed long enough, wouldn't the security men shut down the airstrike?

Or was it possible they didn't have the codes to do so?

In which case, was John just guaranteeing his own death?

Choat tried to stand again, and again John swung the chair. This time, Choat caught the chair with both hands, grabbing two legs. John immediately leaned into the other man, pushing forward with all his weight. Choat was poorly balanced and fell to the stairs, this time with John and the chair on top of him. John kicked, aiming for Choat's crotch, but only managed to plant his foot into the security agent's belly.

Choat grunted and spat.

Bang!

John turned at the sound of the gunshot and saw Diaz on the landing above him. He had dragged Ellie onto the landing, still tied to a chair, and he pressed a gun to the temple of John's daughter.

Ellie was trying to sing, but she was sobbing.

"You like making deals, you stubborn bastard, here it is." Diaz spat blood on the floor. "You get on the train now, I let one member of your family live. You choose."

How much time was left?

"All three," John grunted. "Or I die here, and you have to explain it to English."

Choat pushed up against the chair that pinned him, and John kicked Choat again.

"I'll give you the girls," Diaz snarled. "I'm not dragging your wife up the stairs."

"We're not going tied up."

"The hell I'm going to untie anyone else." Diaz pointed his pistol at John. "But you can walk on your own power."

John was weary to the bone. He didn't think he could knock Choat down again one more time. His heart pounded agonizingly in his chest, his head ached, and his right hand was a limp, useless fish, screaming in pain. He'd gained all the time he could—if it wasn't enough, he had tried.

He nodded and stepped away from Choat.

Choat sprang from the ground, snarling curses. He punched John in the temple, knocking him to the stairs. Pressed against a heated step, John heard Ellie crying. Somewhere in the background, Ruth was singing. Maybe Rock was singing with her.

Choat's pistol lay on the step near John. He put his injured hand on top of it, trying to draw it to himself, but Choat stomped on his hand. John felt himself scream, but he didn't hear the sound of it as the world collapsed into a single shriek of white noise, and then Choat scooped up the pistol.

The empty magazine hit the steps beside John's head.

John looked up and saw Choat totter up the stairs toward his colleague. They were shouting at each other, but John couldn't hear their words.

Diaz pointed his pistol at Choat. They both looked bright orange, in the flames.

Choat raised his own pistol, but he didn't point it at Diaz—he aimed at Ellie.

And then Choat's head exploded. A sudden crater opened in the side of his face that was turned toward John, and then a second and a third, and then blood spouted from his neck, and he toppled over, falling toward John.

John saw Keckley at the top of the stairs with a rifle. Behind him came Korsgaard, Moore, Payne, and Sam, but the audit chief was in the lead, his bullets sawing through Choat.

Then he turned on Diaz.

But Diaz shot first, and blood spilled from the audit chief's shirt.

Keckley tumbled down the stairs, and the men behind him charged. The security men had rifles, but they weren't shooting yet. Sam held something in his hand that wasn't a pistol at all, and he pointed it at Diaz.

Diaz pivoted to shoot his attackers, but fell suddenly to the ground, twitching.

John's hearing returned with the sound of Ellie's screams. He dragged himself slowly to his knees, tasting blood, and climbed the stairs one lurching step at a time.

"Ellie, you're okay," he mumbled. "You're okay."

But he couldn't go to comfort his daughter. He had no idea how much time was left, but it couldn't be long. Moore was wrapping tape around Diaz's hands and ankles. Sam had a knife and was working to cut Ellie free. A taser sat on the floor beside his foot.

"Get this all down for the report," Korsgaard was telling someone.

"John? John?" Ruth called from inside Comms.

"I'm here!" he yelled back.

He knelt beside Keckley. The audit chief's eyes twitched as he stared at the ceiling. He lay swamped in a puddle of his own blood.

"There's an airstrike coming," John said. "I need the code to call it off."

Keckley twitched, kicked with both feet, and lay still.

Sam and Ellie ran into Comms. Moore and Payne scrambled past John holding yellow fire extinguishers, headed for the flames.

John dug into Keckley's ear and pulled out the radio bud. He pushed it into his own ear, not waiting until it was in to begin talking. "Post Chief Carlton, can you hear me? This is John Abbott. Post Chief Carlton?"

"I'm here, Abbott. You want the airstrike override code."

"I'm heading to the console now." John squeezed Keckley's shoulder, mumbling a silent thanks that he wished he'd been able to communicate before the man died, then stood. Sharp pain ran up his spine, sharp pain thudded in his chest, and his head ached. His right hand was still useless, but at least it had finally hit the point where it had taken all the pain it could take, and the pain receptors had simply shut off, leaving the hand numb.

John dragged himself into Comms. At the doorway, Ruth seized him in an embrace.

"Thank you," she whispered fiercely.

"No time," he groaned, and pushed forward to the comms panel. At the console, he fell to his knees and saw his blood spatter on the plastic. "I'm here," he grunted. "I don't see a timer or anything."

"What do you see?"

"The screen is black."

Sam appeared at his elbow. "What do you need?"

"You need to see the screen." Carlton's words were fast, her voice high-pitched. "You have to put codes into three separate entry fields. I don't know how to choose them without seeing the screen."

"I need to see the screen," John said. "Can I reboot the system?"

"It won't reboot while it's counting down to the airstrike," Carlton said. "I think I can see the planes."

"It won't reboot," John said to Sam. He felt helpless. "Diaz and Choat sabotaged the console."

"I can do this." Sam pulled his multitool from his pocket and knelt beside the console.

"The network's down," John reminded him. He felt crushed. "Chief, maybe evacuate anyone you still can."

"Anyone who isn't already out isn't going to make it," Carlton said. "We evacuated *some* people. Damn, but I didn't think my career was going to end this way. I'm going to be an ugly footnote in some book of Company history."

"We won't even make a footnote," John said. "This will all be suppressed."

"Okay," Sam said, "I'm connected. Whoa, this doesn't look good. John, get down here."

John slid to the floor, levering himself on the console. He and Sam hunkered over the multitool, which was connected by a cable to the underside of the comms unit. The multi's screen was red and showed a countdown, which was ticking down less than a minute remaining. It also showed the Greek characters alpha, beta, and gamma, each beside a blank data field.

"Okay," John grunted. "Alpha, beta, gamma. Forty-five seconds left."

"Alpha," Carlton said. "Three one, one two, one six, zero zero."

John repeated the numbers back to her as he thumbed them in with his left hand. "Next?"

"Beta," she said. "Cumberland." She spelled it, and John typed it out. "I can see the aircraft," she said. "Just blips of light, but they couldn't be anything else. Dear God, to see death coming."

The countdown continued, and the multitool's screen gave no indication that either of the entries so far was correct. Sam's hands were shaking as he held the tool up for John, and his breath was quick and shallow.

Fifteen seconds.

"Gamma. Zero two, zero eight, one eight, five eight."

John said the numbers back as he entered them.

When he typed in the final eight, the screen turned green.

All the numbers and letters disappeared.

"Chief?" he said.

A brief silence. "They're going," she said in a rush of exhaled breath. "They're turning away from the post."

"It worked." John collapsed against the console. "It worked!" He looked around Comms. "Rock?"

Ruth helped him stand. "He's putting out the fire with the security men." She hugged him again, and this time he hugged her back. His girls both appeared, forcing themselves into the embrace, and John gathered them in.

"I'm sorry I stink," he said.

"You're alive," she murmured.

"Surprise. Where's Ani?"

"At Nyoot Abedjoo," Sunitha said.

"The bad men kicked Ani!" Ellie's voice trembled. All things considered, though, she was keeping herself together remarkably well. "She was hurt!"

"Ani will be okay," Sunitha said, wrapping her arm around her younger sister. "She's a tough dog."

"Is this over?" Ruth asked.

John eased himself down into a chair that still had loose loops of cord around its legs and considered the question with his family still pressing close against him. What if he stopped right now, did nothing more to pursue the matter of gunrunning at Arrowhawk Post, and simply went about the job of being an accountant?

Choat was right: Someday, the issue would arise again because some other village, or some other Weaver nest, would want to be armed. But that day might be far away.

And Diaz had said that he was taking orders from Director English. What if English decided that John was a threat to him? Would the director send more assassins? Or send another airstrike under some other false pretext? Or simply fire John, since his employment, in any case, was at-will?

John could do something about that. He could record everything he knew, gather up the evidence, including the witnesses who had heard Diaz say he was acting on English's orders, and hide the evidence somewhere. If English knew that the evidence existed, and didn't know where it was, then maybe he would be willing to leave John in peace.

Could John live with that? He buried his face in his hands. Maybe. But even if he could bear it as an ethical matter, how could he prosper and thrive? How could he have the successful trading career he wanted, if the man above him was corrupt, and only tolerated John because he was being blackmailed? And John would live life looking over his shoulder, afraid from day to day that his dead man's switch had been disarmed, and English was about to crush him.

Could he negotiate with English? Something cold pressed against John's temple; it was a glass of water Ruth was offering him. He poured half of it into his hand and splashed it into his face, trying to clear his thoughts. He drank the rest. What would he offer English? A share in the new deal with the Weavers of Bourbon Lake?

Or was there something he could do to actually defeat English?

He decided he would have to try.

CHAPTER THIRTY-FIVE

John watched the landscape whiz past beneath, through the windows of the maglev train.

The fight with Diaz and Choat had been followed first by medical treatment from Dr. Hinkley. John's face still shone from the creams he had had rubbed into it, for abrasion and burns. Then there had been an intense debriefing with Carlton, roping in Rock, Faisal, Sam, Ruth, and others as necessary, to bring the post chief up to date. She had disavowed all knowledge of the gunrunning and, from the shocked expression on her face, John believed her.

Korsgaard had meticulously recorded it all for his reporting.

John also believed Carlton when she said Keckley couldn't have been involved. He was gruff and maybe too hands off, but there was no evidence that he was corrupt. His death in retaking the post rather tended to vindicate him, as well.

Ruth had recounted how Diaz and Choat had broken into Nyoot Abedjoo by night and captured her, along with her daughters and Rock's family, to bring them back to the post and hold them hostage. Only the baby had been overlooked, because Nefreet had hidden her inside a hamper. Along with taking prisoners, the two security men had gone out of their way to kill DeBoe.

Carlton had suspended Rock. "If," she'd added, "any of us survives this, and I have any authority come tomorrow, and this even matters. I understand why you did it, but you can't run guns using Company assets. It's a clear violation of the Code of Conduct. You're going back to Earth, as soon as possible. I'll sign the paperwork to have your family go with you."

"I'm staying here," Rock had said. "This is my home, and I don't need your job. I'll be trading on behalf of Nyoot Abedjoo from now on. With the Company, and also in the country trade."

"I guess I'll see you at the wats, then." Carlton had shaken her head. "If we all survive, et cetera."

She had also promised to pay Faisal everything that John owed him, over John's objections, but with a satisfied nod from Ruth and a delighted oath from Faisal.

The local network had been taken offline the Company House comms panel, and after the debriefing and a short conference, they had left the network disabled. Carlton, Rock, Ruth, Sam, Faisal, and John had each recorded a short statement of what they had witnessed of the gunrunning and had assembled that with relevant financial reports into a single packet of data. In his statement, John had explicitly spelled out his suspicion that Director English was at the head of the gunrunning operation. Diaz had been offered the chance to make a similar statement and had only sneered at them.

Carlton and Korsgaard each kept a copy of the data packet and John and Faisal each had a copy on their multitools.

John and Faisal had then boarded the maglev with Diaz as their prisoner and headed for Henry Hudson Post. John had showered and dressed in Company blue and buff, but he had a split lip and a skinned cheek and a face burned all over and his hand was in a cast. Faisal wasn't in uniform, but he wore a neat pink tunic and trousers; he, too, was swathed with various bandages.

They each carried a shoulder bag with a change of clothing and a pistol. There was no chance of resisting the Security Services of Henry Hudson in a shoot out, but if they ended up staying a night or two in the large post, John wanted to be able to defend himself.

What would English know? What would he think, and what would he expect?

Surely, he knew that the airstrike had been called, and then called off. That seemed to be part of a scheme to eliminate evidence and witnesses, and it seemed to John that English was in on the security agents' plans. He might guess that Diaz and Choat had been killed, but it would only be a guess, and John hoped to keep the director off balance as long as he could.

Pacing back and forth, he tried to cajole Diaz into sending a message on his multi or giving John a password, but the security agent refused. Still, John had the multitool with him, which should mean that English would be aware the maglev was coming back to Henry Hudson, and probably that Diaz was on board.

Diaz himself had his hands bound with adhesive tape, more tape over his mouth, and tape attaching him to his train seat.

Once he regained network access, about halfway to Henry Hudson, John placed two calls.

First, he contacted Bangerter Cheapside. He transmitted the data packet to the Henry Hudson lawyer, and he summarized verbally, as directly as he could, what had happened. He explained the call he would make next, and told Bangerter he thought there was a chance that Security Services would intercept him at the station, or simply blow up the train before he reached Henry Hudson.

Cheapside agreed to watch the train station for John's arrival, and to transmit the data to Earth law enforcement agencies in the event of John's death.

When John terminated the call, his heart was heavy. Did he really have any reason to think that his calls weren't already being monitored? If Director English had the loyalty of rogue agents within Security Services, and if he suspected that it was even possible that John was coming back to Henry Hudson with a prisoner, surely he would have ordered the network monitored.

So unless he was catching English off guard, John had probably accomplished nothing other than to put Bangerter Cheapside's life at risk.

But he had to try.

John's second call was to Internal Audit. This time, he insisted to the synthesized voice that he needed to talk to a live person. He withheld his name—though Internal Audit could probably identify him from his multi—and kept saying, "Pass me to a live operator please," until a different woman's voice came online and said, "My name is Pham. What do you want to tell us about?"

He summarized the story to Pham and transmitted the data packet to her, as well. She said she would make some preliminary investigation into the matter, and would meet him at the train station to take custody of Diaz.

His calls finished, John sat back and took a deep breath. The die was cast.

He cut the tape from Diaz's mouth.

"What made you do it?" he asked.

"You know you have nothing on English," Diaz said.

"I have you," John said. "There is plenty of eyewitness testimony against you, and you'll turn on English."

Diaz grinned. "I'll go home, and enjoy the fruits of my labors. Buy a little house in Florida, something with a nice back garden and a woodshed, not too many gators, and set up my tools there. Make guitars and ukuleles for the rest of my days."

"I wasn't expecting to hear that," John admitted.

"Go to hell, I'm not helping you."

The station platform at Henry Hudson was empty except for a small knot of people at the end, near the elevator. John and Faisal freed Diaz from the pole and then he walked freely, even comfortably, down the length of the platform with them, hands still bound with silver tape.

The people at the end of the platform were an Asian woman with four large men behind her. They wore blue and buff, but not in any configuration John had seen before; their chests alone were dressed in Company blue, and their sleeves and trousers were buff, which made them look paler than Company men usually did. They carried pistols on their hips, one carried cuffs, and two held electric prods.

"Oh, look," Diaz said, "the party poopers."

"I'm Linda Pham," the woman said to John. "Internal Audit. You're John Abbott."

"I am." John felt tired. "This is Faisal Haddad, who was also a witness to many of the misdeeds of Mr. Diaz. You have a short statement from both of us. Should we come in with you now to make longer statements?"

The men left the tape on Diaz's wrists and simply clapped the cuffs over it. The two men with prods stood to either side of him and guided him to stand still.

"At this time, no," Pham said. "We'll reach out if we require more information."

If?

John nodded. "Shall we stick around Henry Hudson?"

"At least for tonight," she suggested.

The Internal Audit team took Diaz away.

Faisal popped his knuckles and took a deep breath. "This feels anticlimactic, Mr. Abbott."

"I don't know how it's supposed to feel," John said, "but if 'anticlimactic' means no one is shooting at us, I'll take it."

"You know what I would take right now is some cheap, hot food," Faisal said. "Something spicy, with rice."

"I'll buy," John said. "And I want you to meet someone."

They found their way to Bangerter Cheapside's office. John could have called, and could have used the map application on his multi, but the lingering dread that he was almost certainly being tracked and bugged left him averse to even touching the device. They only had to ask three people before they find a narrow door to the side of a noodle bar called Wang's, with the words BANGERTER CHEAPSIDE, ATTORNEY AT LAW AND SPECIALIST IN CODE OF CONDUCT AND BYLAWS ISSUES printed on it in bland sans serif font.

They knocked and stood in front of the eye of a door camera, and then Cheapside buzzed them in. At the top of a flight of stairs that leaned to one side, they found Bangerter's offices: one tight conference room with a table and four chairs, a tighter office with a desk and a computer, and a reception area featuring nothing but two ratty sofas. Not inflated foam, John noted. There was no receptionist, or evidence of one.

John introduced Faisal, who bowed. "A pleasure to meet you, Mr. Cheapside."

"Likewise, Mr. Haddad."

Cheapside ushered them into the conference room and shut the door. "This room is a Faraday cage," he told them, squeezing himself into one of the seats. "Electromagnetic signals can't get in and out, so don't waste your time trying to search the network or make calls."

"If English is having me monitored," John pointed out, "then he already knows exactly where I came."

"And, indeed, he probably already knows I have a Faraday cage in my office." Cheapside smiled. "I've had dealings with Director

English before. Still, if there's anything you need me to know, you can tell me in here. And there's at least one thing I want to tell you."

"If it's news that Diaz and English have both been locked up for transport to stand trial on Earth, I'll be very happy."

Cheapside looked John in the eye. "Neither of those things is likely to happen, at all."

"I'm glad you're telling it to me straight."

"I've transmitted your data packet to Earth."

"Uh . . . how? To whom?"

"All the details of the how don't matter," Cheapside said. "But since you know I have a Faraday cage, you can imagine that I might summon someone here to take possession of the data in physical form, on a chip. And you can imagine that the data might be sent by tight beam to Earth, to be captured in an existing database there."

"You mean, the data packet will get to Earth in forty years," John said.

"It's not a great ace in the hole," Cheapside said, "but it may be useful to know that, one day, whatever happens here, your side of the story will be told. And, who knows, you may be able to trade that for something."

"If no one's going back to Earth in chains," John said, "what is likely to come of all this?"

Cheapside stroked the end of his short, fat tie. "The most justice possible, in my guess, would be that English gets demoted and transferred, and Diaz gets retired to Earth."

"That was also Diaz's guess for himself," John said.

Cheapside nodded. "He's been around."

John sighed. "What else did you want to tell me, as my lawyer?"

"I'll go to any meetings you want me at, of course," Cheapside said, "and I'll review any agreements. Especially severance agreements and NDAs. But most importantly, since we're inside the Faraday cage and no one can hear us . . . do you have guns?"

John and Faisal transferred their pistols to their pockets for accessibility. Carrying their shoulder bags with them, they all descended into the noodle bar and took a tiny circular table in the back.

"Ordinarily," Cheapside said, "I sit in the corner, with my back to the wall and full view of the door. Mr. Abbott, why don't you take that seat?"

There was a back door as well, also visible from where John hunched over the table. While they waited for their noodles, John called Linda Pham's number on his multi.

No answer.

He sent her a message: *Please let me know ASAP tomorrow when I should expect to come in and give you a fuller statement.*

The noodles arrived. John's contained prawns and red peppers and he added a squirt of a thick, dark sauce that had a strong umami smell. He was stirring the contents of the bowl with his chopsticks when his multi vibrated, indicating an incoming call.

The multi advised him that the caller was *Director English, Western Wellesley Region.* He showed it to Cheapside, who started a recorder on his own multitool and then nodded.

"John," English said. "I'm glad to hear that you and your family are safe."

John felt trapped under a bright light. "Thank you," he managed to say.

"Let's talk," English continued. "Since you're in Henry Hudson, we should do it in person. Maybe over a cup of coffee, so we can linger a bit. Does tomorrow morning at ten work for you?"

"Did you hear from Linda Pham?" John asked.

"Internal Audit? Yes. I've heard their full report, and yours, on the events at Arrowhawk Post. You must be traumatized. From the sound of it, you took quite a physical beating, on top of everything else."

John's full report?

"Yes," he said.

"I've also heard about the good you've done. There's always a place in the Company for people with talent, imagination, and hustle."

"Is this a meeting I should bring a lawyer to?" John asked.

English laughed. "So ambitious! If we need to negotiate any agreements, we can do that remotely, after the fact. I'll see you at my office tomorrow."

English disconnected.

"What do you make of that?" John asked.

Cheapside shrugged. "How confident are you that he was involved in the gunrunning?"

"Pretty confident," John said. "And Diaz said he was involved."

Though John couldn't quite make all the threads match. Why had the director sent him to investigate the post, if he was complicit in the fraud? Was it possible John was mistaken?

Or had the other members of the gunrunning ring cut Director English out? Was that what had spurred him to sending John? And was John sent because he was new, young, and disposable?

Cheapside slurped a long clutch of noodles. "Well, I'm willing to go in with you, if you like."

John picked out a prawn and nibbled it thoughtfully. "Maybe just transmit to Earth by tight beam that I went in. And if I don't come out, tell my wife."

When they finished eating, John paid, and only then noticed that he'd had a response from Linda Pham: *No further action will be required from you. Thank you, Mr. Abbott.*

CHAPTER
THIRTY-SIX

They walked the lawyer back to his office.

"You mind if I look at something in one of the pawnshops?" John asked Faisal.

Faisal shrugged. "I have no business in Henry Hudson, Mr. Abbott, I am just following you around."

It felt as if months or even years had passed since John had been in this post, but he retraced his steps easily back to the pawnbroker's where he'd left Ruth's jewelry. Someone other than Monson was manning the counter, so John didn't ask to look at the jewels, but contented himself with seeing them through the plastic of the counter.

"Looking for a gift for Mrs. Abbott?" Faisal asked.

"Something like that."

They exited the pawnshop and turned down the narrow alley and its packed commercial traffic. John was baffled by the phone call he'd received from Director English and the text message from Internal Audit and he was wary of being tracked, so he was looking in every reflective surface for blue-and-buff uniforms, or for the repeated appearance of any face that would tell him he was being followed.

The face he saw was Diaz's, just for a moment, and then it blinked out of sight.

"Let me get you a boba tea," he said to Faisal.

"I am not sure I can say no, if you are paying."

The tea vendor had a short line and a large mirror. The mirror was overhead, allowing customers to look down at the baffling array of boba ball flavors and tea varieties, but it was also angled, so John could look behind him.

Where he definitely saw Diaz, lurking in the crowd.

Faisal saw him, too. "We are followed. How disappointing. I was hoping for chocolate boba in a blueberry tea."

"Two chocolate teas," John said to the tea-setty.

"Blueberry teas," Faisal said. "With chocolate boba."

The tea-setty grunted and set to work, scooping boba into two printed cups.

John watched the security agent. Diaz browsed at a carousel of flicks—not current, but all flicks that had been popular before John left Earth—but he wasn't looking down at the promotional cards at all. He was looking at John. John tried to keep his eyes straight forward, locked on the tea-setty, and just watch Diaz through his peripheral vision.

"Milk or sugar?" the tea-setty asked.

"Neither," Faisal said. "John?"

"Right," John said.

"Neither," Faisal repeated himself.

Faisal took both teas and nudged John with his elbow to remind him that it was time to pay. John fumbled with the bills, his right hand still useless, and when he looked up into the mirror again, Diaz was gone.

"Diaz went to our left," Faisal murmured. "You and I should go right."

John took his tea in his left hand and turned right. He looked for more reflective surfaces and didn't immediately see any. He felt his heart rate climbing.

"The tea's not hot," he said, frowning.

"The boba are chilled," Faisal said. "The tea was piping, did you not see the steam? But it immediately chilled to warm. It is a very nice temperature, and the flavor is delicious. You should drink it."

John risked a look back, stopping, stretching, and turning his head. He didn't see Diaz.

"Lord of Lights," Faisal said, "you should drink your tea or throw it away. You only have one good hand, and holding the tea in it is really going to slow you down if we get into a gunfight."

"You don't think Diaz will attack us here in the street?" John gulped warm tea, chewing on the sweet, starchy boba. He felt as if he were gulping breakfast cereal.

"*You* clearly do." Faisal frowned around his own tea, which he held in his left hand. His right hand was in his jacket pocket. "And Mr. Cheapside's best legal advice to us was to carry firearms."

"This is not really how the recruiters described Sarovar System when they came to NYU," John said. "There were more atmosphere yachts and genetically reconstructed dinosaurs."

"Ah, you are thinking of Sarovar Gamma."

"Is it as nice as they say?"

"I have never been, but I would very much like to go. I feel it is a place where I might fit in well. You should ask English about it. I think Company directors vacation there. Or Carlton might know, she is the post chief, and they might get to go to Gamma, too."

The acid in John's stomach wouldn't let him finish the tea, so he dropped it into a waste bin and shoved his hand into his pocket. The cool hatching of the Webley's grip was reassuring.

"I don't see Diaz anymore," he said.

"I am confident it was him."

"We find an out-of-the-way hotel," John said. "And we pay cash. And we turn off our multis, right now."

He texted Ruth: *Going to bed. All is well. I'll update you tomorrow.*

He hated the lie. He hated it worse for the fact that he had just come clean to her for all his lies about working for English. But he hated lying less than he hated the thought of telling her he was in danger.

John paid cash for three skewers of chunks of roasted fowl alternating with cubes of some green vegetable. He asked the kebab-setty for two more swatches of the foil the skewers came in, and the man handed them over without comment. John double-wrapped both his multitool and Faisal's in the foil, and shoved them into his shoulder bag.

"How well do you know Henry Hudson?" he asked Faisal.

"Not well enough to know where a no-names, cash-basis hotel would be."

"Okay, then." John turned left down an alley so narrow that Faisal had to turn his shoulders slightly to fit through. It was a short alley, too, quickly opening into a parallel street, and John was tempted to stand in the opening and wait, forcing Diaz to reveal himself, but he resisted the urge. Despite outnumbering the security agent, he wasn't confident that he and Faisal would win an open fight, so their best option was to evade and hide.

He turned right on the street, passing a pedal-powered rickshaw and then walking close behind a line of falafel and shawarma and gyro carts, and then turned right again, plunging into another alley.

This one was broader, nearly as wide as the street, but it was dark. A shadowy outline of a man loomed up in front of him, and then a second and a third shadow.

"Reddy us your noob, Company man," the first shadow said. "All mat, you shemi home after."

Bang!

The shot was fired by Faisal, and it went straight up. "*You* shemi home, mar," Faisal growled, "or we *semamoo*."

At the shot, the first of the shadows faded instantly into the darkness. At Faisal's snarl, the other two backed away, bobbing up and down until they turned and ran.

"Thank you." Cold sweat poured down John's back. "We're not doing a great job of staying hidden."

Faisal said nothing, but picked up the pace. They rejoined their original alley and turned right again, completing a loop when they passed the tea-setty, who waved at them and smiled. John didn't like feeling so memorable, so he scowled back.

At the next alley, they turned left, and John broke into a ragged run. A strip light at waist level kept the alley from being completely dark, and at the end, John risked a look back—no sign of Diaz, or anyone else in the alley.

He picked a building with a completely opaque plate front and no apparent name other than HOTEL. The presence of men and women in skimpy halters and black lace panties suggested that this was a place that would ask no questions, or at least not press for accurate, documented answers.

He paid cash for a room. When the clerk, a sagging man with gray stubble covering his jaw and scalp, shoved a registry toward him, he scanned toward the top of the page and picked a name, repeating it and the contact details verbatim.

"Nefer second floor?" the clerk asked.

"Nefer," John said.

They took the two keycards offered and climbed the narrow stairs at the back of the lobby; halfway up to the second floor, John crouched and looked out the door again, seeing only a ponderous pair of buttocks squeezed into pink vinyl and black fishnet, and hearing a baritone woman's voice singing an obscene sea chanty.

Their room was on the second floor, at the end of the hall. There was another door across the hallway, and, two meters beyond the doors, a big plastic slab of a window.

The hotel room was a flexi-space. A tiny corner was tiled and contained toilet, sink, shower, and a wall-mounted printer squeezes into two square meters of floor. In another corner stood a larger gray printer-disposal unit and a dark red foam inflatables dispenser, both coin-operated. A single narrow window looked out above the bustling activity in front of the hotel. The plastic of the window was already tinted, suggesting that people on the street couldn't see inside, but John pressed the wall control to darken the tint to opaque.

Then he sat on the floor and buried his face in his hands.

Faisal set his shoulder bag down. "You need sleep. You have been beat up, and imprisoned, and had a long journey. Lord of Lights, that is not the half of it."

John laughed, his face still buried. "You're describing yourself, too."

"Yes, Mr. Abbott, but you have a meeting with the director in the morning."

"We should both sleep."

Faisal nodded. "I shall procure you a bed." He examined the dispenser. "What resistance level do you favor?"

"Stop it, I'm paying." John stood and worked cash into the machine. "I'm dialing a nine for myself. What do you like?"

"I enjoy a soft, fluffy three," Faisal said. "And I will shower, so the smell of kebab and boba oozing through my pores does not keep you awake all night."

John snorted.

Faisal stepped into the shower space and plastic walls slid out to enclose him. The water started. John slumped into his foam bed, wishing that he'd brought a book to read. Or that the room had a flicks player, and he'd bought a chip at one of the kiosks on the street below.

He also wished he knew what was going to happen to him in the morning. Why did Director English want to see him? Why in his office, which was highly visible, and not in some dark corner of a dirty noodle bar? That sounded, improbably, like an invitation from a person with honorable intentions.

But English was wicked, wasn't he? Didn't John know that? Diaz had said that English was the one giving him orders. Was it possible that English was innocent, and did indeed want to talk to John for ordinary Company reasons? To debrief him, and reassign him?

Or maybe send him home to Earth?

Most of all, John worried about Ruth and the girls. They should be staying in Nyoot Abedjoo, safe under Rock's watchful eye, but DeBoe had been staying in the village, and he'd been murdered.

There was a knock at the door.

The shower stopped, the shower printer whirred, and Faisal squeezed out of the corner, a thin spun towel wrapped around his waist. He grabbed his pistol from his bad, crept to the door, and peered through the peephole.

Diaz, he mouthed to John.

John drew his revolver and crouched in the back corner of the room.

Faisal pressed himself against the wall. "I ordered nothing," he growled in a voice a full octave lower than his normal speaking tones.

John heard a clatter from the hallway, and then a heavy thud. Faisal pressed his eye to the peephole and shrugged. John aimed his revolver at the door, right in the center, where a man's chest ought to appear, and gestured to Faisal to open it.

Faisal opened the door and stepped back in one motion, pistol aimed out at the hallway.

Diaz lay on the floor in the hall. He was dead, his face a mass of scorched and charred flesh from which the hideous odor of death by burning was just beginning to arise. A pistol lay on the floor beside him.

Faisal leaned into the hall, and then pulled himself instantly back. "A beam attack came through the window. There is a hole burned right through the plastic."

John tried to remember what he'd seen out the window. "There's nothing out there," he said. "That's the side of the building. It's over an alley."

"Drone attack, then." Faisal shut the door.

They pressed themselves against the walls of the hotel room, weapons in hand, waiting.

Nothing happened.

"What do we do about the body?" John finally asked.

"Nothing. We did not kill him. We did not see it happen. It is the hotel's problem." Faisal grabbed his bed and started dragging it away from the window. "I suggest that if they ask us about it, we say that we had already fallen asleep, and did not even know anything had happened."

"Why are you moving the bed?"

"I still need to sleep," Faisal said, "and so do you. But we better not be in the line of fire of that window, even black as it is."

CHAPTER THIRTY-SEVEN

In the morning, Diaz's body was gone and an opaque yellow epoxy plug filled a hole in the window the size of John's fist. Opposite the window, above an alleyway, was a blank plastic wall. The attack had come from a drone. The prickling feeling of distrust between John's shoulder blades spread.

The front desk clerk didn't utter a peep as they left.

John and Faisal walked a slow loop around the center of Henry Hudson Post. They were looking for faces following them and they were looking for drones on their tail, but they didn't see either. They saw cars, but more commonly bikes, rickshaws—pulled by humans, animals, and robots—and now and then a horse, as people got up and about their day. Drones zipped through the air this direction and that, but none seemed to be following John and Faisal.

They ate eggs with bright yellow yolks fried inside thick slices of white toast, which John promptly vomited into the gutter.

The Henry Hudson Post Company House looked less like a palace or administrative building, and more like a fortress, as John stared up at it. He unwrapped the two multitools from their foil sheaths and took his. He ignored the sudden flood of notifications of new messages and missed calls, except to confirm that none came from Internal Audit or Director English.

He handed his shoulder bag to Faisal, with his pistol inside. "If I don't come back . . ." he said.

"Lord of Lights, you are coming back."

"But if I don't . . ."

"I will get Ruth and the children home to Earth, by hook or by crook." Faisal smiled.

They shook hands, and then John went up into Company House.

A receptionist dressed entirely in blue other than buff strips at his shoulders handed John a keycard and sent him to the elevator at the back of the bank again. He rode the lift up, his head a maelstrom of partially composed speeches of resignation, defiance, pleading, and condemnation.

A second receptionist whispered words into a comms bud in her ear, then pressed a button to open English's door.

John entered the office and found Director English standing with his shoulders to the door, hands crossed behind his back, looking out a broad window. John hadn't had a chance to linger on the view on his previous visit, so he crossed to the window and joined the director as the door hissed shut behind him.

Green forest, golden-yellow in the morning sun, stretched out below them. From this height, which must be a hundred meters up, Henry Hudson proper looked like a small settlement, mere detritus around the feet of the giant Company House. A river bisected the woods in the intermediate distance, and at the horizon, several progressively lighter blue-gray silhouettes of mountain ridges stacked against the sky.

"John Abbott," English said. "You're a talented man."

"That's what I tried to communicate in my résumé," John quipped.

"I figured you could do the audit work," English said. "I didn't realize you would be so dogged, and so hard to kill. I'm very pleased that you survived Diaz's and Choat's attempts to remove you."

"Which time?"

English laughed. "John, what do you value in life?"

"My wife," John said instantly. "My daughters."

English waved his hand. "Everyone says such things. Most men don't really mean them, though I get the sense that perhaps you do. What are you here for? Why come to Sarovar?"

"Freedom," John said.

"All men value their freedom," English said.

"I value *your* freedom," John said. "As well as mine. And the freedom of the country-setties, and the freedom of the Weavers, and Post Chief Carlton's freedom, and everyone else's, too."

"You're principled."

"Compulsion is the basic evil," John said. "I don't want to be enslaved, I won't enslave others. I don't want to be raped, I won't rape. But it isn't really a principled stand, it's built into me. I can't be happy compelling others. Don't you feel the same?"

"Many men are perfectly happy to compel others," English said.

"I guess I'm not many men," John said.

"No wonder people are willing to flock to your banner."

"Nobody's flocking anywhere," John said.

"Does it make you happy if the masses choose to follow you?" English asked. "Strictly of their own free will, let us posit. Do you like being a leader?"

"Is this a counseling session?" This was not at all the conversation John had expected.

"We're debriefing. I want to make sure my man on the ground is all right."

John shuddered. "I'm all right."

"Do you like being a leader?" English asked.

"No," John said. "It's hard to be an example."

"Is that what you think a leader is?"

"A good leader."

English was silent for a while. Had John offended him?

"You want to let people make their own choices," English observed.

"I want to hire good people and leave them alone. Some twentieth-century CEO said that. It's good advice."

"William McKnight," English suggested. "3M."

John shrugged. "I heard it from my Economics professor, Mike Rothman. He also said that the only good business deal was a deal in which all parties were happy, and nobody who wasn't a party to the deal got screwed."

"What about your children?" English pressed. "Do you leave them alone?"

"Mostly," John said, "yes. I want to show my children a good example, be there to answer their questions and protect them, and let them figure out their lives."

"Your children might achieve less, because you're not there, driving them on."

"They also might avoid the neuroses that come from having a parent force their hands in all things."

"How does what you want differ from anarchy?"

"Labels are dangerous," John said. "We can use the same words and talk past each other by assuming too much. But I think that, most of the time, and in most situations, people are better off helping each other. If we all understand that, and we're all free to act, then we'll choose to help each other."

"Have you ever been called naïve?" English asked.

"All the time," John said. "And an idealist. And also an optimist. I don't think I'm any of those things."

"You're certainly atypical. Your mind does not . . . follow the common paths."

"Is the common path the one that led Diaz and his friends to sell guns to the Weavers?" John asked.

"That was an aberration," English said smoothly.

"Was it?" John rubbed his eyes and blinked. "I guess I haven't been here long enough to know."

"But what you did was an aberration also. Maybe a breakthrough. Tell me more about the trade you arranged."

"Can we sit?" John asked. "I'm still a little weak."

"Ah, I promised coffee." English clapped his hands. "Tell me how you take yours."

"One cream and one sugar." John sat in front of English's broad desk. "Nothing special."

English touched an earbud. "Two coffees. Mr. Abbott takes his with one cream and one sugar."

English then sat beside John, on the same side of the desk.

"So the Weavers and the country-setties were in conflict," John said, "because the country-setties were trying to get into the Weave trade, and the Weavers knew it. I saw an opportunity to make them partners instead of enemies."

"You like free trade."

"It's the only truly moral way to interact with other people." John nodded. "And the free market is the only system in which we all succeed by making each other better off. The best way the Company can benefit the various peoples of Sarovar is by respecting all their dignity and engaging with them in free, uncompelled trade."

"I understand that the country-setties will be producing the raw stuff of which the Weave is made . . ."

"It's called 'zenef' in Sedjem," John said. "It's like raw spidersilk from a sort of cave worm."

"So in the process of making your deal, you've learned secrets of Weave production that we've been after for years."

"There was too much hostility." John shrugged. "Among all parties. Not enough trust."

"How did you win their trust, then?"

"I put myself at risk," John said. "Also, I promised to provide an antifungal."

"To the country-setties?"

"To the Weavers. They're desert creatures, and they're living in a wet place." John laughed. "You know, it occurs to me now, that I'm not sure I cut myself into the deal. I guess I assumed that I would have a piece of the action where the Company buys Weave from the Weavers, but if not . . . everyone else takes all the value."

"I'll make sure you're dealt in for whatever there is," English assured him. "So you brought new production online to solve the conflict, and you specialized the parties. Humans produce zenef, Weavers produce Weave, more Weave is produced than before."

"And it's all high quality," John said.

"Selling more high-quality Weave will bring the price down on Earth," English said.

"But we'll sell more of it," John said. "Lower margins, more dollars of profit, more people enjoying the benefits of Weave."

"Except that there's a bottleneck," English said. "Only so many ships going back and forth between Earth and Sarovar. So Weave piles up on Sarovar and rots. Or the cap on how much can be shipped, combined with increased production, means that the Weavers are bid down in how much they can earn for their Weave. Company volumes stay the same, margins go up, but the Weavers make less."

John frowned. He hadn't thought through the fact of the wormhole that connected Earth and Sarovar. "The potential profits should lure investment," he said. "Someone should be attracted to putting their capital into additional freight ships. Maybe ships that are specialized, so they're as cheap as possible and ship nothing but Weave. No passengers. Maybe no human crew, even."

"Someone should do that," English agreed.

"*I* should do that," John said. "Only I have no capital."

"Hmmm."

The coffees arrived and English sipped his, which was a steaming espresso.

"You say the Weavers are desert creatures," English said. "Do you mean they come from the southern continent, Bonaparte?"

"Maybe, although . . ." John shook his head. This conversation had gone in completely different directions from what he'd intended and imagined. "Look, there's another possibility. What if they came from another planet?"

"Fascinating. Sarovar Beta is a desert world, not dissimilar to Mars."

"Or another system." John cleared his throat. "There's some evidence . . . kind of a lot of evidence, actually . . . for starters, it's what the country-setties themselves believe . . . that humans have been here longer than our official records indicate."

"What are you saying?" English leaned forward, eyes flashing. "Humans and Weavers came here together in some ancient spacefaring past? From Earth?"

"I don't even know," John said. "I guess I'm saying someone should be studying this."

"You should be studying it," English suggested. "This sounds like an excellent intellectual pastime for a married Company officer. Especially one who has already built a relationship of trust with the locals."

"Eh," John demurred. "I'm not really the academic type."

He sipped his coffee. It was rich and delicious.

"Have you considered the possibility," English asked, "that you just don't want to take responsibility? All this high talk of principle and mutual benefit, but isn't the bottom line just that you don't want to be bothered? Even this fascinating historical question; you bring it up and say someone should study it, but then you just want to walk away."

"I take responsibility," John said.

"You talk. You'll risk yourself. But in the three-way trade you've arranged, you don't have any skin in the game. You're just the idea man. If others can't keep the trade going the way you've arranged, it collapses, and you aren't hurt."

"That's crazy," John said. "I have nothing *but* skin in the game. I'm in debt, I'm forty light-years from home with no way back, my whole world is here. If the three-way trade I arranged falls apart, my neighbors go back to shooting up my house. And the minute I have any capital to invest, I'll be part of that three-way trade. Or maybe I'll invest in new ships for the extra Weave."

"You wouldn't take the cash and leave? If, say, you had enough to pay off your debts and buy return tickets to Earth for the whole family?"

The words brought John up short. Everything he'd been saying assumed he was going to turn around and go right back to working at Arrowhawk Post, but was that really a likely outcome of this conversation?

Director English's gaze was guarded, giving nothing away. Was this a test? Diaz had wanted to go home, and now Diaz was dead. Had he been killed for trying to leave? Was English looking for some reassurance that John intended to stay? Was English offering to bribe him for his silence?

"I'm here to make my fortune," he said. "I want to pay for my kids' educations, and their weddings, and their first homes. I think that will take years. Besides, if I went home now, I'd have less than a month at this job. That's a terrible thing to put on a résumé."

"I take it you haven't been looking at your multitool this morning," English said.

"I . . . slept in." It wasn't entirely false.

"There are perfectly good reasons why you might not have been reading your multi messages last night and this morning," English said. "But I assume, since you're sitting here with me, that now might be a good time to look."

"Not a very polite time," John said.

"Be impolite." English stood. "There's something there that you need to see." He stood with his coffee, stretched, strode languidly to the window, and resumed gazing at the view.

John saw messages last night and this morning from Ruth, and he felt guilty not having already seen them and responded. He saw a message from Faisal, saying that he was sitting on a bench outside the train station, waiting.

And he saw a message from the Sarovar Depository, indicating that he had received a deposit of sixty thousand dollars.

He stood. "What's this?"

English turned and set his cup on his desk. "From the tenor of your voice, I'm guessing it's sixty thousand dollars."

"I can't be bribed," John said. "I can't be bribed for a million dollars, but that you would make the attempt for just sixty thousand . . . I'm outraged and I'm offended, at the same time."

"It's not a bribe," English said.

"It isn't my *salary*," John said, "I don't make nearly that much. What the hell are you doing, giving me sixty thousand dollars?"

"I didn't give you that money," English protested. "You need to look at the entire message, and not just the notification. That's the payment for your Weave."

John looked at the notice again; English seemed to be telling the truth.

"My broker at Central Transit offered an excellent spot price," the director said. "I took the initiative to accept on your behalf as well as on my own."

"How did you know the amount?" John asked.

"I know how much you shipped," English said, "and I know the price we got. So are you still planning on staying, John Abbott?"

John set his coffee cup on the coffee table. "You've been really interested in exploring my economic and philosophical principles," he said. "You've poked around in my psyche, and you've even dug into my finances. You didn't bring me here to bribe me. If you'd wanted me killed, you obviously could have done it last night."

English frowned. "Wanted you killed? Why would you think that?"

"You know." John rubbed his eyes. "Out with it, Director. What did you bring me here for?"

"First and foremost," English said, "to offer you a promotion."

John sat in awkward silence for long seconds. He felt as if he had pressed the controls to send his groundcar forward, and it had shot backward instead. "To come back to Henry Hudson?"

"Well, tell me if your heart is set on that," English said. "To me, a transfer to Henry Hudson looks premature. First, because there's an obvious bigger promotion to be had at Arrowhawk Post."

John nodded. "I can be second-in-command to whoever the new audit chief is."

"No, you can be audit chief. You're the only accountant we have who has any experience with Arrowhawk's finances. I could bring you back to Henry Hudson, but it would be in a larger organization, where upward mobility is harder, and there's more competition."

"It seems like a lot of work for one person," John said. He was being offered Keckley's position, and if he was alone, he'd have to do all the work that had been DeBoe's, as well.

"You write the job posting, and I'll get you a second person to be your assistant. This will bring a sizeable raise, which in itself may not be a big deal, but it means that you can invest more in the trade."

It was a real promotion, in terms of authority, even setting aside the money. "I won't lie. That's attractive."

"There are other perks," English said. "Periodic trips back to Earth. Access to the shuttle service among the Sarovar worlds—which, I must tell you, include some lovely vacation spots. Atmosphere yachts. Rejuvenation clinics. You can play polo riding genetically reconstructed dinosaurs, John, there are delights you can't find on Earth. A sabbatical every seventh year, which is great for the aforementioned vacation places, or if, for instance, you want to write a book. On the production of Weave. Or on the true history of humankind on Sarovar Alpha, or the origin of the Weavers. For instance."

John took a deep breath. "I don't see myself writing a book. But vacations on resort worlds might be nice."

"The second reason why I think you're better off staying in Arrowhawk is that you've set up this new trading arrangement. It's a good thing, John, you've done good work, but even good things sometimes need a little watching before they can be trusted to stand on their own. I think you'd better stay close to the trading, to run it, especially while it's new."

"Run it and invest in it," John said.

"I presume so."

John took a deep breath. "I don't know if I can do it."

"Keckley had more experience than you, but you've got enough for this job. And you've got the most important qualification."

"What's that?"

"Carlton asked for you."

"You mean, when I was hired by the Company? She liked my résumé or something?"

"No, I sent you to Arrowhawk the first time. But yesterday, I got a request from Post Chief Carlton that she be allowed to fill the vacant audit chief position with you."

"She barely knows me," John protested.

"You know, people don't usually fight *against* promotions." English frowned and consulted his multi. "But if it makes you feel any better about the job, she wrote, 'John Abbott is likely crazy, which I expect is probably what it takes to work out here on the edge of nowhere and find success. Also, his wife is tough as nails. And Janae agrees with me that he's the man for the job.'"

"Janae's her daughter," John murmured.

"I know."

John stood, paced up and down the office, and then turned to face Director English, standing in the door. "But I can't work for you."

English folded his hands in his lap. "Why not?"

"You were behind the gunrunning."

"What are you talking about? I sent you to *investigate* the irregularities."

John scratched his scalp, trying to stimulate his brain into focus. He had too many thoughts flying through his mind at the moment. "I think that's because Jefferson and his friends were taking more than they were supposed to. I think they were supposed to only invest in gunrunning with their own Weave, and pay you a cut. But they skimmed Weave from the Company, which I think hurt you, maybe hit your bonus, maybe made you look bad. Maybe it was going to lead to the whole thing being discovered. I guess they must have been in cahoots with Diaz and Choat, or else the security agents could have given you the true numbers and verified that you were getting robbed. And maybe also the traders withheld your share from that portion, so you were getting screwed, and you sent me to investigate."

"To implicate myself in a serious Code of Conduct violation."

"I think you figured I wouldn't survive. Or maybe, once you had the information you wanted, your plan was always to kill me. I'm new to the Company, I'm disposable, so I could dig up whatever I dug up, and it didn't matter, you'd have Diaz and Choat kill me. Right before you killed *them*."

"*You* killed Choat," English said. "Or at least Choat was killed in your presence."

"But I'm pretty sure *you* killed Diaz. First you shut down the Internal Audit investigation—I don't how you did that, but maybe it was as easy as denying all charges. Or maybe you threatened Linda Pham."

"I didn't kill Diaz. This is all wild speculation." English smiled. "If it were at all true, I'd be very upset with you right now. But you've been through a lot, and you're the hero of the day. I can forgive many things to the hero."

"And I think killing Diaz and Choat was at least an option from the start. And you wanted them to be on hand to kill me, so you sent them down to Arrowhawk after me."

"I know that you think these things. This is what you said in your statement that you gave to Internal Audit. But if Internal Audit had found any evidence suggesting anything at all of the sort you're suggesting," English said, "I would be in a holding cell right now."

"I don't think Internal Audit even looked," John said. "How could they have done anything like a decent job, and finished it the same day?"

"Most of the things you're talking about would leave electronic trails," English said. "Records of communication, travel orders, money transfers, and so on. I think Pham and her team must have looked, and quickly concluded that there was no evidence of wrongdoing on my part. Perhaps they had already been looking to the activities of our rogue security agents, and you handed them the final answers, wrapped up neatly with a bow on top."

"And then they released Diaz to come kill me."

"No one released Diaz to kill you," English said. "We released him to go home. He was supposed to be on a train to Central Transit right now. Here—take a look at the travel order." He showed John the screen of his multi, which did indeed seem to be a travel order for Diaz to go to Central Transit and take the next available berth for Earth.

"Then why did he come after me?"

"He came after you?"

"Last night. Don't pretend you don't know."

English laughed. "John, you helped kill his partner and cost him not only his job, but also his highly lucrative side hustle of selling arms. Are you seriously telling me you don't think Diaz had any *personal* reasons to come after you?"

"Maybe," John admitted, "but I don't think he had the personal resources to *find* me."

"No trains had left the station," English said, "and Henry Hudson is just not that big, and Diaz was an intelligence operative, so he had contacts. You are heaping up imagined mystery upon imagined mystery, when the more likely explanations are exceedingly simple."

"What's the likely explanation for Diaz getting lasered to death in front of me?"

"Ah, I wondered." English shook his head. "I only knew that he was killed last night in a fleabag hotel, I hadn't realized he was in your presence."

"He was in front of my hotel room. He was shot through the window with an energy beam, apparently while trying to get through my door."

"From which you conclude that I was outside the window, clinging to the wall like some pulp-novel avenger, killing Diaz because he had failed me."

"Maybe you had already decided to let me live at that point. Maybe killing Diaz was just hiding your tracks. Maybe you even made that deal with Internal Audit, that if they let Diaz free, you'd solve the problem. Killing him must be a lot cheaper than sending him back to Earth, and with much less risk of discovery."

"Now you're really impugning Internal Audit. I'll get you their files, if it will make you feel better. They investigated Diaz and Jefferson and the others and concluded that they were all guilty of Code of Conduct violations. They investigated me and determined that there was no evidence to substantiate Diaz's accusations. Diaz was released and ordered to Central Transit. Jefferson and the other traders are arriving here by train today, in a couple of hours, as it happens. They're en route to Central Transit, to be sent back to Earth and fired."

"They're rich," John said. "Getting fired is no punishment. You're sending them home to sit on their piles of cash."

English shrugged. "We're a corporation. We can't kill people for Code of Conduct violations. Company lawyers on Earth will decide whether they want to sue Jefferson and his friends to force them to cough up their ill-gotten gains, but the truth is that such lawsuits are usually more trouble than they're worth. We should invest the resources into developing Sarovar, instead. Into developing people like you, and opportunities like your new trade deal. But listen, you think I'm involved in this gunrunning scheme because Diaz said so. But why would you believe him? He was a thug and a killer."

John hesitated. "He ambushed me in Arrowhawk Comms while I was talking to you. It seemed likely that you had told him where to find me."

"Arrowhawk is the size of a peanut shell," English said. "I'm sure Diaz knew where you were at all times, if you were on post."

"And you didn't answer my calls," John said. "I needed help."

"Arrowhawk's network was down," English said. "I tried, and couldn't get through. I'm glad you were able to deal with Diaz despite my failure to help. It shows that I picked the right man for the job."

John hesitated, took a deep breath.

"You're taking my accusations very well," he said.

"You did a good job for me." English shrugged. "I need you to do another job for me. You're an idealist in a very non-ideal world, so I know you're not happy about how some things turned out. You and your family have had a very rough week, so you must be stressed and exhausted. I think when you've calmed down, you'll realize that it can't possibly be the case that I'm the villain you've imagined. And then you'll be audit chief. Youngest audit chief ever to sit in the executive offices of any post of the Sarovar Company, as it happens."

John snaked a finger under his cast to scratch and tried to think.

What was his basis for believing in English's guilt, really? Wasn't it, at the end of the day, only that Diaz had identified English? But Diaz could have been lying. Claiming English was his accomplice could easily have been a way to try to bluff John into submission.

"Did you know about the airstrike?" John asked.

English nodded. "I was alerted immediately that it had been ordered by the Arrowhawk Post command. Comms were out, so I couldn't talk to anyone on the ground to find out what was happening. As you can imagine, I was immensely relieved when the airstrike was called off and communications were restored."

John picked up the coffee and finished the last of it. "I want to talk to Jefferson at the train station."

"That's a great idea," English said. "And I won't accompany you, to make you worry that I'm intimidating your witness."

English extended a hand to shake; John hesitated.

"Come on, John," English said, "shake my hand. If you decide later that I'm guilty, you can take back the handshake. Otherwise, let me congratulate you now on your promotion, and urge you to get back to Arrowhawk Post, so you can get to work."

They shook hands.

"Send me a message when you've decided," English said. "In either case, the train that delivers Jefferson will take you back to Arrowhawk. At the very least, to collect your family and go to Central Transit, if that's your choice."

John walked slowly to the train station, dread and indecision filling his heart.

English wasn't trying to accompany him to control what he said to Jefferson, which tended to suggest that English was innocent. Or did it? There would be surveillance at the station, and English could always have John killed afterward, just as he had had Diaz killed.

Just as John *assumed* he had had Diaz killed.

Or maybe it suggested that English had already bought Jefferson's silence. Maybe all his talk about how costly it was to sue former employees was a smokescreen for a dirty deal that had already been agreed, and English knew that Jefferson would go free.

Except that would leave a witness to English's guilt—maybe three witnesses, alive and well on Earth.

Or had John become paranoid?

He found his way to Faisal.

"You are alive, Mr. Abbott," Faisal said. "I would think you would be happier at that fact."

John chuckled. "I've been offered a promotion to audit chief of Arrowhawk Post. I confronted English directly about his involvement in the gunrunning, and he denied it."

"Convincingly?" Faisal asked.

"Maybe," John said. "He certainly made a very good show of leaving me my free will in the matter. But Jefferson and his accomplices should be coming through the train station here in an hour or so. I'm going to ask him."

"He might not even know, if the whole thing was set up by Diaz acting as intermediary," Faisal pointed out.

"Or he might, Mr. Haddad," John said stubbornly.

"This is your decision," Faisal said, "and I am not going to try to persuade you to act in one direction or the other. But I think I should say that if you are only willing to work with people whom you know to be of spotless benign will and innocent of all selfish or wicked drives . . . you are going to have to work alone, your entire life."

John ruminated on that advice as they waited. He paced in a circle, back and forth along the station platform, rubbing his cast with his uninjured hand, while Faisal stood still and watched the guideway.

The train arrived with a high-pitched shriek, slowing quickly to a stop.

"We'll take this train back to Arrowhawk," John said.

Faisal raised his eyebrows in question.

"One way or the other, we go back to Arrowhawk today," John explained. "The question is whether I stay."

Four armed men in Company blue and buff stepped off the train and unloaded Jefferson, Tasto, and Grandi, all handcuffed and scowling. The last of the security men to step off the train was Payne, who grinned and nodded affably.

"Abbott," he said.

John nodded back.

"They're all yours. As long as you want." The agents chained the three former traders to a steel ring sunk into the floor and then walked away, standing on the other side of the platform to watch and talk among themselves.

Jefferson spat on the concrete. "What the hell do you want, Abbott?"

"I want to know who else was in on your scheme," John said.

Jefferson stared for a while, and then snorted. "The three of us and Gonzalez."

"Who else?" John pressed.

"Diaz and Choat."

"Who else?"

"You know what he's asking," Tasto growled.

Grandi laughed and barked something in Italian.

"The Weavers." Jefferson looked puzzled. "What are you getting at, Abbott?"

"How did you sell the extra Weave you made?" John asked.

"I'm a trader," Jefferson snarled. "That was the easiest part."

"Who gave you the idea?"

"No one gave me the idea, it was *my* plan in the first place." Jefferson shook his head. "I approached Diaz, and he agreed that he could round up some spare weapons. What are you getting at?"

"Hey," Tasto drawled, "if you're going to take all the credit now, how about you go ahead and take all the rap?"

A dull gleam came to Diaz's eye. "You hypocrite, Abbott. You're going to take over the trade now."

"Did Diaz and Choat report to someone else?" John probed.

"You think they would tell us if they did?" Grandi snapped.

"You think they asked *permission* to commit a Code of Conduct violation?" Tasto laughed.

"No." John sighed. "I'm just trying...trying to understand."

"Do it on someone else's time. Maybe someone whose life you didn't ruin." Jefferson spat on the concrete again. "Guards! We want out of here! Get this jerk away from us!"

John turned and walked away, sweeping Faisal up in his wake.

"Mr. Abbott, have you changed your mind? Do you not want to take the train back to Arrowhawk Post?"

"I do," John said. "But first, I need to go redeem my future."

CHAPTER
THIRTY-EIGHT

When John and Faisal stepped off the train in Arrowhawk Post, Carlton stood alone on the platform.

"Do I get to call you 'Chief'?" she asked.

"Is that how it works?" Abbott wondered.

"No, I'd probably just call you 'Abbott.' But you know what I'm really asking."

John took a deep breath. "I'm interested. I need to sort some things out in my head."

"You talk to Ruth yet?"

They began walking slowly down the steps, Faisal at their heels.

"That's one of the biggest parts of sorting things out. But also, I worry that I'm being bought off."

"By me?"

John and Carlton stopped at the door to the Audit office. Faisal waved goodbye and continued down the stairs. Through the closed door to the Medical office, John heard the murmur of Hinkley consulting with a patient.

"I was convinced English was behind the gunrunning."

Carlton nodded. "I heard Diaz blame it on English, too. But if you're thinking English is buying you off with this job . . . English is a wealthy man. He's been trading in Sarovar goods for thirty years. Not just Weave, but all of it. He's got his own chalet on Sarovar Gamma. If he really needed to buy you off, he could do better than give you a crappy little job at a crappy little post at the edge of nowhere."

"You're really selling the offer hard, I see."

Carlton shrugged. "If you're going to take this position, you should see it for what it is. Opportunity and a step up, but also risk. From audit chief of Arrowhawk Post, the only paths up are to take my job, get transferred to a bigger post, or go back into one of the functions of Central Audit. And working in Arrowhawk, your chances of getting attention so that someone will support your transfer are slim."

"Keckley was right," John said. "I need to write a new depreciation manual."

"Keckley was a smart man," Carlton said. "He knew he wasn't going anywhere, but he also knew he could do his job in twenty hours a week, so he did that and then did what he liked with the rest of his time. Not a bad way to live."

"You're saying it's a crappy little job but it can be done in twenty hours a week."

"Not at first. At first, it will take you eighty. Since you have no help, at first it might take you a hundred hours a week. I'll be telling you to knock it off and go home, but you won't, because you're a stickler for getting things right; because you're ethical; because it bothers you when two numbers that are supposed to come out seven come out nine instead. But once things are in order, and you've devised procedures you like to streamline the work, it will become a very manageable role. You've already shown a real aptitude for trading, so maybe you'll go out with Takahashi and Hager in the trucks in your spare time."

"Maybe I'll go on more school field trips with the girls."

"I hear that was quite an adventure, last time."

"Yeah." John thought for a bit. "I will want help. How do you feel about me hiring someone local?"

"What do you mean, one of the traders?" Carlton frowned. "We're down four as it is. I'm going to be posting job descriptions and trying to attract candidates from other posts as well as doing the usual recruiting in schools. I'll want you to help me describe the trade deal you've set up—that should be a strong recruiting point. I'm thinking I might promote Sam Chen."

"He can drive and also trade. It's a good choice."

"You weren't thinking you'd recruit Sam into Audit, I take it?"

"I was imagining one of the country-setties."

"You have someone in mind?"

"No. I just . . . they should have opportunities, too."

"I don't know what they learn in school, but I'm pretty sure it isn't double book-entry accounting."

"I'm pretty sure you're right," John said. "But I would pick someone, and teach that person what he or she needed to know. And I think we could pay less than we pay an offworlder recruit, and still pay a fabulous salary, from that person's point of view."

"Well, that's certainly attractive." Carlton harrumphed. "I don't think the Code of Conduct prohibits it."

"It doesn't," John said.

"It's probably a more interesting way to attract attention from Audit leaders than writing a depreciation manual."

"I don't know," John said. "Depreciation schedules are pretty fascinating."

"But listen, on the point of being bought off," Carlton said. "I don't know whether Director English really wants you in Arrowhawk or not, but *I* want you here."

"Thank you," John said.

"I mean it. We don't have lawyers here, and the nearest full-time compliance people are in Henry Hudson. That means I need everyone to have a good working conscience, but especially I need my audit chief to have personal probity. I need you to care that we're doing things right. Sometimes a little fast and loose, sometimes with a little improvisation, sometimes recklessly, but without cheating. Without being evil. And, at the risk of sounding like Security Chief Korsgaard, reporting everything."

"Keckley wasn't a bad man."

"Keckley was a good man. An excellent man. But he got fooled by some greedy traders and a corrupt subordinate. I got made a fool of, too. It took you coming along and investigating to set that whole mess right."

John sighed. "It was English who sent me."

"And English backed you as my choice for audit chief. And Internal Audit cleared him."

"How did that happen so quickly?" The speed with which English had been cleared, together with Linda Pham's very few words on the subject, were part of what still gave John pause.

"Like I said, we don't have lawyers. We don't really have laws, except that in theory a few U.S. federal laws are applicable. We have the Code of Conduct, and it's Company officials who administer it. That means people can't assert constitutional rights or delay the process with legal demands. Very few people even get to lawyer up because almost nothing gets to a hearing. And so much of what happens is recorded, that usually Internal Audit can review the video on someone's multi, or listen to the audio from a recorder in a conference room, and immediately tell whether there was a violation or not."

John shook his head. "I'm just not satisfied."

"Good." Carlton clapped him on the shoulder. "Don't be satisfied. Be hungry, anxious, and on the lookout. And of course, it might not be that Internal Audit cleared Director English of suspicion ... it might be that they found him very suspicious, but didn't have enough evidence to do anything about it. Or maybe they did take action. Maybe it was all reported to English's boss, and English got fined, or took a pay cut, or was denied a promotion he'd been angling for. Or maybe they're still watching him."

"So, you want me to stay, but you don't want me to have illusions. English might have been profiting from the gunrunning."

"Might have been the mastermind behind it. But so what? He's not asking you to run guns, is he? He's asking you to keep the books for Arrowhawk Post. And by the way, while you're here to do that, you can also make sure that the peace treaty you set up—yes, I know, it's dressed up like a trade deal, but it's really a peace treaty—*works*. If you walk away now, I'd give it three chances out of four that the deal collapses within the year."

"And with me here?"

"Two chances out of four. But I'm a cynic. And maybe, think about this, maybe Internal Audit went to English's boss and English did get disciplined, and part of the consequences he faces for his misdeeds is that he has to keep you on here. Maybe the ethical forces within the Company want you to keep English in check."

"That feels like a stretch."

"Yeah, okay. But *I* want you to keep us all in check. And keep peace here at Arrowhawk. And prosper."

"I want those things, too."

"So stick around. But if you're not going to stick around, you should know that there are a couple of crates of firearms in the warehouse with your name on them. I understand your wife purchased them."

Carlton went down the stairs and out.

John stood in the doorway to the Audit office, shaking his head at the thought that this would become his exclusive domain.

The door to Medical opened and a gray-bearded man with no teeth and a long gray tunic emerged. He nodded to John and left, and then the Surgeon emerged.

"Good, you're back," she said.

"Not sure yet I'm staying."

"Let me check your vitals anyway." She shrugged. "Can't hurt."

The doctor examined him, an efficient process that involved three different handheld scanners as well as fingers to his wrist and a stethoscope between his shoulder blades.

"Nothing to treat right now," she said as she put the stethoscope away into a drawer. "You ought to come back once a quarter. Hell, you're right next door, it won't take five minutes, come by once a month. If anything goes off—heart, whatever—we want to catch it and treat it right away."

John nodded. "Thanks, doctor."

He drifted down the stairs and into the warehouse. On the way, he looked at the scorch marks that blackened two stories' worth of stairs, and the melted light fixtures and door fittings all along that length. The offices, though, seemed to have survived intact. John had really only come to Arrowhawk Post because it had been his job, but he had definitely come with the intent to fix problems.

He'd fixed some problems, but he'd created others. The post was short of traders now, and the stairs needed to be fixed, and there was no one to run the post's accounts.

Unless John himself did it.

And it was because of the post's presence that there were roads, and a doctor with modern tools and knowledge, and a school.

Though the post could use more reliable power.

Which it might get if John stuck around to do the work.

In the warehouse, he found Sam lying on his back on a creeper, torso, head, and arms invisible underneath one of the trucks. John heard Sam whistling, and the clank of metal tools.

John found his two crates and a cart he could use to drag them to his khat. He loaded the crates, feeling the ache that persisted in his muscles and bones from his exertions.

"Is Gary okay?" he called.

Sam slid out from under the truck and grinned. "John Abbott!"

"Alive, against the odds."

Sam set aside his tools and stood. "Gary's fine. He's been at Nyoot Abedjoo since the day of the field trip. Those two security clowns broke in there, but they weren't . . . they didn't bother Gary."

John nodded. "I'm embarrassed that I don't know this, but is it just you and Gary?"

"My wife died years ago," Sam said. "Nothing to be embarrassed about."

"Well, listen, my family's still in Nyoot Abedjoo, too. I thought I might take a truck and go get them. Shall I pick up Gary while I'm at it? I gather things have quieted down at Arrowhawk now."

Sam grinned. "I'll go with you."

"I'll be right back."

John dragged the cart to the family khat. When John opened the gate, he found Nermer standing there, holding his staff.

"Mar Abbott," Nermer said. "Welcome home."

"Have you been guarding the khat while my family's been at Nyoot Abedjoo?"

"This is a dangerous time, and the khat needs guarding."

John carried the crates to his upstairs office and set them on his table. The corroded bronze scythe and leather skullcap still sat there, waiting for him to do something with them. He'd need to buy frames. Or maybe he could get a model human head printed, to display the skullcap on.

Who would investigate the history of the humans of Sarovar Alpha, if not John?

It was a little strange to own so many firearms, but he couldn't exactly sell the guns to anyone, having personally worked so hard to end that trade. Who had sold them to Ruth, anyway? Rock seemed the likely culprit. Maybe he could return them to the Company and get some kind of credit. Or maybe he would teach Nermer to shoot, and arm his khat guard with something more powerful than a stick.

He should take the girls shooting.

He left all the guns in the crate, though, and just took his Webley with him. He told Nermer he'd be back soon, and then strolled back to Company House, enjoying the absence of unmarked white groundcars.

They climbed into the truck and Sam drove toward the post exit.

"I got offered a new job," John said. "Sort of a promotion."

"Funny thing," Sam answered. "So did I." He was beaming.

John smiled. "Really? Tell me."

"I'm going to be a trader," Sam said. "Carlton says I can get seniority credit for my time driving the trucks, since I've seen as many wats as any of the traders, which means I'll jump right over factor and be shipping Weave for my own account."

"Congratulations!"

"I've made okay money," Sam said. "With just the two of us, I save most of my salary. But this will mean I can really get ahead."

"It's going to be busy," John said. "Even with you, the post is down three traders. Everyone's going to be working overtime just to keep up with the existing wats."

"Exciting, right? And I've got my savings to invest. But I was thinking we could do more than that. I was thinking we could take your new system and take it out to other villages and nests. It's one thing to have Nyoot Abedjoo and Antela Anta cooperating, but we can up the production of the entire region."

"Assuming it works in our pilot program first." John nodded. Of course, massively increasing the production of the entire region only increased the urgency of the bottleneck problem at the wormhole. He needed to look into that.

"I owe this to you," Sam said. "I'll ship your Weave anytime, no charge. Even if the rules say there's some minimum charge I have to take, I'll just give it back to you on the side."

"Thanks, Sam. But I'm pretty sure I'll be a trader, too."

"Wow, that's a career switch," Sam said. "But it makes sense. You're the one who negotiated with the Weavers."

"No, I got offered Keckley's job. Audit chief for the post. But I'm pretty sure it means I'll get to trade for my own account."

"Congratulations, Chief!" Sam grinned.

"I don't think people really talk to the audit chief that way."

"Not to Keckley, they didn't. To you they might."

John asked, and Sam let him drive the last five miles along the gravel road to Nyoot Abedjoo. The large gate was open, and John slowed down so that the village's guards could get a good look at him and Sam through the windows before they entered.

Sunitha and Ellie came running up as he stepped out of the truck. He knelt to meet Sunitha at eye level, and so that Ellie could fling herself onto his thighs and wrap her arms around his neck. Ani leaped up and down alongside the girls, seeking attention and getting well-deserved scratching. She was limping, but only slightly.

"Are you ready to go back to Arrowhawk Post?" John asked.

"Is it safe?" Sunitha asked.

"Are the fires out? Are the Weavers gone?" Ellie asked.

"What about the men with guns?" Sunitha added.

"Arrowhawk is safe again," John said. Ruth was approaching over the village green, so John handed Ellie the plastic envelope containing her jewels. "Will you take this to Mother? She doesn't expect it, so yell 'Surprise!' or something."

Ellie raced off with her commission.

"How are Mom and Ellie?" John asked Sunitha.

"We all worried about you. Mom said extra-long prayers. Ellie cried herself to sleep a couple of times. But I was pretty sure you'd make it back."

"Oh yeah? Why is that?"

Her faux English accent suddenly appeared. "You're just that sort of person, Father. You're the one who always comes back."

"Is that okay?"

The accent dropped. "That's a great thing to be, Dad." Sunitha hugged him, and John stood.

Ruth arrived and John hugged her, too. She looked a little dark under the eyes, and her skin was pale and tight.

"You haven't been sleeping," John said.

"Not very well. I . . ." She held up the plastic sleeve with the jewelry inside. "What does this mean?"

John offered his hand. "Let's go for a walk."

They walked in silence down to the lakeshore holding hands, and then paced slowly around its marshy fringe. When John finally talked, he updated his wife about his trip to Henry Hudson, the job offer, and his conversation with Carlton.

When he had finished, they walked in silence again.

"Well," he eventually said, "I guess I thought you would have something to say."

"Do you want to hear it?"

"I'm asking."

"You hid things from me."

John took a deep breath. "Yes."

"I understand that it was awkward that you were investigating your fellow employees, so there was sensitivity in what you were doing. But you could have told me. You could have told me some of it, at least."

"I thought that would only make it awkward for you. And maybe dangerous. And I was under instructions not to tell anyone. And specifically not to tell you."

"It did get dangerous. It got dangerous when the Weavers came after me and my children, and then again when those two security men kidnapped us. And my being ignorant didn't protect us. When you had to go out late at night, you should have told me where you were going."

"Even if I was going somewhere risky?"

"Especially then. So that I could pray for you." She touched John's cheek with her hand.

John sighed and nodded.

"You're not a spy, John. You're an accountant. You can tell me the whole truth."

"The whole truth is mostly boring," he said. "It's mostly depreciation schedules and revenue booked in the wrong period and allocating power bill costs."

"Tell me the boring stuff, too," she said. "All of it. But especially the parts where you or we are in danger."

John nodded.

"So now tell me whatever it is about your trip to Henry Hudson that you've been holding back."

"Internal Audit took Diaz from me at the train station," John said. "Then they let him go, and he came after me. Me and Faisal. He followed us around Henry Hudson, and then when we thought we'd lost him, we checked into a hotel room."

"*Thought?*"

"He knocked on our door shortly after that. I think he was going to shoot us, because he had a pistol in his hand. Or at least, he was prepared for hostilities. But someone else shot him."

"Someone else who?"

John shrugged. "We didn't see. Through the window, with an energy gun, someone shot Diaz right in the head and killed him. Probably a drone."

"I'm not sad he's dead," Ruth said.

"No one is," John agreed. "English denied knowing anything about it."

"Do you believe him?" Ruth asked.

"I didn't at first," John said. "But then I accused him to his face, and he . . . he took it. He answered for himself."

"You're persuaded he's innocent?"

John sighed. "I'm persuaded that he doesn't want me killed, and that he wants me back in the job at Arrowhawk Post. And I think it's possible he was involved in the gunrunning, but I can't prove it."

"If he killed Diaz to protect you, that makes me feel fondly toward Director English."

John smiled and nodded. "But if he killed Diaz to cover his tracks and protect himself, he could just as easily do the same to me next time."

"Only if you're an accomplice who has become inconvenient."

"Or an accountant who is asking the wrong questions, or turns up evidence of more wrongdoing."

Ruth thought about this. "I don't think that's going to happen. If anything, if there's evidence of wrongdoing on his part, he's putting you far away from him, so you won't find it."

John felt silly that the thought hadn't occurred to him. "Maybe that's it. I can help him and the Company make a success out of Arrowhawk, and, for the moment at least, I'm far away and harmless in a remote corner of Wellesley. Literally the most remote corner there could be."

"I think that's it," Ruth said. "So the question is, can you live with that?"

"Someday, I'll cross his path again," John said.

"Maybe years in the future. Maybe he'll retire before you do. Maybe he's innocent, after all, and you'll never clash again."

"Maybe."

"Can you live with those possibilities?" Ruth asked. "Can you live with the maybes that result from standing in the center of the swarm of possible explanations?"

"That's rather poetic." John considered. "I can live with it, as long as I get to live with you."

"If you're with me . . . really *with* me," Ruth said, "then I want to stay here and make our life. You've already become a sort of hero, and you've made a big career step. Now we just need to make a home."

"I'm not sure what the raise actually amounts to," John said, "but I bet we could hire a housekeeper. We could get a tutor for the girls, too."

"I like them in school. I like that they have friends from Nyoot Abedjoo."

"So do I," John said.

She held up the jewelry in a sleeve. "Does the fact that you're getting a raise mean that we don't need to pawn these again?"

"We made enough profit to buy the jewels back and still have a nest egg to invest." John laughed. "A small nest egg. Although I think we should also get a printer-disposal unit and a cleaning drone. And we still have the arsenal you bought."

"I thought we were going to need it to ransom you."

"I appreciate that. Now Nermer can go armed to the teeth. And so can you and the girls."

"Wearing my grandmother's jewels. I shall be the envy of all Arrowhawk Post—and the terror of it as well."

John handed Ruth his multitool and she typed out his acceptance message to Chief Carlton. Then they turned and began walking back toward the village and the truck. The girls saw them coming and ran to meet them, dog racing by their side.

SAROVARI PIDGIN
WORD LIST

aa – here

ab – to stop, a pause, cessation

aboo – to brand, mark

adoo – to be excited, be happy, be eager

aha – to fight, stand up

akoo – supplies, gear

amem – grasp

ank – life, live

aroo – to ascend

asha – many

at – room, small building

atep – burden, load

ba – the elk with ram's horns

bak – worker

been – bad

beenoo – badness

beet – sweet cane syrup

beeyaoo – ore

boo – place

dashar – red

dashroo – Weavers

demi – touch

eefed – sheet, bolt

een – interrogative particle, begins yes/no questions

eenet – get

eeoo – island

eeret – do

ees – see 'nee ees'

eetroo – river

eez – tomb

em – is, are, be; 'em' plus a verb is present or present progressive

et – food, esp. bread

341

gemmy – find
genen – soft
gereg – lie, trick, deceit
got – have, bring, carry
ha – descend
haab – send
habet – writing
hams – sit
hanket – drink, esp. beer
hanoo – home, house
harad – child, children
hatty – lion, wild cat
haw – body, flesh
hay – measuring tool, multitool
hedj – white
hedmoo – seat
heet – rain
hefat – snake
hefty – prisoner
heka – king, ruler, magic
hemet – think
henteet – south, southern
heper – become, exist
her – before a verb, indicates the imperfect or imperfect progressive
heroo – now
het – thing, something
hetep – content, peaceful
hezzy – sing
hyanet – travel by sea, sail, swim, row
hur – inferior
ib – heart, soul, mind
iker – good, excellent
inoo – trade goods
ishest – exclamation of surprise
iti – father
ja – storm, wind
jat – to cross
jeba – finger

jert – hand
jes – own, self
joo – mountain
ka – herd beast
kamat – black
kat – craftsmanship, work, make
ken – extend
keres – to bury
khat – enclosure, walled building
mar – boss
masha – army
mat – peace, truth
maw – water, sea
mech – to fill, full
mechet – north, northern
medjer – block
mee – please
menyoo – herdsman
meri – want, love, like
mesach – a lizard
mesedj – hate
meshroo – evening
messy – give birth
mik – look, listen (interjection)
min – now
mitet – copy
mitoo – equal
miut – mother
mo – see
moot – die
neb – everyone, each, all
nebba – have
nechem – take
nee – negation
nee ees – emphatic negation
nefer – good
nehem – yell
nen – no, not

netet – that
noob – gold, cash
nyoot – post, settlement, nest
-ooee – very, exceedingly (adjectival suffix)
oor – weak, small
pa – this, this one
par – house
patpat – trample
pecher – run
pehyaret – circle, clearing
pesa – cook
pet – sky, space
poo – it
ra – day, today; in front of a verb, communicates future or intent
rach – know, learn
reddy – give, place, put
remen – shoulder
remetch – people
ren – name
rood – skin, pelt
saah – toe, toes
sachah – remember
sakkab – cool, cold, grow cold
seba – gate, door
sebi – criminal
secher – plan, idea; to fell
sedjem – to talk, speak; to speak trade pidgin
sedjer – to sleep
sef – yesterday
seger – silence
seksek – destroy
semamoo – kill
semoon – probably, maybe, perhaps
sen – kiss, smell
senet – a boardgame
sensen – fraternize
seshem – job
seshmem – hot, heat up

setep – choose
setty – guy, person
sha – start
shay – Hausman's Bear, a six-limbed, bearlike thing
sheboo – food
shed – vehicle; boat, truck
shemi – go
shendeet – kilt
shesroo – fabric, esp. Sarovari Weave
shezep – image
shoot – darkness, night
shta – far
sneb – healthy
snedj – fear
soohet – egg
soori – drink
soot – but
stas – drag
ta – land, earth, dirt
tatemoo – everyone
tchazat – lift up
tchezmoo – dog
tem – do not
twaoo – beseech
ur – great
wa – one
waadj – wave (water)
wadj – command
wah – stop
waham – again, repeat
was – power
wasah – broad
washab – answer
wat – road, journey, trading voyage
waw – Company employee
weba – trust, believe
wedja – decide
wenem – eat

wenen – exist
wep – open
yaash – pilot
yach – then, next
yah – the larger moon of Sarovar Alpha
yarih – the smaller moon of Sarovar Alpha
yash – call
yooms – lie, deceive
yoot – come
za – protect
zach – write
zee – go
zenef – blood, the raw material of Weave